ON THE OUTSIDE

BOOK 9 IN THE RYAN KAINE SERIES

KERRY J DONOVAN

CHAPTER ONE

Daylight cut through the oppressive darkness, carving through the gap around the only outside door in her cell. It painted three bright stripes on the concrete floor and forced Sabrina up from the blessed comfort of sleep. She turned over, and the springs on the ex-military cot squeaked in aggressive complaint. The wafer-thin foam mattress provided little protection against the metal that tried, throughout the night, to slice her to ribbons.

Reluctant in its lethargy, her mind swam against the flow, battling the tide of despair, arms pulling, legs kicking, until she finally dragged herself to the surface, into wakefulness.

Counter to the hopes promised in her dreams, she awoke in the same grimy dank place—her cell.

Each time she moved her hand, the iron manacle that attached the chain to her wrist chafed her skin a little more. The protective cloth she used—a piece torn from the sleeve of her nightshirt—had fallen loose during the night. The wound felt as bad as it looked. It

1

wept blood and a yellow-green pus. Assuming she lived long enough for the wound to heal, it would leave a scar.

Sans doute. No doubt.

The questions remained. Why had the colonel kept her alive? He did not usually spare the lives of those he believed worked against him. Ruthlessness had been his *modus operandi*.

Clutching the coiled chain tight to her thigh, Sabrina arched her back and tried to ease the tension that had formed between her shoulder blades. The movement did nothing but allow a biting cramp to attack her muscles. Every muscle in her body ached, cried out for warmth. The warmth of food, of nourishment.

Grit scratched her eyes and crunched when she ground her teeth. She tried to swallow, but a dry throat made it a near impossibility.

All her own fault. Such an idiot. As *grand-père* Mo-Mo often said, one day, arrogance would be the end of her.

Sometime during the past few weeks, she had spoken to the wrong person. Greed had turned that person against her. Or maybe the betrayer came from closer to home.

But who?

Sabrina sighed.

Identifying the individual responsible for the treachery would be a challenge for others. As a task, it fell outside her capabilities. At any moment, she expected a member of the Creed to drag her away to her death. Hopefully, it would be quick. Quicker than the slow death of dehydration or starvation.

Why had it taken her so long to discover the cause of the missing inventory? The clues had been there from the very outset, but her covert investigation had been blocked at every turn. Only by pure luck did she stumble upon the first crack in the fortress of silence. One fissure led to another, and eventually they coalesced into a canyon. Death and destruction became a trail leading to the colonel, the Doomsday Creed, and this very place. She had only lacked the evidence to convince the authorities to move in and close down the band of home-grown terrorists.

One day. Perhaps two. That was all she required. But it was not to be.

In the dead of night they came for her. They overpowered and drugged her, and they spirited her away to this grubby cell. Three nights and two days ago.

Merde à leurs cœurs noirs! Damn their black hearts!

The hours stretched out interminably and each moment, the death she expected failed to materialise. All she had were her thoughts, which turned relentlessly in on themselves, becoming more and more distorted as the hunger and thirst took effect. Her stomach tightened, grumbled, rebelled against the deprivation, and her throat constricted in pain from the lack of drink.

L'eau. Water.

What would she give for a tall glass of cool, clear water? A drink to extend her life for one more day.

No. Think of something else.

The treachery.

Who had turned against her? Who had turned her over to the Creed?

The names on the list were many, and crossed at least two continents. Too numerous to determine in her weakened state.

Why had they acted against her?

The obvious answers came easily enough. Either greed, or a belief in the cause espoused by the colonel, or both. Greed seemed the more likely option, since the cause was hopeless—the dream of a lunatic. The missing weapons and ammunition were worth millions of dollars on the black market, and the colonel possessed very deep pockets.

Sabrina, sitting on the edge of the bed, doubled over and clenched her belly against the next attack of raging cramps. More and more, thirst and hunger dominated her waking thoughts, making it difficult to think logically.

She cast her eyes to the ceiling. One solitary lightbulb suspended from a cable attached to a rafter. She had never seen it alight.

Time passed evermore slowly. Her mind wandered.

Concentre-toi, Sabrina. Concentrate.

Tex might arrive at any moment, and she did not want him to see her weakness, or to see her cry. Not that tears would actually form. Dehydration would not allow it.

Yes, she needed to concentrate on Tex and his slack-jawed partner, George.

Focus upon Tex. Use anger as a driver. Fight. Stay alive for as long as possible. Help will come. Please God, help will come.

The first time she saw the blond-haired mountain of a man, he slammed open the door to her filthy prison cell and stood in the opening. So tall, he had to stoop when passing through the doorway to avoid striking his head. Shoulders so wide they almost blocked the opening, and his huge silhouette stood out dark against the blinding sunlight. Behind him, head poking through the gap, stood a squat, ugly young man. He had an underslung jaw, a shock of uncombed hair, and carried a pump-action shotgun pointed at his toes.

When the big man stepped inside, sunlight seared her eyes so painfully she had to close them tight and turn her head away. He stood inside the threshold, unmoving while she recovered enough to look up at him.

"Hey there, little lady," he said. His soft Southern drawl made him sound almost friendly. "My name's Tex. I sure am glad to meet you, ma'am."

When he made the greeting, he touched his forehead as though tipping his hat to her.

Still shielding her eyes, she stared up at the man who remained well out of reach. The youngster with the shotgun hovered just outside the doorway.

Tex leered at her, taking in her state of undress. The men had snatched her while she slept, and she sat on the cot barefoot, wearing only a silk nightshirt and shorts. The translucent cloth left little to his imagination.

"I said, 'Hey there, little lady'," Tex snapped, teeth bared, all pretence at civility disappearing in an instant. "Answer me, damn you!"

Sabrina swallowed and tried to speak, but she could not drive any words through her parched throat. Instead, she looked up at him and nodded.

Once satisfied he had her full attention, Tex smirked. He took a set of keys from the pocket of his dusty jeans, selected one, and used it to unlock the only other door in her cinderblock cell—a door she had tried, and failed, to open since the start of her incarceration. She assumed it to be the door to another cell. Many times, she had knocked upon it but had received no response.

Tex turned the handle and pushed. The door creaked inwards to reveal a toilet and a washbasin.

Tex ducked low and entered the closet. He rested a hand on the tap.

"Thirsty?" he asked, still smiling.

Again, she could only nod.

From the moment Tex entered the cell, the ugly one with the shotgun had not taken his eyes off her. His lower lip glistened with drool and he wiped it dry with the back of his free hand.

Ensuring she could see his actions clearly, Tex fitted a plug into the drain and twisted the handle of the tap. It squeaked open and clear water trickled into the bowl, filling it slowly. She couldn't tear her eyes from the flow, which sparkled in the sunlight streaming through the small, frosted glass window on the far wall of the closet.

Miraculously, her mouth watered at the sight and allowed her to swallow.

"Yes," she croaked.

His smile grew even wider. Brilliant white teeth stood out against his dark suntan.

"Well, come get some, honey," he said, beckoning with a hand as large as a shovel.

She stayed put—sitting on the edge of her cot. Wary.

"What's wrong, Frenchie? Scared o' little ol' me?"

Sabrina stared him down. She said nothing.

"Aw, honey. There ain't no need to be afraid of ol' Tex. I ain't gonna touch you none. Here, I'll prove it."

When the water reached the lip of the bowl and started to dribble over the sides and puddle on the filthy concrete floor, the huge man turned off the tap.

He said, "Go on, honey. Help yourself," bowed gracefully, and backed out of the cell, locking the door behind him.

Sabrina jumped up from the bed and raced to the closet. She reached all the way past the inner door before the chain stretched taut and the manacle tore into the flesh of her wrist. It brought her up short—short of the basin, but not the toilet.

She screamed out in pain and frustration.

Outside, behind the locked door, Tex let loose a huge belly laugh.

"What's wrong, Frenchie? Chain too short? Shame that. A cryin' shame!"

The cell door opened, and once again, Tex blocked the sunlight with his huge frame.

Sabrina backed away to her cot, hugging her injured arm tight to her chest.

His braying laugh echoed throughout the cell and drove deep into her head. The one with the shotgun shifted his gaze from her to Tex and back again as though he was struggling to understand the joke.

"Serves you right for bein' so eager, Frenchie."

"Why am I here?" she croaked.

"That's what happens to people who work against the Creed. You brought it all on yourself, honey."

"What do you plan to do to me?"

"Gonna tenderise you a little, then you'll find out."

Still laughing, he backed out of the cell, barged the smaller man out of the way, and locked the door again. She sat on the cot, crying silent, dry tears, listening to his footfalls crunching on gravel and disappearing into the distance.

CHAPTER TWO

On the fourth day of her incarceration, after more taunting visits from Tex on days two and three, the man who had turned into a monster in her mind opened the cell door once again. Tex was accompanied, as always, by the ugly, drooling lad with the shotgun. Of similar height to Sabrina but much wider, the lank-haired youngster rarely took his eyes off her, although he never entered the cell.

"Howdy, Frenchie," Tex said, standing just inside the cell with his fists planted on his hips. "How you doin' this fine day?"

She looked away and refused to answer.

"What's up, girlie? Cat chewed off your tongue?"

She glanced up at him. Her eyelids, gummed up with sleep and chalk-dry, grazed her eyeballs. Still, she refused to say anything. Even if Sabrina had anything to say, she doubted speech would be possible in her state of desiccation. Her tongue stuck to the roof of a parched mouth and grated when she pried it free.

"Thirsty?" Tex asked.

He held up a one-litre bottle of water and shook it at her. It gurgled merrily in his giant fist.

More torture.

Anger bubbled up inside her, hot and bitter. If the big man would only take three steps closer, she could reach him. Gouge out his eyes with the long fingernails she had sharpened to points on the rusty metal of her army cot.

"No, really," Tex coaxed. "This time I ain't kidding. Here you go."

Gently, he tossed the plastic bottle onto the foot of her bed, well within reach. Its liquid contents reflected the yellow sunlight, forming starbursts in her compromised vision.

"Don't trust ol' Tex, huh?"

Sabrina sneered at him and shook her head.

"Suit yourself, but you've got an hour to drink yer fill and spruce yourself up afore I come get you. The colonel's made time in his busy schedule to see you, and you wouldn't want to upset him none. I can assure you of that." He turned to George and nodded. "Go on, dummy. Toss 'em in there."

From outside, George threw a large paper grocery bag into the cell. It bounced off the foot of the bed and fell to the floor.

"Darn it, George," Tex laughed. "You never could throw worth a dang, boy."

"D-Dark in there, Tex," George said, his expression downcast, hangdog. "I-I done m-missed m-my aim."

George stammered and spoke much more slowly than expected, as though trying the words out for size in his head before speaking them aloud. Sabrina suspected the youngster of having a learning difficulty of some kind. Given time, she might be able to use such a nugget of information. But how? As yet, she did not know.

Tex stomped closer and snatched up her wrist before she could react. He jabbed a key into the padlock and twisted. The hoop clicked open, and he removed the padlock. The manacle split in two and dropped to the floor, tearing the new scab from her wound.

She was free! For the first time in days, she was free.

Sabrina sprang to her feet and pounced, screaming and clawing at his blue Texan eyes.

Tex dodged aside. Laughed. Drove a clubbing right fist into her belly. She doubled over. Coughing, gasping for breath, she sank to her knees on the hard floor.

"See that, George?" Tex said. "She ain't lost none of her fight. Gotta love that in a woman."

Still fighting for breath, eyes tearing, Sabrina stared up at him.

"*Putain!*"

"I got no idea what that means, honey, but I'm guessin' it ain't a word my momma would have used. However, I'm a forgivin' man and won't take it to heart. Now," he said, pointing to the bag, "put them clothes on and make yourself presentable. The colonel don't take kindly to unnecessary shows of the flesh. And only drink the water in the bottle. Don't be tempted to take none from the tap. That there water's from the well and it's tainted. Only fit for washin' your hands and flushin' the toilet. Hear me?"

————

When Tex returned with George in tow, Sabrina felt stronger, almost human. Although it had taken much more willpower than she thought available to her, she had sipped the water slowly rather than empty the bottle in three or four huge gulps. She hid the half-full bottle in the darkness behind the bed, determined to eke it out.

To her surprise, the paper bag George threw to the floor contained her own clothes—hiking boots, socks, underwear, a pair of jeans, and a heavy plaid shirt. The bag also contained a hairbrush and a small, individually wrapped bar of soap.

Before dressing, she washed in the cold water and used her old nightclothes as a towel. Despite the dire warning Tex gave, the water smelled and tasted clean and fresh. Was he playing with her mind again? More torture?

The unperfumed soap stood in for shampoo, and the hairbrush managed to pull out the tangles in her shoulder-length hair. With no mirror available, she had no idea what she looked like and didn't really care. The water revived her a little, but the hollow void that was her bruised and grumbling stomach reminded her of the desperate need for food, and the dire nature of her situation.

Imprisoned and facing death, she needed to gather all her wits about her if she were to survive.

Minutes after she had finished dressing, the door opened and Tex entered, smiling wide. Behind him, George lowered his head and stared at her through thick and bushy eyebrows. The cast in his left eye made it difficult to determine exactly what he was looking at.

"Well hi there, Frenchie," Tex said. "You sure scrub up real nice. Here, take a bite out of this."

He underhand lobbed her a small, green and scabby apple.

Sabrina breathed on it, polished it on the thigh of her jeans, and bit into it. Sour. A crab apple. She grimaced.

Tex guffawed.

Rather than spit out the bitter pulp, she stared directly into the deep blue eyes of her tormentor and kept chewing. Although tart and unpalatable, the apple contained sugars, and sugars meant energy. If she chewed for long enough she might avoid stomach cramps.

Tex snarled. He grabbed her upper arm and dragged her out of the cell into the cold sunlight. She blinked against its harshness, but held tight to the apple and continued chewing—drawing out every last morsel of nourishment.

The instant her eyes cleared, she recognised the location as Camp Pueblo. A place she had identified during her investigation as worthy of further inspection. She had studied detailed satellite reconnaissance photos of the facility and knew the layout well.

A disused military base, it had been abandoned by the US Army in the eighties and allowed to fall into decay. Sometime within the past decade, it had become the Arizona headquarters of the Doomsday Creed. Colonel Caren had leased the site from the Army through a shell corporation and had paid almost nothing for it.

Camp Pueblo nestled in a large clearing in a river valley between a range of densely wooded mountains. Built along traditional lines, low buildings—some built from clapboard, some from cinderblock—encircled a large drill square. A two-metre-tall, rusted chain-link fence topped with razor wire surrounded the perimeter of the three-acre site.

The mid-morning sun beamed down on them from a sky so clear and blue, it reminded her of childhood holidays spent in the Pyrenees—as did the biting easterly gale that whistled through the mountains looming above and around them. She shivered against the chill and breathed deep of the sweet, clear air—high altitude air so clean and clear, the mountains appeared close enough to reach out and touch. Branches of the fir trees whipped and bent under its gusting breath.

The beauty of the setting stood out in sharp contrast to her sense of foreboding. She was about to meet Colonel Caren, a man who left a trail of destruction in his wake, and had done so for three decades.

She felt very small and extremely fragile beside the huge Texan, and hoped she gave off the same sense of vulnerability. It might help her in some way.

With George pointing the shotgun at her back and keeping close behind, Tex took a weed-strewn gravel path that led from her cell and skirted around the back of a row of single-storey barracks—ten in total. The unraked gravel crunched under their boots.

After a fifty-metre tramp, they fell under the shadow of a double-height clapboard building with an A-frame roof. From the satellite images, she had identified it as one of a dozen storage hangars occupying one third of the whole camp. It stood beside the PX building—the base retail store, now disused and crumbling.

Again, she shivered as another heavy gust hit her square in the back and threatened to knock her from her feet. A cloud of ruddy brown dust swirled up from her ankles and tickled her nose. She sneezed and winced against the pain shooting from her tender stomach.

Somehow, one day, Tex would pay for that cowardly punch to her belly. One day soon.

They stepped out from the shadow of the hangar and onto the

drill square—an open space the size of a football field—its concrete surface cracked and covered in decades of accumulated dirt and dead leaves. The colonel certainly took no care in the appearance of his headquarters. Perhaps he considered Camp Pueblo mere temporary accommodations.

A company of forty or so men, their camouflaged uniforms mismatched, stood in three long rows—three platoons. They faced the two-storey, brick-built administration block, murmuring quietly amongst themselves. The imposing building stood proud and alone, the only construction on the northern side of the camp. It had been built into a low hill and commanded an imposing view of the camp. Four wide steps ran down from the entrance and stopped at the apron running around the whole of the drill square. A red, white, and blue flag fluttered atop a flagpole, the ropes twanging against the metalwork. Sabrina could not identify the flag. It certainly was not the "stars and stripes" of the United States banner.

Tex pulled her by the arm and, as they stepped onto the parade ground, the murmuring quietened and all eyes followed them towards the main building.

Once they reached the narrow space between the soldiers and the apron in front of the administration block, he tugged her to a halt and gripped her arm tight enough to create more bruises and restrict the blood flowing to her hand. Another reason to wish the large Texan a slow and painful end. Sabrina tried to free her arm from his grip, but she had no chance. The Texan outweighed her by at least one hundred kilos.

"Stop fighting me, Frenchie," Tex said through the side of his mouth. "You'll only hurt yourself."

"If you kill me, Ryan will find you and tear you apart."

Tex looked down at her, left eyebrow arched.

"Ryan? Who's he?"

"He's the man who will end your life, *cochon*!"

Tex snorted and looked around at the group of stern faces.

"Point him out to me, Frenchie," Tex grunted. "Which one is he?"

Sabrina swallowed the apple pulp. It went down smoothly.

"You will not see him coming. Of that, I can assure you."

Smiling, he leaned closer, snapped out a straight jab. A fist the size of a boulder smashed into her chest. The impact pushed her onto her back, stunned and unable to breathe. Tears flooded her eyes and her vision swam. Blood roared in her ears.

"Shut your stupid mouth, bitch," he hissed, teeth clenched. "Don't rile me!"

Sabrina flipped onto her stomach and scrambled to her hands and knees. She placed the flat of her hand against her chest and pressed, forcing down the sheer blind panic.

Respire. Breathe.

Open-mouthed, she gasped, sucking in the cold, thin air. Slowly, her breathing recovered and her heartrate slowed.

Stupide!

Why antagonise such a beast who enjoyed nothing more than torturing her? An animal with no heart.

Moments later, with her sternum still throbbing, the double doors of the administration building burst open. Colonel Caren, and two other men Sabrina recognised from their mugshots as Creed Captains, marched out onto the entrance porch.

A deep-voiced man in the crowd shouted, "Atten-hut!"

Boots thumped into concrete as the company stamped to a ragged attention.

Silence fell. Ominous. Powerful. Even the wind seemed to hush.

The captains descended the steps, marched out into the sunshine, and took up their positions in front of Sabrina and Tex. They stood three metres apart, staring hard at her. As the only woman on show, her vulnerability increased.

Colonel Richard Caren remained on the porch in the deep shadow. He had a barrel for a chest, held his wide shoulders back and stiff, and sucked in a taut stomach. He stood at ease, feet apart, arms behind his back. Eyes glistened in a square head as he took in his audience, his followers. His men.

Sabrina waited, barely able to draw breath.

CHAPTER THREE

Still on her hands and knees, Sabrina waited.

The whole company seemed to hold its breath.

Thirty rapid heartbeats passed before the colonel stepped out into the light. From the porch, he loomed over them, nodding and smiling in benign magnanimity.

"At ease," he ordered, quietly.

No need for a man of his authority to shout.

Once again, boots ripple-stamped, the parade ground trembled under the impact, and the company stood at ease.

The colonel's chest expanded in pride. He nodded his approval and said, "Stand easy, men. Covers off."

His people removed their multi-coloured berets, relaxed their shoulders, and shuffled their feet, but remaining in position.

"You," the colonel said, "are the finest group of white men anyone has ever had the honour to lead. I am proud to be your commander."

The same gruff voice from the crowd called out, "And we're proud to be with you, sir. Three cheers for the colonel! Hip, hip, hip!"

The militiamen cheered, "Hoorah!" three times in near unison. When they'd finished, the colonel raised both arms and patted the air for silence.

"Thank you, men. We've travelled a long journey, but our patience has brought its rewards. Hear me, now. Our self-serving government of mongrels, cowards, and weaklings has betrayed us for too long. Its time is running run out. We, the Creed, are pure-blooded, white Anglo-Saxon protestants. Proud of our heritage. We have promised to defend our homeland with our lives. Am I right?"

A ragged chorus of "Yeah" and "Hoorah" rang out from the company.

"Am I right!" he repeated. His voice rose in volume and he thumped a fist into his chest, eyes bright.

The men roared louder.

At Sabrina's side, Tex howled at the sun.

Folie. Madness.

Colonel Caren shouted over the noise.

"The darkies, the spicks, the mulattos, the kikes, the towelheads, the commies, and the snowflake liberals have been spreading their vile weakness throughout our proud country. The Hispanic invasion of Texas is only one small example of the insidious ways these low-life creatures are preying on our generosity and our hospitality. They are weakening our blood, raping our women, and enslaving our children. It stops here!"

The increasingly agitated group cheered wildly. Tex punched his fist into the air and roared.

Sabrina glanced around her. The glassy-eyed people were lapping up the histrionic nonsense. The ridiculous nature of the overblown rhetoric belonged in the Nuremberg Rallies of the 1930s, not in the beautiful wilds of the Arizona mountains.

"*Folie*," she muttered. "*Folie pure.*"

As if in protest, another cloud of dust billowed up on a cushion of angry air. Sabrina blinked the grit from her eyes and spat it from her mouth.

Colonel Caren railed on for fifteen more minutes, whipping his people into a frenzy before stopping abruptly and calling for silence with his outstretched arms and patting hands.

"Thank you, my friends. Thank you. The moment we've been waiting for, planning for, preparing for, is drawing ever closer. Thanks to the work of so many supporters of our cause, we have amassed a powerful arsenal of weaponry. Before long, we will be ready to launch Operation Homeland."

He paused, nodded, and again the people roared. Again, he raised his hands and silence fell.

"However," the colonel said, "as you know, government agencies —the jackals—have been working against our just and holy cause. They use outsiders, lackeys, to tear down our hopes and prevent us reaching our goals." He pointed at Sabrina. "Jackals like the woman before you! Stand up and let the army of the Creed see you for what you are—a Judas!"

Tex grabbed Sabrina by the hair and yanked her to her feet. She reached up, grasping at his fist, trying to pry his fingers loose. To ease the pain, she stood on tiptoes. He laughed at her feeble efforts until her scratching nails drew blood. He snarled and shook her head, tearing tufts of hair from her scalp.

"*Lâche!*" she screamed. "Coward!"

Red-faced, Tex growled and slapped her hard across the face. She ducked, but in her fatigue, reacted too slowly and failed to avoid the full force of the crunching blow. It struck hard and knocked her from her feet. She landed on her hands and knees, gasping for breath.

"See how the mongrel fumbles in the dirt?" Colonel Caren bellowed. "See how she grovels at our feet?"

"Give her the Creed's justice!" a man yelled.

"String her up!" another called.

"Kill the whore!"

"Quiet!" Caren roared. "This isn't a lynch mob. That's not our way. The Creed has laws. Laws enshrined in our manifesto, and, by God, we're going to abide by them. If I see fit, the woman will be tried in a Creed court of law, presided over by me. She will receive Creed justice. If found guilty of plotting against us with deliberate malice aforethought, by a jury of my peers, only then will she be punished."

Every eye in the compound turned towards her. Their hostility rolled over her in heated waves. Sabrina climbed to unsteady feet. She would not grovel before them.

The captain standing to the right of the colonel, a short, middle-aged man with thinning grey hair and a round belly, leaned close and spoke quietly. Caren nodded.

"As Captain Boniface has just pointed out, we might well put her to death. Unless ...." He paused for effect, and silence fell as a metal curtain. "Unless we can find another use for her."

He stared at Sabrina and waited for his people to finish venting yet more of their spleen.

"Lieutenant Scarborough," the colonel called, facing Tex, "can you think of a fitting use for her?"

"Yes, sir," Tex answered, shooting her a lewd grin. "I surely can. She's a fine-looking piece of ass. The whorehouse is always on the lookout for new meat."

The men cheered.

"A very good idea, Lieutenant," the colonel said, scratching his chin as though considering the idea. "And one we might consider down the line. However, an alternative would be to hold her hostage and keep her fresh. Her grandfather will likely pay handsomely for her safe return. What say you, *Sabrina LeMaître*?"

Sabrina gasped.

He knew her real name! How?

Very few people in the US knew her true identity. Less than a handful.

Someone had given her away.

"Well?" the colonel shouted. "What say you, Ms LeMaître?"

"I say you are a madman!"

Tex lashed out. His open hand caught her across the face again. She staggered backwards, but this time, managed to keep her feet. Where the blow landed, her skin glowed red hot. Her teeth had cut the inside of her cheek, drawing blood. She spat. The blood stained the dusty parade ground bright red at the feet of the enormous Texan.

Tex closed in and shouted in her face. "Speak to the colonel like that again, and I'll kill you, bitch." He raised his right fist, making ready to deliver another blow.

She backed away and turned to the Creed soldiers.

"This is madness," she said. "You are all insane!"

George, who until that point had kept well away, smiling in dull confusion at what was happening around him, held his shotgun out horizontally and used it to corral her back towards the centre of the arena.

Tex snatched hold of her hair again and pulled her tight to him.

"Lieutenant Scarborough," the colonel said, raising his hand as a stay of execution, "that's enough for the moment. Take her away and keep her confined until we can arrange the Court Martial. And make sure she's well fed and watered. I want her to look fit and healthy for the video. We'll show her grandfather how well the Creed takes care of our prisoners. We are not towelheads. No one's going to accuse us of behaving like ISIS." He turned to the pot-bellied man at his side. "Captain Boniface, make arrangements to contact Maurice LeMaître. He's had four days to sweat her absence. He'll be malleable enough by now. He'll pay a handsome price for her."

Colonel Caren dipped his head and the shorter man hurried away, taking his taller, slimmer companion with him. The colonel returned his attention to his troops.

"That's all for now. Go about your duties and prepare for war!"

The herd cheered long and hard. The same man in the crowd called out, "Atten-hut!", and the men stomped to another rippled attention. Colonel Caren saluted, turned about-face, and disappeared back into the darkened administration block.

"Dismissed!" the soldier with the voice of gravel yelled.

The men stamped to the right, marched three paces away, and dispersed to go about their business. Many who passed close enough, stared at her and mouthed obscenities. It did not bode well for her ultimate freedom. *Grand-père* Mo-Mo might indeed pay a ransom, but

Sabrina was certain that Colonel Caren had no intention of releasing her.

Tex wrenched her hair, pulled her closer. She yelped and arched her back to reduce the strain. Tears stung her eyes. The metallic taste of blood filled her mouth.

"*Cochon*! Let me go!"

"You heard the colonel's orders, honey," Tex whispered. His breath heated her stinging cheek. "You're going home to your comfortable little cell."

Tex dragged her along, holding her tight against him. They returned to the warehouse, retracing their steps from earlier. George unlocked the door to her cell and stood back. Tex released her hair and thumped her in the back. She lurched inside, and the door slammed shut behind her. Moments later, the small hatch in the door opened, and Tex grinned at her through the narrow bars.

"I'll send one of the women with food and water. Gotta keep you healthy for the whorehouse." He laughed and banged the hatch shut.

In the near darkness, Sabrina felt her way to the cot and eased herself down. She pulled the crab apple from her pocket, bit off a small piece, and started chewing. The apple juice stung the cut on the inside of her cheek, but the blood dulled its bitterness, making the pith slightly more tolerable.

As her eyes grew accustomed to the darkness and her surroundings became more and more visible, her mood lifted. Since the arrival of Tex earlier that day, her situation had improved. If Colonel Caren could be believed, Captain Boniface would contact *grand-père* Mo-Mo. Which meant the Creed needed to keep her alive until the payment—whatever it might be—had been made. To do that, they would have to give her food and water.

She had been given a reprieve.

A great deal could happen in the time it took *grand-père* Mo-Mo to pay a ransom. A great deal.

One further realisation improved her mood. Tex had not replaced the manacle. Her hands were free and she wore fresh, clean clothes.

Yes, things had indeed improved since that morning.

CHAPTER FOUR

Thursday 18th May – Sabrina
Camp Pueblo, Arizona, US

After an interminable wait in her darkened cell, which she spent sucking all the sugar from the core of the crab apple, the lock clicked and the door screeched open. Sabrina barely had enough time to hide the water bottle behind her back before George stepped aside and a young woman entered, carrying a tray. Without meeting her eye, the woman placed the tray on the foot of the cot and rushed out of the cell. She cast a furtive glance at George before hurrying away.

The tray contained a metal bowl covered with a metal plate on top of which were two slices of white bread, cut thick, unbuttered. At their side stood a mug of steaming coffee.

"G'on, eat up, afore it gets c-cold," George whispered from the other side of the doorway. "Ch-Chicken stew. I-I ... h-had me some earlier. T-Tastes real good."

"Thank you, George."

She lifted the plate from the bowl and the delectable aroma of warm food made her mouth water and her stomach grumble. She drooled almost as much as George.

The youth edged closer and to one side until only one eye poked around the jamb.

"D-Don't eat too quick, mind. E-Else you'll maybe g-get gut-ache."

"Thank you, George," Sabrina repeated.

She placed the tray on her lap, enjoying the warmth it imparted onto her thighs. After so long without food, the stew really did smell wonderful.

She took the plastic spoon—the only utensil on the tray—and dipped it into the lumpy liquid. George had not lied. It tasted good. The vegetables—potatoes, carrots, and turnips—melted in her mouth, the taste extraordinary. She chewed the meat slowly, luxuriating in its flavour and texture.

"G-Good, huh?" George asked, exposing more of himself in the doorway. More than half. Although he did still cling to the doorframe as though too frightened to let go.

Still chewing, Sabrina smiled.

"It certainly is."

"I-I made sure they g-gave you more meat," George said quickly, tripping over his words. "O-On account of you not eatin' for so long. Y-You is real h-hungry, huh?"

"Yes, George. I am really hungry. Why don't you come in and talk? I am lonely, also."

"N-No. Th-That ain't allowed." George shook his head violently. "Tex would wh-whip me, if'n I did that."

He reached for the door and slammed it shut. Keys jangled on their chain, one rattled into the lock, and the mechanism clunked.

"S-Sorry, miss," George called through the keyhole, "but I ain't allowed to s-say nothin' to you. Eat up, I'll b-be back for the t-tray later."

———

A long time after she had mopped up the last of the delicious stew with the bread, hours afterwards, George opened the cell door and the same girl who had delivered the food took away the tray. Again, she neither looked directly at Sabrina, nor did she speak.

"Y-You talk funny," George whispered once the girl had left.

"That is because I am French."

"Long way off, huh?"

"France is in Europe."

George nodded, his excitement clear. "I know all 'bout Europe. Seen it on a m-map at school. It's got that c-country what looks like a boot."

"That's right, Italy. Europe is many thousands of kilometres from here."

A frown creased his forehead. "Kilometres? Them's like m-miles but sh-shorter, yeah?"

"Exactly, George. One hundred kilometres is approximately sixty miles."

George nodded and his face became animated.

"That's like from here to P-Pine Creek an' back!" He pointed in the general direction of the setting sun and excitement rattled through his words. "T-Tex told me that wh-when we set off in the Jeep to fetch you here."

His expression changed from excited to hang-dog and his head dropped.

"What's wrong, George?" she asked, quietly, not wanting to scare him away.

If she could keep him talking, gain his trust or friendship, she might make him an ally. She needed all the friends she could find.

"I ain't s-supposed to t-tell you nothin'. Not even allowed to t-talk to you. Tex wouldn't like it none. 'Sides ...." His words trailed off and he started chewing on his lower lip.

"Besides what, George?"

He glanced off to his left, no doubt worried about being overheard.

"Besides, we s-snatched you from your bed. You was s-sleeping nice and peaceful." He shook his large head. "That weren't nice."

"No, George. It was not nice, but I forgive you."

His frown deepened, and he tilted his head to one side like a puppy asking a question.

"You do?"

"Yes, George. Tex made you take me, so it's not really your fault."

His grateful smile made him look like a very young boy.

"Hey, George!" Tex shouted from a long distance away. "What you doing, boy?"

George seemed to shrivel in on himself, and his face crumpled in fear.

"G-Gotta go," he whispered and reached for the door. "Don't tell Tex I said n-nothin'. Okay?"

"I promise, George," she said as the door slammed and the lock clicked.

"I-I ain't done n-nothin', T-Tex. Honest," George shouted, his words fading along with his shuffling footsteps.

"You dummy. Think I don't know what you're up to, boy?"

A loud slap rang out, and George yelped.

"No, Tex! I ain't d-done nothin'. Don't hit me no more."

"You fancy her, boy?" Tex asked, his voice taunting and growing louder and he drew closer to the cell. "Gimme the keys, dummy."

"I-I ain't no d-dummy, Tex. I speak good. R-Real good."

Tex bellowed out a sarcastic laugh. "You speak good, do ya?"

"Yeah, I does."

"Where's them keys?"

Keys rattled, the lock clicked, and the door crashed open. Behind Tex, shadows stretched long across the parade ground. Not long to wait until sunset.

Tex cast his eyes around the cell before fixing his angry gaze on Sabrina. He sniffed.

"You been talking to poor George?"

She refuse to meet his eyes and kept her mouth closed, still relishing the aftertaste of the food. She had secreted one slice of bread under her pillow—just in case.

"I asked you a question, Frenchie." He clenched his big hands into fists and stepped further into the cell. "Answer me, damn it."

She looked up at him and nodded.

"I thanked him for the food. That's all."

Tex glanced around the cell once more and sniffed again.

"Enjoy yer food?"

"*Oui, merci.* Yes, thank you."

"Make the most of it. You never know when the next hot meal's gonna turn up."

"The colonel said—"

"It don't matter what the colonel said. I'm in charge of the prisoners, and I decide who gets what."

"Prisoners? There are others?"

Tex grinned and lifted a shoulder. "That's for me to know and for you to find out, Frenchie. Remember what I told you 'bout the water!"

He slammed the door, laughing as he locked it.

Sabrina crossed her legs, leaned back against the blockwork wall, and settled in for another unending night. At least the odious man had forgotten to chain her up again. She could use the toilet as and when she needed it, unfettered by the restriction.

As for the water in the tap ... was he telling the truth?

———

Sometime later—it could have been two hours, could have been longer—her attention was drawn by someone scratching at the door. The small observation hatch in the door creaked open.

"M-Miss?" George whispered. "Y-You still awake?"

She jumped from the bed and felt her way to the door in the near total darkness.

"Yes, George."

"Y-You don't need to pay no m-mind to Tex. He's just messin' with ya. That water's fresh and pure. Straight up out of the m-mountain.

And here. T-Take this." He pushed something through the bars. "I-It's a magazine for when it's light. G-Got some n-nice pictures in it ... a-and stories too. Thought you m-might like it to help p-pass the time. But don't let Tex see it. G-Good place to hide it is under your m-mattress. Th-That's where I hides my special things. You know?"

Sabrina took the rolled up offering and clutched it to her chest.

"*Merci*, George. Thank you."

"It ain't n-nothin'."

The hatch closed and darkness returned, this time almost total.

She felt her way back to the bed, holding tight to her treasure. Unexpected tears stung her eyes and a lump formed in her throat. The generous act of a total stranger overwhelmed her. Not only had George shown her kindness, he had unwittingly given her a weapon. Now all she required was the correct opportunity. If she waited and watched, surely one would come.

———

Woken as usual at 07:00 hours by the clumsy bugler who made an unholy mess of sounding "Reveille", Sabrina rolled off the cot, removed her shirt to keep it fresh, and performed her regular morning yoga routine topless. Suppleness was key. When the moment arrived, she would be ready. Thirty minutes or so later, fully warmed and as loose as possible given the situation, she washed using the tiny rectangle of soap. She dried herself with her old night-clothes and dragged on the fairly clean shirt once more. She returned to the cot and unfurled the magazine, which turned out to be a copy of *Monster Truck World*—five months out of date. As George suggested, plenty of pictures graced the pages, but the articles on engine rebuilds and suspension upgrades failed to draw her in, but did, at least, help pass the time.

Outside her cell the sounds of a waking army camp filtered through the walls and door and drew her attention. Shouted orders. Troops performed close-order parade ground drills, marching in time. Small-arms fire echoed from a nearby shooting range. They all vied for her attention. So much so, that she almost missed the sound of a key scraping in the lock.

Heart thumping, she rolled up the magazine as tight as it would go, gripped it firmly in her hand, and hid it behind her back.

Dieu, aide et protège-moi. God, help and protect me.

The door opened and Tex stepped inside. The same girl from the previous day entered behind him, carrying another tray. This one held a steaming bowl of porridge and a cup. Without looking at Sabrina, the girl placed the tray on the cot and hurried away.

"How you doin', Frenchie? Sleep well?"

Sabrina lifted her chin in a nod and glanced at the bowl, hoping he might think her desperate to eat. If he took the hint and chose to torture her some more, the bully might lower his guard.

Tex stepped closer.

If he took one more step …

Outside, close by, a huge diesel engine roared into life. She jerked in shock.

"What's up, honey? Did the big truck scare you?"

He shuffled a pace closer. Stood right in front of her, his midriff at face height. She whipped out the rolled up magazine and drove it into his groin as hard as she could.

Air and spittle whooshed out of him and he doubled over. Sabrina jumped up and drove the magazine into his face, again and again. Blood spurted from his nose.

Tex reached up, trying to protect his face from the blows. She drove her heel into the point of his chin. His head snapped back and cracked against the floor. His eyes rolled up into his head, then closed. Tex lay in a ball, still. Briefly, she considered attaching the manacle to his wrist, to see how he enjoyed the experience, but it would have taken too long.

She turned, dived through the open doorway … and ran straight into George and his loaded shotgun. They fell in a tangled heap of arms, legs, and exploding shotgun. Both barrels blasted simultaneously. Close. Deafening. Hot powder scalded her face, stung her eyes.

She lay on top of George, stunned, ears ringing, gasping for breath.

People shouted. Yelling. Cursing.

George pushed her off and rolled away. Someone grasped her hair and pulled. Muffled shouting reached her buzzing ears.

"Bitch! You fucking bitch."

An open-handed blow stung her cheek and snapped her head to the left. A second slap landed on her other cheek, and a third. A fist drove into her stomach, winding her. She lost control of her limbs. Her arms and legs turned to jelly, and she slumped towards the ground, but the grip on her hair held her up. It tugged, yanked, jerked her upright.

"Come here, bitch!"

Tex dragged her into the cell and threw her to the floor. She slammed onto the concrete, landed on her tailbone, and cracked her left elbow. Numbness spread down her forearm and into her hand. For a moment, she could not move her fingers, then pins and needles tingled through her hand. Relief. No broken bones.

Tex stood over her, hair dishevelled, chest heaving. Livid red welts coloured both sides of his face. Blood streamed from his nose and ran down his chin. He stood still for a moment, fuming. Then, arms thrown wide for balance, he planted his left foot one step towards her and pulled back his right, ready to launch a kick that might end her life.

"No!" George screamed and hurtled through the doorway and threw himself at Tex. "L-Leave her b-be!"

He threw his arms around Tex, wrapping him in a bearhug. Off balance, Tex toppled sideways and they crashed against the wall. The impact broke the hold and George stumbled backwards. Tex recovered quickly and slammed his hammer fists into the boy's face. George scrambled away, no match for the giant of a man.

"Run!" George screamed at Sabrina. "Quick!"

Sabrina tried to scramble to her feet, but she might as well have been wading through mud. Her arms and legs refused to work properly. As she focused on crawling towards the open doorway, the corner of her vision caught sight of Tex standing over George and kicking him in the head again and again. The blows landed with sickening force.

George stopped moving, his head a bloody, pulpy mess.

Sabrina pushed herself to her wobbly feet and lurched towards the door. A hand grabbed her shoulder and spun her around. A fist struck her face.

Darkness swirled around her.

Noise faded into silence and she toppled into a merciful nothingness.

CHAPTER FIVE

Pain blossomed and shrank. Each time she moved, the hurt returned anew. Agony piled upon agony. Groaning and shuffling continued in the darkness. Someone whimpered. Sabrina could not tell who was making the noises, but did not think it was her.

George?

Was he still in the cell?

Sabrina tried opening her eyes, but only the right lid worked well enough to allow in any light. The other, swollen shut, remained closed, the eye dark.

A shadow appeared in the doorway. It moved towards her. She jerked awake and squirmed away, towards the corner of her cot and imagined safety. A chain rattled and the manacle rasped against her wrist, digging in, opening the part-healed wound. She raised her left hand, and the chain rattled again.

Trapped. Chained. Hopeless.

Hot tears spilled from her eyes and rolled down her face, stinging her bruised and swollen cheeks. She tried not to sniffle.

"Think you could escape, huh?" Tex growled, standing over her, close and intimidating.

He kicked the frame of the cot. She flinched.

"Hit me, would ya!"

Another kick jolted the cot.

"Kick me, huh? I should rip your head off, bitch!"

She lifted her head. Pain flared, running from her neck into her right shoulder. When she breathed deeply, her ribs hurt, but it did not feel as though any ribs were broken. Heavily bruised only. Bad, but it could have been worse. Much worse. At least she still lived.

Yes, she still lived, but ....

"Where is George?"

Tex shot out a huge hand. His fingers encircled her throat, constricting, squeezing, throttling the life from her. Unable to breathe, she gagged, kicked out, but he twisted and her booted feet struck nothing but empty air. She reached up, clutched his wrist with both hands, dug her sharpened nails into the exposed flesh. They scratched, cut, drew blood. He yelped, pulled his hand free, held it up to his face. Blood dripped from the ripped flesh.

"Fucking bitch!" he yelled and raised the hand again.

"Lieutenant Scarborough! What's going on here?"

Colonel Caren appeared in the doorway. The stodgy Captain Boniface stood behind him. Tex dropped his hand and stood to attention, his whole body rigid.

"Well?" Caren shouted. "Answer me, damn it!"

Tex swallowed hard. "Questioning the prisoner, sir."

"Interrogating prisoners is beyond the scope of your remit, *Lieutenant*." He stood close to Tex, looking up at the taller man, who ground his teeth but kept silent. "What exactly happened here yesterday? I've yet to receive your written report."

"Prisoner tried to escape, sir. I prevented it."

"She tried to escape? I gathered that much, Lieutenant. What happened?"

"She had help, sir."

"Who from?"

"George, sir. The cretin gave her a magazine, sir. She attacked me with it and tried to run."

"Cretin? Cretin?" The colonel raised his heels from the floor and lowered them again. "Now listen to me, Lieutenant Scarborough, Private Tucker swore allegiance to the Doomsday Creed and as such, deserves all the respect due to each and every member. When you insult one member of the Creed, you insult us all. You insult me!"

"Sir, yes, sir. My apologies, sir."

"Don't let it happen again!" the colonel barked.

"Yes, sir. I mean, no, sir. Sorry, sir."

The colonel studied Tex's injuries and shot a glance at Sabrina, his eyes alive with what? Mirth?

"Such a tiny a woman did all that damage to your face with an itty bit of paper?"

"She ... rolled it up and used it as a sap, sir."

"Begs the question who's the sap, doesn't it?"

"Sorry, sir?"

"Maybe I should invite her to join us and you two can swap places, Lieutenant Scarborough."

"Private Tucker helped her, sir. Jumped me and told her to run."

"Is that so? He's a traitor, you say?"

"Yes, sir. I do."

Colonel Caren nodded and glanced at Sabrina again.

"In which case, you need to present your accusations to the adjutant in writing. If Captain Andersen considers that there's a case to answer, he will raise the charges and they will be heard by a General Court Martial. Is that clear?"

"Sir, yes, sir!"

"Do you still wish to accuse Private Tucker of treason, Lieutenant?" he raised an eyebrow. "But remember, if the accused is acquitted, he has the right to bring charges of intentional malice against his accuser."

Tex squinted sideways at Sabrina before fixing his bloodshot eyes on the colonel.

"Permission to talk freely, Colonel?"

"Of course. Speak up, son."

"Can we take this matter outside? Somewhere the prisoner can't hear, sir?"

"Why shouldn't she hear this? We have nothing to hide." His gaze followed the direction Tex looked, and he smiled at her.

Sabrina took her opportunity.

"All this talk of honour and martial law," she said, "it's a joke. You are all criminals and murderers. You kidnapped me and are holding me for ransom. How honourable is this?"

Colonel Caren turned to face her fully for the first time since entering the cell.

"Ms LeMaître," he said, pulling back his shoulders, "we are at war with the Government of the United States. In war, honourable men sometimes have to resort to dishonourable acts. It is unfortunate perhaps, but—"

"War? You are at war?"

Sabrina shuffled to the edge of the cot and jumped to her feet, ignoring the riot of pain exploding through her body with every movement. "This is how you justify your torture?"

"Torture? What torture? Before your escape attempt, we treated you well."

"You do not consider a public beating as poor treatment?"

"Under the circumstances, that particular chastisement was a necessity. Justifiable."

"Justifiable chastisement?"

"You sassed the colonel in front of the men!" Tex shouted.

Colonel Caren raised his hand for silence. Tex shut his mouth, glared at her, swollen faced, and pumped out his chest.

"Not only is he a coward," she said, keeping her voice quiet and even, "but he is also a sadist!"

Sabrina raised her hand to display the wound on her wrist.

"Your Lieutenant chains me to the wall," she said, "and he gives me only enough slack to reach the toilet. I cannot reach the *lavabo*—the washbasin. He starves me for days and leaves me without water. And then he beats me." With her unchained hand, she pointed to her face. "Torturing women. This is acceptable in your *war*?"

"You attacked me!" Tex said, sounding pitiful. He turned to the colonel again. "Like I said, sir. She attacked me with a rolled up magazine, one George gave her against my express orders. And when she ran—"

"Enough." The colonel cut his hand through the air, and Tex snapped his mouth closed again. "We shall discuss this later."

"But, sir. This is all—"

"Lieutenant Scarborough, you are dismissed!"

"Sir, yes, sir."

Tex stood to attention, whipped out a salute, which the colonel returned, and marched out of the cell. He sidestepped past a smirking Captain Boniface and left in disgrace, tail tucked firmly between his legs.

Sabrina sneered at the back of the scolded Lieutenant.

"If that man represents the Doomsday Creed, I pity you, Colonel Caren."

The leader of the Creed sighed. "In my position, Ms LeMaître, I have to take whatever I can get. Can't afford to be too choosy at this formative stage. Still"—he rubbed his hands together—"let's talk about more pressing matters, shall we?"

Her legs gave out on her and Sabrina sank back onto her cot.

"Where's George?" she asked, staring up at the man in charge of the Creed. The man in charge of her destiny.

"Don't worry about young George. He's in good hands."

"Where is he?"

He pointed over his shoulder, in the general direction of the hangars. "We took him to the infirmary. He's being well cared for. I'll let you see him when he wakes—depending upon the outcome of our discussion, of course."

"Is he still unconscious?"

The colonel nodded.

"For how long?"

He shrugged. "He's out for the count, but his breathing's steady, and his heart rate's strong. The boy's going to be okay."

Sabrina clenched her hands into fists.

"Tex—I mean Lieutenant Scarborough kicked him in the head many times. He needs a hospital. There could be internal bleeding. He may die!"

The colonel shook his head.

"Uh-uh. A trip to the hospital's out of the question. Civilian doctors ask too many questions. Questions I don't want to answer." Caren shrugged and added a sigh. "Fatalities are inevitable. Such are the fortunes of war."

"But George is young. He has no place in your army. No place in *any* army. Why did you accept him into your Doomsday Creed?"

Caren sighed. "Had no choice. His mother, my sister, died in an auto accident more'n ten years ago. I've been looking after the kid since he was eight."

"George is your nephew?"

"I don't tend to shout about it, but he is. Poor boy doesn't have anyone but me to take care of him."

"Allowing your nephew to die of head injuries is no way to take care of him, Colonel Caren."

He held out his hands in a sign of helplessness. "As Charles Darwin said, it's a case of the survival of the fittest. If George doesn't make it, I can't be held responsible."

"Then you are definitely a criminal."

"Many great leaders are seen as criminals when they first lift their heads above the parapet, Ms LeMaître. But I don't want to talk about that any further. We have another issue to deal with."

Sabrina quailed inside, but tried not to show it on her face.

"What issue?"

"One that relates to your current situation," he said, signalling to his associate. "Captain Boniface, if you please."

The pudgy captain fully entered the cell, carrying a large video camera with a built-in light attached to a folded tripod stand.

"Now, Ms LeMaître," the colonel said, "would you like some time to prepare yourself before we start filming?"

"Prepare myself in what way?"

He smiled.

"Well, I don't know. Perhaps you'd like to make yourself more presentable? Run a brush through your hair or something? I'm afraid we don't have access to any makeup, though."

He dropped the smile.

"You wish me to look less like someone who has been beaten by your sadistic jailer?"

Colonel Caren scowled.

"Okay, in that case, we'll carry on. Captain Boniface, make ready, if you please."

The captain spread out the legs of the tripod and settled the video camera in front of the cot. He hit a button and the built-in light flared, dazzling her. She closed her eyes and turned her head away.

"Shucks," the captain muttered, "always doing that. Just one moment, Colonel."

"Take all the time you need, Captain. Ms LeMaître's going nowhere, and this needs to be perfect."

Sabrina blinked the orange afterimage from her eyes and watched Captain Boniface angle the light upwards and fiddle with some of the controls.

"There," he said. "Perfect focus and the lighting's good, too. Hides the worst of the bruising. Can't do nothing about that cut lip or the closed eye, though. Ready when you are, Colonel."

The colonel unfolded a newspaper and tossed it to her.

"It's today's *Arizona Daily Star*. Hold it up so your grandfather can see the date clearly."

Sabrina hesitated. She did not want him to grow suspicious of an overly rapid compliance.

"If I do so, will you allow me to see George?"

"I shall certainly consider it."

Sabrina lowered her eyes, simulating fear.

"*Merci.* Thank you," she whispered.

Assez bien. Good enough.

She wished to send the video message as much as the colonel did.

"Very well." He cleared his throat and spoke firmly. "Okay, here's how this is going down. You'll read out a statement I've prepared and answer any questions I ask clearly and concisely. You will speak only in English. If you try to give any hint of who we are or where you're being held, I'll stop the recording. Then, I'll invite Lieutenant Scarborough back in and tell him to slice off one of your fingers or an ear, which we'll send to you grandfather as proof of life. It will also confirm our intent. Do I make myself clear?"

She allowed her lower lip to tremble.

"I-I promise not to say anything untoward."

"Excellent. And please feel free to explain away your cuts and bruises as you see fit. Perhaps you'd like to tell him they were the result of an accident." He stuck out his chin and tilted his head to one side. The bones in his neck cracked. "Captain Boniface, am I out of shot?"

"Yes, sir."

"Okay. Start filming."

The flabby man pressed a button and nodded.

"Hold it up," Colonel Caren ordered, pointing to the newspaper on her lap.

She opened it to the front page and held it under her chin.

"Good. Now, state your name and the organisation you work for."

She swallowed hard before responding.

"I am Sabrina LeMaître. I am employed by European Small Arms and Personal Protection, A/S, and I work directly for my grandfather, Maurice LeMaître."

Colonel Caren frowned, but let her embellishment pass unremarked.

"Read this."

He removed a folded sheet of paper from the breast pocket of his tunic and stretched out to hand it across. He made sure only his arm appeared in the light.

Sabrina opened the paper and scan-read the short statement.

Blood drained from her face and bile rose from the pit of her stomach.

Mon Dieu. He is not serious.

She stared up at the madman, wide eyed. He smiled down at her, oozing confidence and certainty.

"Read it!" he ordered.

She coughed, took a deep, halting breath, and read the paper verbatim.

"Grandfather, I am being held by the Defenders of Liberty and Justice." She licked her cut lip and took another breath. "They will release me unharmed when you send them all the necessary access codes and security schedules to Brown and Company's regional research and storage facility in Arizona. If you contact the police or the federal authorities, or if you do not comply within five days, the Defenders will kill me and dispose of my body in such a way that no one will ever find it." She raised her eyes to stare into the camera lens. "Please help me, Grandfather."

Colonel Caren nodded his acceptance and held out his hand. She returned the note.

"The newspaper, too," he said. "I haven't finished reading it yet."

She tossed him the paper.

"Very good. Now, you can tell your grandfather how well you're being looked after."

She took a deep breath. The time had arrived.

"The Cree—Defenders are treating me adequately. I am eating and drinking well, and I am ... healthy."

Colonel Caren scowled again and tapped a finger to his cheek.

"These cuts and bruises"—she waved a hand in front of her face —"are the result of a fall. It was an accident and entirely my own fault."

"Good," the colonel said, nodding. "Very good. Now, given the parameters we discussed earlier, is there anything personal you'd like to say to your grandpa to help him make his decision?"

She stared at him in disbelief. The arrogant, over-confident man had just given her the opportunity she had been praying for.

"*Grand-père* Mo-Mo, please do not worry about me. Over time, these bruises will fade. They are even less serious than the damage the seagull caused to your new silk shirt in Nice. Please do as these people ask."

The colonel sliced his hand in front of his throat and Captain Boniface turned off the recorder.

"What did you mean by that seagull bullshit?"

Merde!

She swallowed hard and shook her head.

"My grandfather is an old man. Very weak. Very sick. I do not know how my ... situation will affect his health. The seagull story is an old family joke. I was trying indicate that I really am well and in full control of all my faculties."

The colonel shot a sideways look at his subordinate before returning his harsh gaze to her.

"Tell me the story. Explain the joke."

"Many years ago, grandfather and I were on vacation in Nice when a seagull defecated all over his brand new silk shirt. He was very angry, but I could not stop laughing. At the time, I was very young. It is a story we tell over and over again."

The colonel sniffed. "Not particularly funny."

"Family jokes rarely are, Colonel. It is like the story of a fisherman. The tale grows more outlandish with each retelling."

After an endless pause, Colonel Caren nodded.

"Yes," he said. "I take your point. Very well, it's acceptable."

As the colonel turned away, Sabrina tried to keep the look of triumph from her face.

"Thank you, Captain. You can send the ransom demand as it stands. Send it this evening."

Captain Boniface nodded and said, "Yes, sir." He collected his equipment and left.

Before she could do anything more than consider leaping on the colonel and using him to barter for her freedom, a tall, dark-haired man with sergeant stripes stitched onto his sleeves showed himself in the open doorway. He looked her up and down, leered appreciatively, and rested a hand atop the sidearm sticking out from the holster on his hip. His action made it clear that she had no option but to sit still and wait.

"I had hoped to send a video to your grandfather that didn't show any injuries," the colonel said, "but I imagine your present condition will add an extra sense of urgency to the situation and ensure our demands are met. There's nothing more motivational that seeing a loved one in distress."

"That does not seem to matter in your case, Colonel Caren. If it did, George would be in hospital right now, not lying in a bed in a filthy building, possibly bleeding into his brain."

The colonel stiffened.

"Don't you dare try to guilt me into action, woman! The camp has a first rate infirmary."

"I saw the state of that building when your pet ape dragged me to the parade ground yesterday. It is derelict. A disgrace."

Colonel Caren smiled. "But on the inside, it's a fully equipped infirmary. There are hospital beds and first class medical provisions. Uncle Sam himself would be happy to use it as one of his field hospitals. Furthermore, we have ... obtained the services of a fully qualified medic who is providing the best treatment possible. I can assure you, I provide nothing but the best for members of the Creed. Anyway, I don't have all day. We need to move forward."

Again, he rubbed his hands together.

"Before we do that, might I ask a question?"

The colonel opened his hands to give tacit permission.

"Your ransom demand, you are serious?"

The colonel smiled, cold and hard.

"Deadly serious."

"It is impossible. My grandfather would never—"

"Perhaps not." He shrugged. "However, when he sees the video of your injured face ... it might encourage a change of heart. You'd better hope he does the right thing, Ms LeMaître. If he doesn't, it won't end well for you."

He left without saying another word. The sergeant winked at her before slamming and locking the door, leaving her in the unlit cell, alone with only her dark and milling thoughts for company.

What on earth would the maniac do with the material stored in the Brown and Company laboratory? In his hands, such a weapon would be a game changer for the Doomsday Creed.

CHAPTER SIX

Maurice LeMaître picked up the portrait photo from his desk. In its silver frame, it weighed heavily in his hand. Taken on the day she received her doctorate, the beautiful face of his granddaughter smiled out at him, her dark eyes shining and alive with justifiable excitement. A certified genius, she had completed her doctorate one year ahead of schedule, and had stunned the lecturers with her groundbreaking, topic-defining thesis—not one word of which Maurice had fully understood. The title and abstract included phrases such as "internet security paradigms", "whip-smart algorithms", and "optimising search strings in digital subsets", whatever any of that meant. With commendable patience, the darling girl had tried to walk him through the headline elements of her research, but Maurice was a simple man, an engineer. He did not have a clue and ended up nodding along to her explanation, pretending to understand, but being genuinely delighted with her success and her enthusiasm.

He pushed himself out of his chair, remembering not to groan from the effort—Sabrina teased him remorselessly when he grunted like the old man she knew he really was—and carried the photo to the window. It showed him a bright day of early summer in the most beautiful city in the world. The city of light and love.

Named after his darling daughter, Sabrina's mother, *Tour Celeste*, ESAPP's new fifteen-storey chrome and silvered glass headquarters had none of the panache of the original, shambling city centre buildings. The board's preferred choice, *La Tour ESAPP*, had been suggested by the branding agency it had hired to provide the company with a "root and branch" corporate makeover.

La Tour ESAPP!

How prosaic. The very idea.

The agency wanted to charge five hundred thousand euros for the design concept and the logo, which used italics to show ESAPP as a "forward thrusting and modern entity". They also wanted to change the colour of the logo from PMS reflex blue—the colour on the French flag—to Nile Green. Their argument? It would highlight the green credentials of the company.

Utter nonsense.

How he and Sabrina had laughed at the bare-faced cheek of the agency who wanted huge payment for doing almost nothing in return.

Without telling Maurice in advance, Sabrina had taken it upon herself to investigate said agency. The wonderful child did something clever with the technology she understood so well and discovered that ESAPP's Senior Director of Strategy and Partnerships secretly owned forty percent of the branding organisation.

Being able to expose such a conflict of interest had been a revelation to Sabrina. She told Maurice that she had never felt so alive or so useful to the company—useful to him personally. From that moment forwards, Sabrina Faroukh had been "born". ESAPP's very own secret security officer.

Their in-house spy.

At first, she concentrated on investigating the many inventory losses that arose in a company the size of ESAPP, which had so many disparate factories and storage facilities throughout the world. The time she spent embedded undercover inside the SAMS IT department—where she met, and ultimately helped, the infamous Captain Ryan Kaine—had cemented her role and indirectly led to her current predicament.

Maurice stared through the window of his new office and bit back the tears.

The view contained little of the original he had enjoyed from his old office. He could barely see the magnificent Eiffel Tower in the smog-shrouded distance, nor the glorious serpentine meanderings of *La Seine*, only the occasional glint of the sun reflecting off the water as it flowed through the city he loved. But Maurice paid scant attention to the wide and tree-lined *Avenue de Wagram*, the main artery into the city centre.

Where are you, my darling girl? Where?

In the five days since her last report, he had sent out subtle enquiries to some of his usual contacts in the security world, but could not say much, for fear of adding to Sabrina's danger. Then the video arrived. The hideous video and the hidden message within. The video that changed everything.

As a result, Maurice contacted a man he knew only by reputation and had never met in person. A man Sabrina trusted with her life. A man wanted by the authorities throughout Europe for a crime against humanity—a crime he did commit, but not knowingly.

Maurice stared down at the picture of his beloved granddaughter, the only family he had left, and edged away from the window, the view unseen. He returned the photo to its position, pride of place on his desk, and lowered himself into his comfortable leather chair.

The portable telephone on his desk vibrated—his unregistered and private telephone—shocking him into action. Few people knew the number. One being ... Sabrina!

He snatched it up, fumbled with unresponsive, arthritic fingers, dropped it to the surface, and picked it up again. Finally, his thumb found the receive button and pressed. A text message. He reached for his reading glasses and perched them on his nose.

. . .

Ten minutes. Griffin.

Not Sabrina, but the next best thing.

Enfin. At last!

He hit a combination of keys to activate the application Sabrina had developed and uploaded onto his portable. It would delete the message and scrub the device forensically clean. In their business, unsecure data could cost lives, and in this instance, potentially the life of his beloved grandchild.

Maurice puffed out his cheeks, exhaled deeply, and tried to rub life into his numb face. He did not wish "Monsieur Griffin" to view him as a wizened and beaten old man, even though he felt exactly that way.

"Enough," he said, speaking to the photo, "crying will not bring you back to me."

He leaned forwards and depressed the switch on his desk intercom. Its mechanical buzz in the outer office failed to filter through the sound-proofing built into the reinforced walls of his inner sanctum. His protective shell. Its bullet resistant glass would stop armour-piercing rounds. The head of ESAPP would be safe from anything but a missile launched from a passing helicopter.

Alain Dubois, the man paid handsomely to protect Maurice and other senior employees from harm, told him he would be safer in the underground security bunker, but who wished to spend their working life as a troglodyte?

"*Oui, Monsieur LeMaître?*" Katherine answered his call.

"Katherine, I am expecting two guests, *Monsieur et Madame* Griffin. They will arrive at the reception desk within the next few minutes."

"*Guests, Monsieur LeMaître? You have nothing in the calendar for this afternoon. This is most irregular. Is Alain aware of the change in protocol?*"

"It is a last minute social engagement, Katherine. The Griffins are old family friends from the UK. I have added their details to the system. Make sure they are made welcome."

"But of course, sir."

"They are not to be delayed or searched in any way. Is that clear? They would be mortified, s would I."

"But of course, sir," she repeated, but sounded doubtful.

"Have Alain show them to my express elevator. And please organise some refreshments. Coffee, tea, and a selection of soft beverages."

"As you wish, Monsieur LeMaître."

"And finally, do you have any social engagements this evening?"

"None that I cannot postpone, sir. Will you be needing me later?"

"That is possible, Katherine."

"In which case, sir. I am entirely at your disposal."

"As usual, Katherine, you have my eternal gratitude. I do not know what I would do without you. I will let you know if you are required as soon I am able. *Merci beaucoup.*"

He clicked the button and reclined into his seat.

While he waited, Maurice stared lovingly at the photo.

"Il viendra, ma chérie. He will come for you."

His granddaughter had the dark eyes, the classical beauty, and the natural wisdom of her mother. From her father, she inherited a raw intellect and a questioning mind. These traits, when combined with her innate sense of honesty and generosity, produced a perfect human being, and one of which any grandfather would be immensely proud. However, beneath these extraordinary physiological and intellectual characteristics hid a weakness—the thirst for excitement and the implacable desire to see justice done. His darling Sabrina would throw herself into the middle of a fight if she felt the justification, and would ignore her personal safety at the same time. As a result, she constantly ran into danger, as exemplified by her association with his impending guests.

The danger she now faced, where would it lead?

Où es-tu, ma chérie? Where are you?

A dark cloud rolled in front of the late afternoon sun, cutting the brightness of the office and reinforcing the gloom that had overtaken his emotions.

The buzz of the intercom interrupted his thoughts.

"*Oui*, Katherine?"

"Your guests have arrived, sir. They are in the *ascenseur*."

"*Merci*, Katherine. Please bring the refreshments in five minutes."

The intercom clicked into silence. Moments later, the yellow light above the stainless steel door to his private express elevator blinked on and its accompanying electronic ding made sure Maurice could not miss the signal. The *ascenseur* rarely operated without him being inside, only Sabrina had permission to use it without Maurice in attendance.

He planted his palms on the tabletop, pushed himself to his feet, and awaited the arrival of a man he never expected to meet in person. A man he never wanted to meet in person

The *ascenseur* sounded again and the light turned green. Seconds later, the door slid back to reveal an inconspicuous-looking couple. The man poked his head out and scanned the room with a practised sweep of his eyes, before stepping aside and allowing his companion to exit the mirrored compartment first. Not only was Captain Ryan Kaine a careful man, he also had impeccable manners.

An officer and a gentleman?

CHAPTER SEVEN

The couple presenting themselves to the world as *Monsieur et Madame* William Griffin were of a similar height, around one-point-eight metres. Above average height for a woman, average for a man. Ryan Kaine held himself erect, his bearing military. Less physically intimidating than Maurice would have expected of a Captain who had led a troop of the Special Boat Service, whose operations were legendary and similar in scope to its French equivalent, the Action Division of the DSGE. Although physically unremarkable, his military record stood for itself.

The captain wore a pair of stiff-soled walking boots, once highly polished but currently scuffed and worn, creased trousers, and a long-sleeved shirt buttoned at the cuffs. Wavy dark hair, greying at the temples, covered his ears and flopped over a pair of all-seeing brown eyes. A full beard softened his chin and covered much of his rugged but handsome face. A backpack dangled by its strap from one shoulder, and his eyes remained restless, aware of everything.

Lara Orchard hid behind the dowdy clothing of a middle-aged woman—comfortable-looking walking shoes with low heels, a tan trouser suit hanging loose about a slim body. Her pale pink blouse was open at the neck, but not plunging. She wore her long brown hair tied back into a low and loose ponytail. Her makeup had been skilfully applied, designed to conceal rather than enhance her natural beauty. Subtle and smart. Intelligent hazel eyes shone bright and took in everything within the office without appearing to do so.

Superficially, they made an unremarkable couple, but closer study revealed much, much more.

The sun chose that precise moment to peek out from behind the clouds and backlight Lara Orchard's hair, showing shades of auburn hidden within the brown.

Maurice stepped around from behind his desk and approached his guests, right hand outstretched in welcome.

"*Madame* Orchard, *Capitaine* Kaine, welcome. And thank you so much for coming so quickly."

Kaine stiffened at the use of their real names, forever cautious. How difficult it must have been for him to relax his guard when everyone he met might be an enemy, prepared to hand him over to the authorities, or worse.

"Fear not, *Capitaine*. This office is completely secure. Sabrina herself designed and installed the electronic shield. A metallic mesh is embedded into the walls and random automatic sweeps test for devices that may have been smuggled in by visitors or office staff. On top of which, Alain Dubois, our Director of Corporate Security, conducts regular scans to search for listening devices."

"Monsieur Dubois?" she asked. "Is he the gentleman who met us in the foyer?"

"Indeed, he is."

"A *Quebecois*?" Kaine asked.

Maurice tried not to show his surprise. Most non-French assumed Alain to be an American.

"Yes, that is correct. Alain was indeed born in Quebec. How did you know?"

"I've worked with a few French Canadians in my time. Recognised the accent."

Maurice nodded in appreciation.

"Like you, Alain has a military background. He was a member of JTF2. You have heard of it?"

Kaine nodded.

"Joint Task Force 2. A special operations group in the Canadian Armed Forces," he said, addressing his pretend wife.

He turned to Maurice and added, "Good people. Well trained."

Maurice allowed himself a smile.

"Alain has worked many years for ESAPP. He is indeed a good man. Reliable and efficient."

"Forgive me, *Monsieur* LeMaître," Kaine said. "I need to check things for myself. Just one moment, please."

Maurice expected the security conscious man to remove a scanning wand from the backpack and wave it around the office as Alain took great pains to do each time Maurice hosted a business meeting, whether with colleagues or rivals. But no, the captain simply reached a hand up to his ear and tapped it once.

"Alpha One to Base. Come in. Over." He spoke quietly, his expression serious.

He repeated the radio summons, glanced at his companion, and shook his head.

"Nothing. Not even our little friend can hear us."

A slow smile formed, and his whole body seemed to relax.

Madame Orchard returned his smile, its warmth genuine and brightening her whole face. "He's going to be a tad miffed."

"I'd put money on him trying to break through whatever barriers Sabrina's installed right now and pulling out his long hair when he fails." Kaine turned to face Maurice. "Excuse me, *Monsieur* LeMaître, we have a very good friend who's every bit as gifted as Sabrina as far as technology is concerned. This is one of the very few times his comms unit has failed us. A bone-conducting earpiece." He waved a hand to his ear by way of explanation."

"Ah yes," Maurice said, stepping even closer to his guests, "you are talking about the reclusive hacker who goes by the name Corky. *N'est-ce pas?*"

"You've heard of Corky?" she asked.

"Only through Sabrina. Who speaks very highly of him."

"Speaking of Sabrina, *Monsieur* LeMaître," she said, "your message said she has disappeared. How can we help?"

Again, Maurice smiled. Clearly, the captain had not told her everything. As agreed during their private telephone conversation, Maurice would maintain their arrangement and spin a tale that was only partly true.

"Please, call me Maurice. We are to be friends, I think." He took her hand in his and shook it briefly and formally. From experience, he had learned that the British were reluctant to greet each other with a kiss on the cheek, and kissing the back of the hand had fallen from favour many decades ago.

"*Enchantée*, Maurice, *et je suis* Lara," she replied, her accent impeccable.

"Thank you, Lara, for responding to my summons." Maurice half-bowed and turned to face Kaine. "And you, *Capitaine*."

"Please, Ryan," he said, grasping Maurice's hand in a firm and calloused grip. "If Sabrina's in trouble, we'll do anything we can to help."

"*Merci*, Ryan, Lara," Maurice said, pointing them towards the softly upholstered chairs in front of the window with one of the best views of the city. "You have had a long journey, I think. Might I offer you some refreshments before we begin? Coffee, or perhaps, tea. ... No, Lara. Do not look so aghast. My personal assistant, Katherine, was taught how to make tea by an English ex-patriate of my acquaintance. It is quite palatable, or so I have been led to believe."

"Thanks, Maurice, " she said, "tea would be lovely."

Ryan led Lara to the sunlit area and they stood, admiring the spectacular panorama.

Maurice glanced at his wristwatch. Almost five minutes had elapsed since their arrival.

Precisely on schedule, Katherine knocked on the door and

entered, carrying a heavily laden tray. She placed it on his desk, frowned at Maurice, but nodded a smile at his guests, and left without speaking.

Maurice bent to lift the heavy insulated teapot, which rattled on the tray as his gnarled, arthritic hands failed him once again. Lara rushed to his side and reached for the pot.

"Please, Maurice," she said gently. "Allow me. I know how Ryan takes it. Rather fussy about his tea, is my Ryan. Will you have something?"

She offered only empathy for his frailty, and Maurice appreciated the gesture.

"A small, black coffee would be perfect. *Merci*."

Ryan waited for Lara to pour the drinks and helped her carry the dainty cups and saucers to the occasional table sitting in front of the large window, surrounded by the comfortable chairs. Ryan sat only after they had, choosing the seat with the best view of the large office. Never totally relaxed, always *en garde*. Maurice appreciated that most of his defences would be targeted towards protecting Lara rather than himself—as the contents of their private conversation had confirmed.

Ryan finished his tea quickly and lowered the cup to the saucer.

"Please, Maurice," he said, twisting in his seat, dragging his eyes away from the window and focusing them fully onto Maurice, "tell us what you can in as much detail as possible."

Maurice raised his cup and took in the enticing aroma, desperate to take just the slightest sip, but thought better of it and returned the cup to its saucer. These days, strong coffee, no matter how delicious, played havoc with the lining of his stomach and he suffered severely as a result. Both his doctor and Sabrina warned him off the delightfully seductive poison. As did the ever-protective Katherine. Hence the warning frown she delivered when bringing the refreshments.

Staring at the bird's-eye view of Paris, hoping it would give him strength if not comfort, Maurice took a deep breath and began.

"Some weeks ago," he said, hearing the weakness in his voice and clearing his throat to compensate, "we, that is Sabrina and I, were made aware of certain ... discrepancies in the affairs of one of our subsidiaries in the United States."

He paused and pulled his focus onto Ryan. He and Lara sat close together, looking every bit the married couple their false identities proclaimed them to be. Comfortable in each other's company. Supportive.

Humans needed company—especially in adversity. With Sabrina held captive, Maurice had no one to call on for comfort. Not even Katherine.

"Are you familiar with the global footprint of ESAPP and our subsidiaries?" He looked from one to the other.

"We are," Lara said. "We had plenty of time for research during our journey here."

"In a previous existence," Ryan said, "I actually worked for ESAPP, at least, indirectly."

"Is that so?"

Ryan nodded.

"I conducted a field test on a prototype of one of your sniper rifles. The Razor SMX—a potential rival to the Accuracy AWM."

"Ah, yes. Of course. We contracted DefTech Limited on a number of occasions. Your former company produced exemplary work. Forgive me, but I am unaware of the results of that particular trial. As a matter of professional interest, how did the SMX perform?"

"Acceptably," Ryan answered somewhat noncommittally.

Maurice made a mental note to dig out the report in question, as soon as Sabrina was back. Her safe return took priority over everything else.

"Forgive me, I digress. The ramblings of an old man. As I was saying, certain discrepancies came to light in our US supply chain that could not be dealt with remotely. A local audit team discovered the irregularity, but were unable to identify its source."

"What exactly was the issue, Maurice?" Lara asked, leaning forwards in her chair, forearms resting on her knees.

"Certain items ... military items ... disappeared from the inventory."

"Your company lost some of its guns?"

"Put simply, that is correct, Lara." Maurice frowned and shook his head.

"The weapons were stolen?" Ryan asked.

"We believe so."

"But you didn't know for sure?" Lara said, surprise showing on her symmetrical and attractive face.

"The situation is rather complicated."

"Were the weapons taken from your secure storage facilities or when in transit?" Ryan asked.

"Again, at the time, we had no idea."

"How is that possible?" Lara asked, leaning even further forwards.

"This really is rather embarrassing, my dear. Most embarrassing. Allow me to explain the background. Colfax-Lacy Industries is one of our subsidiaries. Based in Cleveland, it has been an armaments manufacturer since the American Civil War.

"Originally, Colfax-Lacy supplied cannon and shot for the Union Army and has worked for the US Department of Defense since its inception. However, in recent decades, the company has diversified into other areas of the military supply chain. A significant and highly profitable part of its current workload is to refurbish damaged or obsolete military hardware for sale into the civilian sector.

"Colfax-Lacy also decommissions weapons confiscated by various police departments throughout the US Midwest. The company owns and operates a number of storage facilities and two large plants to crush these weapons. They also have a blast furnace to melt down and reuse the raw materials. You might say that Colfax-Lacy is quite literally, refashioning swords into ploughshares," Maurice said, permitting himself another slight smile.

"An ecologically sound member of the arms industry?" Lara asked, her voice laden with irony.

Ryan frowned and shook his head almost imperceptibly, but said nothing.

"That particular aspect of the Colfax-Lacy Industries portfolio is what led us to acquire the business, Lara. At ESAPP, we pride ourselves on our green credentials. Now, where was I?"

"The inventory issue," she said.

"Ah, yes. As you can imagine the logistics involved in transporting such inventory throughout the US is somewhat complicated, as is the paperwork. Many agencies play a part in overseeing the operation. The DoD, the FBI, and the ATF are all involved on a national, federal level. And this bureaucracy is further complicated by local and state organisations. Our storage facilities are bonded and ... Well, suffice to say, the bureaucracy and paperwork is extraordinarily complex."

"And open to corruption?" Ryan asked.

Maurice lowered his head and reached for the coffee. Surely one little sip would not hurt? He pulled his hand away. Yes, it would.

"So," Lara said, "in a nutshell. Some guns had gone missing and you didn't know how. Nor did you know who stole them?"

"That was correct at the time the situation came to light. But things have moved on since then."

"Since Sabrina started doing her thing," Ryan said, making it a statement, not a question.

"Yes, that too, is correct. After expending a considerable amount of time interrogating the Colfax-Lacy computer infrastructure—and without consulting me—Sabrina decided to investigate in person. She built a new identity for herself and inveigled her way into the Colfax-Lacy IT department. She did not tell me anything of her plans until *after* she had started working in America. At the time, I was under the illusion that she was visiting friends in Bordeaux."

Ryan nodded. He was not surprised.

"How long ago was this?"

"Late last January."

Lara jerked upright.

"Are you saying Sabrina has been undercover for four months and you've been out of contact for all that time?"

Maurice raised both hands to placate her. "Not at all, my dear. Sabrina reported to me daily through her secure communications system." He pointed towards the portable telephone lying on his desk, attached to the charging cable. "In all that time, she did not miss a single day. Months passed and she found nothing. And then, three weeks ago, she made a breakthrough. One moment, if you please."

Without grunting—which took rather more self-control than he wished it to—Maurice stood and made his stiff-kneed way to his desk. He removed the tiny data storage device from the drawer he always kept locked, and returned with it to the seating area by the window. In his short absence, Ryan must have felt the heat of the low afternoon sun, since he had rolled the sleeves of his shirt part way up his forearms. A fresh scar stood out pale pink above his left wrist, no doubt the legacy of a recent injury, and his right forearm bore a faded tattoo—a winged dagger. His flat stomach and the way his biceps stretched the fabric of his shirt sleeves showed that he maintained much of the formidable levels of fitness he would have attained during his time in the military.

At first glance, Ryan Kaine appeared small, a lightweight even, but the strength and power that lay beneath the clothing would be obvious to anyone who took time to study him closely.

"This flash drive contains every report Sabrina ever made in relation to her investigation. I assume you know how to access the data?" He handed the little device to Ryan, who passed it directly to Lara.

"We do," Ryan said.

She placed the unit into an internal compartment in her leather handbag and locked the clasp.

"Please take great care with the information. The life of my grand-daughter may depend upon what you discover therein."

"So," Ryan said, "this breakthrough. What can you tell us?"

"In brief, Sabrina traced the missing inventory to a small town in Arizona. A town whose name is Pine Creek."

"I'm guessing Sabrina hotfooted it to Arizona?"

"That is correct, Ryan. After resigning from her job at Colfax-Lacy on medical grounds, she changed identities and travelled to Pine Creek, posing as an artist who wished to paint the local scenery. Apparently, the landscape in the area is truly extraordinary."

"Would Sabrina be able to pass herself off as an artist?" Lara asked.

Maurice straightened. "But of course. It is a gift she inherited from her *grand-mère*, my late wife. She is very talented, as you can see." Maurice pointed to the painting that took pride of place on the wall behind his desk—a night-time scene of Paris which included the city lights reflecting on the slow flowing river.

"Magnificent," Lara said, "I noticed it right away. Your wife painted it?"

"No, that is one Sabrina created from the roof of our old offices. She is very talented, no?" Despite himself, Maurice allowed his chest to swell with pride.

"Beautiful," Ryan said, momentarily glancing up at the painting before returning his gaze Maurice. "So, she travelled to Pine Creek?"

"Yes. And from that point on, her reports became more and more ... guarded, as though she wanted to keep certain information from me."

"Are you sure these reports came from Sabrina?" Lara asked, demonstrating that she was far more than simply a hanger-on.

"Absolutely, Lara. Without doubt. We always begin our telephone conversations with questions and answers that no one else can possibly know. Without doubt, the telephone calls and text conversations were from her."

"But she seemed more reserved than usual?" Lara asked.

"Exactly so. It was as though someone was listening to her side of the conversation. Then, five days ago, she stopped calling and her reports ceased to arrive. Ryan, Lara, I am worried sick for her."

And now the lies and half-truths must begin.

CHAPTER EIGHT

Kaine studied their host carefully. The slight tremor afflicting his right hand had increased with Maurice LeMaître's agitation. The way Sabrina's grandfather grimaced when he stood and the bony knuckles Kaine felt when they shook hands confirmed the old man suffered from arthritis. Why he continued to work when money could not be an issue, Kaine couldn't even imagine. Perhaps he had no one to take over the company and was waiting for Sabrina to mature enough to take the reins.

The way Maurice's eyes glistened when he said, "Ryan, Lara, I am worried sick for her," spoke volumes. The catch in his voice demonstrated his pent up emotion.

True to form, Lara reached out and took the old man's hand in hers. She said nothing, but the touch of sympathy and empathy was typical of her.

"Did she tell you where she was staying or what she planned to do?" Kaine asked.

Although he appreciated Lara's empathy and caring nature, they had to move the process along.

Maurice blinked and inhaled deeply.

"When she arrived in Pine Creek, she took a room in a boarding house. From what I could gather, it is within walking distance of a saloon whose name matches the town. That is all I know."

Kaine nodded. At least he had a place to start looking. He glanced at Lara. Her expression told him she knew which way his thoughts were heading. The main challenge he had was working out a safe and certain way of leaving her in Paris while he headed off to the US alone. After what had happened to Danny, he wouldn't take her across the pond with him. No bloody way.

The idea of placing her in danger again tore him apart inside. He hoped she couldn't read his mind too clearly. The last thing in the world he needed at this point was a stand up, full volume fight with the only woman he'd ever really loved.

"How have you left it?" Kaine asked, returning to the script he'd agreed with the elderly man.

"In what respect?"

"I imagine a man who sits at the head of a global organisation such as ESAPP has influence in the highest circles. Have you put out any feelers?"

"Forgive me, Ryan. What are 'feelers'?"

Thus far, Maurice's English had been flawless, and, despite their special arrangement, Kaine couldn't escape the feeling that the old man was being deliberately evasive.

"Five days ago, your granddaughter dropped off the grid. I can understand why you might not want to talk to anyone in Colfax-Lacy or the Pine Creek Sheriff's department, but please don't tell me you haven't spoken to someone in authority. You must have personal contacts in the DoD and the FBI."

Maurice lowered his eyes to the table where Lara still held his hand. His grip seemed to be even tighter if the whiteness of his swollen knuckles was any indication. Lara's expression hadn't changed. Kaine doubted the elderly man's grip strength was powerful enough to cause her any discomfort.

"Indeed I have, Ryan. And the results are not as I would have expected."

"Really?"

The old man lifted his head and locked eyes with him.

"You must understand, I could not raise the alarm officially in case it placed Sabrina in greater danger or led to her exposure. The day after Sabrina failed to make contact, I spoke via video call with Louis McGregor, the Director of the FBI, whom I have known personally for a number of years. Briefly, I outlined the situation. He said he would instruct the head of the FBI Arizona field office in Phoenix to instigate discreet enquiries."

Maurice frowned and broke eye contact.

"What happened?"

Maurice met Kaine's gaze again. His eyes had cleared and a steely glint appeared that had not been evident before. Maurice LeMaître was so much more than a feeble old man.

"Louis promised to have the Phoenix SAC"—he turned to Lara and explained—"that is the Special Agent in Charge, a man called Allman Griezmann, to contact me immediately."

"And what did Mr Griezmann have to say?" Lara asked.

"Mr Griezmann called me the same day and assured me he would send his best agents to Pine Creek and let me know what they discovered. Although he has called me every day since, he has told me very little." Maurice clenched a gnarled fist. "The man speaks in clichés, Ryan. He says a great deal but tells me nothing. It feels as though he is, 'blowing smoke up my ... tailpipe', as the Americans might say."

"Have you tried contacting Director McGregor again?"

"Of course I have!" Maurice snapped, sitting up straighter, "but each time I call Washington, I am told Louis is in a meeting and cannot be disturbed. The private number I have for him transfers me to voicemail. The only person I have spoken to is the Deputy Director Jordanna Hallam." He paused for breath.

"And?" Lara asked.

"The woman is even worse than SAC Griezmann. She spouts nothing but cliché after anodyne cliché. Ryan, Lara, I am absolutely convinced the FBI is not telling me all they know, which is why I called for you."

Inwardly, Kaine smiled. Maurice was playing his role to perfection.

Lara nodded her understanding.

"Doesn't ESAPP have protocols for missing executives? You said your man, Alain Dubois, is capable. You didn't consider involving his department?"

"Yes, Alain devised our in-house protocol for hostage situations, but, as far as I know, this is not a hostage situation. Not at the moment."

He broke eye contact with Lara and glanced at Kaine, who made sure Lara couldn't see his nod.

"Furthermore," Maurice continued, "there are certain issues related to ... internal security."

"What exactly do you mean by 'issues'?" Lara asked, turning to Kaine.

Maurice released his hand from hers and sat up straighter.

"It is not easy to explain, but during our last conversation before she travelled to Pine Creek, Sabrina said that she had discovered something about the missing weapons that she tracked back to Colfax-Lacy, and maybe even the heart of ESAPP itself. I questioned her on the matter, but she would not be drawn. Sabrina said she needed proof before she could make any accusations.

"In her first report, from Pine Creek, she became much less talkative. When I tried to press her, she laughed it off and said she was being overly dramatic. She did, however, swear me to secrecy and promised to tell me more as soon as she could. She also promised to keep in touch. But there is one thing more. During her final call, she mentioned you, Ryan, although I did not realise it at the time. When Louis failed to answer my calls I became really worried. I started reviewing all she had told me. Her words kept rattling around in my head, and it was only then I decoded her message. You see, Ryan, she referred to you indirectly, and not by name."

Kaine stiffened. Although he'd known the truth, not this fabrication, Lara hadn't. She would expect him to react in a certain way to the revelation, and he didn't want to let her down.

"What exactly did she say?" he asked, lowering his tone, to make it appear as though he was hearing the information for the first time.

Maurice closed his eyes, presumably to help his memory. "When I think of the days I wasted before contacting you—"

"Maurice! What did she say?" Kaine repeated.

The old man's eyes snapped open. "She said, '*Grand-père* Mo-Mo, do not stand beneath any seagulls. Remember the wonderful holiday in Nice when the seagull dropped a nasty mess on your shoulder. It was so funny.' That is what she said as precisely as I remember it."

"Did that particular incident actually happen?" Lara asked, confusion narrowing her eyes.

"Yes, it happened as she described it. We were strolling along the *Promenade des Anglais* in Nice. She was only nine years of age. Beautiful, enthusiastic, and deeply inquisitive. And a gull did indeed make a frightful mess on the shoulder of my new shirt. She laughed hysterically as I cursed and peeled the shirt from my body." He smiled at the fond memory. "It became a tradition to tell the story at family gatherings and make great fun of the pompous and foolish old *grand-père* Mo-Mo." He sighed. "As I said, I thought nothing of it until after Sabrina failed to report for a third day. It was only after the FBI started giving me the cold shoulder—and yes, I am aware of the pun—that I made the connection."

"What connection?" Kaine prompted, although he already knew.

"As a young child," Maurice said, running off at another apparent tangent, "Sabrina showed a precocious interest in ornithology. She developed an encyclopaedic familiarity with the subject. During the brief vacations I was able to spend with her, she would demonstrate the depth of her knowledge whenever she could. I treasured that time and learned a great deal about birds—especially seabirds." He paused and looked deeply at Lara. "No need to look at me like that, my dear. These are not the silly ramblings of an old man, they are entirely relevant."

Lara's beautiful face wrinkled slightly. Whether in thought or offence, he couldn't tell. "Maurice, the thought never entered my head. I just wondered where you were heading."

"It is simple, Lara. You see, the term 'seagull' is a actually a misnomer. There is no such species. It is an informal way of referring to any member of the *Laridae* family of gulls. Sabrina would never have used the term 'seagull' by mistake. The very idea would be alien to her. She would have considered it as talking down to me. And that, she would never do."

Kaine knew exactly where Maurice was heading with his *ramblings* and, by the light of understanding he recognised in her eyes, Lara could see it, too.

"Maurice," she said quietly, "exactly what member of the *Laridae* family delivered the unfortunate 'message' to your shirt?"

The elderly man's eyes lit up and he pointed his index finger towards the ceiling. "Aha, the penny has dropped, I think. Can you guess?"

She glanced at Kaine before saying the words, reluctantly. "It was a herring gull?"

Kaine shivered.

The mere mention of *Herring Gull*—the fishing boat Kaine had hired to carry him out to the North Sea and act as a launchpad for the missile that destroyed Flight BE1555—released enough stomach acid to sear his innards. The memory of that horrific night would never, could never leave him. Along with the eighty-three innocent passengers, *Herring Gull* had also died that night, destroyed by the explosives that were intended to kill Kaine, too. That evil night, he survived by pure luck, but without Sabrina's help he would never have been able to deliver justice to the real culprit, Sir Malcolm Sampson. Kaine owed Sabrina a debt he would never be able to repay.

"*Exactement*, my dear. *Exactement*," Maurice said, lowering the pointing finger and using it to tap his temple. "And the moment my befuddled old brain made the connection, I contacted you through the website of *The 83 Trust* that Sabrina created. *Et voilà*, here you are. I hoped and prayed you would not let us down."

"What can we do to help?" Lara asked, speaking for them both.

"You will?" Maurice asked, looking from Lara to Kaine.

"Of course I will," Kaine answered.

Lara snapped her head around to glare at him.

"*You* will?"

Kaine shook his head. "Slip of the tongue, love. I meant *we'll* help. Of course we'll help," he said to Maurice. "In fact, we'll do everything we can."

Maurice raised both arms in the air and let them fall, the hands slapping his bony thighs.

"As Sabrina said, you are indeed a man of honour. I knew you would offer your services. In fact, I was so confident, I have reserved two first-class tickets for you on the next Air France flight into the US. The aeroplane departs Charles de Gaulle airport at seven o'clock tomorrow morning, and there is a short stopover in Los Angeles."

"There's no earlier flight?" Lara asked.

Maurice shook his head. "Unfortunately, you have missed the last flight today. Tomorrow is the best we can do. Ordinarily, I would put our company jet at your disposal, but under the circumstances ...."

"It might raise too many red flags?" Kaine suggested, helping their joint cause.

"*Exactement*, Ryan. The warning signals would be too loud. We cannot risk the information reaching whoever Sabrina was worried about. We could not pretend the flight is for me. These days, I rarely travel abroad as my health does not permit me to take many high altitude flights. My doctor would have palpitations if she thought I had ignored her advice."

"Hmm,' Lara said, her shoulders sloping, "I didn't expect to be flying across the Atlantic tomorrow morning."

"Is anything wrong, my dear?"

"Not really. It's just that we only packed for an overnight stay in Paris. And we've not had time to book a hotel."

Maurice waved a hand in the air. "That is not a problem, Lara.

ESAPP maintains a permanent suite in *Le Mandarin Oriental, Paris*. You must stay the night. I have already made the arrangements. As regards to your wardrobe, Lara, ESAPP will provide you with a generous allowance—"

"Thank you Maurice, you are too generous, but we wouldn't consider it. It's just that at this time of the year, Phoenix will be hot and humid. We haven't packed for those conditions."

"*Le Mandarin* is close to many fashionable clothing boutiques, Lara. And Katherine, my assistant, will act as your personal shopper for the evening. Forgive me but, before meeting you, I did not know how well you spoke French."

"*Je parle un peu français*," she said with what was, to Kaine, a perfect accent.

"Ah, I see. But perhaps you would enjoy the experience more with Katherine at your side? You and she are of a similar age, and I am absolutely certain she would be a much better shopping companion than would Ryan."

Again, Lara glanced at Kaine. This time, she laughed.

"You are absolutely correct, Maurice. Shopping for clothes with Ryan is like a military operation. No fun at all." She turned to face Kaine fully and gave him the benefit of her full blown smile. "Do you mind, Ryan?"

Kaine held open his hands. "Why on earth would I?"

"You'll be on your own for the evening."

"All evening? Hang on there a minute. Don't you get carried away and buy out the whole of Paris."

He winked. Kaine didn't mind if she spent thousands. They had plenty in their private account and Lara deserved a whole load of pampering. In any event, he'd prearranged the whole thing with Maurice anyway, and secretly enjoyed the thought of her having a somewhat normal experience for a change. At least until she discovered the truth.

"While you're at it, do you mind picking me up a couple of T-shirts, a lightweight jacket, and a pair of summer chinos?"

She sighed and shook her head.

"If I have to, I suppose."

She leaned closer and pecked him on the cheek.

Maurice broke out another genial smile. "It is settled then. And ESAPP will pay, of this I insist. And Ryan will not be alone while he awaits your return. Assuming he does not mind spending the time in the company of a feeble old man," he added, turning to Ryan.

"It would be an honour and a delight. And it would give me more time to pick your brains regarding Sabrina's investigation."

Maurice used the chair's arms to push himself to his feet.

"In that case," he said, "I will summon Katherine and make the introductions."

Slowly, he made his way to the desk, pressed a button on the intercom, and spoke quietly.

"Are you sure you don't mind?" Lara asked, facing Kaine. "We haven't had long to soak in the Parisian atmosphere."

Kaine leaned closer. "We'll have all night, love. There'll be plenty of time to sleep on the plane. It's an eleven-hour flight. And, from what I remember, first class seats are fully reclinable. We should be comfortable enough."

Although it was for her own good, he felt as guilty as all hell for lying to her.

"And besides," he added, "when was the last chance you had to spend time with a woman of your own age? Recently, you've been spending your whole life around a bunch of crusty military types."

Losing Danny, whom she treated as an errant younger brother, had affected her as badly as it had Kaine and the rest of the team. Lara would benefit from a change of pace, and it would give Kaine the opportunity he needed.

The office door opened and the woman who'd brought the refreshments entered the office. She wore a beautifully tailored trouser suit and high-heeled, open-toed shoes. Parisian elegance personified. She stepped alongside Maurice and smiled at them.

"Katherine," he said, "may I present *Madame et Monsieur* Griffin, Elizabeth and William. They are friends of Sabrina, whom she met during her time in London."

Kaine relaxed, relieved that Maurice had remembered to use their temporary names. Despite his physical infirmities, his mind was a razor.

They shook hands with the personal assistant who seemed not the least put out to take on the role of personal shopper.

"Good evening, Elizabeth—"

"Beth," Lara said. "Please call me Beth."

"*Enchantée*, Beth." She leaned back to take a good look at her client for the evening. "We shall have an excellent time. You have a wonderful figure, slim and tall. After we are finished, the makeover will be transformative."

"Thank you, Katherine, but I'm not looking for a makeover. I just need something light and suitable for trekking through the Arizona desert and perhaps its mountains."

Katherine's mouth fell open, but closed again an instant later.

"Beth," she said, shaking her head, "even in the wilderness, one can have *panache*."

"I'll take your word for it." Lara laughed.

Katherine relaxed and her smile became less forced.

"Nonetheless, we shall still have a wonderful time. Are you ready to explore *Le Triangle D'Or*? After all, Beth, it is the place where every woman dreams of shopping when in Paris, is it not?"

"It is a little late in the day. Will we have time to browse?"

"Lara, my dear," Katherine said, her smile widening, "I have already made the arrangements. In Paris, the name Maurice LeMaître opens many doors, and keeps them open for as long as is necessary."

Lara turned to face Kaine. With her back to Katherine, she lifted her eyebrows. "See you at *Le Mandarin* in a few hours?"

"Take your time, and have fun."

"Maurice," Lara said, holding out her hand, "*merci beaucoup pour votre hospitalité*. It's been absolutely delightful to meet you at long last."

She leaned close to the frail man and kissed him on each cheek in the European manner. He gripped her elbow and eased her towards the door.

"Go," he said, "enjoy yourselves. And Katherine, no expense is to be spared for either of you."

"*Merci, Monsieur LeMaître.*"

Katherine offered Kaine the slightest of bows, said, "*À bientôt, Monsieur Griffin,*" and led Lara away with barely a backwards glance. Before the door closed, the two women were already engrossed in deep conversation.

Thank God.

He never thought Lara would fall so easily for the gentle bribe. It confirmed how much she needed to be taken out of herself. Danny's loss had affected her more than she'd let on. Hopefully, she'd forgive his deception one day, but he didn't relish the idea of defending his position on his return.

As the door sighed against its jamb and cut off the women's friendly chattering, Maurice turned to face Kaine.

"Ryan," he said, "now that I have engineered her absence according to your instructions, we are free to talk, *n'est-ce pas?*"

CHAPTER NINE

SATURDAY 20TH MAY – Early Evening
ESAPP HQ, Paris, France

With Lara on her way, Kaine relaxed and turned to Maurice.

"Sorry to have asked you to arrange that slight subterfuge, but Lara has to stay here, in Paris. I can't take her with me."

"You are worried for her?"

Kaine hesitated before answering. Danny's loss still hurt badly. It would take time for the wound's raw edges to scab over and then to heal fully.

"I lost one of my men recently, and I can't risk placing Lara in danger. She has to stay in Paris. Can I rely on you to keep her safe?"

"But of course, Ryan. I am sorry to hear about your operative, your friend, but Lara will be under my constant protection for as long as it is necessary. I will open my Paris residence to her. It has a comfortable guest suite and my personal security team will be at her disposal. I have already explained the situation to Alain Dubois—"

"You've done what?" Kaine snapped.

He jumped up, reached for his mobile, and prepared to chase

after the women. If necessary, he'd drag Lara back to the office and hold off flying to Arizona until Rollo arrived.

"Please, *Monsieur* Kaine, Ryan," Maurice said, making calming gestures with his open hands, "do not exercise yourself. Alain knows nothing with regards to the situation in Arizona. I briefed him only in the broadest possible terms."

"What did you tell him?"

"Only that you are a business associate and Lara—*Madame* Griffin —needs our protection while you are in the Far East negotiating a sensitive munitions deal on behalf of ESAPP and an unnamed UK company. This situation is not unique, Ryan. It has happened a number of times in the recent past. Alain Dubois is a good man. He can be trusted to protect Lara. You have my word."

Kaine took a steadying breath. He didn't like placing Lara's safety in the hands of strangers, but he saw no alternative in the short term.

"She is very special to you, Ryan. Not simply a protégée, I think."

Kaine nodded. "Very special. You'll forgive my anxiety?"

"But of course," the elderly man said, reaching out to clasp Kaine's upper arm. "Lara is as special to you as Sabrina is to me. I understand your feelings exactly."

"So you won't mind if I have one of my men stay with her in my absence?"

"It will not be necessary," Maurice said, tilting his head to one side, "but if it makes you feel better, so be it."

"Thanks for being so understanding, Maurice. Can I have a moment?"

Kaine turned away from the old man, pulled out his phone, and dialled a secure number. Rollo answered immediately—hands free— and listened to Kaine's instructions without interruption. The call took less than a minute. Kaine returned the mobile to his pocket and breathed easier.

"My man, William Rollason—Rollo—lives in France. He's driving through the night and should arrive before dawn."

"He knows where to go?"

Kaine gave Maurice a thin smile.

"Yes, Maurice. He knows where all your houses are. I told him to drive straight to your city residence. He'll introduce himself as Lara's elder brother, Harry. I assumed you wouldn't mind."

Maurice LeMaître issued a Gallic shrug and topped it with a headshake. "He is a military man, this Rollo?"

"Yes, but don't worry, he's properly housetrained."

A heavy frown deepened the wrinkles on the old man's brow.

"*Pardon, mais qu'est-ce que c'est,* 'housetrained'?"

"A poor English joke, Maurice. It simply means he knows how to behave in public. He will not embarrass you or annoy your staff."

"Ah, I see. Forgive me, but this poor elderly Frenchman often finds your English sense of humour unfathomable."

Kaine nodded his understanding. He found the French penchant for visual, slapstick humour anachronistic and incomprehensible.

"So," Kaine said, drawing a line under the merits and demerits of international comedy, "may I see the ransom video?"

"*Mais oui.* You can see it on the big screen. If you do not mind, I shall visit the rest room. I have seen the film more times than I wish to."

He moved behind his desk, picked up a remote control, and pressed a button. A wall panel to Kaine's left slid back to reveal a large flat screen TV. The image showed the ESAPP logo, in the colours of the French flag.

Maurice handed Kaine the control.

"Simply press play," he said, wiping his eyes with a handkerchief he'd removed from the pocket of his vest, "but please wait until I have left the room."

Only after the old man disappeared behind a door so well hidden that Kaine hadn't noticed it before, did he hit play.

The ESAPP logo faded and a bright light snapped on, illuminating a damaged face Kaine barely recognised. Bruised, swollen, and bloody, Sabrina had taken a beating.

Bastards.

He gritted his teeth and balled his hands into fists.

Off camera, a deep voice with an American accent said, "Hold it up."

Sabrina jerked and held a newspaper up to her chin, *The Arizona Daily Star*, dated Friday, May 19th. Yesterday.

"Good," the man offscreen said. "Now, state your name ..."

———

The video didn't last long, less than three minutes, but it told Kaine enough to know that the man holding her meant business. Sabrina's stumble over the name of the group holding her captive had been intentional, but only someone who knew her well would have picked it up. He'd bet his trigger finger that the so-called Defenders of Liberty and Justice either didn't exist, or, if they did, had nothing to do with Sabrina's abduction.

Whoever *was* actually holding her, "the Cree—", had made a number of mistakes. The compounded errors showed an overconfidence bordering on stupidity.

First, instead of making a new, error free recording, they'd allowed Sabrina's intentional error and her message regarding the seagull to go through. Second, they'd sent the information via the internet, which opened the possibility for tech-savvy individuals— like Corky—to identify the IP address of the sender, and through it, their location. Third, the man offscreen who barked the orders had allowed his voice and arm to appear on the hi-res digital recording. The same tech-savvy individual might be able to identify the speaker's voice. If it had ever been uploaded to the internet, Corky would match it to the one on the ransom video and identify its owner. Fourth and finally, the kidnappers had allowed Maurice five days to gather the information they demanded, which gave Kaine until the following Tuesday to find her.

Four days, less travelling time. It would be a stretch, but with Corky's help, it might be possible.

What Kaine did—if and when he found her—would depend

upon the situation on the ground, but whoever dished out the punishment to her face would pay. Damn right, would they pay.

Kaine had time to replay the recording twice more and power down the screen before Maurice returned.

"Thank you for humouring an old man," Maurice said, resting his hand on the desk for support.

"Who else has seen this?"

"Only the two of us."

"You haven't sent it to the FBI?"

"No, the kidnappers told me not to. Do you think I should?"

Kaine paused. What should he say to that?

"I'm sorry, Maurice. You have to make your own decision. The FBI have plenty of experience in negotiating with kidnappers and they have the technology to pull information from the recording, but ..."

"But?"

"But so does ESAPP. You haven't shown this to Alain Dubois either?"

"Indeed, I wanted to, but in her message, Sabrina mentioned only you. If she wanted me to involve Alain, she would have found a way to tell me. Before bringing in my people, I have been awaiting your arrival. The past six hours have been torture."

"I can imagine."

"Please help me, Ryan. Should I send the recording to the FBI?"

"Yes, I think you should. And as soon as possible. And set your best digital investigation team on the recording. The more people working on this the better. The moment I'm away from here, I'll ask Corky to analyse the data."

The old man sagged against the desk. He appeared ready to collapse but somehow found the strength to hold himself upright.

"But, before you do, how am I actually getting to the States?"

Maurice stretched out an arm to expose an understated gold Cartier. "A car and chauffeur are waiting in the basement garage for you. He will take you to *Le Bourget*, where a Gulfstream G550 will be able to transport you direct to Arizona inside of nine hours. I suggest you fly direct to Tucson, which is closer to Pine Creek than Phoenix."

"Whose plane is it?"

"It belongs to a Saudi Crown Prince who owes me a personal debt of honour. No questions have been, or will be, asked. The aircrew think you work for me and they are currently unaware of your actual destination. The aeroplane is fully fuelled and the pilot will file a flight plan only when you are airborne. I trust these arrangements are satisfactory?"

"Perfect."

"Is there anything I have forgotten?"

"The file?"

Maurice tapped his forehead with the meat of his hand.

"*Zut!* My memory."

Using his left hand for support, Maurice made his way behind his desk and pulled a thick file from the same drawer from which he'd removed the flash drive.

"Here is the printout of every report Sabrina filed relating to the Colfax-Lacy investigation. It is comprehensive. I have also included a second flash drive of all our telephone conversations, starting from three weeks before she reached Pine Creek. Prior to that time, our conversations were private and will shed no light on her investigations. Of this, I can assure you. The drive also includes the ransom recording." He sighed and it looked as though he found it difficult to swallow.

"Aboard the G550 is a fully equipped office with internet access via satellite. You will be able to play the recordings *en route*. Finally, there is a document shredder. Please destroy the papers when you are finished. Does that cover everything?"

Kaine scratched the side of his neck.

"Can't think of anything we've missed right now. I'd better be off, then."

"Will you be able to contact me?"

"No. I'll be staying dark the whole time. It's the only way I operate."

Kaine offered his hand. The old man brushed it aside and leaned close to hug Kaine and kiss his cheek. Once finished, he pulled away and tears glistened in his cloudy brown eyes.

"Bring her back to me, Ryan. She is all I have."

Kaine placed a hand on the old man's shoulder.

"I'll do my very best, Maurice. You have my word."

"This, I know, Ryan."

Kaine squeezed the bony shoulder gently.

"Look out for Lara."

"Do not fear for her, Ryan. Your man, Rollo, and I will take the greatest care of her."

"I didn't mean that, Maurice. I meant, take care of yourself. When she finds out what we've done, she'll be spitting nails. Glad I won't be around to face the initial firestorm."

Maurice wiped away his tears with the tips of his fingers.

"Can I believe my ears? One of the most skilled special forces operatives the British military has ever produced is in fear of the slender Lara Orchard?"

"Yep, I am," he said. "But I fear for you the most. In fact, part of Rollo's job will be to protect you from her wrath." Kaine smiled and added, "By the time I return with Sabrina"—*hopefully*—"she'll have had enough time to cool down."

"You jest, *mon ami*?"

"Only a little."

Kaine pointed to the burnished steel doors in the corner of the plush office. "Should I use the private lift?"

"*Mais bien sûr.* Please allow me."

Maurice accompanied him to the lift and pressed his left thumb to the fingerprint scanner. The alarm dinged and the lift door slid open immediately.

"Press the button marked 'BB'," Maurice said, pointing to the panel inside the door. It is an express lift which will take you directly to the basement parking garage. Your car is a dark blue Lexus and the driver is Pierre. *Au revoir, mon ami, et bonne chance.*"

Kaine stepped inside the polished lift and hit the button. The door hushed closed on the frail old man.

CHAPTER TEN

Saturday 20th May – Early Evening
ESAPP HQ, Paris, France

The lift whistled down the fifteen floors so quickly, it took Kaine's stomach a second to catch up with him, and left him wondering how the old man coped with the descent speed. From the third floor, the brakes applied a gently increasing pressure and the lift slowed to a gentle stop at the sub-basement. The doors whispered open and Kaine stepped into a bright, clean underground garage. Immediately ahead of him, a dark blue Lexus waited, facing an ascending ramp. A squat man in a peaked cap stood to attention at the rear passenger door, holding it open and ready. The chauffeur's face betrayed little expression, but his stiff-shouldered, straight-backed posture suggested confidence and hinted at a military background.

"Pierre?" Kaine asked.

"*Oui, monsieur.*"

"Do you speak English?"

He didn't want anyone to know he understood French and spoke it reasonably well. The moment he'd left Maurice LeMaître's penthouse, he'd moved into operations mode. As such, all information was currency and had to be treated as valuable.

"Certainly, sir."

Still holding the door handle, Pierre eased away and ushered him inside with a wave of his free hand. Kaine hesitated. Something felt wrong.

Pierre glanced to his right, behind Kaine. A presence registered in Kaine's consciousness. He backed away from the chauffeur, spun, and stood with his back against the car's boot, arms raised.

A tall figure stepped out from behind a support column. He wore casual clothes—black baseball cap, dark blue polo shirt, jeans, and walking boots—and held out his open hands in a gesture of appeasement.

"Take it easy, Mr Griffin," he said, removing the cap and lifting the shadow from his face. "It's me, Alain Dubois. We met earlier. In the lobby."

Kaine kept his arms raised.

"Yes, Mr Dubois," he said, keeping his eyes on both ESAPP's Director of Corporate Security and the driver—not the easiest of tasks. "I remember you. Barely recognised you in civvies, though."

Dubois' thin lips stretched into the hint of a smile. A smile that failed to register in his blue eyes. He nodded to Pierre. The chauffeur returned the nod, tipped his hat to Kaine, and marched away, closing the passenger door before he left.

"What the hell are you doing here? You're supposed to be protecting my wife."

Kaine tried to keep his voice even, but the thought of Lara wandering the streets of Paris with Maurice's personal assistant—a woman who looked as though a stiff breeze might knock her over—sent a tremor down his spine. He reached into his pocket for his mobile, but Dubois raised a hand.

"Relax, Griffin. Your *wife* is perfectly safe."

The emphasis Dubois placed on the word "wife" drew Kaine's attention and was made worse by the fact he'd dropped the title and had started calling him "Griffin".

"Right now," Dubois continued, "two of my very best men—former Legionnaires—are watching Mrs Griffin and Katherine spend the old man's money."

"Does Mr LeMaître know about this change in plans?"

Dubois ignored the question.

"And in case you're wondering," he continued, the knowing smile returning, "Katherine is no ordinary secretary. She, too, is one of my people. A well-trained and highly experienced bodyguard. One of the very best exponents of *aikido* I have ever seen. As I said, your *wife* is in safe hands."

Again, he added the strange emphasis. Kaine's hackles prickled. Did the smoothly confident Canadian know the truth?

Kaine pulled out the mobile and dialled.

"I assume you're calling her?"

Kaine blanked him and raised the mobile to his ear.

"In which case, please tell her to ask Katherine to introduce her to Armin and Ricardo. I'll wait."

"Bill?" Lara answered, sounding a little breathless. Traffic noise in the background, including blaring horns, indicated they were outdoors.

"Hi darling," Kaine answered. "Can you talk?"

"Not really. Katherine and I are window shopping. What's wrong?"

"Ask her to introduce you to Armin and Ricardo."

"You mean the two men who've been following us since we left the ESAPP building?"

"You spotted them?"

"Of course. Katherine told me they were bodyguards for our protection. They're keeping their distance, though."

"Describe them."

She paused for a moment before answering.

"Both tall. Over six feet. The taller one is black, with a shaved head and a beard. The other looks Scandinavian. Blond hair, blue eyes. Broken nose and a scar over his right eye. Both look competent, professional. Why?"

"Just a sec. Hold on."

He hit mute and stared at Dubois.

"Describe your men."

The *Quebecois* sighed and shook his head in exaggerated patience. His description of the bodyguards matched Lara's well enough. Kaine released the mute, and the traffic noise returned.

"Beth? You there?"

"Yes, is everything okay?"

"Never better. Just wanted to make sure you were okay. Take your time. Enjoy yourself. I'll see you later."

"I will. Love you."

"Me too."

Kaine ended the call and returned the mobile to his pocket.

"Okay," he said. "Now tell me what's going on?"

"I'm driving us to *Le Bourget* and we're both taking the Gulfstream to the States. Now," he said, marching to the driver's door and opening it, "you can either get in and let me explain on the way, or stand there with your thumb up your arse. What's it going to be?"

Dubois offered yet another smile—this one seemed designed to alleviate any perceived offence—and slid behind the wheel.

Kaine cocked an eyebrow and made an instant decision.

"Well, since you put it that way ...."

He jumped into the front passenger's seat. Before he could pull the door closed, Dubois fired up the powerful engine and took off at race pace. The front tyres squealed as they bit into the concrete and the car climbed the steep exit ramp.

The Lexus burst out of the underground carpark, turned right at a green traffic light, and picked up speed. So late in the evening, Parisian traffic had eased, and Dubois took full advantage of the near-empty streets. He gambled on amber the whole way along *Avenue Foch* before turning right onto the eight-lane *Boulevard Périphérique*, heading north.

While Kaine engaged his seatbelt and pressed himself hard into the back of his leather seat, the speedo climbed to a hair-raising ninety-five kph, and Dubois had the Lexus weaving in and out of the traffic. Around them, car horns blared and headlights flashed, but Dubois seemed oblivious to the anger he left in his wake.

"Dubois," Kaine said, having to raise his voice as they thundered beneath yet another booming overpass, "*Le Bourget*'s a private airport, and the Gulfstream's a private plane."

"Yeah, I know. And your meaning?" Dubois asked, thankfully keeping his eyes on the road as he undertook a panel van advertising French pastries.

"It won't take off without us."

He shot a lightning glance to his right and winked.

"What's wrong, Griffin. Scared?"

"Nope, you're clearly an advanced driver, but why risk being stopped by the gendarmes?"

This time, Dubois' answering laugh contained a little mirth.

"This is one of Maurice LeMaître's personal vehicles, Griffin. There isn't a cop in Paris who'd stop this car. The poor guy would find himself transferred to the sticks in the blink of the *Directeur Général*'s eye."

"I wondered why you weren't taking any notice of the speed traps."

They reached a long straight. Dubois gunned the engine even harder. Their speed hit one hundred and ten kph and they rumbled beneath one more overpass.

Tower blocks passed at an impressive speed as they reached the flyover section, heading out of France's capital city. Streetlights bathed the road in amber. Headlights flashed white, brake lights bloomed red all around, and the city disappeared behind them.

A sign announced the exit to *Porte de Clignancourt*, and Dubois maintained his speed. A map of the main routes around Paris that Kaine had recently committed to memory confirmed they were heading towards *Le Bourget*. He relaxed a little more.

"Okay," Kaine said, twisting to study the driver, whose expression hadn't changed much since his last smile, "you promised me an explanation. Out with it."

They drove under a large blue sign to *Charles De Gaulle* airport and carried on towards Orly.

"I've taken a leave of absence."

"What?"

"You're not deaf, Griffin. You heard me."

"You haven't answered my question, Dubois. Why are you here?"

The *Quebecois* shot Kaine a lightning glance before returning his eyes to the road and performing yet another dangerous undertake.

"What would you do if you discovered someone you cared for a great deal had gone missing and your boss told you to babysit another man's wife?"

"Excuse me?"

Dubois gritted his teeth and gripped the steering wheel tight enough to crease the leather. His first sign of real emotion—anger mixed with frustration.

"I joined ESAPP nearly fifteen years ago. I've known Sabrina all that time. Watched her grow up, for God's sake."

"You're just friends?"

"More than just friends," he muttered and fell silent for a moment, as though too embarrassed to go further.

"She's an impressive woman," Kaine said.

An enigmatic smile found its way to Dubois' face.

"Beautiful, too. She grew into someone very special. The thought she might be in trouble turns me inside out."

"So, you're risking your job to find her?"

Another glance. Dubois' blue eyes darkened.

"My job? Crap. I've been headhunted by the world's richest people. Could walk into any job I choose, but ...."

"But?"

"Without Sabrina, work means nothing." He swallowed. "And that's all I'm saying on the matter."

A blue sign on an overhead gantry instructed them to take the middle three lanes to *Le Bourget*. The traffic swelled and forced Dubois to ease his foot off the throttle a little. He took turns blaring his horn at drivers who had the temerity to slow him down.

After a few minutes' silence where Dubois had to negotiate even heavier traffic, he spoke again.

"We can either join forces, or work separately. Either way, I'm going to the States to bring her home. It's your call."

Kaine took his time to respond. The only thing he knew about the *Quebecois* came from the concise bio on ESAPP's website and from Maurice's brief, but glowing report. During the flight, he'd ask Corky to run a deep dive, but for the moment, he could find no reason to reject the man's offer.

The road curved around to the east and they headed towards the darkening horizon in silence. They left the A1 and joined the E19, this time, heading northeast.

"Our objective is to find Sabrina, yes?" Kaine asked.

Dubois nodded.

"Nothing else matters to me. Nothing."

Kaine rubbed a thumb along his chin.

"Who's running the show?" Kaine asked.

Operational issues needed to be addressed from the outset. The last thing Kaine needed was any doubt as to the chain of command.

"You are ... Unless you do something to put Sabrina's life in greater danger. I promise you, I'm just here to help. That work for you?"

A green road sign pointed them towards *Le Bourget*. Dubois took the slip road onto the N2 which soon morphed into the N17, and then became the D317.

"For the moment. All I want is to find her safe."

"Me too."

They took a left turn onto a private road and Dubois slowed the Lexus to his version of a crawl, which still smashed the speed limit for the local road. He screeched the Lexus to a stop in front of a green bomb-proof gate that guarded a white single-storey building, *AirXII Business Jets*.

Dubois swore in French, ground his teeth, and, showing huge impatience, blasted the car's horn twice. The gate slid open, slowly. Too slowly for the *Quebecois*, who revved the engine and lifted his foot from the brake before the gate had reached its half way point. The Lexus surged forwards, narrowly missing the gate's leading edge and the need for a new paint job. Dubois parked across two spaces, killed the engine, and leaped out. He grabbed a backpack from the rear passenger's seat and headed towards the terminal building, carelessly leaving the car doors open. Kaine climbed out and followed his lead. If ESAPP's Director of Corporate Security didn't care about losing one of Maurice's personal cars, neither did he.

The glass doors to the terminal building slid open and they were met by a tall, elegant woman. She wore a close-fitting business suit, and a hat with the logo of a company Kaine didn't recognise. She smiled at them and fell into step beside Dubois, chatting to him in French. Kaine played the ignorant foreigner, but it was clear that Dubois and the woman knew each other. She referred to him by his first name and he replied in kind. She introduced herself to Kaine as Elise Dupain and already knew him as Griffin.

They hurried through a deserted building. Her stiletto heels clacked on the highly polished marble floor tiles and the sound echoed off the marble walls. Kaine was almost disappointed not to be yomping over a red carpet.

After a fifty-metre route march, they paused while another pair of automatic doors briefly delayed their progress.

On the other side of the exit doors, a two-berth golf buggy stood waiting. Elise showed him to the front passenger seat and climbed behind the wheel. Dubois hung off the rear foot rail, hands clinging to the roof strut.

"Mr Griffin, please excuse the humble golf cart," Elise said, her accent pure Parisian. "Normally, our clients would be driven straight onto the apron, but these circumstances are—"

"That's okay, Ms Dupain. This is perfectly adequate."

She followed close to the side of the terminal building before turning sharp right at an indeterminate point and heading straight to a blue-liveried Gulfstream G550.

Mumbling something about the need to "visit the head", Dubois jumped from the cart, jogged up the steps, and ducked into the aircraft.

Always in a rush.

Kaine climbed out of the cart, smiled at their escort, who'd probably been summoned from her home simply to drive a pair of apparently ungrateful passengers a few hundred metres when they could have walked or driven themselves.

"Thank you, Ms Dupain. Please forgive my overeager young companion for his impatience."

She smiled.

"Alain has always been a man in a hurry, Mr Griffin. There is nothing for which you need to apologise. Please have a safe and pleasant flight."

She smiled, tucked an errant strand of windblown hair under her hat, and drove away without a backwards glance. Since arriving at the airport, at no time had anyone stopped them or asked for identification. There seemed little need for passports in the rarefied atmosphere of private jet transport.

How the top one-percenters live.

He climbed the five steps at a much more sedate pace than Dubois, and, like Dubois before him, had to duck under the small opening to enter the fuselage, where he could stand without stooping.

The instant he set foot in the cabin, his walking boots sank into the lush charcoal-coloured carpet, and the smell of leather and teak hit his nostrils.

Half way along the empty mid cabin, four white leather, fully reclinable seats faced each other—grouped perfectly for a mid-flight business conference. Towards the cockpit, four more seats surrounded a teak dining table. Unless Kaine missed his guess, the bulkhead door isolating the tail from the rest of the cabin would lead to the galley, bathroom, and sleeping quarters. Kaine sighed at the opulence encapsulated in a flying bus that cost a mere sixty million pounds just to own and shedloads more to operate.

Still, who was he to sniff? He didn't turn up his nose at a flight that would shave more than ten hours from his journey from Paris to Tucson and make it in one easy-to-handle trip.

Given the chance, he could probably grow accustomed to such luxury.

Before he could decide which seat would be his home for the flight, the bulkhead door opened and Dubois entered. He had to duck even though the cabin height exceeded six feet.

"Sorry about dashing off like that." He offered Kaine a slightly embarrassed smile.

"Caught short?" Kaine asked.

"Not quite, Mr Griffin."

He took his left hand from behind his back. In it, he held a Sig Sauer P226—Kaine's weapon of choice. He pointed it at the floor between Kaine's feet.

Dubois dropped his smile.

"Or should that be, Captain Kaine?"

CHAPTER ELEVEN

SATURDAY 20TH MAY – *Evening*
Le Bourget Private Airport, Paris, France

Kaine stiffened. Held his open hands out to the sides.

Shit!

After so many months on the run, to be captured by a smiling *Quebecois* in the cabin of a multi-million-pound jet was so damned infuriating. Separated by three metres, Kaine had no chance of rushing the Canadian. Even an amateur would be able to fire before Kaine reached him, and Dubois was no amateur. For the same reason, the main fuselage door at his back—so close he could feel the wind blowing through the opening—might as well have been a mile away.

Dubois stared at him, po-faced. He had Kaine cold.

Kaine held his breath. Nothing to do but await his moment. If fate gave him a chance, he'd be ready.

"What now?" Kaine asked, keeping his arms away from his sides. Balanced and prepped.

Dubois frowned and followed Kaine's glance. He stared down at his hand, and his face registered shock.

"Damn," he said in apparent surprise. "Forgot I was carrying this for a moment."

With his right hand, he grabbed the Sig's muzzle, turned it and held it to Kaine, handle first.

Kaine didn't move.

"Go on, Captain," he said, still smiling. "Take it. It isn't loaded."

Prepared for anything, Kaine leaned close and cautiously removed the gun from Dubois' hand.

Light. Too light.

No magazine. He pulled the rack to confirm his impression. The gun was empty.

Dubois started laughing.

"Man, the look on your face! Wish I had my camera handy. What a picture!"

Kaine clenched his fists.

"Explain yourself, Dubois."

The *Quebecois* held up both hands, palms facing forwards. His laughter died.

"Sorry, Captain Kaine. My bad. No harm, no foul."

"I'm waiting for that explanation, damn it. What the hell's going on here?"

"All in good time, Mr ... Griffin." He smiled and added a wink. "We've got nine and a half hours to catch up. Fancy a drink?" He pointed forwards, to the galley.

"I'd rather beat you to a pulp," Kaine growled.

"You could try," he said, nodding slowly. "You could try. Might make a good fist of it, too. I know your rep. But how would butting horns get us any closer to finding Sabbie? And that's all either of us wants, right?"

Sabbie?

"That may be, but let's get one thing clear," Kaine said through clenched teeth.

"And what's that?"

Kaine paused to make sure he had the grinning *Quebecois'* full attention.

"The next time you point a gun at me, you'd better be prepared for the consequences."

Again, Dubois raised his hands in surrender, his expression serious and apologetic.

"It won't happen again, Captain. You have my word. All I want is Sabbie home safe and unharmed."

Kaine stared the younger man down. He really would have liked to take him apart, piece by piece, but, although he'd have felt a whole lot better, it probably wouldn't give him the answers he wanted.

A lock clicked loud in the deathly silence. The door to the cockpit opened and a short, wide-hipped woman stepped through the walkway and entered the fore cabin.

"Good evening, Mr Griffin, Mr Dubois," she said, nodding to each in turn, her accent pure BBC newsreader English. "I'm Captain Avery, your co-pilot for the flight. We'll be taking off very shortly."

Avery glanced at the Sig, but its presence didn't seem to throw her off her stride. No doubt she'd witnessed many strange occurrences in her rarefied occupation. She moved into the mid cabin, closed and locked the main fuselage door, and turned towards them, addressing Kaine the principal, rather than Dubois, the employee.

"As per Mr LeMaître's request, we aren't carrying cabin crew on this flight. Please help yourself to any refreshments you require from the galley." She pointed forwards. "Should you need anything else, Captain Credence and I are at your disposal."

She studied the Sig again, and a frown deepened the wrinkles on her high forehead.

"It's unloaded, Captain," Dubois said, serious and official. "We know what would happen to cabin pressure if we fire a gun in here when we're in the air. Isn't that right, Mr Griffin?"

Kaine slipped the Sig into his pocket.

"Indeed we do, Mr Dubois."

Avery turned towards Kaine once again.

"We'll need to file a flight plan, sir."

"Tell the flight controller we're heading to LaGuardia Airport, New York. I'll give you the actual destination when we reach cruising altitude."

"Very well, sir."

She nodded and returned to the cockpit.

When the catch finally snapped on the cockpit door, locking them out, Dubois rubbed his hands together and headed forwards, to the galley.

"Don't know about you," he said, not looking behind him, "but I need a beer. Care to join me?"

"No thanks. When am I getting that explanation?"

Dubois stopped and spun on his heel.

"Will you please pull that poker from up your ass. We're all friends here. If I wanted to give you up to the authorities, you wouldn't have left ESAPP Tower. We're on the same side, you and me. Now, come on. If you don't have a drink with me, it's going to be one hell of a long flight."

Short of reverting to Plan A and trying to beat the information out of the smart-arsed Canadian, Kaine could see he had no alternative but to concede defeat, for the moment.

"In that case, I'll make myself a coffee," he said, having no intention of drinking anything he hadn't made himself—or taken from a sealed container.

Minutes later, a high-pitched whine of the twin engines winding into life told Kaine the crew had completed their pre-flight checks. An electronic ding sounded and the light above the cockpit door changed from green to red.

Captain Avery's disembodied voice invited them—ever so politely—to take their seats and fasten their seatbelts. Kaine walked his piping hot and delicious freshly-ground coffee to one of the seats in the mid cabin. Dubois, carrying a bottle of Danish lager, took the seat opposite, his back to the cockpit.

Kaine dutifully coupled the seatbelt across his lap and cinched it tight. Dubois left his undone.

"Take-off speed's a little over one hundred and fifty miles per hour," he said, as though Kaine didn't already know. "If we get into trouble at that speed, a lap strap isn't gonna save us. Take it easy, Captain."

By the time they reached cruising altitude and Kaine had given Avery their true destination—Tucson International Airport, Arizona—Dubois had finished his first bottle of beer and opened a second. Kaine nursed his coffee and never took his eyes off the Canadian. He prided himself on his patience, but Dubois had the knack of stretching it to the limit—and he didn't need to try very hard.

Dubois crossed one leg over the other and leaned back in his seat.

"Okay," he said, his expression as serious as it had been since the Gulfstream's wheels left the tarmac, "I guess you've suffered enough. Ask your questions and I'll answer them as fully as I can."

Kaine took a deep breath.

Where to start?

"How do you know who I am?"

Dubois shrugged.

"That's good. Start off with an easy one. To be perfectly honest, Sabbie told me."

Kaine shook his head.

"Not a chance. She wouldn't do that."

"No, not directly. But, like I said, Sabrina and I are very close. I worked it out from what she *didn't* say as much as from what she *did* say."

"Explain."

"Sure, sure." He drained his bottle and placed it in the cup holder built into his seat's armrest. "When she returned from London, she briefed Maurice and the rest of the security team—including me—about her time working undercover at SAMS. Interestingly, she skirted over Sir Malcolm's part in the plot to destroy the plane you ... er, inadvertently shot down."

Dubois had the good grace to flinch and lower his head as he mentioned the flight.

"Of course, your name and face was spread all over the news media at the time, but Sabbie was surprisingly close-mouthed about the affair. It got me thinking—and asking questions. I followed your story. Read every article ever written about the downing of Flight BE1555, and every sighting of the notorious terrorist, Ryan Kaine of the SBS.

"Eventually, I asked her about it straight out. She was reluctant to talk, but I sort of wheedled the truth out of her. Eventually, she told me all about how Sir Malcolm set you up. Swore me to secrecy."

"And you agreed?"

"Of course. I'd do anything for her." After a few brief moments, he added, "I love her."

A simple statement, plainly delivered.

He flushed, lowered his eyes, and studied his fingernails. For the first time, Kaine noticed how well manicured they were. Alain Dubois took great care of his personal grooming, with not a strand of his brushed back, light brown hair out of place.

"Then," Dubois continued, talking to his hands, "you pretty much dropped out of the headlines. It was as though the media grew bored of writing about you and the news cycle moved on. Sabrina stopped talking about you, and I never pressed her for more information. Thought it was better for everyone concerned if we drew a line under it. After all, you are morally innocent of any wrongdoing."

The Gulfstream's intercom signal dinged and Captain Avery told them they'd reached their optimal cruising altitude and speed—fifty-one thousand feet and eight hundred and fifty kph—and would be landing in Tucson in eight hours. Again, she wished them a pleasant flight.

"Okay," Kaine said, "keep going. What do you know about Sabrina's current mission?"

"Nothing. She didn't tell me a thing. When she left, I had to quiz the old man—I mean, Maurice, about it."

"What did he tell you?"

"Only the bare bones. That she'd gone undercover again to find out what happened to some missing inventory."

"How did you react?"

"Damn it, how'd you think I reacted! I went apeshit. For God's sake man, *I'm* in charge of corporate security, and *I'm* responsible for the safety of all our employees. All of them. It felt like I was being kept out of the loop because ...." He paused, shaking his ahead as though unwilling to complete the thought.

"Because they didn't trust you?"

Kaine's suggestion drew another pained expression from the *Quebecois*, who'd finally looked up from examining his fingernails.

"Yeah, exactly," he said, clenching his fists. "And that's what I told Maurice. Offered my resignation over it, too. I mean, the woman I love was putting herself in danger, by doing *my* job! Goddamn it. It made me so mad, and ... scared for her."

He pulled in a deep breath and shook his head again.

"Anyway, Maurice rejected my resignation and promised to keep me fully informed. I believed him, too." He added a grimace to another headshake. "How naïve was I?"

"In what way?"

"When she disappeared, Maurice kept it from me for three fucking days! Tried to handle things himself, the stupid old goat." Dubois caught himself and waved a hand in the air. "Sorry, I didn't mean that. When Sabbie stopped calling, Maurice must have been terrified. When it comes to his granddaughter, he's an open book. Ordinarily, I would have noticed his change in personality, but I was in Marseilles, firefighting for the company. He should have called me back, clued me in, but .... Damn it, water under the bridge, eh?"

"When did Maurice tell you?"

"This morning, when I got back from Marseilles. I damn near exploded. Then he told me about the FBI not returning his calls. And that's when I stepped in. I've got contacts in the US and sent out some feelers."

Kaine stiffened.

"You did what?"

Dubois flapped his hand again, an action intended to instil calm, but had become intensely irritating.

"Cool it, Captain," he said. "I know how to fly below the radar."

"And what did you learn?" Kaine demanded through a tight-lipped frown, trying to keep calm.

"Nothing. The Feds are keeping close-mouthed about it. I was in the middle of planning a trip to Arizona, to follow Sabrina's trail when you and your 'wife' arrived. I recognised you right away. Of course I did. It hit me like a punch in the gut."

"What did you do?"

Another wince followed.

"This is where I have a little confession to make."

"Go on."

"When I met you in the lobby, I dropped a bug in Ms Orchard's jacket pocket."

It took all Kaine's self-control not to react.

"I heard everything you said in the penthouse. Which is how come I met you in the basement."

"Sneaky," Kaine said, for want of something better.

Dubois snorted.

"Maurice is real paranoid about his privacy. He had Sabrina and me install the screening in his offices. When he told me about his unexpected guests—Sabrina's friends from London—I guessed it might be you. And knowing what you'd suffered since last September, I assumed you'd be as paranoid as Maurice and run your own sweep for bugs. Didn't think you'd check Ms Orchard's person, and I was right."

"How did your bug transmit through the screen when mine couldn't?"

Dubois smiled again.

"Like I said, Sabrina and I installed the system. We know how to open the back door."

Kaine tensed. Dubois had shown a real flare for the security game. No wonder he was in such demand. But he didn't know everything. Lara had left the office before Maurice and he discussed the ransom demand and Kaine had watched the ransom tape. Dubois couldn't know about the kidnapping.

How would he react when—if—Kaine played him the recording?

Probably go ballistic.

Not that Kaine was going to say anything before reading Dubois' CV. And even then, he might hold back, depending upon what he learned.

Dubois raised his right index finger and pointed it at Kaine.

"When we land in Tucson, don't try blowing me off, Captain. I'm with you on this whether you like it or not. What d'you say? Partners?"

He stretched out the hand. Kaine stared at it.

"Don't leave me hanging, Captain. When we get to Arizona, you'll need some backup. As a Brit, you'll stick out like a wedding guest in a gimp mask, but as a Canadian, I'll blend in real easy." His accent broadened into something less Canadian and more Californian.

Kaine relented. He leaned forwards and took hold of the offered hand. The handshake was firm and brief, without any overt tests of strength or power. No histrionics.

"So," Kaine said after they'd relaxed back in their seats, "does Mr LeMaître know where you are?"

Dubois checked his watch and nodded.

"By now, he will. I sent him a time-delayed email, told him my plans and asked for his blessing."

"Will he give it?"

"Hope so. Why don't we ask him?"

Dubois swivelled his seat and pressed on a leather panel in the bulkhead. It popped open and he unclipped a satellite phone from its cradle. He dialled a number from memory and waited.

"Maurice?" he asked after a momentary delay. "Yes, it's me. You received my email?"

Dubois grimaced slightly and held the phone away from his ear while Maurice shouted loud enough for Kaine to hear a few choice French expletives.

After a few minutes, Maurice calmed enough for Dubois to return the phone to his ear.

"Yes, sir. Mr Kaine's sitting in front of me now. I'm guessing he wants to speak to you." After another slight pause, Dubois smiled and handed the phone across.

"Ryan, is that you?" Maurice asked, panting from his recent exertions.

"Yes, it's me."

"Alain recognised you. Please forgive me, I had no idea."

"Not to worry. It's done now."

"How did he know, Ryan?"

"Long story, and it's not important. Do you trust him?"

"Implicitly," Maurice shot back instantly.

Kaine watched Dubois closely when he asked and while Maurice answered.

"In retrospect," Maurice continued, "Sabrina and I should have worked with Alain from the outset. If we had done that, perhaps she would not have been taken. Alain thinks I do not know about his feelings towards her, but I'm not so blind an old man that I cannot see what goes on in front of my own eyes." His voice broke. "I know what they mean to each other. Had Alain known of her latest adventure in advance, he would have tried to stop her. You can rely on him, Captain. He is a good man. Highly skilled at everything he does."

After a brief pause, the old man added, "Dare I say, he is as highly skilled as you are, Captain Kaine?"

Perhaps.

"Maurice, can you instruct one of your IT staff to send Dubois' personnel file to the Gulfstream? I want everything you have on him. Everything. Not that I don't trust your judgement, you understand. It's just that I like to know who I'm working alongside."

"I understand completely. In your position, I would require the same thing. The file will be with you shortly."

"Thank you, Maurice."

"Please bring my granddaughter home, Captain." Another catch broke into his words.

"I'll do my best. *À bientôt*, Maurice."

He ended the call and returned the phone. Dubois snapped it back into its compartment and closed the panel.

"Right then," he said, "what's next?"

"Next," Kaine said, "I read your personnel file."

"And after that?"

"If I'm satisfied with what's in the file, we'll have a chat."

Dubois smiled.

"Sounds like a plan to me." He pulled on the armrests and eased out of his seat. "Let's get you that file. The sooner you start reading, the sooner we can start working together properly."

I'll be the judge of that, son.

CHAPTER TWELVE

SATURDAY 20TH MAY – Evening
51,000 feet above the Atlantic, Gulfstream G550

Dubois' unredacted résumé arrived within ten minutes of Kaine ending the call with Maurice.

He started reading it while drinking his second excellent coffee, and the high-pitched whine of the twin jet engines faded into silence. The whole time he read, Kaine kept half an eye on the Canadian, who'd finished his third beer and, instead of moving on to a fourth, made himself a coffee, and drank it while eating a premade cheese and salad baguette. At the same time, Kaine's new companion had his eyes fixed to the screen of his mobile.

Halfway through reading the résumé, Kaine relented and opened a sealed baguette of his own and ate it with a bottle of alpine water. The baguette tasted delicious.

The CV spared no detail. It outlined Dubois' early years and his advanced educational qualifications. At eighteen, Dubois entered the Canadian army as an officer cadet and left as a captain eleven years later. After three years in service, he transferred to Joint Task Force 2, and received his tan beret after passing out towards the top of his training cohort.

As part of the Canadian Special Operations Forces Command, JTF2's primary mission was counter-terrorism. During his own time in service, Kaine had worked alongside JTF2 units on a number of occasions. They always acquitted themselves well.

Kaine scanned the rest of the report. Dubois had served with distinction in many of the same theatres of war as Kaine had done.

2004 – Haiti – deployed to defend the Canadian embassy and secure the local airport when rebels ousted the Haitian president.

2005/6 – Iraq – member of Operation Lightwater, tasked with hostage recovery alongside the SAS. Kaine was in Iraq at the time, but hadn't run into the tall *Quebecois*.

2007 – Afghanistan – received a commendation for trying to save the life of a Master Corporal who fell from the roof of a communications tower. Under heavy fire, Dubois dragged the man to safety and gave first aid, but unsuccessfully. The Master Corporal died and Dubois was evacuated to the nearest field hospital, where he received treatment for a bullet wound to the thigh.

2010 – Canada – JTF2 had a role in securing the Winter Olympics, which turned out to be Dubois' last operation before resigning his commission to join ESAPP and earn the big money.

Dubois had left JTF2 before Operation Mobile during the Libyan Civil War, which was a shame, since both the SAS and the SBS were involved in many joint skirmishes. He and the *Quebecois* would likely have met.

According to the ESAPP company bio, Dubois' sidearm of choice was the ES9 *Tempête*, a 9mm semi-automatic with an uncanny resemblance to Kaine's preferred Sig P226.

Kaine studied the man opposite, whose eyes lifted from his phone and fixed on his.

"You finished?" Dubois asked, pointing to the laptop they'd found in the small but well-equipped office in the rear cabin.

"Pretty much, *Captain* Dubois," Kaine answered, giving a brief nod.

"Happy with what you read?"

"Special Forces is a small world. I'm surprised we've never met before."

Dubois pulled in a deep breath through his nose and let it out through his mouth.

"Me too."

"We were both in Kandahar in '07," Kaine probed.

"We were?"

"Tough gig."

Dubois nodded. "Tough enough."

Kaine had made up his mind. He closed the file and slipped the flash drive Maurice gave him into the USB socket.

"Okay," Dubois said, "enough of this reminiscing or you'll have me in tears. Are we cool now?"

Kaine nodded.

"We're cool."

"So, you gonna tell me what I missed after your 'wife' left on her shopping trip?"

Again, Kaine nodded.

"You're not going to like it."

"I'm a big boy, show me."

Kaine scrolled through the folders on the drive until he found the one he wanted. He opened the file, handed the laptop across, and studied Dubois' reaction to the ransom demand.

Although he couldn't see the screen, with the volume set to max, Kaine could heard every word spoken on the recording, including the kidnapper's harsh American twang.

Colour washed from Dubois' face and his eyes glistened in the low light. He clenched his jaw and said nothing. When it ended, he played it all the way through for a second time. Still he didn't speak.

After the third uninterrupted viewing, he played the recording for a fourth time, stopping it at various points and narrowing his eyes before continuing.

"What are you thinking?" Kaine asked when Dubois had finished the fourth run through.

Dubois pulled in another deep breath.

"I'm thinking when I find the guy who hurt Sabbie, I'm gonna tear him apart."

You'll have to stand in line, mate.

"You picked up her stumble?" Kaine asked.

"When she started to say 'Cree' and changed it to 'Defenders'?"

"Yep."

"Why?"

"Your reaction suggested you knew what she meant."

"Did it?"

"Don't piss me about, Dubois. As you said earlier, we're on the same side."

Dubois blew out a sigh.

"Yeah, I guess I did." Still, he hesitated.

"So?" Kaine asked, with more force.

"Sabbie's one smart cookie. Rarely makes a mistake. I reckon she was sending us a message."

"Do you know the people she means? The native Americans— The Crees?"

Dubois shot him a grim smile and shook his head. A lock of light brown hair fell over his brow and he raked it away with his fingers.

"No way. I reckon she was pointing us towards a group of right-wing nutters, the Doomsday Creed."

He broke off and started tapping away at the keyboard and working the touchpad.

Kaine waited a few moments before his patience broke.

"And?"

"Give me a sec, Captain Kaine," Dubois said and carried on typing, eyes on the screen not the keyboard.

A few moments later, he said, "Yep. I knew it. That's the asshole in the video," and spun the laptop so Kaine could see the screen.

It showed a video of a man in the uniform of a colonel in the US Army, standing on a dais, addressing a unit of soldiers on parade. Kaine reached forwards and released the mute on the speaker.

"...proud of serving with each and every one of you fine *men*." He emphasised the word, "men".

The camera scanned around to pick up the faces of the assembly, both men *and* women. The colonel carried on talking for a few minutes before dismissing the troops. He half turned to the officer on his right, a female major, and sneered as he ignored her salute. He turned, about face, leaving her standing alone on the stage. The disrespect he showed a fellow officer said much more about his attitude to women than his words, and confirmed they were intentional rather than a mistake.

"Who is he and how did you know he's the man on the ransom tape?" Kaine asked, fixing Dubois with a hard stare.

Dubois pursed his lips and returned Kaine's gaze, unintimidated. A good sign.

"Colonel Richard Caren. That film"—he pointed to the laptop— "was taken back in 2010, on the day he 'retired' from the service. He retired before he could face a Court Martial for his attitude to women in the service, which is prehistoric, by the way. As for how I knew it was him on the ransom tape, it's my job."

Dubois spun the laptop to face him again.

"Stop being so bloody cryptic, Dubois. Explain yourself."

"Before ESAPP acquired Brown and Company, Maurice asked me to run a threat assessment on them. I visited the site and ran a security audit on the personnel and the physical infrastructure." He paused and looked past Kaine and gave a middle-distance stare over his head—accessing his memory.

"And?"

"Clearly, I gave them a clean bill of health or ESAPP wouldn't have moved on the company."

"Where does this Colonel Caren come into the picture?"

Dubois pointed to the laptop again.

"If we had direct access to the ESAPP infrastructure, I'd let you see my report, but the security protocols wouldn't allow it. Guess I have time to give you the CliffsNotes version.

"Brown and Company's primary expertise lies in the development and testing of personal protective equipment—body armour, all-inclusive biohazard suits, gasmasks, and the like. A couple years before the ESAPP acquisition, Brown's won a DoD contract to develop equipment to protect military personnel against the fallout from dirty bombs.

"As part of its research, the company upgraded its research facility in Arizona to store and utilise fissionable material, including americium-241, caesium-137, and plutonium-238."

Kaine closed his eyes. He could see where this was heading.

"Upgrading their storage facility to secure the material stretched Brown's finances to breaking point and left them wide open to a hostile takeover. That's where ESAPP came into the picture. As I said, I ran a full audit. It looked pretty good, but, as you can imagine, Uncle Sam's not particularly keen on allowing parts of their defence infrastructure to fall into foreign hands. Especially when it involves nuclear material."

He paused for a breath before continuing.

"Before I could set one foot in the laboratory, I was 'invited' to the FBI's Arizona field office for a 'meet and greet'." He frowned, no doubt at the memory. "They made it clear it was an invitation I could not refuse."

"So, the FBI hauled you over the coals?"

Dubois raised an eyebrow and shook his head.

"Not at all. They were actually really polite. Couldn't have been any nicer. The guy in charge, a guy named Griezmann, showed me into his office and took me though some intelligence they'd built up on persons of interest. Colonel Caren, that guy"—again, he pointed to the laptop—"rated number two on their list of local home grown terrorists. Turns out our Colonel Caren is the leader of a bunch of right-wing nutcases who are—"

"Determined to overthrow the US Government and seize power for themselves?" Kaine interrupted. He'd heard it all before.

"Not quite. The Doomsday Creed demand the right to self-determination. They want a Homeland of their own and plan to set it up in Arizona."

"That's an interesting twist. Why Arizona?"

Dubois shrugged and pulled his eyes back into focus.

"Who the hell knows? Caren was born in a one-horse town called, Copper Strike. Arizona's one of the biggest copper producers in the US."

He pulled the laptop closer and started typing again.

"Here's a map of the area. Brown's facility is forty-five miles northeast of Copper Strike."

He pointed to a place on the map, a section of southeast Arizona. With one road in and one road out, Copper Strike lay less than one hundred miles northeast of Tucson, and in the middle of a range of hills, the tallest being Mount Garrett.

Kaine's senses prickled when he followed the AZ-366 for about seven miles north east of Copper Strike and read the name of the nearest town of any size in the area—Pine Creek.

"Damn."

Dubois stiffened. "What?"

Kaine hesitated.

How much should he tell a man he barely knew? Just because Maurice LeMaître trusted the Canadian didn't mean Kaine had to. On the other hand, the way Dubois reacted to the ransom demand— with barely suppressed rage when he saw Sabrina's injuries— couldn't have been more genuine. Furthermore, as the Canadian said, in Arizona Kaine would be an outsider. Having Dubois onside would be a distinct advantage. He needed to take the risk.

Up to a point.

"Sabrina told Maurice she'd followed the missing inventory to Arizona. More specifically, that place." He tapped the screen. "Pine Creek."

Dubois gritted his teeth.

"Sabbie was in Pine Creek when she disappeared?"

"Seems that way."

Dubois listened in silence until Kaine finished telling him the little he learned from Maurice.

"That bit on the tape about the seagull," Dubos said, "that's why Maurice called you in, rather than tell me?"

"You heard the story before?"

"Yeah, but she always called it a herring gull not a—" He hit his forehead with the meat of his hand. "Damn it. I'm a fool. *Herring Gull*'s the name of the boat you were on when you shot down that plane."

Dubois jerked his head back and held up the same hand in a gesture of apology.

"Sorry, man. Didn't mean to bring that up. Crass of me. I'm usually more sensitive, but ...."

"Yeah, I understand. It's a tough situation. Apology accepted."

They fell into a brooding, thoughtful silence while Kaine tried to work out a strategy. He had no idea what Dubois was thinking, but he appreciated the fact that the Canadian didn't waste time ranting and raving or chewing the deep pile carpet.

Dubois finally asked the question Kaine didn't really want to answer.

"What's our next move?"

"Good question."

"Any ideas?"

"Hundreds, but I'd like your input first."

"The rulebook says we should send the ransom tape to the Feds and let them handle the negotiations, but ...."

"But?"

Dubois gripped the arms of his seat so hard he creased the leather and risked doing them permanent damage. He raised pained eyes to Kane.

"Fuck's sake, these nut jobs have Sabbie! You saw what they did to her. We've only got a couple of days to find her before .... Shit!" Barely in control, he took a steadying breath. "I've dealt with hostage negotiations before, but this ... She's been tortured, for God's sake!"

Kaine gave him a moment to gather himself before speaking.

"The man you met in Phoenix, SAC Griezmann, what did you make of him?"

Dubois' nostrils flared as though he'd stumbled into a latrine the morning after the canteen had served a particularly severe curry.

"Nothing but a desk jockey. Struck me as a guy who'd run a mile to avoid making a tough decision. Wouldn't want to carry the can for making a mistake. Why?"

"With all Maurice LeMaître's clout, I'm wondering why Director McGregor stopped taking his calls."

Dubois released his grip on the armrests and eased forwards in his seat.

"What are you suggesting?"

Kaine shook his head.

"Nothing, I'm just rolling the information around in my head. Asking questions."

"Spitballing, huh?"

"That's right."

Dubois scratched the tip of his nose for a moment before nodding.

"Okay, I see what you're getting at."

"And what's that?"

He nodded again.

"The old man said Sabbie's attitude changed when she reached Pine Creek, right?"

Kaine took his turn to nod. "And she stopped giving him any details about the case."

"Yeah. That's right."

"And she kept you out of the equation, too."

"But she called you in, and you're an outsider."

"That's right. She did."

Dubois flushed bright red.

"Are you accusing me of—"

Kaine raised his hands to quell what promised to be a loud and defensive outburst.

"Take it easy, Captain," he interrupted "I'm not accusing you of anything. We're just spitballing, remember?"

"Yeah." Dubois' chin jutted. "Spitballing. Go on."

"From the outset," Kaine continued, "Sabrina and Maurice were worried about internal security at Colfax-Lacy Industries."

"Yeah. With missing inventory, first thing we do is figure it's an inside job until we can prove otherwise."

Kaine waited for him to finish before saying, "Sabrina claimed to have found the leak but said she needed more proof before she acted."

Dubois pursed his lips.

"Goddamn idiot, putting herself in danger like that. When we get her home, I'm gonna ...."

He broke off and shook his head. Tears glistened in his dark blue eyes.

"So, what does this tell us?" he asked, slowly.

"She started in Cleveland, Ohio and moved to Pine Creek, Arizona. Which means, she crossed state lines—"

"Which makes it a federal issue!" Dubois blurted out.

"Colfax-Lacy ships ordnance throughout the Midwest. Its business is always going to be a federal issue."

"Yeah, good point."

An idea struck Kaine from out of the blue, but he didn't want to get ahead of himself.

"I've just had a thought," he said, trying to keep his racing thoughts under control. "The FBI are keeping tabs on this Colonel Caren, yes?"

"Sure. So what?"

"So, they might know where he is."

The light of understanding dawned in Dubois' eyes, which seemed to turn them a paler shade of blue.

"Damn, I should have thought of that myself."

"You're too close to it. One of the benefits of me being an 'outsider'."

Dubois pulled back his cuff and read the time on his watch.

"Twenty-three hundred hours, Paris time. Makes it fourteen hundred in Phoenix. Griezmann might be in his office. I'll give him a call."

He reached for the side panel but Kaine held up his hand again.

"Before you do that, let's think this through, okay?"

Dubois pulled his hand back and tilted his head to one side.

"What's there to think about?"

"Just, take a moment. What do we know so far?"

The *Quebecois* ran his fingers through his long hair once more.

"Okay, but let's make this quick. While we're up here at fifty thousand feet sitting on our thumbs, Sabbie's rotting in a cell. We've only got a couple of days before the deadline."

"Yes, I know, but I keep coming back to the same two questions."

"Which are?"

"Why has Director McGregor stopped taking Maurice's calls? And why didn't Sabrina contact the FBI when she found the link to Pine Creek?"

"And what answers do you come up with?"

"Maybe she did."

"Sorry?"

"Maybe Sabrina *did* call the FBI."

Dubois ground his teeth and closed his eyes for a moment. When he opened them again, they were even more angry.

"For God's sake. Now you're trying to tell me the FBI's involved in her kidnapping?"

"No, I'm not saying that at all. I'm saying they might be working on the case already. If Sabrina *did* tell the FBI about Pine Creek, they might have tried to warn her off. You know Sabrina better than I do. Would she have listened to them?"

Dubois' shoulders sagged and he dropped back into his seat.

"No, of course she wouldn't. The silly fool would have gone ahead anyway. Damn it, I've had another idea."

"Go on."

"Knowing her like I do, she might even have volunteered to work undercover for the Feds. I wouldn't put anything past her. She loves the buzz of an investigation. Do you really think the Feds are involved?"

Kaine shrugged.

"No idea. I'm just—"

"Spitballing," Dubois said. "Yeah, I heard you."

"There's at least one other question that needs answering."

"What's that?"

"Before I ask it," Kaine said, being deliberately evasive, "let's see if we agree on something."

"Okay, sure."

"If Sabrina set up a false identity, a legend, it would be good, right?"

"Not good." Dubois snorted. "It'd be perfect. Not even the FBI would be able break it."

Kaine gave him a knowing smile.

"Agreed," he said. "So how did Colonel Caren discover her true identity?"

Dubois blinked.

"Jesus Christ. Someone told him!"

"Yes, that's right, Alain," Kaine said, nodding slowly. "Someone told him."

CHAPTER THIRTEEN

SUNDAY 21ST MAY – Overnight
51,000 feet above the Atlantic, Gulfstream G550

Kaine and Dubois studied each other carefully and the seconds dragged out for a full minute.

"But who?" Dubois demanded, fists clenched tight, leaning forwards again, elbows digging into the arms of his seat. "Who the hell would have given her up?"

Who indeed?

"How many people knew her real identity?" Kaine asked, staring hard at the Canadian.

Dubois returned the stare with a scowl. He didn't waver, didn't even blink.

"Don't you bloody look at me like that!"

"Like what?"

"Like you think it was me!"

"Reel your neck in, Captain. I'm not accusing anyone. Just asking the question."

"For fuck's sake, Sabbie and I love each other, man. We're looking to get married next year. On top of which, I didn't even know where she was until this morning. I've been in Marseilles for the past two weeks, remember."

"So, I repeat the question. How many people knew her real identity?"

Dubois relaxed his hands and blew out his cheeks.

"Okay, right. Sorry. Guess I'm a little sensitive right now. Let's see … Apart from Maurice, I have no idea who else knew. I suppose Brad Schwartz, the Chairman of Colfax-Lacy would have known, since he was the one who raised the initial concern. And Director McGregor and Deputy Director Hallam of the FBI would have known, since Maurice contacted them both. Al Griezmann, too. And the agents he sent to Pine Creek looking for her."

"No," Kaine said, shaking his head. "That doesn't work. Maurice didn't contact the FBI until *after* Sabrina disappeared."

"Yeah, yeah. Sure." Dubois paused for a second, then raised an index finger. "Unless, as you say, Sabbie *did* contact the Feds before heading to Pine Creek. Maybe she *was* working with them. Christ, this is a nightmare."

Kaine understood the argument and agreed. The more they dived into the weeds the more complex the situation became.

"Just goes to confirm that we're on our own here," Kaine said. "If one of the Feds is working with Colonel Caren and finds out we're on our way—"

"Sabbie's as good as dead."

Kaine nodded. "Agreed."

"So what are we going to do?"

Kaine took his turn to rake a hand through his overlong hair.

"I do have one idea."

Dubois opened his fists and flexed his fingers, his eyes glinting and alive.

"Go on. Spill."

"What are you prepared to do to get her back?"

"Anything necessary," Dubois snapped.

"Would you break the law?"

"In a heartbeat," he answered without hesitation. "Why? What's on your mind?"

Kaine took his time, making sure he formed the statement correctly.

"The threat assessment you ran on Brown and Company ...."

"What about it?"

"You've been to their research lab? You know the players and they know you, right?"

"Yes. To all three."

"How easy would it be for you to get hold of the information the colonel's looking for?"

Slowly, Dubois' grim smile returned. The first time he'd raised any sort of smile since viewing the ransom tape.

"Despite going AWOL, I'm still ESAPP's Director of Corporate Security. As such, I have access to all Brown's facilities. All I need to do is turn up unannounced and say I'm calling a snap security check. I call them all the time and without warning. Which is the whole point. Keeps everyone on their toes. In fact, that's what I was doing in Marseilles this past three weeks."

"And, if it comes down to it, you're prepared to give the colonel the information?"

This time, Dubois did hesitate, but not for long.

"If necessary, yes. I will."

"Let's hope it isn't necessary, then."

"Yeah," Dubos said, nodding. "Let's hope."

"You know the US Government will consider releasing the codes and the security schedules to the Creed as treason? If we're caught, we'll face a capital charge."

"Better not get caught then," Dubois said, not missing a beat.

"No, we'd better not."

"And while I'm stealing the access codes to Brown's research labs, what are you gonna be doing?"

"Me?" Kaine asked.

"Yeah, you, *Captain.*"

"After learning all I can about the Doomsday Creed on that

laptop, I'm going to pay a visit to the *Pine Creek Saloon*. By the time I reach the town, I imagine I'll be a tad thirsty, don't you?"

Dubois' grin widened.

"Yeah, I bet you will be."

"Can I have the laptop?" Kaine held out his hand.

"Would you mind using the desktop in the office? I'd like to run my own searches. After a couple of hours, we can compare notes. That make sense to you?"

"It does."

Kaine liked the idea of being alone for a while without making it obvious. It would give him the chance to chat to Corky without being overheard. Corky wouldn't take kindly to the idea of a stranger earwigging their conversation, and upsetting the techie wizard was the last thing Kaine wanted. The shy little man was worth his weight in oval cut diamonds.

Dubois held up a hand.

"Before you go, I need to show you something."

Dubois stood and headed towards the front of the cabin. He collected the backpack he'd taken from the Lexus and returned to his seat in front of Kaine.

"While we're off doing our separate things," he said, opening the pack, "we'll need a way of keeping in touch. Take a look at this baby."

From the pack, he pulled out a large plastic box and placed it on the table between them with hushed reverence as though it contained something of great value and importance.

"What's this?" Kaine asked, intrigued.

"This baby," Dubois said softly, "is the next generation battlefield communications system. ESAPP's R&D team in Nantes has been working on it for years."

He slid open the lid to reveal a foam-lined, compartmentalised box. Each of the two smaller compartments contained an earpiece, and the two larger sections held the drive units.

Kaine almost burst out laughing. The drive units were enormous things half the size of a house brick.

"What do you reckon? Neat, right?" Dubois said, removing one of the earpieces and holding it up to the light.

"I've seen earwigs before," Kaine said, dryly. "What's so special about these?"

Dubois shook his head.

"You ain't seen nothing like these, buddy. These are prototypes. The only two in existence. Bone conduction, silent operation, microwave transmission and reception, satellite interface ...."

The Canadian proceeded to wax lyrical about his "baby", and Kaine feigned interest, trying to appear suitably impressed by the devices.

"Impressive, huh?" Dubois said, after they'd spent a few minutes familiarising themselves with the system's operation and agreed on their individual call signs.

"Yep. Pretty damned good if they work in the field."

Dubois handed Kaine a leather case containing his unit.

"We've run field trials from here 'til Sunday. This kit works good."

"In all terrains? Arizona isn't Nantes. Pine Creek's in the mountains."

"I've tested these things in the Alps. They work as advertised."

"Hope you're right. Either way, they're better than anything I've got." Kaine lied and didn't feel bad doing it. "And on that note, I'm heading to the office."

Using the arms of his chair, Kaine pulled himself to his feet. At the same time, the plane's port wing dipped as the jet banked, forcing him to throw his arms out to the sides to retain his balance. Lightning fast, Dubois leaped to his feet and raised his fists in defence.

The Gulfstream levelled out and Kaine opened his hands in submission.

"Whoa there, son. Take it easy."

Dubois shot him an embarrassed smile and lowered his arms.

"Sorry, Captain. Guess I'm a little jumpy."

Kaine nodded. "That's understandable. Are we cool?"

"Yeah. We're cool. These flights don't usually suffer turbulence at this altitude."

Dubois returned to his seat, sighing as the soft leather upholstery deformed to engulf his large frame.

"By the way," he said craning his neck to look up at Kaine, "if we're going to be working together, how's about using our Christian names. You call me Alain, and I'll call you Ryan."

Kaine grimaced and shook his head.

"Uh-uh. That won't work."

Dubois' brow wrinkled into another frown.

"Why not?"

"My name's Bill, remember? Bill Griffin."

"Oh sure," Dubois said. "I'll remember when we land. But, for the duration of the flight, you're Ryan. Okay?"

"No. From now on, I'm Bill."

The Canadian sighed.

"Okay. If you insist."

Kaine dipped his chin, said, "I do," and headed for the compact office in the rear of the plane.

———

Some two and a half hours later, Kaine exited the office to find Alain Dubois stretched out in his reclined chair, eyes closed, mouth open, snoring gently. Kaine nodded in appreciation. Like most experienced and highly skilled special forces operatives, the Canadian had learned to take pre-operation power naps at the drop of a hat, irrespective of his personal investment in the mission.

During his time in the office, Kaine had forced two large black coffees down his throat to help keep himself awake long enough to brief Corky and for him to clone the software of ESAPP's comms system. The kit Corky had developed with the help of Rollo and others was far superior and more compact than ESAPP's gear, not that Dubois would ever know—at least not from Kaine.

While Corky was doing his thing, Kaine ran some internet searches of his own and ended up scrolling through hundreds of hits related to Colonel Caren and his Doomsday Creed. Nothing he read told him much more than he already knew, or assumed.

As Kaine took his seat, Dubois woke and rubbed his face. His expression turned a little sheepish but Kaine shook his head.

"Don't worry about it, Alain. We all need our sleep."

Dubois stretched out a long yawn.

"I've been awake forty-eight hours straight. Needed a nap before we land. Find anything interesting?" He nodded towards the office.

"Bits and pieces, but no definitive location. The Creed doesn't exactly entice the most impressive members of the gene pool. Definitely not what you'd call a savoury bunch. At least a dozen Creed members have been jailed for everything from disorderly conduct to violent affray. One received a long sentence for manslaughter. Nothing's been linked directly back to the colonel, though. He seems to be the only one with any brains. What did you find?"

Dubois rubbed more life back into his face and smacked his lips. "My mouth tastes like the floor of a hamster's cage. Gonna brush my teeth, freshen up. What'd you ask again? Oh yeah. The Doomsday Creed's populated by a bunch of lowbrows, alright. And you're right about Caren being the brains of the outfit. Fancies himself as a political visionary, too. Stood for state governor the year he left the army, but lost big time."

"How did he fund the campaign? Shadowy backers?"

Dubois stuck out his lower lip and nodded.

"In part, but Caren comes from old money. His family's one of the richest in the state. Owns a couple of high-producing copper mines and huge areas of land north of Tucson. The Caren clan have been running Renshaw County since long before the Civil War. Richard Caren's the last in the line. Inherited the family fortune when his father died in a hunting accident." Dubois raised a hand to forestall Kaine's telegraphed interruption. "Before you jump to any conclusions, the colonel was on tour in Afghanistan when his old man croaked. He's innocent of that particular crime."

Dubois snorted.

"Turns out Richard Caren Senior wasn't as proficient with a

hunting rifle as he should have been. Blew his own leg off when he fell out of his hunting hide. Bled to death in minutes. Blind drunk, at the time, too."

Kaine nodded.

"That's what I read. So, the colonel owns most of Renshaw County, Arizona?"

"That's right. Thousands of acres of farmland and huge tracts of forest. He owns a few logging operations in the high mountains and runs a couple of lumber yards. One's in Pine Creek. The other's in Copper Strike. Rents out farmsteads all over county."

"I read that, too."

"And he could be holding Sabbie in any one of those places. Goddamn it!" He rolled out of his seat and headed for the rear cabin. "Sorry, I need the latrine."

Kaine sat back in his seat and allowed his mind to wander. Where was Sabrina, and how was she doing? How the hell were they going to find her? His thoughts ran around in ever decreasing circles, getting him nowhere but leaving him more and more frustrated.

Moments later, Dubois returned. He'd changed into shorts and a muscle T-shirt and looked ready for a workout.

"Got me a regular wakeup routine," he said, interpreting Kaine's expression and predicting his question. "Need to set myself up for the day." He jerked a thumb over his shoulder. "Latrine's free if you need it. There's fresh towels in the shower and a new toothbrush by the sink. Help yourself to whatever you need."

One thing for certain, Alain Dubois could be generous with other people's belongings.

Kaine pointed to the backpack he'd brought with him from the UK and dumped on the empty seat beside him.

"I'm good, thanks. Used to packing for unexpected trips."

Dubois shot what Kaine took to be a sympathetic smile.

"I guess you'd have to be."

The comms system dinged pleasantly, and the information panel above the cockpit door lit up. Captain Avery's disembodied voice wished them a pleasant evening.

"We'll be landing in seventy-five minutes," she said in her cultured British accent. "The time in Tucson right now is 20:47, yesterday evening." The intercom allowed the smile in her voice to stand out clear. "The temperature is a gentle twenty-one degrees, with moderate humidity. We will activate the seatbelt sign ten minutes before landing. Captain Credence and I hope you've had a pleasant flight."

The comms chimed again and the information panel dimmed. Kaine adjusted his watch back the nine hours to allow for Arizona time, CET.

Dubois tapped his diver's watch.

"Way ahead of you, buddy."

Being called "buddy" by a relative stranger didn't sit all that well, but Kaine let it pass.

"Better take my chance for a shower while I can," he said, collected the backpack, and left the cabin.

By the time he returned, feeling as refreshed as it was possible to be after so many hours without sleep, Dubois had taken up a prone position on the carpet. Kaine stood in the doorway, watching the *Quebecois* run through an impressive set of floor exercises.

He finished with twenty-five, perfectly executed clapping press-ups followed by another twenty-five leg thrusts. Excellent exercises for a confined space, calculated for effectiveness and efficiency. Sweat poured off the man, soaking into the towel he'd spread out over the expensive carpet.

Kaine felt old and tired just watching the younger man work.

Dubois breathed deeply a few times before rolling onto his back and standing. When he saw Kaine watching him from the doorway, he jumped.

"Oh," he said, "didn't see you there."

Really?

Kaine had lost count of how many times some younger hotshot had tried to impress—or intimidate—him by flexing his powerful muscles and building up a muck sweat.

What it was to be so young and thrusting.

Stop it, Kaine.

He dismissed the thought as uncharitable. Dubois had had other things on his mind and might well not have noticed Kaine's return from the shower.

"You okay?" Dubois asked.

"Yes, thanks. Going to make myself some breakfast before we land. Or is it supper?"

"Yeah, time zones confuse the hell out of me, too." He towelled the sweat from his face. "I need a shower. Give me ten and I'll join you in the galley."

———

Although the galley's fridge-freezer held enough supplies to make a full English breakfast, Kaine didn't fancy cooking anything more complicated than porridge—made with milk and sprinkled with dried sultanas and brown sugar. The complex carbohydrates would provide enough slow-release energy to last through the Arizona night.

They ate in the main cabin, in brooding silence, Kaine lost in his thoughts, and Dubois, head lowered and focused on his food.

With three warmed and butter-filled giant croissants wolfed down, Dubois pushed his empty plate to the side of the fold-away table. He dabbed his thin lips with a cotton serviette, threw it on the plate, and cupped his coffee mug in both hands.

"So," he said, leaning back, "we've got fifteen minutes before we hit the runway. What's the plan?"

Kaine swallowed the last of his porridge and washed it down with a swig of cooling coffee. The food felt heavy in his stomach. Perhaps he should have gone for the croissants as well.

"How long's it going to take you to reach Brown's site?"

The big Canadian shrugged.

"Five, six hours, maybe."

"Really? Doesn't look that far on the map."

Dubois snorted. "True enough. As the crow flies it's only a

hundred and fifty miles, but the facility's on the northeast side of Mount Garrett, and the last fifty miles are rough mountain roads. Not much more than dirt tracks in places. Pretty tricky to drive at night, which is why I forced myself to take that shuteye earlier."

"So, are you planning to time your arrival for first thing in the morning?"

"Nope. Don't have time to wait for the niceties. I'll roll up in the small hours. Put the fear of God into them."

"They work through the night?"

"Nope," he said, smiling again, this one wicked. "They operate days and evenings but keep a full-time security presence, twenty-four-seven. They have to. It's written into the DoD contract. I plan to shake them up pretty good."

Kaine grinned back.

"You're a bad man."

"Sure am. But keeping the scientists and admin staff off balance will work for us."

"Sounds like a plan, and it'll stop them asking awkward questions."

Dubois puffed out his chest.

"I'll be the one doing the questioning. They'll hate me for it, but I don't give a shit. All I care about is getting Sabbie back—and kicking the crap out of the guys who hurt her."

Dubois drained the last of his coffee and set the mug down on top of the plate.

"You'll be heading straight to Pine Creek?" Dubois asked.

"More or less. I'll pull off the road and catch up on some sleep before arriving tomorrow morning. Assuming I can hire a car in Tucson this time of night."

"The cars are already lined up," Dubois said. "I hired a couple of Ford Explorers. We need SUVs since we're both heading into the mountains."

"Good thinking. Thanks."

"It's all courtesy of ESAPP." He checked his watch again.

"Assuming we land on time and your passport and legend stand up to immigration checks—"

"They will."

Kaine had every faith in Corky's paperwork. It had never let him down so far.

"You sure? US screening's pretty tough these days. They run fingerprint checks an' all."

"I'm certain." Kaine held up his hands. "These fingerprints will track back to William Griffin, retired Royal Marine Commando and current director of ESAPP. Ryan Kaine's fingerprints don't exist anymore. Not on any official database."

Dubois' eyes bugged.

"They're gone? How in the hell d'you manage that?"

"You don't know?"

"Know what?"

"Your future wife's damned good at what she does."

Sorry Corky, but your secret's safe with me.

CHAPTER FOURTEEN

Sunday 21st May – Sabrina
Camp Pueblo, Arizona, US

The sunlight around the cell door dimmed as day slid towards another evening and into the inexorable, endless night. The inept bugler sounded "Retreat" at 17:00 hours and "Taps" at 21:00 in a pitiful and mocking attempt at a show of military discipline. The one saving grace of the whole ridiculous charade was that it served to tell Sabrina the time.

Outside, the noises of humanity faded as the people settled down for their sleep—a sleep that would not come easily for Sabrina.

To pass the time, she ran through all she knew of Brown and Company, and the knowledge filled her with dread.

Giving a person with delusions of grandeur, such as Colonel Caren, access to radioactive material when he already possessed the means to disperse it would be a total disaster. *Grand-père* Mo-Mo would never countenance such a thing, not even to save the life of his only granddaughter. It would not be an option for him.

How long had she been held captive? Four days? Five? Six?

Why had the FBI not freed her already? They surely knew where the colonel was holding her. Her contacts in the Bureau must have known that Camp Pueblo was his base of operations. Where else would the Creed be holding her? The first day after her abduction, when she had failed to report in, her primary FBI contact should have raised the alarm. Even now they should be organising a raid to free her and close down the camp. After all, the Bureau had the fire-power and, with the information she had provided, they surely had the evidence to obtain a warrant to search the camp.

So where were they?

Why did she still languish in a filthy cell?

Sabrina slowed her overly rapid breathing and refused to allow herself to sink into despondency. Self-pity would not help the situation. She had hope.

When *grand-père* Mo-Mo received the ransom demand and the cryptic message hidden within, he would send for Ryan, a man she could rely upon. A man who would risk everything to save her.

Il viendra. He will come.

Although what a man alone in a foreign country could do against such heavy odds, she could not imagine. Even if that man were Ryan Kaine.

Gravel crunched outside her cell.

For the first time since the start of her captivity, the single, bare light in her cell clicked on. Blinding in its unexpectedness, it seared her vision. She raised her arm to protect her eyes against the sudden glare. Dull and yellow, but bright enough to dispel the darkness from the corners of the dirty little room, Sabrina blinked until she had grown accustomed to the glow.

The lock clunked and the cell door creaked open.

Colonel Caren marched in, stiff-backed and upright. Unlike Tex, he did not have to duck to pass under the frame of the door.

"I—George needs your help," the man said without preamble.

She lowered her arm and the chain rattled loud in the cramped confines of the cell.

"Excuse me?"

"Do you still want to help him?"

"George?"

"Yes! That's who I'm talking about."

"I ... thought you had a doctor."

"She's ... no longer available, and George is in a bad way. Rambling."

"I am neither a doctor nor a nurse. Is there no one else to take care of him?"

"If there was anyone else, I wouldn't be here, woman!" he snapped. "Are you going to help or not?"

"Why will you not take him to the hospital, as I advised?"

"Don't start that again. I've already given you my reasons. Well? What's your answer?"

She blinked hard and held out her left hand.

"Release me, and I will do what I can."

"Sergeant Graham!"

The colonel snapped his fingers and the same dark man from earlier appeared in the doorway. As tall as Tex, Graham ducked to avoid cracking his head on the cross frame.

"Yes, sir?" he asked, his voice deep and booming.

"Take her to the infirmary."

"Yes, sir."

The sergeant pulled a bunch of keys from his pocket and crossed to the cot. He unsnapped the padlock and her manacle fell to the floor, taking with it the cloth Sabrina used to protect her wrist. The scabs sticking to the cloth tore loose, and the deep abrasion started weeping again.

"I will need some antiseptic cream and a dressing for this," she said, showing the colonel her injury.

He wrinkled his nose and shied away from the wound. For a military man, he did not seem to enjoy looking at torn and damaged flesh. No doubt, he preferred to keep at a safe distance from the battlefield. In which case, he should perhaps promote himself to general—an armchair general.

She did her best not to sneer at his reaction.

"There's a dispensary in the infirmary. Help yourself to whatever you can find. If you need anything else, talk to Sergeant Graham. He's my junior aide-de-camp."

Graham took one pace backwards and stood at attention in the corner of the cell.

"Where is Tex? I mean, Lieutenant Scarb—"

"He's performing a little errand for me. Why?"

"Is he being punished for his treatment of me and George?"

The colonel gave her a lop-sided smile. "Lieutenant Scarborough is a passionate supporter of our cause. Sometimes, he can get a little ... shall we say, overly enthusiastic in the performance of his duties."

"He is out of control. A vicious madman."

As are you, Colonel Caren.

"He has his orders, Ms LeMaître. I can assure you, he will not mistreat you again. That's why I thought it best to keep you two apart. It'll give tempers time to cool a little."

"You do not trust him to obey you?"

The colonel stiffened and jutted out his chin.

"My people follow their orders to the letter. If not, they are punished in the manner outlined in our Military Code of Conduct."

"You have a Code?" This time, she snorted.

"Of course! As has every constitutionally formed military unit in history. Ours closely matches that of the Army of these United States, and we are all proud to honour it."

"And all of your people obey this code?"

"Of course."

"So why did you feel the need to separate Lieutenant Scarborough and me? Did you not trust him to follow your orders?"

"As I told you, the lieutenant has another task to perform."

"Am I permitted to ask another question?"

"Make it quick."

"Your people have all read this Code of Conduct?"

"They have."

"I am surprised all your people read."

He scowled. "Now you're being facetious."

"Really? I told you what Tex did to me." Again, she held her hand up, highlighting the damage to her wrist and face. "Is this how your Code instructs you to treat your prisoners?"

"You tried to escape, woman!"

"And George," she continued, "did he—your own flesh and blood—deserve to be kicked in the head until he became insensible?"

Colonel Caren glanced sideways at the sergeant at her mention of George being a direct relative, but Graham failed to react. Either he did not understand her, or he already knew of the familial relationship.

The colonel swatted the air between them, his action dismissive. "That's enough, woman! This isn't a debating society. Just look after George and the others and we'll get along fine until your grandfather comes through with his part of the deal."

"He will not accede to your demands."

"We shall see. Sergeant, take her to the infirmary and treat her with the respect she deserves."

"Sir, yes, sir!" Graham barked and added a crisp salute.

Colonel Caren returned the salute and left the cell without giving Sabrina another glance.

The moment they were alone, Graham grabbed her by her upper arm and growled, "Let's go, honey."

She tore her arm from his grasp, aggravating the pain thudding through her shoulder and head.

"I am not your 'honey', Sergeant!" she hissed. "Treat me with respect. You heard the colonel."

"Yeah." Graham sneered. "I heard what the old man said, and I know how to *respect* traitors to the cause like you."

Facing another sadist like his friend Tex, Sabrina closed her mouth and lowered her arms. She was in no condition to defend herself against another vicious brute. In this situation, discretion would serve her better than outright hostility.

"You lead," she said, looking up sideways at him and speaking softly, "and I shall follow."

Graham sorted, said, "Har, har," and thumped her between the shoulder blades, pushing her towards the door.

She stumbled outside. Graham took hold of her upper arm and they retraced the route that she and Tex had taken the previous day.

Eventually, after two long minutes of being dragged along the gravel path and sucking in the cold night air, they reached the shadow of the hangar that Colonel Caren referred to as the infirmary. It loomed over her, the clapboard walls rotten and the pitched roof sagging. Behind it, the orange glow from a dozen floodlights illuminated the deserted parade ground.

In the surrounding darkness, the tree-clad mountains had turned from beautiful and protective, to looming and ominous. They surrounded the camp, leaning in, powerful, aggressive, suffocating. A stiff breeze whistled through the trees, bringing with it the sharp tang of pine resin. She paused and looked up. Above the fractured hills, a billion bright stars twinkled in a clear and moonless sky.

Graham thumped her back once again, and she staggered forwards, barely able to prevent herself from falling face first into the dirt.

"C'mon, woman. I don't got all night."

Slowly, she turned to face him.

"Will you give me a moment, please?" she said, trying to reach his softer side—gambling that he had one. "I have been cooped up in that cell for days. Being outdoors is ... refreshing."

Sabrina stared up at him, wide-eyed, pleading. She moved closer and reached a hand towards his chest. When he first entered the cell the previous day, Graham had looked at her in such a way as to suggest he might find her attractive. Sabrina had no aversion to using whatever advantage she could find to win the support of such a man.

"Please?" she repeated. "Allow me one more minute."

Graham cleared his throat and glanced over her shoulder.

"Okay," he said softly. "If I give you a minute out here in the fresh air, what'll you offer me in return?"

She stepped even closer and placed her hand over his heart.

"What would you like?" She breathed the question, softly.

Beneath her palm his heart thumped slow and strong, showing no signs of excitement or arousal.

He reached up, clutched her hand in a fierce grip, and squeezed.

Despite herself, Sabrina squealed. She tried to free her hand from the crushing grip, but Graham was too strong.

"You think I'm stupid, woman? Think I'm gonna fall for that 'come hither' horseshit? If I want anything from you, I'll take it. Whether it's on offer or not."

His free hand snaked out and up.

Sabrina ducked in time for the slap to glance the top of her head rather than land full force. She brought her knee up between his legs, but he jerked sideways. Her blow missed its target, and struck his outer thigh.

Graham twisted her wrist outwards, pulled her arm away from her body, and slammed his fist into her left breast. Pain shot through her whole body. She doubled over, gasping for breath. She had never felt such paralysing agony. Breath wouldn't come. Acid bile roared up, burning her throat. Vomit erupted from her gasping mouth and splashed on the hard-packed earth at her feet.

Graham released her arm and jumped back. She dropped onto her hands and knees, emptying her stomach of half-digested chicken stew and bread.

"Fucking bitch. If you've puked on my boots, I'll—"

The sound of her own vomiting drowned out the rest of his threat. Seconds later, fingers entwined in her hair, and Graham yanked her to her feet, roughly.

"Get a move on, bitch."

He dragged her towards the hangar, angling them straight to the double doors. He pushed one of the doors open wide and threw her inside. She stumbled over the sill but kept her feet, and stood in the rectangle of light created by the parade ground floodlights.

Standing in the opening, Graham raised his forearm to his mouth and breathed through his sleeve. He pushed her further into the darkness and leaned inside to throw a switch on the wall. Three bare bulbs illuminated a large and dingy room.

Sabrina gasped at the desperate sight.

Dust covered the concrete floor and hung in the air. Sabrina gagged as the stench of vomit, sweat, and decay hit her nose.

Two rows of rusty beds, the same design and age as the one in her cell, stood out from the side walls, their heads against the wall, feet pointing towards the centre to form an aisle. Most were empty, but five contained a human form draped in a stained and dirty sheet. All were women. Four of the patients lay on their backs, deathly still, hair hanging long and lank about their faces. One woman sat up, leaning against a pair of thin pillows, coughing into a bloodstained cloth.

So much for the colonel and his lie. Far from the clean, well-maintained infirmary he promised, Sabrina found herself in the midst of a torture chamber, a dungeon.

She hurried towards the conscious patient, but the woman held up her hand to stop her approach.

"No ... stay ... back," she gasped, breathing raggedly after each word. "Highly ... contagious."

Sabrina stopped dead and spun to face Sergeant Graham. From somewhere, he had pulled out a medical mask. He busied himself hooking the straps around his ears and settling the cloth over his nose and mouth.

"Where is my mask?" she asked, closing on him.

He stiff-armed her away, his fist thumping into her breast once again.

"There ain't enough to go around. You'll have to make do with bandages or something." He waved a newly gloved hand into the gloom.

"*Mon dieu*! Who are these women?"

"Nobody important. Camp followers, is all. Whores mostly."

"What illness do they have?"

He shrugged.

"No idea. They've all got coughs and a rash. Looks like the 'flu, but I've never seen it come on so fast or be so"—he sniffed behind the mask—"fatal."

"Fatal? Oh my Lord. People have died?"

"Four, since last week. Plus them two today."

He pointed to the still forms lying on beds on the far side of the room.

"We ain't had a chance to clear them out yet. Tex and a few of the men are building the bonfire right now. We burned the others, too. Colonel Caren said burying them would likely contaminate our land forever. Since the first death, the old man put the infirmary in quarantine."

"What does the colonel expect me to do?"

"Look after his nephew, is all. Nothing anyone can do for them others."

"This is madness! The colonel should call in the Centre for Disease Control. They have protocols for outbreaks such as this. Treatments. These women do not need to die."

"Shut up, woman. The CDC's funded by the US Government! They're the ones who prob'ly created this damned bug in the first place. Colonel says the CDC has poisoned our water, too."

"And you believe him?"

"Colonel Caren used to work at the Pentagon. He knows what's going on. There's your evidence, right there!"

He pointed to the bodies before unclipping the strap on his holster and pulling out his handgun—a Smith and Wesson M&P Shield. US-built, the 9mm semi-automatic closely matched the ESAPP Strike P99 in performance, but far exceeded it in price.

"Get over there!"

He pointed the weapon towards the far corner where a weak overhead light failed to dispel the gloom completely. She hesitated for a moment, but the fear in his eyes showed her that the sergeant wanted to spend no more time in the plague house than absolutely necessary.

As she approached the gloom, the area became more clear. A portable privacy screen, similar to ones used in real hospital wards, stood out from the wall. She moved closer. In a bed behind the screen she found George. Bloodied and battered about the head and face, he lay on his back, groaning. Nobody had taken the trouble to clean his face.

Before she could reach George, Graham raced forwards, took hold of her damaged wrist, and held up the open loop of a handcuff.

"No! Please."

"Colonel's orders."

He snapped the cuff and squeezed the ratchet closed around her damaged wrist.

"No. It's too tight!"

"Tough."

He attached the other cuff to the final link of a long chain piled on the dirty floor. Its far end was attached to a steel plate anchored to a vertical wall post.

"How can I work like this?"

"You'll figure it out."

Graham backed away, pointing the gun at her chest. "Take care of George and you might still get out of here alive."

He hurried away, pulling the door shut behind him. The lock clicked. Sabrina stood still, chained inside a plague house, hardly daring to breathe.

What could she do?

George groaned. Louder this time.

Remembering how she had injured her wrist the first time, she took hold of the chain and pulled it behind her before rushing to his side. She placed the back of her free hand against his forehead and breathed a relieved sigh. His skin felt cool to the touch. He had no fever.

She leaned closer.

"George? Can you hear me?"

He moaned but otherwise, did not respond.

The woman in the next bed coughed.

"Hey ... you there ..."

Sabrina left George to his groaning and stepped around the screen to address the woman.

"Yes?" she said, keeping as much distance as possible. "How can I help?"

"I ... I'm burning ... up. Water ..." The woman waved to an internal door Sabrina had so far failed to notice. "Bottles ... not ... the faucet."

Behind the door, Sabrina found a small room lit from the outside by a single window. She threw the switch on the wall just inside the door and a bulb exploded into a light so bright, it hurt her eyeballs. It took a few moments for her vision to adapt.

The room contained a small office desk and chair, both metal. Two of the walls were lined with shelves, one of which was stacked with medical books and journals. On one shelf, she found unopened bottles of spring water. On another, she found piles of worn but clean linen and balls of cotton in sealed plastic bags. A metal drawer unit alongside the desk contained medical equipment, some of which had seen better days. They included an open box of surgical gloves, a pair of round-nose scissors, a stethoscope with perished rubber tubing, and an ancient blood pressure cuff. At the back, hidden behind the pressure cuff, she found real treasure in a box of disposable scalpels, their blades covered in plastic sheaths.

Merveilleux! Wonderful!

She pocketed one of the scalpels, hoping it might come in useful at some stage, and continued her search.

The middle drawer contained sealed bandages, miscellaneous dressings and swabs, and an open cardboard box of wooden tongue depressors, which Sabrina would rather burn than stick in the mouth of a sick person. In the bottom drawer, she found a stock of cardboard bedpans and urine bottles.

Next to the unit stood a lockable and colour-coded medicine trolley. She found a bunch of keys on the desk. None would fit her handcuffs. One did open the trolley, but all the compartments inside were empty. There was not so much as an aspirin.

In the room, Sabrina had found the pharmacy of which the colonel had been so proud. A pitiful thing. Totally inadequate.

After pulling on a pair of the blue medical gloves, Sabrina took two bottles of water, a pile of cloths and a plastic basin, and carried them back to the "ward". She helped the woman—who answered to the name Mary Abbot—sip from the bottle and laid a dampened cloth on her forehead. Before Sabrina could ask any further questions, Mary drifted into a disturbed sleep.

George groaned again and mumbled something in his delirium. Sabrina returned to his side and used a fresh bottle of water and a fresh cloth to clean his facial wounds. Clear of blood and dirt, his bruised and swollen face looked much improved.

Sabrina turned away and visited each of the beds in turn, checking the condition of each occupant as best she knew how.

Apart from George and Mary, she found two alive, all had high temperatures, shallow breathing, and rapid pulse rates. It took her a few minutes to pluck up the courage to approach the two beds farthest away. She had never been in the same room as a corpse before and had no idea how she would react.

She pulled back each grubby sheet in turn.

Both bodies were grey, their skin sunken. They looked to be middle-aged, but, in life, could have been younger. The skin at their throats was cold to the touch and still. No pulse.

Sabrina covered them with the dirty sheets and rushed back to the room to discard the gloves and wash her hands with a bottle of liquid sanitiser she found at the back of a shelf.

She considered dousing herself in the yellow antiseptic fluid she found on another shelf, but decided it might be a step too far—and probably too late. Instead, she used the sanitiser to disinfect the furniture before dropping into the chair, folding her arms on the table, and resting her head on her forearms. She had to adjust her position a number of times before finding an angle that did not press upon a wound.

The last thing she remembered before closing her eyes was trying not to sob too loudly and disturb her patients.

Her patients!

Mon Dieu.

The word tortured her. Acid churned in her stomach.

Ryan, où es-tu? Ryan, where are you?

CHAPTER FIFTEEN

In the distance, muttering reached her consciousness.

Sabrina twitched. Her neck creaked and her tongue stuck to a bone-dry mouth.

"M-Miss ...."

Sabrina jerked awake. Harsh light stabbed her eyes. She had failed to switch it off.

She stretched out her arms, but the handcuff tugged at her wrist, and she snatched it back before tearing away even more skin. Her neck ached from lying awkwardly and livid red marks from her cheeks and forehead stood out dark on her forearms. Lord alone knew what her face looked like with the swelling, the cuts, and the bruises. She dared herself to peek in the mirror attached to the inside lid of the medicine trolley, but recoiled at the idea and slammed it down rather than upset herself any further.

She tried blinking away the sleep but grit from the inside of her eyelids scraped her eyeballs and made matters worse. A quick dousing of a flannel with water and a gentle dabbing would make her feel a little better, but ... something had woken her? What? The crick in the neck probably.

Cot springs creaked and a drowsy voice called out, "M-Miss LeM-Maître? I-Is that you?"

Sabrina spun on her chair. Aching muscles reacted against the sudden movement, and she gritted her teeth against the storm of pain.

Outside, in the darkened infirmary, George sat up in his cot, leaning on his elbow, his battered face creased into a deep frown.

"George!"

She jumped out of the chair and raced from the room, nearly tripping over the chain dragging on the floor. She stopped short of his cot.

"George. How are you?"

He gave her a weak and painful smile.

"G-Got a m-myself one f-fierce headache."

"Yes, I can imagine. Lean back and relax. I shall bring you some water."

He reached out to her.

"N-No, don't go!"

"It is okay, George. You need to drink something. I shall be right back."

She left him, only to return a few moments later with a fresh bottle of water, which she helped him to sip.

He had flopped back against a thin pillow, the back of his head resting on the harsh metal frame of the bedstead.

"W-Where am I?"

"The colonel calls it the infirmary," she said softly, "but I would call it a filthy store room."

"T-The inf-firmary? Oh m-my G-God. T-They put me in the d-death house!"

George jerked up and squirmed towards the edge of the bed. He tore the sheet from his body and tried to stand.

She held up her hands to block his escape. He squealed, dug his bare heels into the thin mattress and worked his way back from her until squashed into the corner, where his bed met the clapboard wall.

"George, calm down."

"B-But those w-women, they're s-sick, an' what they's g-got ... i-its c-catchin'."

"But it is too late, George. You've been here for so long, if you were going to contract something, it will already have happened. Keep your distance from the other patients and you should be okay."

Tears flowed from his wide eyes and rolled down his puffy cheeks.

"I-I'm gonna d-die!"

He buried his head in his hands, shoulders shaking in time with his wailing. Only then did Sabrina notice the cuff around his wrist and the chain to which it was attached. The colonel had meant what he said about maintaining the quarantine. No one entering the infirmary would leave without his permission—at least no one alive.

She rested a hand on his bobbing shoulder.

"George, you must try to be calm. I am with you. Together, we will find a way out of here."

He lifted his head from his hands.

"How w-we gonna d-do that?" He rattled the chain on his wrist. "W-We's in c-chains."

"If there is a way, we will find it, and if not ... others may help."

George leaned to one side and tried to see around the screen.

"Others? Wh-Who'd you m-mean?"

"The Creed kidnapped me, George. People will be searching."

Sabrina would say nothing more. She was not ready to tell George anything she did not want the colonel to know. For now, her association with the FBI and her message to *grand-père* Mo-Mo had to remain a secret.

"Just 'cause y-you was k-kidnapped don't mean people's gonna c-come lookin' for you. Not here, they ain't. You ain't the first."

Sabrina stepped closer.

"George, what do you mean by that?"

The young man tilted his head to one side and his frown deepened.

"Where d'you t-think we got the doc?" He used his chin to point at Mary. "An' all the rest of them w-women?"

Sabrina spun and pushed the screen away. Mary had neither moved nor spoken since she had re-entered the "ward".

"What are you saying, George? Were all these women abducted?"

He dipped his head in a nod.

"Sure they w-was. C-Colonel said they w-were fallen women who'd b-be b-better off w-working for the C-Creed than s-sellin' they-selves for money."

Sabrina shook her head in disbelief. Could it be true?

"The colonel took the doctor, too? Are you certain?"

"Sure he did. Once they s-started g-gettin' sick, he needed s-someone to take c-care of them."

"But she's a medic. She would be missed. You cannot simply take someone as high profile as a doctor and think to get away with it. Did no one come looking for her?"

"'C-Course not. The colonel ain't s-stupid. W-We never take the women from close by. We l-liberate them from different p-places. The colonel calls it 'c-casting our net w-wide'."

Sabrina turned around and tore away the screen. It toppled and crashed to the concrete floor, throwing up a little cloud of dust. Mary still did not stir. Sabrina feared for the worst, but when she pressed her gloved fingers to the throat of the stricken woman, she found a weak pulse.

Barely hanging on, but at least she was still alive.

She tested the pulses of the other three women but found that another had succumbed to her illness during the night. She gasped, blessed herself, making the sign of the cross in scant reverence to the passing of yet another innocent victim. Three corpses now lay at rest in the makeshift infirmary that had become a mortuary. Colonel Caren and his Doomsday Creed had so much to answer for. So much.

Sabrina paused for a brief moment to gather her dark thoughts before snapping out of her malaise and searching her surroundings. The overhead lights barely illuminated the long, low room.

Against one wall, she found a chair with a broken back and

carried it to the bedside of the doctor. She sat near the head of the bed and studied the woman carefully. Her gaunt face and grey, sagging skin suggested a woman in late middle age, but that might have been the ravages of the illness. Mary could be anywhere from thirty to fifty years of age. Pimply red splodges discoloured her upper chest, and ragged, shallow breathing told of a lung disorder, but that was as far as her diagnostic skills would take her. She could have spent time in the office, reading books, but a crash course in medical practice would be of little use when Mary, a qualified doctor according to George, had been unable to save her patients.

The situation could not have been any more perilous. Sabrina desperately wanted to grant Mary the restful peace of sleep, but time would not allow it.

Sabrina reached out her hand and gently shook a bony shoulder.

"Mary," she whispered. "Mary, can you hear me?"

"Wh-Whatcha d-doin'?" George asked from his place at the far corner of his bed. "D-Don't get too close to her or you'll catch it, too."

Sabrina shot him a silencing glance.

"She might know what the illness is, and I might be able to force your uncle to get us proper treatment."

"The colonel don't c-care 'bout these w-women. He ain't g-gonna waste no time treatin' us."

"He might do, if I offer to give him what he wants."

Colonel Caren did not know it, not yet, but *grand-père* Mo-Mo was not the only person outside of Brown and Company who could gain access to their laboratory and its high-value storage facility.

"Mary ... can you hear me?" Again, Sabrina touched the overly warm shoulder.

Her breathing faltered and Mary opened her eyes.

"Where ....? Oh, it's you. Thought ... I was dreaming."

She struggled to lift her head and sit up.

"Wait one moment."

Sabrina took two pillows from the empty beds and used them to prop Mary upright.

"Mary, my name is Sabrina."

"They ... took you, too?" Mary asked, glancing at the chain attached to Sabrina's wrist.

Sabrina nodded.

"How long ago?"

"Four, five days. It is difficult to say. What about you?"

"No idea. Weeks. Are you a ... doctor or ... one of the ... others?"

"Neither. I am an ... IT consultant." A small lie, but Mary did not need to know the truth.

"Why ... you here?"

"It is a long story. What is wrong with you? Do you know?"

Mary's eyes rolled up, her lids fluttered and closed, and her head lolled back against the pillow.

"Mary, stay awake. I need you!"

Sabrina took the cloth from Mary's forehead, wet it and replaced it. Mary's eyes opened, glassy and unfocused. Her head lolled to one side. Sabrina stood over the bed and shook the sick woman's shoulders.

Mary rallied again. She licked her cracked lips.

"Water ... please."

Sabrina placed the bottle to her lips and allowed her a sip.

"What is your diagnosis, Doctor Abbot? What is the treatment?"

Using her title and surname had the effect Sabrina intended. Mary sat up straighter and her eyes found focus.

"Typhoid," she gasped. "But this is a new, much more ... virulent strain. I've ... never seen it so ... contagious ... or fast-acting."

Typhoid?

Sabrina shuddered.

"What is the treatment?"

Mary's eyes closed for a few seconds. Sabrina thought she had lost the moment, but Mary muttered, "Antibiotics. Should have saved them, us, but ... but ... the colonel wouldn't provide any drugs. He ... he's a ... lunatic."

Mary coughed weakly, doubled up and vomited a foul-smelling yellow bile over the side of the bed. Sabrina jumped to her feet and backed away. The wooden chair scraped on the concrete floor and toppled over. Like the privacy screen, it threw up a little cloud of dust as it hit the floor.

Why had Mary not tried cleaning the infirmary in the weeks of her captivity? Basic hygiene and sterilisation rules would have a helped. Might they have saved the women?

"That's g-gross," George said, his damaged nose wrinkling.

Someone hammered on the doors. Sabrina turned in time to see and hear them both screech open. Two figures dressed in hooded coveralls, gloves, goggles, and face masks entered, pushing a wooden hand cart. Tex and Sergeant Graham, wearing facemasks and gloves, stood behind them, handguns drawn.

"Right, Frenchie," Tex said, pointing his semi-automatic at her chest, "better step back. It'd be a pity to have to shoot you. I wouldn't kill you, of course. No, sir. The colonel wouldn't be too pleased if I did that before your granddaddy came across with his payment." He lowered his aim. "Just a little flesh wound would do. Maybe take out a knee. Not fatal, but painful as all hell."

He laughed. At his side Sergeant Graham stared straight at her, expressionless. She hated each man equally and wished them both a slow and painful death.

When Ryan arrived ....

Sabrina edged closer to George who sat upright in his bed, trembling.

The two covered men pushed the cart into the infirmary, breathing heavily though the masks. They picked up the first body, threw it into the cart without ceremony, and repeated the process with the second dead woman.

"Check the others," Tex barked.

One of the men peeled back the sheet of the third body and nodded.

"This un's gone, too," he said, nodding to his partner.

They added her to the others, taking the same lack of care. With their gory task complete, they hurried away with the cart.

"How you doin', George?" Tex asked from the opening. "Good to see you're awake. No hard feelings, I hope."

George stiffened, but did not reply.

"You shouldn't have gotten in my way, son," Tex continued his taunt. "Mind you, them bruises ain't done nothing to harm you in the looks department."

"Leave him alone, *cochon*!"

"Shut your mouth, bitch. Don't forget, I'm the one with the gun."

Sabrina stood up taller.

"Yes. I see that. You are very courageous standing there pointing a gun at a boy and a woman in chains. So brave." She raised her chained hand and beckoned him inside. She hid her right hand behind her back. In it, she held the scalpel. With her thumb, she flicked off its protective sheath to expose the finely honed blade. "Put away your gun and come inside. Show us how brave you really are!"

Tex sneered and shook his head.

"Uh-uh. No way, Frenchie. I ain't settin' foot in that place. Don't wanna catch no plague. You just sit tight and enjoy what little time you got left."

"It is not the plague, you buffoon! It is typhoid. It can be treated with antibiotics and by sterilising this building. Nobody else has to die!"

Tex laughed. "Yeah, that's what the doctor said, but the colonel didn't believe her. She'd have said anything to get out of there. Typhoid's a disease for the wops and the wetbacks. This here is the United States of America. We don't got typhoid. Eradicated it decades ago."

"Please," Sabrina said, hand outstretched, chain jangling. "Let me speak to the colonel."

"No way, Frenchie. Colonel's busy right now. He's preparing to give them bodies a proper send off. Gonna speak Bible words over them, too. He's good like that, is the colonel. All heart."

"Listen to me, man. Tell the colonel if he sends someone for the medicine, I can give him what he wants."

"Lying bitch. You're the same as the doctor." Tex turned to Graham. "Lock 'em in, Sergeant. We have us a bonfire to light."

"Sir, yes, sir."

139

Graham slammed the doors on the cackled laughter spewing from the mouth of the vile Texan.

"Coward! *Cochon!*" she screamed, but Tex continued laughing and Graham joined him.

Sabrina kicked out at the chair and sent it skittering into the empty bed next to Mary, who failed to stir. To calm herself, Sabrina checked the pulse of each remaining patient and tried, without great success, to make them drink.

"M-Miss LeMaître?" George asked following a few moments of pulsating silence.

"*Oui*—yes, George?"

"Are w-we g-gonna die in here?"

She righted the chair and carried it to the side of his bed. "No, George. You and I will not die. I have friends on the outside. They will be looking for me."

"Y-Your grandpa?"

"*Oui.* Amongst others."

"O-Others?"

She began to answer but stopped. Could she risk telling him?

"What others, Miss?"

"George, can you keep a secret?"

"Y-You c-can trust me, M-Miss LeMaître. I ain't never s-spilled a s-secret in my life." He crossed a finger over his chest. "I-I swear to G-God!"

The innocence in his eyes made her want to help him. Give him some hope. But the young man was deeply tied in with the Creed and she did not know how far she could trust him. An obfuscation of the truth would suffice.

"George," she said, leaning closer and lowering her voice, "my grandfather knows people in authority. The moment he receives the ransom demand, he will contact the FBI and they will come to rescue us."

George opened his eyes wide and shook his head wildly.

"No! No! He c-can't talk to the F-Feds. He c-can't. The colonel's g-gonna be mad. He's got the sh-shield. If the Feds c-come, he'll use it."

Sabrina held up her hands.

"George, calm down."

He jumped from the bed and stood barefoot, swaying slightly. "No. If the F-Feds c-come ... The s-shield. It's b-bad. Real bad."

She stood and held the boy by his upper arms. He stopped swaying and stared blankly at her as though not recognising who she was.

"George," she said as calmly as possible, "what is this shield?"

"Uh-uh," he said, shaking his head again, this time under more control. "C-Can't tell you."

"Why not, George?"

"I-It's a secret, a-and I never gives up a secret. Not never."

CHAPTER SIXTEEN

SUNDAY 21ST MAY – *Morning*
Pine Creek, Arizona, US

The sun breaking through the surrounding fir trees glowed behind Kaine's closed eyelids and eased him into a gentle wakefulness. He yawned long and hard and rubbed the sleep from his eyes.

The dashboard clock on the brand new, leather upholstered Ford Explorer read 05:43. Far too early to hit the trail and roll the final twenty-five miles into Pine Creek. As a stranger in a small town, he'd stick out so much that a low key arrival would be out of the question.

Kaine grabbed the bottle of water he'd picked up at a truck stop on the I-10 just outside Williston, pulled his rucksack from the passenger seat, and cracked open the driver's door.

The crisp mountain air brought tears to his eyes and breathed fresh life deep into his lungs. He dropped the backpack onto the bonnet and broke the seal on the bottle. While sipping the still water, he took time to breathe and take in the scene. What had appeared an ominous, brooding place when he'd parked overnight had blossomed into a place of serene beauty, being slowly warmed by an amber sun.

Kaine took another deep pull from the bottle, swilled out his mouth, and spat the water onto the tan earth. A tiny rivulet ran downhill for a few centimetres until the bone dry earth blotted it up.

Birds called out in the canopy all around, and critters rustled the undergrowth. Otherwise the Dry Canyon Picnic Grounds lay still and silent. Judging from the tranquillity and the freshness, he was the only human for miles.

He dug through the contents of the backpack until he found the necessaries. Minutes later, with his business completed, his teeth brushed, and his mouth fresh, Kaine stood ready for the day ahead.

The rucksack contained the barest minimum equipment he felt capable of smuggling through Tucson Airport's stiff security, including two pairs of his exceptionally expensive, state-of-the-art glasses. He pulled one pair from their protective case and slid them on. Currently, the lenses were clear, but they would darken in bright sunlight the same way as any standard photochromatic lenses. The prime difference between these and any other pair of shades lay buried deep within the thick yet fashionable frame. Each arm contained a host of electronic wizardry and a long-life battery guaranteed to last at least ten hours on a single USB charge.

Kaine tapped the left arm once.

"Alpha One to Base. Are you receiving me? Over."

"*Hi there, Mr K. How you diddling?*"

Kaine closed his eyes for a moment. For reasons best known to himself, Corky refused to maintain correct comms protocol, irrespective of how often Kaine chided him about it. Still, Corky had designed and built the comms system, which gave him a massive degree of latitude.

"Ready to head in soon. How do these glasses work exactly? Over."

"*Tap the right arm twice and see what happens.*"

Kaine followed the instruction. Instantly, the left lens changed focus, forcing Kaine to use his dominant right eye.

"Whoa. That's strange. Over."

"*It's a digital camera.*"

"What can you see? Over."

"Whatever you're looking at."

"How?"

"Neat, huh? Corky's played a blinder here. Bifocal eye tracking sensors built into the frame triangulate your gaze direction. Distance sensors alter the lens power using advanced liquid crystal augmentation to adjust the focus. The system's linked to a camera and the data is stored in a high-density—"

"Okay, Base. That'll do. You lost me at 'bifocal'. Over." Kaine allowed a smile to colour his voice.

"You is a technophobe."

"We can't all be certified geniuses. Is there any way I can view the camera pictures remotely? Over."

"Sure you can, Corky uploaded a camera app to your mobile remotely. Without a satellite pickup signal, the range is two kilometres."

"That's excellent. Thank you, Base. Changing the subject, did you finish your deep dive into our new friend? Over."

"Yep. Sure did."

Kaine waited for Corky to elaborate, but the hacker kept unusually quiet, probably waiting for a drumroll.

"What did you find? Over."

"Not a single thing. Far as Corky's concerned, the Canadian's squeaky. Pure as the driven. Didn't find nothing more than a few speeding tickets."

Kaine nodded to himself.

"That's hardly a surprise. From the way he drove last night, I reckon Alain Dubois thinks he's Gilles Villeneuve."

Or his son, Jacques.

"What about our target? Did you find a potential location? Over."

"Still working on it, Mr K. Loads of data to sift through. If Corky finds anything, you'll be the first to hear about it. Now, wanna know how to contact the Canadian without having to use ESAPP's piece of crap comms unit?"

"Yes please, Base. Over."

"Tap either arm three times and you'll be spliced into the ESAPP infrastructure. Do the same thing when you use the earpiece alone."

"Will he know I'm on your system? Over."

"Not on your life, Mr K. And don't you dare tell him nothing about Corky. Not one thing. Get it?"

"Of course not. Over."

"Good. Corky's got enough on his plate without being dragged into someone else's problems. What, with you and the Doc, Mr J, and Sean, Corky's—well ... you know. Pretty stretched. Anyway, before I bugger off for my supper, there's just one more thing. The satellite coverage where you are is spotty. If the international comms drop out, you'll still be able to talk to the Canadian so long as you're within a few klicks of each other and there ain't a mountain between you."

"Understood, Base. That's good to know. Alpha One, out."

To familiarise himself with the camera's operation, Kaine spent time scanning the immediate picnic grounds, looking both near and far, and viewing the recordings on his phone. Once satisfied he could work the system effectively, he climbed back into the Ford, ate a sports cereal bar, and finished the rest of the water. Not the best breakfast he'd ever eaten, but definitely not the worst.

By the time he'd performed his minimum warm-up exercises and freshened up using the camp's facilities, the sun's warmth had penetrated the trees and the first humans had arrived to fill the air with excited jabbering and the mouth-watering aroma of frying bacon.

The dashboard clock read 09:35, and the car's built-in GPS system gave him an ETA of 10:55.

Operation Sabbie could finally begin.

CHAPTER SEVENTEEN

Sunday 21st May – Morning
Pine Creek, Arizona, US

The AZ-366 wound up the southern slope of a fir tree and brush-studded mountain, but straightened as it reached a dusty plateau. For the last mile of the run into Pine Creek, the two-lane road ran die straight and pan flat until it reached the outskirts of a town whose welcome sign called itself the "Biggest Little City in Renshaw County, Az. Popn. 13,635."

Kaine slowed the Ford to well below the speed limit and drove all the way along Main Street without stopping. It took less than ten minutes. His target, the *Pine Creek Saloon*, occupied a large plot on the western outskirts of town, a few hundred metres from the posted "city limits". He drove past the saloon without slowing further, taking in the building and its surrounds.

Flat-roofed and stucco-clad, the white-painted saloon looked peaceful enough, and the cars parked around the side showed it as open to Sunday morning trade. Crude, hand-painted signs attached to the wooden three-pole fence guarding the frontage boasted,

"Breakfasts served all day," and "Coffee strong enough to stun a rodeo bull".

Kaine smiled to himself and kept on driving.

Once through to the edge of town—the edge leading straight into the mountains—he pulled into a side street to make the turn. Although he'd yet to see a single vehicle since leaving the camping grounds, Kaine thought better of pulling a U-turn on the main road. Who knew what sort of law enforcement operated in Pine Creek? He hoped not to draw the attention of the local sheriff unless it was absolutely essential to finding Sabrina.

Thirty seconds later, he turned into the saloon's lot, and parked around the back, under the shade of a large Ponderosa pine. He grabbed his rucksack, opened the door, and climbed out into a pleasantly warm day. A dozen or so dust-caked SUVs dotted the parking lot, showing that the citizens of Pine Creek weren't averse to spending their Sunday mornings in one of the town's hostelries.

Maybe the bull-stunning coffee was worth getting out of bed for. Either that, or the saloon stayed open through the night and the drivers hadn't left. Time would tell.

He stepped around the side of the building and climbed up the two steps onto a wide, covered porch, heading for the entrance—a classic pair of batwing doors. In this theme park version of an Old West saloon, he half expected to hear the tinny notes of an off-key honkytonk piano. Again, he smiled to himself.

As he closed on the entrance, the batwings crashed open and a huge man dressed as a cowboy poured out, stinking of booze, stale sweat, and even staler tobacco. Tall, wide-shouldered and pot-bellied, he had to duck under the door frame or hit his head. Two other men appeared behind him in the doorway.

Kaine backed up, but not fast enough to avoid Cowboy's shoulder-charge.

"Sorry," Kaine said, although he wasn't at fault.

"Hey! Watch where you're goin', boy!"

Cowboy thrusted out a hand to brush him aside, and Kaine twisted at the waist. The man's hand met nothing but fresh air. He lost balance, missed his footing, and stumbled down the steps and out into the sunlight. He narrowly avoided ending up flat on his face in the dust.

"Oops," Kaine said. "You okay there, mate?"

Cowboy spun around and glowered up at Kaine.

"You ignorant little—"

"Hey," Kaine said, raising his hands, "no cause for that, mate. It was an accident. No harm, no foul."

"You got in my way!" Cowboy snarled.

He formed fists and made to rush up the stairs, but two other men pushed out through the doors and out onto the porch, staring at the scene.

Kaine sized up his position. He'd been in similar situations before and needed more elbow room.

He stepped off the porch, dropped his backpack to the dusty ground at his feet, and positioned himself to see all three men easily.

Cowboy wore a black, wide-brimmed hat, tilted back to show a shiny white forehead above a line of sunburned skin. Beneath a black leather waistcoat, his red and white plaid shirt stretched tight over the beer belly, and his dusty jeans had seen better days. His highly tooled, light brown cowboy boots hadn't been cleaned in forever.

Kaine wanted to be impressed, but didn't have the energy. Instead, he dipped his head, used the tip of a finger to slide his special glasses lower down his nose, and looked over the top of the frame.

Cowboy leaned to his left as though fighting to keep upright in a stiff breeze.

"What's going on here, Duke?" said the larger of Cowboy's two friends—another hulking bear of a man, but this one had red hair, a wispy beard, and flinty blue eyes.

"This fucker," Duke said, pointing at Kaine, "tripped me, Birdy. I coulda broke my neck."

"He did, huh?" Birdy asked. "That right, Duke?"

Coming from such a large man, Birdy's high-pitched voice seemed incongruous, and the rapidly spoken words carried a degree of mania, suggesting a man with a short fuse.

Kaine fixed what he hoped looked like a genial smile to his bearded face and squinted into the low sun. He stepped around his backpack and shifted a couple of paces to win himself a better view. Cowboy turned with him, tucked in his chin, and looked sideways. His dark eyes glinted in the sunshine.

"It was an accident," Kaine said, still smiling. "Let me buy you a beer to smooth things over."

Duke snorted.

"A beer, he says," the big cowboy nodded. "The pissant wants to buy us a beer. What d'you say, guys? We gonna accept his offer?"

"No, no," Kaine said, raising a finger in the air. "I don't mind standing you a beer, Duke, but I'm not buying a round for the whole saloon. I'm not made of money."

Duke nodded to his friends. Each occupied as much space as Cowboy and each was similarly dressed. Kaine shook his head. He'd wandered into a Western Frontier theme park but didn't have time for the guided tour. Sabrina needed him.

"Seems like we got ourselves a cheap asshole," Cowboy said through a loud guffaw. "What you reckon, Birdy?"

"Sure seems that way, Duke."

"What d'you say, Johnny?"

The third man—lean, dark haired, clean shaven and in his early-twenties—glanced at each of his companions and shook his head slowly. He took a couple of paces to his side and leaned against one of the posts supporting the porch roof. He hooked his thumbs into his belt and kept them there.

Sensing no immediate danger from Johnny, Kaine focused his full attention on Duke and Birdy, who had descended the steps and taken a position on Duke's left flank.

Slowly, Kaine lowered his right hand and let it hover at waist level. He brought the other hand up to meet it. An innocuous move designed to put him in a better position to defend himself without making it overtly threatening.

Duke spat into the dirt. The dark brown, tobacco-filled glob missed Kaine's hiking boot by a matter of centimetres. He jerked his foot away and grimaced.

"Nasty," Kaine said. "Was that absolutely necessary?"

"Watch yer mouth, smartass," Duke growled.

"Yeah, watch yer mouth, smartass," Birdy repeated, almost in falsetto.

Johnny shook his head again and sighed.

Kaine tried to see through the etched glass of the saloon's large window, but the sun showed nothing but a reflection of him, the three men, and the dusty road behind them. Kaine stood alone against two hulks. He'd faced worse odds in his time.

He took a breath, held it for a moment, and released it through his mouth.

Pissant? Arsehole? Smartarse? And they don't even know me.

He could play the situation any one of a number of different ways, most of which would end up drawing even more attention to himself. Although Duke didn't happen to be wearing a badge or carrying any ironware, Kaine had no way of telling how close to the local sheriff's department the man might be. In small towns such as Pine Creek, everybody knew the town drunks and would probably back them over a stranger.

On the other hand, he didn't fancy being on the receiving end of a thumping. To find Sabrina, he needed all his faculties intact and allowing these idiots to dish out a beating wouldn't make things any easier.

The situation created a bit of a quandary. If he couldn't play the tough guy, he'd have to do it another way.

"I only stopped by for breakfast," Kaine said, aiming for plaintive. "I don't want any trouble."

Duke formed fists, his swollen knuckles cracked under the effort. If the action was intended to intimidate, it failed.

"You don't want no trouble? Well, tough luck, son. You've found yourself a whole heap."

Duke pushed his face even closer, wafting more whiskey-laden breath towards Kaine. To compensate, Kaine leaned away and started breathing through his mouth.

"Like I told you, Duke," Kaine said, still keeping his voice low and slow, "I'm not looking for trouble."

Duke looked confused as though wondering how Kaine could possibly know his name. He stood even taller and sucked in his gut.

"Pissant!"

Kaine winced.

He'd used that one before.

Must have a restricted vocabulary for insults.

"You're heading for a stomping."

Kaine swallowed and allowed his grin to falter. "I-I'm sorry you feel that way, sir."

Duke guffawed loud and long, and turned to his redheaded sidekick. In doing so, the big cowboy left himself completely vulnerable to a left cross, should Kaine decide to end the inevitable confrontation before it started. On the other hand, taking Duke out of the picture quickly and decisively would lead to questions Kaine preferred not to answer.

He held back.

"Hear that, Birdy? This scrawny little asshole just called me 'sir'."

"I sure did, Duke," Birdy said. "You, a 'sir'? Ain't never heard nothing funnier in all my life. Pissant, he is alright. Talks funny, too."

Duke glanced sideways at his buddy, as though unsure what to make of his response. He clearly couldn't decide the extent to which Birdy had insulted him, too. Kaine sighed. Neither of these idiots would trouble the scorers too much if they ever sat a Mensa test.

"Birdy," Duke said, "are you sassing me?"

"Me?" Birdy slapped a hand to his large chest. "Hell no. Why would I do that?"

Duke grunted, hitched up his jeans, and turned to face Kaine again.

"Hey, dumbass. Are *you* sassing me?"

Kaine swallowed, showing as much fear as he deemed suitable under the circumstances.

"N-No, sir. Not at all," he said, offering another weak smile. "I-I'm not looking for trouble, sir."

Duke further tightened his gut and stood even taller.

"What *are* you lookin' for?"

"Like I said, all I wanted was breakfast. But, I've lost my appetite. If you don't mind, I'll be on my way."

Without losing sight of the big man, Kaine bent at the knees, scooped up his backpack, and hugged it to his chest.

Duke's expression hardened. "Yeah. As it happens, I do mind." He raised a hand and beckoned Kaine closer with gnarled fingers. "C'mon, asshole. Come get yours."

"As I keep saying, I don't want any trouble."

Duke sneered. "What you want and what you get don't necessarily add up to the same thing."

That's deep.

It turned out that Duke was a philosopher. Who'd have known?

Kaine pointed behind Duke and Birdy to the surveillance camera fixed above the saloon's entrance, its lens pointing straight at them.

"You know we're on camera, right?"

Duke shot a glance up at the building before returning his focus to Kaine.

"That's a dummy, you dummy," Duke said, laughing. "It ain't gonna save your sorry ass."

"Oh dear," Kaine said, hugging the Bergen even tighter. "Looks like I really am in a certain amount of distress, doesn't it?"

Duke frowned, hesitant for the first time since he'd made the approach.

"That accent," he said. "You a Brit?"

"Yes," Kaine said, nodding eagerly, making it appear as though he thought his nationality might have earned him a reprieve. "Yes, I am."

"What's a Brit like you doing in my town?"

"Just passing through."

Duke smirked. "Just passing through?"

"Yes, that's right. I'm just passing through. So," he said, cowering beneath Duke's hard gaze, "Pine Creek is your town? Does that mean you're the mayor?"

Birdy snickered. Johnny winced and scratched his chin, but maintained his neutrality and kept leaning against his post.

"Nope," Duke said, "just a concerned citizen. Me and my buddies like to keep our eyes and ears open for trouble."

Trouble? Moi?

"Do I *have* to answer your questions?"

Duke stiffened again. "You do, if'n you want to keep them shiny white teeth in your head."

"Yes, Duke, I-I understand."

Duke frowned. "Hey, how come you know my name?"

"A little Birdy told me." Kaine shot Duke another glance. "Sorry, that's what passes for a joke in England. I tell jokes when I'm nervous."

Duke snorted.

"You Brits ain't nothing but a bunch of faggots. My granddaddy died in France saving your chickenshit country from Adolf."

Kaine sighed. The UK-US special relationship clearly hadn't reached as far as Pine Creek, Arizona. He'd find no reprieve from that quarter.

He cast his eyes around a small town with delusions of grandeur. Main Street stretched out in a straight line, running northeast and southwest. Two wide lanes of cracked and heavily patched concrete ran through the centre of the place, separating single-storey buildings, mostly constructed from adobe and painted white in deference to the attack of the summer sun.

In the distance, a stoop-shouldered couple crossed the otherwise deserted street, too far away and too elderly to intervene.

No help from any quarter.

"I'm sorry for your loss," Kaine said, for want of something more original to say.

"Duke," Johnny said, speaking for the first time, "this isn't right. Two against one doesn't look good."

"What you mean two against one. You playing chicken?"

Johnny straightened. "You don't have any reason to call me chicken, Marmaduke Albemarle. Haven't I proved myself often enough? This here Brit doesn't look like a troublemaker to me. Seems more like a tourist. Are you certain you're playing this right?"

"Thanks, Johnny," Kaine said. "I appreciate your help."

"Uh-uh." Johnny shook his head. "Ain't helping no one. This isn't my fight, is all."

"Shut yer mouth, Johnny," Birdy squeaked. "Duke knows what he's doin'."

"Does he?" Johnny asked.

Birdy sidled around behind Kaine and, still hugging the Bergen, Kaine shifted sideways to maintain his view of both men. He forced his lower lip to tremble.

"Yeah, Johnny," Duke growled, "I know what I'm doing."

Wait for it.

The momentary pause stretched out to infinity.

Way off to the south, the air horn of a haulage truck blasted out an angry two-tone Doppler blare. A gust of wind woke the dust, forced it into mini twisters, and drove them along the street. Kaine narrowed his eyes and blinked away the airborne grit. His glasses helped.

Duke shouted, "Now!"

In a coordinated move, Duke lurched closer, fists raised. Birdy screamed and dived forwards, arms wide, trying to wrap Kaine in a bearhug. He aimed to pin Kaine's arms at his sides while Duke attacked from the front.

The bearhug failed.

Kaine's backpack stopped Birdy's hands meeting at the front and making a crippling grip.

Duke growled, leaned in, and threw a straight, piledriver left.

Kaine squealed, buckled at the knees. The powerful blow scraped the top of his head and landed flush on Birdy's nose. The punch snapped Birdy's head back, breaking the ineffectual bearhug.

Birdy shrieked and crumpled into a heap on the dirt-strewn

ground. His eyes rolled up into his head, blood pumped from a flattened nose, and his mouth sagged open.

On his hands and knees, Kaine scrambled away, the backpack apparently hampering his attempts to stand.

Duke roared, his anger and frustration clear.

"You chickenshit asshole! Look what you done to Birdy!"

He aimed a vicious kick, the pointed-toes of the cowboy boots primed to crush Kaine's ribcage.

From the ground, Kaine cried, "No, please!"

He jerked and twisted. The boot connected with his backpack, and bounced off harmlessly.

Duke raised his foot to stomp Kaine's head.

Kaine screamed and pushed both arms away from his chest. The backpack struck Duke's locked supporting knee, snapping it out and back. Duke howled, collapsed, and fell on top of Birdy. Air burst out of both men, who lay in a bunch of thrashing, flailing arms and legs.

Kaine finally dropped the backpack and tried scrambling away. His boots lost traction in dust and the left heel "accidentally" caught Duke on the chin. Eventually, his foot gained traction and he lurched to his feet, whooping in great faltering gasps of dusty air. Once upright, Kaine backed away from the downed men and cowered in the shadows, coughing and clasping a wooden post for support.

"Oh my God," he wailed, staring at Johnny for backup. "What just happened?"

Eyes wide, mouth hanging open, Johnny shook his head.

"If that don't beat all."

"Sorry?" Kaine asked, still gasping.

Johnny pushed away from his post and strolled towards Kaine, thumbs still hooked into the belt loops of his jeans. As he reached the floundering idiots, he paused and chuckled.

"Never seen anything like that in all my born days."

The chuckle turned into a great belly laugh and the younger man turned to face Kaine. "You're either the luckiest man in Arizona, or the most skilful."

Kaine pushed away from the post and stood, trembling.

"Don't know what you mean." He held out his hands, both shook so much he could have been suffering from a fever. "I've never been so scared in all my life. Violence terrifies me."

Johnny swatted away Kaine's statement and held out his right hand. Kaine hesitated for a moment but saw nothing but open friendliness in the younger man's eyes. He took the offered hand and they shook.

"Drink?" Johnny asked.

"Yes please. I need one." Kaine swallowed. "What about those two?"

He pointed to Duke and Birdy, who had managed to untangle themselves. Duke was on his backside leaning against a sun-bleached wooden bench, one leg bent at the knee, the other straight out in front. On all fours, Birdy retched into the gutter, blood still dripping from his nose.

Johnny sighed loud and long.

"Doubt they'll be in a state to do anything for the next little while."

"Shouldn't we call an ambulance? I think Birdy's nose is broken, and Duke's knee doesn't look too good."

Johnny slapped Kaine on the shoulder. "You're all heart, Mr ...?"

"Griffin," Kaine said, "William Griffin. My friends call me Bill."

"Jonathan R Manchester III, but people around here call me Johnny." He held out his right hand again. "I'm right pleased to meet you, Bill Griffin."

"Likewise, Johnny." After another brief handshake, he added, "What about that ambulance."

The younger man pointed towards the saloon. "I'll ask Marshall to handle that."

Kaine stiffened. "There's a marshal in the saloon, and he didn't stop those two spoiling for a fight?"

Johnny laughed again.

"No, you don't get it. He ain't 'a' marshal. It's his first name. Marshall Guthrie. C'mon, let's go make his acquaintance. He'll be tickled pink when I tell him how you took apart the city's toughest and meanest hombres."

Those two are Pine Creek's toughest and meanest?

It didn't say much for the rest of the town.

"I did nothing of the sort."

"I know, but that ain't the way I'm gonna tell it, Slugger."

Damn.

After all his hard work and skill, he was still going to earn a reputation as a tough guy.

CHAPTER EIGHTEEN

Kaine picked up his pack, clapped the dust off it, and followed Johnny up onto the porch and under its welcome shade. The younger man pushed through the batwing doors and held one open for Kaine.

They stepped over the threshold and back a hundred and fifty years in time—into the Old West.

As he'd suspected, a themed saloon.

Circular tables topped in tattered green baize and surrounded by hard wooden chairs dotted the floor, but left plenty of gaps to allow access to the highly polished bar. The inevitable honkytonk piano stood off on one side, lid down and silent, thankfully.

The dark wood counter stretched out across the whole width of the room, fifteen metres at least. A couple of dozen wrought iron bar stools with uncomfortable-looking wooden seats lined up against the wood panelling, standing guard. Most were empty.

Kaine climbed onto one of the stools and balanced the backpack on the stool to his left. Johnny took the stool on his right. The whole way through the cavernous and near-empty bar, Kaine kept sight of the entrance through the horizontal mirror hanging behind the full length of the bar. Etched with the saloon's name, *Pine Creek Saloon and Grill, Proprietor Marshall C. Guthrie,* the mirror enabled Kaine to keep constant watch on the batwings in case the two bozos recovered more quickly than expected. The strategically placed mirror made their extended walk through the bar feel much safer.

Off to Kaine's left, four men in cowboy rig, their hats removed and hanging on the backs of their chairs, played poker. They paused the game long enough to watch Kaine and Johnny cross to the bar before the heaviest of the players hacked out a cough, and said, "Hey, we playing cards or what?"

The others grunted and returned their attention to the table. The fresh-faced man sitting opposite the impatient one took four chips from the top of one of his neatly piled stacks and threw them onto the heavy pot.

He said, "I'll see your hundred and raise you two."

Kaine tuned out the rest of the game. Playing for such high stakes required deep concentration. The poker players presented no threat and he still had the mirror. None of them could do a thing without him seeing them move first. He settled on the stool and waited.

A door behind the bar and off to one side opened and a stocky man about as tall as Kaine stepped through. He had a thick head of white hair parted in the middle and tied back into a long ponytail, and sported a white Kenny Rogers beard. His ivory-coloured cotton shirt had a ruffled front, and a black shoestring tie added to the image of Kenny Rogers in his guise of the Gambler.

"Hey, Johnny," the barman said, "you back so soon? Who you got for me?"

Johnny turned and held up a hand. "Marshall, this here's Wild Bill Griffin, the roughest, toughest hombre west of the Pacos. Well, west of London, England, at least."

"Morning, Mr Griffin. What can I get you?"

Johnny answered for Kaine. "After wrangling Duke and Birdy into submission, I reckon he'll need a stiff whiskey, Marshall. Make it a large one. I'll have a beer."

The barman stood up straight and snapped a look at the entrance.

"Them two birdbrains give you an overly warm welcome, Mr Griffin?"

Kaine winced and offered up a little shrug. "A little, Mr Guthrie."

The barkeep snapped upright. "You know my name?"

"Johnny told me, and"—Kaine pointed to the etched mirror behind the bar—"I imagine that's you?"

Guthrie turned to look then laughed.

"Sure is, Mr Griffin. You don't miss much, do you? So, you want that whiskey?"

"It's on me, Marshall," Johnny said, clapping Kaine on the shoulder once more.

Kaine jumped, as though from the shock.

"Better not since I'm driving."

"One small whiskey ain't gonna do much damage," Johnny said, still chuckling.

"You'll need a drink to slake your thirst on such a hot day," Marshall added. "How 'bout something else? Something long and cold?"

Kaine frowned in thought. "I don't suppose you sell sarsaparilla?"

"What?" Marshall's eyebrows shot up and ran away behind his frizz of white hair.

Kaine lowered his head and sent him an apologetic grin. "Always wanted to say that ever since watching cowboy movies as a kid."

Marshall slapped the counter.

"Hey," he said, "you're okay, Wild Bill. In answer to your question, we've got all kinds of soda, but there ain't no call for sarsaparilla these days."

"In that case, I will have a small beer."

"You got yourself a favourite?" He waved at the dozens of taps fixed to the counter.

"Something local would be nice to wash away all this trail dust."

"Plenty of breweries hereabouts, but Coldwater Gold packs plenty of taste."

"Sounds good. I'll give it a try."

Guthrie grabbed an old-fashioned glass mug from the shelf below the counter and tugged on a tap with a hand-written label. It delivered a pale yellow liquid with a thick foamy head. Guthrie poured another, letting the first settle, then flicked away the excess foam with a spatula. He topped it up and slid the glass across the counter to Kaine, handle first.

Next, he finished pouring the second beer and passed it to Johnny.

Guthrie and Johnny watched carefully as Kaine took his first tentative pull. Cold, crisp, and clean, and he could actually divine some flavour. Pleasant, not that strong, and unlikely to cause too many ill-effects.

"Nice," he said, smacking his lips. "Very nice."

His response seemed to please Guthrie well enough, and his host shot some cola into a tall glass from a nozzle attached to a flexible hosepipe.

"Cheers," he said and held it up.

They touched glasses. Kaine took another small sip and turned to Johnny.

"What about an ambulance?"

"Ambulance?" Guthrie asked, stretching his neck.

"I told you," Johnny said. "Wild Bill Griffin here just gave Duke and Birdy a licking. Tore 'em apart with his bare hands, he did."

Kaine swallowed hard and shook his head. "It wasn't like that, Mr Guthrie. Not even close."

"Never seen anything like it," Johnny continued, ignoring Kaine's interruption. "Took down Birdy first. Broke his nose. Then he busted Duke's knee."

"That's not what happened," Kaine said, "and you know it. I was terrified. Thought I was a dead man."

"Nah," Johnny said, "they'd have maybe roughed you up a little, but they'd never have killed you. Too much paperwork." He laughed long and hard.

Kaine explained what really happened, playing up how terrified he'd been the whole time.

"So," Guthrie said, "you fainted and Duke broke Birdy's nose?"

Kaine gave up a sheepish nod.

"And Duke twisted his knee when he kicked my backpack," Kaine added, cringing. "I got lucky."

"That how it really went down?" Guthrie asked Johnny.

"Yeah," Johnny answered reluctantly, "but my way of tellin' it's better."

In the mirror, the bright patch of light over the batwing doors darkened and two sorry-looking specimens filled the space. Duke had his arm draped over Birdy's shoulders, heavily favouring his injured leg. Birdy, his yellow and green lumberjack shirt spotted with blood, staggered under the load. They pushed through the batwings and shuffled into the bar.

"You broke my nose, man," Birdy wailed at Duke. "An' now I gotta carry your sorry ass?"

"Didn't do it on purpose. The asshole fainted, I tell ya."

The two men crabbed sideways and dropped into the nearest empty chairs.

"How many times I gotta tell you two bozos?" Guthrie shouted. "You keep drivin' away my customers an' I'll go out of business. Now quit it."

"Hang it, Marshall," Duke said through a grimace. "He started it! Tripped me up and sassed me some."

Guthrie smiled wide, and his dark blue eyes glistened in the subdued lighting thrown by electric lights tricked out to look like nineteenth century oil lamps.

"You need me to call an ambulance?" he asked.

"Nah," Duke answered, glaring at Kaine, "bring a bottle and two glasses. That's all the medicine we need."

Johnny leaned closer to Kaine and whispered, "Good idea for them to self-medicate. Whiskey's much cheaper than the ER."

He winked.

Guthrie walked a tin tray with a full bottle, two shot glasses, and a pile of paper towels to Duke and Birdy's table. He poured the first two measures, which they knocked back in one. Each grimaced as the whiskey hit the back of their throats. After they'd finished gasping, Guthrie leaned close, jabbed his finger into the table, and talked so quietly Kaine couldn't make out a single word.

A couple of minutes later, after pouring a second "medicinal" measure each, Guthrie replaced the stopper on the bottle and returned to the bar with it. Both clearly chastened by Guthrie's dressing down, the two men downed their second—and final—drink, struggled to their feet, and left. This time, Duke managed to leave entirely under his own steam, limping heavily as he departed.

"Don't mind them none," Guthrie said. "Duke always did like to play Sheriff, but with him having flat feet and the eyesight of a gopher, he never could pass the physical."

A hearty laugh started at his toes and rocked up through his entire rounded body. Halfway through the chortle, the door behind the bar opened again and a woman entered. About five foot nine, heavily made up, overfilling her tight jeans and tasselled shirt. Kaine struggled to work out the woman's age, which could have fallen anywhere in the range from forty to sixty.

The moment she entered, Guthrie stopped laughing and opened his arms, but she ducked under his offered embrace.

"Not in front of the customers, Marshall. You know better'n that."

"Gee, honey. If a man can't hug his wife in his own place of business, what sort of a world we livin' in?"

"Get away, you old fool," Mrs Guthrie said, slapping his arm.

"They always like that?" Kaine asked Johnny quietly.

"Sure are. Sweet, ain't it," Johnny said, speaking through a snort.

"Quit that, young man," Mrs Guthrie said, smacking the counter with a hand full of heavy silver rings and showing how the counter had gained so many of its scratches.

After Guthrie had served a couple of bareheaded range hands at the far end of the bar, he returned and stood beside his wife. He wrapped an arm around her waist and she moved close against him.

"This here's a Brit. Name of Griffin," Guthrie said, smiling. "Griffin, this my wife, Billie."

"Billie?"

"Short for Wilhelmina," she said, rolling her eyes as though she'd grown tired of the reaction.

Kaine nodded a smile and took a longer draw of Coldwater. It still tasted good.

A shout from one of the card players near the piano drew Billie's attention. Guthrie released her waist and she answered the call for service. After she left, Guthrie refilled Johnny's glass and pointed at Kaine's.

Kaine threw a hand over the top of his beer and shook his head.

"No thanks. I'm good for now."

Guthrie sniffed. "Ain't likely to grow rich off of your custom, am I."

Unlikely.

Raucous laughter from the card players drew their attention. Billie, hands on her wide hips and head thrown back, laughed along with them. She straightened and touched the shoulder of the young man who'd called her over.

"Cal Davis," she said, still laughing hard, "you really ought to know better."

She turned and sashayed back to the bar. She took up a station at the far end of the bar and started filling the order.

"Well, I'd best be going soon," Johnny said, picking up his glass, "Got me some packing to do."

"Heading back up to Flagstaff?" Guthrie asked.

"Yep. Classes start bright and early," Johnny answered and turned to Kaine. "I'm studying philosophy along with a bunch of students who don't care to listen." He drained his glass in one long extended pull, slammed it down on the counter, and pulled a banknote from a pocket in his waistcoat. "Will a ten cover it?"

"Surely will."

Guthrie palmed the note, turned away, and rang up the total on the old-fashioned bar till. The cash drawer dinged open, Guthrie slipped the note under a sprung clip and slammed the drawer closed again. He didn't give any change.

Kaine smiled and shook his head. Once again, he had the distinct impression of being in the middle of a theme park or in a time warp. He turned to face Johnny.

"Are you likely to have any trouble from Duke and Birdy?"

"For not helping them out?"

Kaine nodded and Johnny shrugged.

"Nah. I'll be okay. Leaving town in a couple of hours and won't be back until the end of the semester. Those fools will have forgotten all about this little fracas by the time I'm back. And if they haven't, well ... I have other friends in town. Duke and Birdy don't represent the whole of the Pine Creek population. Not by a long way."

He held out his hand.

"Nice to meet you, Wild Bill Griffin. It's been real interesting."

They shook hands for the third time and Johnny left. Kaine doubted he'd see the youngster again. He checked his watch. Time was flying, but he wasn't ready to leave Pine Creek. Not for a while.

CHAPTER NINETEEN

SUNDAY 21ST MAY – Midday
Pine Creek, Arizona, US

Guthrie returned from serving a group of newcomers. He grabbed a spotless towel and a sparkling glass and started polishing. Ever the showman.

"Mind if I ask you a question?" Kaine asked.

Guthrie nodded. "Fire away."

"Are they playing poker for real?"

"Nope. The chips are fake. In this state, gambling ain't legal outside of a casino, unless it's for charity, like the Lotto. That there game of poker is for background colour." He gave Kaine a theatrical wink.

"Have I walked into a theme park?"

"That's what we're shootin' for," he said, his expression turning serious. "It's coming up to the start of the main vacation season and the tourists love this rig." He waved a hand in front of his outfit, pointed to his hair, and leaned closer. "Don't tell no one, but this here's a wig I only wear when I'm in the saloon."

"Looks pretty realistic to me," Kaine said, and held out a hand, making to tug at the ponytail.

Guthrie jerked out of reach and laughed again. "Yeah, you're right. It's real. Ain't no foolin' you, is there, Mr Griffin?"

Kaine let the question pass but glanced around the place and threw out a compliment. "It's really looking the part in here."

The barman beamed and took Kaine's comment as a request for more.

"Thank you, sir. Me and Billie started by redecoratin' the saloon, then we relaunched the annual rodeo. Now, we run cattle drives and trail riding for the city slickers."

"Impressive." Kaine tilted his beer in salute.

Guthrie raised a finger to tip his non-existent hat.

"Thank you kindly, sir."

"Credit where it's due."

"Where are you headed, if you don't mind my askin'?"

"No, I don't mind at all. Doing the tourist thing and going where the wind takes me. Sorry," he said, adding an apologetic smile, "but I thought I'd make my way up to the Grand Canyon. I hear it's worth a visit."

Guthrie sniffed and added a stiff-shouldered shrug.

"You mean it isn't?"

"Oh, it's nice enough," he said, his tone dismissive.

"Much else worth visiting locally?"

"Depends on what you're interested in."

Kaine took his turn to shrug. Time to tread carefully. He didn't want to raise any interested eyebrows.

"Actually," he said, shifting on his stool which proved every bit as uncomfortable as it promised, "I'm a bit of a military historian. I like visiting old battlefields and museums and the like. One of the reasons I headed up this way from Tucson was that I saw Camp Pueblo on the map. Google says it's abandoned so I thought I'd take it in on my way through. Easy to find, is it?"

Guthrie grimaced. "Camp Pueblo's way up in the mountains over difficult roads."

"That's all right, I'm driving an SUV."

Guthrie shook his head with finality.

"Wouldn't do you no good, my friend."

"Why not? Nothing to see?"

"Oh, there's plenty to see if you like worn-out clapboard huts and concrete bunkers overgrown with weeds."

"Actually, that's exactly what I like. You see, I take photos for my album. Planning to publish a book. Would I need permission from the army to shoot off a roll of film?"

"Nah. Army closed the base down years back. They've got nothing to do with the place no more. You'd need permission from the colonel."

The colonel?

Despite the surge of excitement, Kaine forced out a thoughtful frown.

"Somethin' wrong, Mr Griffin?"

"Sorry, I'm just a little confused. The army has nothing to do with the camp, but I need a colonel's permission to take some photos?"

"Yeah, I suppose it does sound a bit strange. I'm talkin' 'bout the new owner," Guthrie said, lifting his bearded chin. "Colonel Caren. Richard 'Dickie' Caren owns half of Mount Garrett and most of Copper Strike."

Kaine nodded. "I saw the signs to Copper Strike on the way into town. Worth a visit?"

Guthrie sneered. "Nah, all they got is a gas station and a small grocery store. You'd be better off staying here for a couple days and exploring Pine Creek. Good nightlife here, if you ignore them two morons." He nodded towards where Duke and Birdy had been sitting.

"So, this Colonel Caren," Kaine said after a momentary lull in the conversation, "is it worth me calling him for permission to visit?"

"Nope. No point."

"You sure?"

"Yeah. Well, let's put it this way." Guthrie leaned in closer and lowered his voice. "Since leaving the service, most of us locals think Dickie Caren's lost his mind."

"Really?"

"We sure do. He's raised himself a private army of … well, Dickie calls 'em 'patriots'. If you know what I mean." Guthrie tapped the side of his nose.

Kaine shrugged. "Not really. I'm not from around here, remember."

"Sure enough. Sure enough," Guthrie said, smoothing out his soup-strainer moustache. "Let's see now. You know what a 'prepper' is?"

Kaine glanced up at the ceiling with its cracked plaster stained yellow from tobacco smoke. He assumed the staining was a paint effect, since smoking in public spaces had been banned in Arizona for more than a decade.

"A prepper? Aren't they people who stockpile food and ammunition in preparation for the end of the world?"

Guthrie waggled his head from side to side.

"That's about it, only"—he flinched, leaned even closer to the bar, and lowered his voice further—"Dickie Caren and his army, the so-called Doomsday Creed, are a little more *proactive* about it." He glanced around the bar to make sure their conversation stayed private. "At least that's my interpretation of the Creed's actions."

Like Guthrie, Kaine searched the bar for eavesdroppers and spoke just as quietly. "Proactive? In what way?"

Guthrie shook his head and pulled away.

"Nope. I've already said too much. You'll have to forgive an old gossip flapping his lips. I'm just shooting the breeze. All I will say is the Creed ain't welcome in Pine Creek no more. Costs too much to rebuild the damage after their visits. And you should stay well clear of Camp Pueblo."

"The Creed's a rowdy bunch?"

"And then some. Got to the stage where the sheriff an' his deputy had to pay the colonel a visit to ask him to keep his so-called soldiers in line."

"How did that go down?"

Guthrie took a deep breath before answering.

"Way I heard it, Dickie Caren called Sheriff Hawksworth a stooge of the Federal Government and threatened to run him out of the camp on a rail."

"How'd the sheriff react?"

"Ah now," Guthrie said, giving another theatrical wink, "the way Cal tells it"—he threw a nod in the direction of the poker players—"Cal's the deputy, by the way. He's the youngster with all them poker chips. Anyway, Cal said the Hawk nodded at the colonel and backed away."

"Colonel Caren ran off the local law officers?"

Guthrie slapped the counter. "He sure did. In actual fact, there weren't much else the sheriff could do, faced with more'n thirty heavily armed men and them being on private property."

"So, this Colonel Caren's above the law?"

Guthrie stiffened. "What's your interest in this, Mr Griffin?"

Kaine raised his hands in apology. "Nothing at all, Mr Guthrie. You were the one who raised the subject. I was just being polite." He took up his beer and pulled in a big mouthful.

"Oh, yeah. So I did. Sorry, Mr Griffin. It's just that the topic of the Creed sort of looms large in the conversations hereabouts. The storekeepers are keen to keep their business rollin' in, but the rest of the Pine Creek population ain't so happy about them being so close."

"So," Kaine said after another sip, "I was right. They do get a little rowdy?"

"Yep."

"Does Pine Creek have any other industries? I mean, can a town this size survive on tourism alone?"

"There's farming and lumber. But neither of them's exactly a thriving industry these days. Too much competition from overseas. Cheap foreign labour and imports." A pinched expression appeared on his chubby face. "There's a quarry as pulls out the best marble in the state. Brown and Company—the weapons manufacturer—used to operate a test firing range a few miles from here, but they moved to Global Plains when the army closed down Camp Pueblo. Global Plains is the other side of Mount Garrett. That's where they test ordnance. Sometimes, when the wind's in the right direction, you can hear the explosions in town."

"Sounds interesting. Does Brown employ many locals?"

"Nah," Guthrie said, curling his upper lip. "The place is closed up tighter than a beaver's butt, if you pardon my language. Operated by some organisation out of Washington. Pentagon most likely. They only hire from the best universities and their people are vetted all the way up the wazoo. Hell, even the maintenance and cleaning staff need government approval." Guthrie leaned even closer, tapped the side of his nose again, and lowered his voice to a conspiratorial whisper. "You ask me, there's some *top secret* shit going on in that place."

"Sounds intriguing."

"Not that I mind top secret, you understand. After all, Uncle Sam's got plenty of enemies, and I don't just mean them towelheads in the Middle East, neither." Guthrie pointed towards the west, clearly having no understanding of the cardinal compass points. "No, siree. There's plenty of people wanting to take a pop at the US Government."

"Really? That's a little worrying." Kaine feigned interest, hoping the old blowhard would keep talking since information was power.

Guthrie scrunched up his face. "Sorry, Mr Griffin. You don't need to hear my politicking. Tell me a bit about you. Can't get enough of hearing that accent of yours."

That's a shame.

"Nothing much to tell, really." Kaine finished his beer.

"Ready for another?"

"Better not since I'm driving."

"One more won't put you over the limit, and there ain't no highway patrol for miles."

Kaine stole a glance at the Coldwater tap and its uninformative handwritten label. "What's the alcohol content?"

Guthrie grinned. "Weak as water. You can have a second and still drive safe, if that's what you're worried about. Stay away from the Choctaw Dark Ale, though. That stuff will have you horizontal in a heartbeat if you ain't used to it."

The pump next to the Coldwater tap sported a professional label, CDA, and its logo featured the feathered headdress of a native American chieftain.

"Another Coldwater it is, then."

"And I'll join you. A little too early in the day to be starting on the whiskey."

Guthrie produced two fresh and bubbling glasses. He took a healthy glug from his and waited for Kaine to take a mouthful.

"You mentioned trail dust earlier, Mr Griffin. Been on the road long?"

Kaine shook his head. "Not that long. I flew into Tucson International late last night. Truth is, I got a little lost on the road and had to spend the night in my hire car."

Guthrie's eyes widened.

"You stopped on the side of the road?"

"No, no. I pulled into some picnic grounds, twenty-odd miles from here."

"That'll be Dry Canyon." Guthrie up-nodded. "Pretty place."

"Yeah, but that's how come I look so rough. Haven't had a shower since leaving home two days ago."

"And then you up and run into them two saddle tramps?"

Kaine smiled, but didn't answer.

"You've had one hell of a time, Mr Griffin. As part of the Pine Creek Welcoming Committee, what can I do to make it up to you?"

"Really, Mr Guthrie, there's no need—"

"Nope, I insist. After all, them idiots spent the night drinkin' in my saloon, and I feel part responsible for what they done. That beer's on the house. How 'bout that?"

"Thank you. That really is too kind, Mr Guthrie."

"Call me Marshall ... Mr Guthrie was my pop."

"Well, in that case, Marshall, my name's Bill."

"Please to make your acquaintance, Bill."

Kaine drained his glass and lowered it to the bar. He stood and grabbed his backpack from the next stool.

"And on that note, I'll take my leave of you. I suddenly feel like an old, old man in need of a shower and an afternoon siesta. All that excitement ...." He sighed and arched his back. "Don't suppose you can point me in the direction of the nearest motel? I didn't notice one on my drive through town."

Guthrie stood back and looked Kaine up and down, taking in his worn jeans and travel-creased shirt. "You looking for flophouse or five star? Sorry to be blunt, but I wouldn't want to steer you wrong."

"Somewhere in the middle would do nicely."

"In that case, head back out through the door, turn right, and walk 'bout one hundred yards. Jim-Bob Masters keeps his rooms clean and tidy, and he don't charge the earth, neither."

Kaine checked his watch again. 12:47. Time was passing, but he'd made some progress. Camp Pueblo seemed ripe for a surreptitious overnight visit.

"You sure he has a room free?"

"If you like, I'll give Jim-Bob a call."

"If it's not too much trouble."

A belly laugh rippled through the helpful man's whole frame. "Ain't no problem at all. Jim's my brother-in-law. In Pine Creek, we like to keep business in the family."

Kaine smiled along with his host. "Makes sense."

"Sure does. Jim-Bob's gonna have a room fixed up for you in two shakes. Leave it with me."

"A hundred yards, you say?"

Guthrie nodded. "That's right."

"My car's parked outside in your lot. Is it okay if I leave it there overnight?"

Guthrie shrugged. "Makes no never mind to me, Bill. Be as safe here as outside Jim's place. Folks around here respect other people's property. Mostly."

"Not worried about the car. It's only a rental. I just didn't want to block up a parking space or outstay my welcome."

"No chance of that, Bill. Now, since you won't be driving, how 'bout that other beer?" Without waiting for an answer, he poured a fresh measure and slid the fresh glass across the bar. "Enjoy."

Kaine climbed back onto his stool and grabbed the glass.

"Thanks, Marshall. I appreciate it."

He took a sip.

Guthrie threw him a dismissive wave.

"It ain't nothing, Bill. Now, give me a moment. I'll be right back."

The old man turned his back on Kaine, headed for the anachronistic wall-mounted phone with a tangled flex, and dialled. Kaine sipped his beer and resumed his study of the growing crowd in the helpful mirror. Since he'd taken up his prime spot on the stool, customers had been arriving, in family groups mostly. They headed straight to tables in the dining area and kept Billie and a recently arrived waitress busy.

Although the saloon could hardly have been described as full, Kaine considered it a healthy crowd for a Sunday afternoon. Two more bar staff—a man and a woman—had turned up to bolster Guthrie's efforts behind the bar. Both were young, attractive, and dressed in character.

As the crowd increased, so too, had the background noise.

In the dining area, the cutlery and crockery clinked and scraped as the food—served in huge piles and on plates the size of tea trays— was ordered and consumed. It smelled great and made Kaine's mouth water.

Guthrie hung up the phone. Smiling, he turned to face front.

"Room's all booked up for you, Bill."

"Thanks, Marshall."

The barman's smile faded as his gaze fell on the entrance.

"Goddamn it," he said. "What does the Hawk want?"

"Who?" Kaine asked.

"Sheriff Hawksworth."

Kaine's heartrate spiked. He took another deep gulp of beer and returned his focus to the mirror.

Now what?

In the reflection, Kaine watched a tall, middle-aged man in a lightweight business suit and a white cowboy hat push through the batwings and hold them open. He paused in the threshold for a moment, looking towards the bar.

Guthrie shook his head and grunted.

"The old windbag never shows up this early on a Sunday. Wonder who or what rattled his cage?"

The sheriff removed the white hat and turned the walk from the entrance into a form of Royal Progress, waving and smiling a greeting to the patrons, most of whom he seemed to be on first name terms with. As he stopped alongside Kaine, his slightly rounded stomach pointed towards Guthrie, forcing open his jacket and exposing a holster and the Sig it held.

Kaine stiffened.

"The usual, Sheriff?" Guthrie asked, reaching for a pint glass, his earlier warm smile appeared slightly forced.

"No thanks, Marshall. I'm here on business." The sheriff glanced at Kaine and nodded. "Afternoon, sir."

"Afternoon, Sheriff."

Guthrie nodded towards Kaine. "Mr Griffin, let me introduce you to the town's lawman, Sheriff Ed Hawksworth. Only the town calls him the Hawk on account of—"

"My name, not my eagle eyes."

Kaine tried to look impressed and a little intimidated. "Good afternoon, Sheriff. Nice to make your acquaintance." He made to offer his hand, but withdrew it when Hawksworth leaned away and reprised his frown.

"You the Brit what just rolled into town?"

Kaine dipped his head.

"Yes, sir."

"You lookin' for trouble?"

"No, sir," he said. "Not at all."

Not for trouble, but I am looking.

"Sure seems that way. I already received a complaint about you."

Kaine swallowed hard and made it show.

"Way I hear it, you beat up two of our upstanding citizens,"

Hawksworth said, his eyes two chips of diamond glinting under the lights.

"If you mean Duke and Birdy—"

"Yeah, that's exactly who I mean."

"They attacked me, Sheriff. I didn't do anything."

"That's true enough," Guthrie said, jumping to Kaine's defence.

"You saw the … incident, Marshall?" Hawksworth asked.

"Nope. I was out back. But young Johnny Manchester told me it was Duke and Birdy who started the ruckus. And Duke was the one who threw the punch that busted Birdy's nose."

"That how it went down?" Hawksworth asked Kaine, sounding doubtful.

Kaine lowered his head again and looked at the lawman through hooded eyes. "Yes, sir."

"And if I call Johnny Manchester on my cell, he'll back up your story?"

"Yes. At least, I hope so."

"That's exactly what he told me, Sheriff," Guthrie said, adding a confirmatory nod.

Hawksworth studied Kaine for a moment, the diamond chips even harder and colder than before. He shot Guthrie a look that carried even less warmth, if that were possible.

"Wait here, Mr Griffin," the lawman said. He tipped a nod at Guthrie, tugged his mobile from its clip on his belt, and strolled across the room to the poker players.

"Am I in trouble?" Kaine asked, making sure to add a quake to his voice.

"Prob'ly not."

"That 'probably' doesn't sound all that encouraging, Marshall."

"Don't you worry about it, Bill. The Hawk can be a hard-nosed SOB, but he plays it straight down the line."

"Why's he going over to the card table?"

"He prob'ly wants to talk it over with Cal Davis, the town's deputy. The Hawk knows Cal's been here all day. Usually is on his days off since he's practising for his annual vacation in Vegas."

The sheriff reached the poker table and Davis pressed his cards face down on the baize and pushed himself to his feet. Hawksworth said something Kaine couldn't hear over the general hubbub. Davis nodded a couple of times, looking at Kaine the whole time.

Hawksworth dialled a number on his mobile and raised it to his ear. After waiting for what seemed like an age, the lawman shook his head and clipped the phone back onto his belt.

Davis asked a question, which the Hawk answered and took a long time over it. Davis turned his eyes on Kaine, nodded, spoke again, and pointed to the table Duke and Birdy had collapsed into earlier.

The sheriff tilted his head, said something else to his deputy, and made his way back to Kaine and Guthrie.

"Everything okay, Sheriff?" Guthrie asked.

Hawksworth ignored the barman and focused his attention on Kaine.

"Johnny didn't answer his phone."

"He said something about packing for a trip to Flagstaff," Guthrie offered, helpfully.

"Marshall," the sheriff said, not taking his eyes off Kaine, "butt out. This is police business."

Kaine drew his hands up to his chest. "Am I in trouble, Sheriff?"

Hawksworth raised one shoulder. "A complaint's been made, Mr Griffin. And I need to investigate. I'm going to ask you to take a little trip with me down to my office. You'll need to make a statement."

"Hawk," Guthrie said, "is that really necessary? I got him booked in with Jim-Bob. Can't this wait until morning?"

The sheriff faced the bar for the first time since returning from the poker table. "Marshall Guthrie, what part of 'butt out' escaped your understanding?"

Guthrie ground his teeth. Dark red blotches bloomed on his already florid cheeks.

Kaine scanned the saloon. At least twenty customers stood between him and the nearest exit. No chance of escape, not without risking injury to innocent bystanders. He raised his near-empty glass. "Is it okay if I finish my beer first, Sheriff?"

"Assuming you can do it in one swallow." Hawksworth's right hand reached inside his jacket, heading towards the Sig. "Don't even think about using that glass as a weapon, sir."

Kaine frowned and pulled in his chin. "A weapon? Why on earth would I do that?"

"No idea son, but anyone who can face down Duke and Birdy without taking a licking makes me nervous."

Hell.

As instructed, Kaine downed the rest of his beer in one go. He had no other option. At the poker table, Deputy Davis grabbed his hat from the back of the chair and set it on his head.

Kaine's heart sank. He couldn't think of a thing to do or say to extricate himself from the mess.

In the UK, he'd managed to avoid incarceration for the better part of a year, but after less than a day in the States, he was about to be frogmarched towards lockup.

What the hell was he going to do about it?

CHAPTER TWENTY

SUNDAY 21ST MAY – Afternoon
Pine Creek, Arizona, US

The slow walk through the saloon, flanked by the sheriff and shadowed by the deputy, reminded Kaine of basic training way back when. Only this time he only had to suffer the curious gazes of the customers, not the merciless towel flicks on his exposed back and buttocks delivered by his fellow recruits. He'd suffered the pain and embarrassment once and once only. During basic training, his questioning the malicious orders of a bullying instructor had led to the whole squad suffering a loss of privileges. It also led to his facing the time-honoured punishment—running the gauntlet. The experience taught Kaine a valuable lesson. After that lesson, whenever he wanted to question anyone further up the food chain he did it in private to give the officer in question enough wriggle room to save face.

The lesson came in handy in most situations, including this one. The right time to make a stand would likely present itself at some stage, but this wasn't it.

They pushed through the batwings and the sheriff led Kaine to a late model, dust-covered Ford Interceptor Police Utility. Cal Davis followed close behind, but rather than backing up the sheriff, he turned right and strolled along the covered porch. At the end, he trotted down the steps and disappeared around the side of the building, heading towards the rear parking lot.

Interesting.

Meekly, Kaine turned towards the Interceptor's rear passenger door.

"Where you headed, Mr Griffin?"

"You don't want me in the passenger cage?"

"Why? Are you a criminal?"

"Well, no, but I thought ...."

"You thought I was arresting you?" Hawksworth smiled, and this one seemed more genuine.

"You aren't?"

"Nope. Whatever gave you that idea?"

Kaine shrugged. "The part where we made the walk of shame through the saloon."

The sheriff's smile broadened. He opened the nearside front passenger door for Kaine and ushered him in.

"That was for Guthrie's benefit. I didn't want to give him the wrong idea."

Holding off the obvious follow-up question, Kaine climbed up into the cab, eased into the comfortable front seat, and strapped himself in. Hawksworth scooted around the front of the SUV and settled behind the wheel.

After he'd fired up the engine, which bubbled and roared with barely restrained power, Kaine's patience gave out.

"What idea *did* you want to give him, Sheriff Hawksworth?"

The Hawk winked, snicked the car into drive, and gently rolled the car away from the saloon, heading east.

"Let's table the conversation until we reach my office, Mr Griffin. We'll be more comfortable, and I can get me some fresh brewed coffee."

"I'm definitely not under arrest?"

"Nope."

"You just want my statement?"

"Nope. Don't need anything but a few minutes of your time."

"I'm intrigued, Sheriff."

"Good. That's what I hoped."

As they pulled away from the saloon, Kaine caught sight of another Police Interceptor leaving from a different exit, throwing up a cloud of dust. Wherever he was headed, Deputy Davis wanted to reach it in a hurry.

Kaine tried to relax his shoulders. It wasn't easy.

Hawksworth cruised along Main Street as though he was on patrol. It gave Kaine plenty of time to contemplate the turn of events and take in the small town that had the audacity to call itself a city.

Either side of the street, single-storey buildings, mostly white painted adobe, but some built from dark red brick, lined the road. The shops stood closed for the sabbath, rusted metal shutters lowered. The town stretched out along Main Street, but didn't seem to go too deep. A few narrow side streets broke the pattern, but they seemed to peter out into brush and scrubland sparsely populated with spindly fir trees.

"Where are we heading?"

"Uptown."

"So, the saloon's downtown?"

"That's about the sum of it."

The sheriff indicated right, turned into 7th Street, which was even less densely inhabited than 8th.

After a slow five hundred metres, they reached a stop sign at a crossroads. Hawksworth indicated left, pulled to a halt, and looked both ways on the deserted road. He was either the most careful police driver on the planet or was taking an inordinate amount of care to demonstrate it. Single-storey homes separated by wide and well-kept plots dotted the left. Open brushland stretched into the distance on the right and ran into the nearby foothills. Next up came the mountains.

The sheriff pulled out and turned left into Pine Avenue. They reached the junction with 5th Street and turned right. Much the same outlook applied—low-level residences on the left, open scrubland on the right until the road curved around to the south and became Maple Grove.

Ahead on the right, just after the apex, a large, two-storey building sprang out of the parched and dusty ground, defended by a steel fence topped with shiny razor-wire. Tarnished steel gates presented an impressive barrier to entry. Two flagpoles stood either side of the once grand but now rather tired entrance. One flew the Stars and Stripes, the other supported a red, yellow, and blue flag with a single central star with the sun's rays spreading up and out. The Arizona State flag, Kaine assumed, but chose not to ask for confirmation.

Hawksworth turned the Interceptor into the short driveway, rolled down his window—letting in a blast of hot, dry, and dust-filled air—and punched a sequence of numbers on a bright new keypad. He didn't hide the numbers he pressed, but Kaine chose not to remember the code. He could see no reason to ever want to gain illicit entry to such an official-looking building any time soon.

Breaking out ... now, that might be a different matter.

The security gates rolled apart, and the sheriff closed the SUV's window before feeding more fuel into the engine. The aircon struggled to compensate for the hike in temperature, but Hawksworth headed straight for the long shadow cast by the building's overhanging roof and parked in his designated spot.

To the side of the entrance, a grey stone column supported a polished brass sign, proudly announcing the place as the Pine Creek Municipal Building, built in 1978.

"Impressive," Kaine said and meant it.

For a town—city—as small as Pine Creek to have such an imposing administrative building when most of the structures he'd seen so far had been single-storey and in need of more than a lick of paint to mask the decay was certainly noteworthy.

"Amongst other things, it hosts the police and fire departments.

Built with state funding and a bequest from a group of the local patriarchs. We're lucky to have it. Ready?"

"To brave the dust?"

"Yep."

They opened their doors simultaneously and, head down and eyes narrowed, Kaine followed his host to the entrance. Fifteen seconds later, Kaine counted each one while trying to hide in the sheriff's lee, they'd made it inside to the cool and quiet of an all-glass booth.

Hawksworth removed his hat, exposing a head of slicked-back salt and pepper hair which curled at the base of his neck, and shook off some of the dust. He used the hat to brush off his shoulders and legs. Kaine copied the Hawk's actions with his baseball cap.

When in Rome.

Once sufficiently dusted, the sheriff pushed open the inner door and they entered a large, unmanned reception area. A desk stood opposite the entrance doors, protected by security glass. Kaine took in the hushed silence.

"Gretchen's prob'ly in the can. Follow me, Mr Griffin."

Hawksworth led him down a long hallway. They passed a dozen closed doors and turned down another corridor. Eventually, he pushed through a pair of swing doors and into a large office with half a dozen messy but currently unoccupied desks. He led them between the rows to another door, this one solid wood. A sign on the door read, Sheriff's Office. It opened into a cluttered room a quarter the size of the one they'd just left. It had a single window overlooking the carpark, and contained one desk, three chairs, and a bank of filing cabinets along one internal wall. A huge Arizona state map covered the wall behind the desk, with the skewed rectangle of Renshaw County shaded in orange.

"Take a pew, Mr Griffin. This won't take long," Hawksworth said, pointing him towards a visitor's chair on the near side of the desk.

Kaine obeyed and dropped the backpack on the thin carpet.

"Before we settle down," Hawksworth said, "mind if I have a quick look-see?" He pointed to the pack. "Standard procedure."

"Certainly," Kaine said, hoisting it up off the floor and handing it over. "Be my guest."

Hawksworth lowered the pack to the desk. He took everything out and searched each item thoroughly. He even checked the pack's lining but, as Kaine expected, he found nothing of interest.

In terms of packing for a trip, Kaine knew what he was doing.

"Sorry 'bout that, Mr Griffin, but ...."

"Procedure?" Kaine asked.

The lawman nodded.

"Yep. I'll let you repack it since you'll do a much better job of it than me."

Kaine stood and gathered his stuff, leaving Hawksworth enough room to reach his chair, but rather than taking his seat behind the desk, the sheriff stepped out the way he'd entered and closed the door behind him. When the lock clicked, Kaine's hackles rose.

He spun and reached for the handle.

Locked.

Hell!

He'd walked straight into a trap.

CHAPTER TWENTY-ONE

Sunday 21st May – Afternoon
Pine Creek, Arizona, US

Kaine briefly considered picking the lock on the door, but he'd walked into a police precinct—albeit an apparently empty one—and didn't want to risk annoying any nervous and gun-toting cops.

Thinking better of doing anything provocative, Kaine returned to his seat and spent the next few minutes repacking his bag, relieved that Hawksworth had missed everything of importance. Performing such a simple task gave Kaine time to centre himself and time to think.

If he *had* walked into a trap, he'd have to find another way out of the mess. Maybe playing dumb would work, along with innocent bluster. If he waited and watched for long enough, an opportunity to escape would present itself—probably.

Once he'd finished repacking, Kaine sat, hands on knees, and tried to slow his racing heart but, after an excruciating ten-minute wait, he jumped up and headed to the door again.

"Sheriff?" he called.

No response. With nothing constructive to do, he started pacing the room.

Four paces until stopped by the filing cabinets butting up against the inner wall.

Stop.

Turn.

Four paces back to the window.

Stop.

Stare through the glass and take in the sun-bleached carpark for a count of five.

Turn.

Repeat.

Five more minutes passed before the lock clicked again and the door opened. Kaine stopped pacing and turned, his back towards the file-covered windowsill.

Sheriff Hawksworth, wearing what looked like an apologetic smile, popped his head though the open doorway.

"Sorry it took me so long, but I got interrupted. Sorry I locked you in, too. Didn't mean to do that. Force of habit." The smile increased in power. "Stems from my days as a prison guard. Can't help myself sometimes."

Kaine made a great show of breathing out a sigh. He didn't for one minute believe Hawksworth had locked the door by mistake, but couldn't see the point in arguing the toss.

The lawman stepped fully into the room and pointed over his shoulder.

"Better come with me, Mr Griffin. There's some people as wants to meet you."

"Who might they be?"

Hawksworth smiled. "Let's wait for the introductions. Save ourselves a heap of time that way. C'mon."

The lawman waved Kaine out of his office and pointed towards a door on the far side of the bullpen.

"Like I said, there's some people as wants to meet you."

"I don't know anyone in Arizona. At least, I don't think so."

Hawksworth's knowing smile caused Kaine's defences to spike.

"Where exactly are we going, Sheriff?"

"Follow me, sir. And don't fret none. You aren't in any trouble. Not as far as I know."

The sheriff negotiated his way around the empty desks. He pushed through the closed door without knocking, and they entered a well-lit and cavernous room that piqued Kaine's interest immediately. It had been setup as a lecture theatre, complete with a stage, on which stood a long table and a dozen chairs. The table ran at a forty-five degree angle to the front of the stage.

Three men and one woman gathered on the left side of the table, facing the auditorium which contained seven rows of ten chairs—all unoccupied. Each wore a white shirt, dark trousers, and shiny black shoes. The men wore dark ties, but the woman's shirt was open at the throat, revealing a small gold cross on a chain. Each had an open laptop on the table in front of them and a holster clipped to their belt.

They had "Government Agents" written all over them.

The wall at the back of the stage carried an enormous electronic whiteboard that displayed a satellite image of what looked like a large military camp set in a clearing and surrounded by densely wooded mountains.

No prizes for guessing where that is.

As Kaine and the sheriff entered the auditorium, the man sitting at the head of the table addressing the others—spikey grey hair cut into a military flattop—stopped talking. All four heads turned to face them, and they watched as Kaine and the sheriff strode down the aisle running along the side of the lecture theatre.

Hawksworth climbed the four steps at the side of the stage two at a time.

Not knowing what else to do, Kaine followed him up.

"This the guy?" Flattop asked Hawksworth.

"Sure is."

"Don't look like much in the flesh," said the heavyset black man in his late forties sitting beside to Flattop.

"Looks can be deceiving," Hawksworth said, nodding towards Kaine, who stood in the wings for want of a better place to stay. All eyes at the table focussed on Kaine, and he understood what it must have felt like to be a lab specimen.

What the hell's going on here?

"Wanna do the introductions?" Hawksworth asked.

Flattop pursed his lips.

"Guess so. Griffin, come in. Sit," he said, nodding to one of the spare seats around the table, his manner not even slightly welcoming.

Kaine didn't move from the safety of the wings. Instead, he crossed his arms and leaned back against the wall.

"I'm okay here for now, thanks. What's happening?"

"No need to be so defensive, Griffin. We're all friends here," Hawksworth said. "Take a seat."

Kaine chewed on his lower lip and shook his head.

"Is this the way you treat all your visitors to Arizona? First, I'm accosted in the street by a couple of thugs. Then, I'm dragged out of a saloon by a sheriff and locked in a—"

"I didn't drag you out of nowhere," Hawksworth butted in. "An' I explained the locked door. Now come and sit down."

"Quit the grandstanding, Griffin!" Flattop barked. "You know real well what this is all about. Sit the hell down like the sheriff said." He jabbed a stubby finger to the empty chair next to the woman.

"Who are you people?"

"We're the FBI."

"And the ATF," the big guy in the seat next to Flattop added.

Kaine allowed his jaw to drop and his eyes to bug.

"You're what?"

"You heard," Big Guy grunted.

"But I'm just a tourist."

"Quit that, Griffin," Flattop said. "We know who you are and why you're here. We're wasting time. Mark." He snapped his fingers at the third man and jerked his thumb in Kaine's direction.

Mark, an overweight thirty-something with shimmering blue eyes and wavy brown hair, levered himself out of his chair and stomped towards Kaine. For his part, Kaine unfolded his arms and raised his hands. They'd made their point. Time to play ball.

"Okay, okay. I'm coming."

Mark returned to his seat and Kaine hurried to take the chair next to the woman who, like him, wore glasses. However, he doubted hers contained the same interesting equipment as his pair. Petite and of Asian descent, she scowled at him through lenses corrected for short-sightedness as though disgusted by his body odour.

He couldn't really blame her. Since arriving in Arizona, he'd slept in a car and rolled around in the dirt with a couple of Good Ol' Boys. After that, he'd drunk beer in a saloon and hadn't had time do anything more than slap off some of the Arizona dust. His aura would definitely improve following a shower and a change of clothes. Still, at least she didn't hold her nose or order him to change seats.

"Sorry," Kaine said to the woman, "I'd sit downwind, but there isn't so much as a breeze in here."

She ignored his disarming smile. The other Feds remained stiff and po-faced.

"Sorry again. I tend to crack bad jokes when I'm nervous."

Still no response.

"Tough audience," he said to Hawksworth, who'd taken the chair on Kaine's right.

"This is serious, Griffin," the sheriff said, voice low. "Button your lip."

Kaine mimed buttoning his lip as instructed.

Flattop glowered at Kaine for a full three seconds before coughing up the introductions.

"Griffin, I'm Al Griezmann, of the FBI. Special Agent in Charge of the Phoenix Field Office." He named the table's other occupants from near to far as, Senior Special Agent Del Beddow of the ATF, and Special Agents Mark Steiner and Mei Chang of the FBI.

Almost a basketball team of specialness.

Kaine nodded at each in turn.

"Do you mind telling me what's going on, Mr Griezmann?" Kaine asked, adding an embarrassed smile. "Something must be serious if the FBI has sent so many of its people to a small town like Pine Creek."

Hawksworth slapped Kaine's upper arm with the back of his hand and shot him a wintery smile. "Pine Creek's a city, Griffin. And don't you forget it. If any of its citizens hear you callin' it a 'small town', I won't be able to hold 'em back."

"Oh dear, I imagine another apology is necessary. Just take it as read that this here Brit"—he dug a thumb into his chest—"is an ignorant fool who's going to keep making an idiot of himself." He cleared his throat. "Might I ask what I'm doing here? Am I in trouble?"

Griezmann glanced at the heavyset SSA Beddow and dipped his head. Beddow sat up straighter and glowered at Kaine while the SAC leaned back in his chair.

Forty-something and built like a pro American footballer but with a thickening waist, Beddow styled his dark hair with a side parting that could have come straight out of a 50s cop show. He shook his head.

"Let's cut the innocent act, Major Griffin. We all know who you are and why you're here. The horseshit ain't gonna wash." He glanced at the woman. "Would you mind running the tape please, Special Agent Chang."

Major Griffin?

They knew his identity, at least his false one.

Stay awake here, Kaine.

To his right, SA Chang tapped a button on her laptop and the image on the whiteboard changed from the satellite view to one closer to ground level. It mirrored every laptop screen on the table— at least all the ones Kaine could see.

The scene, picked out in crystal clarity, showed the frontage of the *Pine Creek Saloon* and three figures standing in the sun outside. A fourth figure leaned against a porch post, keeping in the shade. A shortish, slightly built man stood facing two larger others. The single man hoisted a backpack from the dusty ground and hugged it to his chest while two of the others closed in.

SA Chang hit another key on her laptop and the ensuing fight played out in slow motion.

Kaine studied the screen, fascinated by watching himself at work. He'd seen videos of himself when in training and on bodycams during live fire ops, but never as a civilian, and never while pretending to be defenceless. On screen, he appeared awkward and unbalanced—exactly the way he'd wanted it to look.

After the fight ended, Chang restored the playback to normal speed and Kaine watched himself and Johnny Manchester shake hands and enter the saloon. As the action outside continued, the two beaten and bewildered men took an age to pick themselves up out of the dirt. They also kept asking each other what just happened.

Birdy, blood streaming into his mouth and down his chin, kept accusing Duke of breaking his nose, while Duke insisted it was an accident and continued to gripe about his knee.

SSA Beddow dipped his head once more. Chang worked her laptop again and the screen turned blank.

"I suppose you're going to claim you got lucky?" Beddow demanded, fixing his dark and brooding eyes on Kaine.

"Well, yes. That's right, I—"

"Cut the bull, Major Griffin. We know all about you and your employer, ESAPP." Another nod to Chang and Kaine's mugshot appeared on the screen above an outline of his CV. It read well, covering all the salient points:

Name: Griffin, William Peter.

DOB: 23/05/1967.

Wife: Griffin, Elisabeth Amanda.

Occupation: Deputy Vice President of External Security, ESAPP, reporting directly to Maurice LeMaître.

Military background: Royal Marine, Major (Ret).

Home address: Isle of Dogs, London

. . .

"In case you were wondering," Griezmann said, "you've been on our radar since the moment you arrived in Pine Creek. We identified you through your rental car."

So much for letting Alain Dubois hire the cars.

At least the *Quebecois* hadn't used Kaine's real name.

Small mercies.

Kaine returned Griezmann's stare with a blank one of his own.

"So, you knew who I was, but were happy to stand back and let me face a thumping?"

"We're not here to pull your nuts out of the fire," SA Steiner snapped.

"Thanks," Kaine said. "And I love you, too."

SA Chang snickered and turned it into a cough. She tried to hide a micro-smile with her hand, but failed.

Kaine liked her already.

Beddow frowned at Griezmann, as though annoyed at having to cede the floor to the tubby man, and took over again.

"We were happy to let you bumble about so long as you didn't get in our way, but when you arranged a room at Jim-Bob Masters' place, you forced our hand."

Kaine raised an eyebrow and turned to Griezmann at the head of the table.

"You've been tapping Marshall Guthrie's phone?"

Griezmann nodded. "Since a week before Sabrina LeMaître"—he pronounced it Lee-Maytree—"went missing."

"You've been what?"

Kaine formed fists, but managed to keep his voice in check.

"You heard me, Griffin. Pull in your horns for a minute while we explain."

"Well get on with it then."

Flattop glanced from Steiner to Chang, ignoring Beddow, which told a tale in itself.

"Special Agent Chang," he said, "if you don't mind. From the top, please."

CHAPTER TWENTY-TWO

Kaine twisted in his seat to face SA Chang. She held his gaze and didn't falter.

"A little over three weeks ago," she said, her accent East Coast, and her voice deeper than her stature would have suggested. "April 29 to be exact, we had a walk-in at the FBI's Field Office in Phoenix. I was on duty and interviewed a woman claiming to have knowledge of the large scale theft of weapons from an armaments company in the Midwest—"

"Colfax-Lacy Industries?" Kaine offered.

She nodded. "Yes, that's the one."

"Did you believe her?"

"Not at first, we get our fair share of hoaxers looking for attention, but she had some documentation and was extremely convincing."

"Convincing enough for you to take it up the line?"

"Yes."

"Then what happened?"

For the first time since SA Chang started talking, she broke eye contact to glance at Griezmann.

"Come on now. Don't be shy," Kaine pressed. "What happened next?"

Chang took a breath, but Griezmann jumped in before she could answer.

"To cut a long story short, Special Agent Chang briefed me, and I called Ms LeMaître into my office and spoke to her personally."

"You spoke to Sabrina LeMaître yourself?" Kaine pronounced the surname correctly, in a gentle effort to educate the SAC.

"Sure did."

"And what did you think?"

"At first, we—I thought she was being fanciful but, since her claims were so serious, I tasked Special Agents Steiner and Chang to investigate."

Chang glanced at Griezmann and something flashed between them. A challenge?

"And what did you discover, Special Agent Chang?" Kaine asked, ignoring the dumpy SA Steiner, who sat hunched over his laptop, twiddling a ballpoint pen, and looking sideways at Kaine.

"The information Ms LeMaître provided seemed to be valid—"

"Which is when I set up a JTF with the ATF," Griezmann interrupted, puffing out his chest. "That's a Joint Task Force."

"I know what a JTF is."

Moron.

Kaine struggled to keep his emotions in check. The SAC couldn't have been much more condescending and arrogant if he tried.

"Yeah, yeah. I guess you do."

"When exactly did you set up this JTF?"

Griezmann interlaced his fingers and rested his forearms on the desk. He shot a shifty glance at SSA Beddow.

"Well?" Kaine demanded, adding an extra note of intensity to his question.

SA Chang found her voice again.

"Two days ago," she said, at barely more than a whisper.

Kaine closed his eyes and tried to keep his growing rage under control. It wasn't easy. Somehow, these people had hung Sabrina out to dry and they weren't prepared to admit it. Not easily.

"So," he said, breathing deeply, forcing himself to speak quietly and slowly, "you set up this Joint Task Force *before* Maurice LeMaître contacted your director, but *after* Sabrina had been missing for what? Two, three days?"

Chang lowered her eyes.

Sweat popped out on the SAC's forehead although the temperature in the air conditioned auditorium couldn't have stretched much higher than twenty degrees.

"Am I missing something, *Special-Agent-in-Charge* Griezmann?"

Griezmann closed his mouth, and his jaw muscles worked hard to keep it clamped shut.

"Well?"

The SAC disentangled his fingers and placed his hands flat on the table in front of him.

"When Ms LeMaître and I first talked," he said, eyes lowered, speaking to the table, "I ... might have given her the impression that she ... needed to help us find more evidence."

"You might have what!"

Kaine leaned forwards, preparing to jump to his feet, but the sheriff grabbed his forearm and pressed it to the table.

"Easy, Griffin!" he said, speaking quietly. "This is getting us nowhere." He released Kaine's arm. "Now, keep your cool and let's move this thing along."

Without taking his eyes from Griezmann, Kaine settled back into his chair.

"So, SAC Griezmann," Kaine said, teeth clenched, "you sent her off to do the FBI's work for you and left her hanging out to dry?"

Griezmann's head jerked up and they finally locked eyes.

"Damn it, I did nothing of the sort. She might have taken it on herself to investigate further, but if she did, it was off her own bat—"

"Jesus, man. That's even worse. You had her working undercover without any backup—"

"Damn it, I gave her my personal cell number. Told her to contact me or Special Agent Steiner the second she found anything concrete."

Kaine turned his attention to the dumpy one.

"And did she contact you, Agent Steiner?"

The sweating Steiner licked his lips, and the ballpoint slipped through his fingers. He failed to look up from his laptop.

"Uh, no. Not once."

"Basically, you primed her and then left her to fend for herself."

"Well, we're stretched really thin," Steiner said. "Always are. We've got plenty of other cases on our desk."

"So, SAC Griezmann," Kaine said, ignoring Steiner's weak excuses, "since Sabrina LeMaître disappeared, you've been sitting with your thumb up your—"

"Goddamn it, Griffin!" Griezmann shot back. "Don't speak to me like that. I'm the Agent in Charge here. You're here under sufferance. Piss me off any more and you'll find yourself buried up to your neck in a deep, dark hole. You get me?"

Kaine stared the man down.

"Bollocks!"

"What?" the SAC spluttered. "What did you say?"

"You heard me. I said, 'bollocks'." Before Griezmann could respond with the inevitable bluster, Kaine continued. "I'm here because you need to save your career. I'm here because you screwed up and because your Director's being leaned on by Maurice LeMaître, who has the ear of the Secretary of Defense, and ultimately, the President himself. You need all the help you can get! Now cut the crap and tell me what you're doing to find Sabrina."

Kaine stopped talking, worried that he'd overplayed his hand. He'd made the tenuous link between Maurice LeMaître and the US President but had no real idea how much pull Maurice really had on this side of the Atlantic.

Kaine stared hard at the SAC, who barely held his ground. A thrumming silence stretched out, broken only by the air hissing through the air conditioning vents dotted around the room, struggling hard to keep the auditorium cool.

SA Chang spoke again.

"We think we might know where Ms LeMaître is being held," she said, tapping at the keys on her laptop.

The electronic whiteboard lit up with the original satellite image.

"That's Camp Pueblo, right?" Kaine asked.

Beddow jerked upright.

"How the hell do you know that?"

"So it *is* Camp Pueblo," Kaine said, eyes still focused on the whiteboard, trying to memorise the layout, which seemed to match the basic configuration of most US military bases.

Chang nodded and opened her mouth to speak, but this time, SSA Beddow butted in.

"Now, hold it right there." He turned to Griezmann. "Al, are you really gonna let her read him in on this?"

The SAC rubbed his chin with the back of his hand and looked decidedly uncomfortable. Kaine's outburst had hit home and the man was playing off the back foot. Everyone in the room knew the FBI had dropped the ball and were, in part, responsible for Sabrina's abduction, and Kaine wouldn't hesitate to use their discomfort to his advantage.

"Don't really see any harm in it, do you?" Griezmann said at last.

"Yeah, I do," Beddow shot back. "Griffin's not only a civilian, he's a foreign national. I don't know about you guys in the FBI, but the ATF doesn't take kindly to outsiders busting in on our operations. Especially foreign assholes who don't announce themselves ahead of time." He turned from Griezmann to face Kaine. "Who the hell do you think you are? Stumbling around like an amateur in your size eleven boots—"

"Actually, I wear size nines," Kaine interrupted, speaking quietly, but clear enough to be heard by all. "Unless shoe sizes are different in the States." He gave Beddow what he considered a disarming smile. "As for the stuff about being a foreigner, it shouldn't matter. All I'm interested in is the safe return of Sabrina LeMaître. I don't give a damn about your inter-agency disputes—"

"Bullshit!" Beddow snapped, underlining his interruption by slamming the flat of his hand on the table. The resulting crack rattled his water bottle and made his laptop jump. "If it was up to me, you'd be in a cell right now, awaiting trial for interfering with a Federal investigation."

The big man paused for breath, giving Kaine time to speak.

"Special Agent Beddow—sorry, I mean, *Senior* Special Agent Beddow," Kaine corrected himself, adding another smile, "despite our obvious differences, I'm still prepared to offer my assistance. You'll find me rather useful. As a matter of fact, I have a great deal of experience in hostage retrieval situations. I do know what I'm doing."

Beddow jumped to his feet and leaned over the table.

"You arrogant little pissant!"

Kaine leaned back and held up both hands, wagging an index finger at him.

"SSA Beddow, you have a charming way with words."

"Quit that, you two!" Griezmann snapped, waving Beddow back into his chair. "This isn't getting us anywhere. Time to lay some cards on the table, Major Griffin. SSA Beddow is correct, we could arrest you right now and tie you up in legal red tape for the duration, but your company carries a great deal of weight in powerful circles."

"As I said," Kaine agreed.

Griezmann sighed and shook his head slowly.

"And as you said, ESAPP's chairman has asked for our help, and since ESAPP's weapons were the ones stolen in the first place, I'm allowing you some latitude. That being said, any more of your bull and you'll find yourself in Sky Harbor Airport, Phoenix, so fast your feet won't touch the ground. And after that, I'll have you on the next UK-bound plane so quick your head will spin. Understand?"

Any more cliches to throw at me?

"Yes, Mr Griezmann. I understand completely."

"Now, answer our questions fully and everything will be fine."

"Fair enough, fire away." Kaine lowered his head.

Beddow glowered at him through thick eyebrows that could have done with the same gel treatment as his hair. "Don't tempt me, bud."

Bring it on, big fella.

"What were you doing at the saloon?" Griezmann asked, shooting a quelling glance at Beddow.

Kaine removed his glasses and pinched the bridge of his nose before pushing them back into place.

"Okay, Mr Griezmann. Cards on the table. The minute Maurice LeMaître lost contact with his granddaughter, he brought me in. Then, when your director stopped returning his calls, our alarm bells started ringing. We thought you weren't taking the case seriously enough."

"That isn't true, Griffin." Griezmann opened his hands and waved them at his subordinates. "As you can see."

"At the time, we had no idea what you were doing," Kaine continued, ignoring Griezmann's flaccid interruption. "And don't forget, all this happened *before* we received the ransom demand. The fact you tried to hide your cockup and kept us out of the loop didn't help. Is there any wonder I tried to keep a low profile when I arrived in Pine Creek?"

"We don't tend to broadcast our ongoing investigations to everyone, even if he is the missing person's grandfather. And we certainly don't talk to every passing Brit. There are security implications."

Kaine nodded. "I can understand that, but while Maurice LeMaître sent your director the ransom recording, I decided to make a more direct approach."

"And started bumbling around under our feet," Beddow said, sneering.

Kaine let the jibe pass. He and the big ex-football player might be heading for a showdown, but an auditorium inside a police precinct was neither the right time nor the right place.

"We knew Sabrina had taken a room in Pine Creek," Kaine continued. "She didn't mention the hotel's name but said it was within an easy walk of the saloon, which is why I headed straight there without contacting you first." He paused for a second and waited to catch Griezmann's eye. "There's another reason I failed to introduce myself to the authorities."

"Which is?" the SAC asked, frowning in anticipation of yet another verbal attack.

"I don't know how Colonel Caren discovered Sabrina's true identity. Someone might have told him." He glanced a Special Agent Steiner. "Basically, I didn't know who to trust."

Still don't.

"Wh-What the hell are you suggest—"

Kaine raised his hand and cut Steiner off mid-sentence. "What's wrong, Special Agent? Guilty conscience?"

Steiner shook his head and both his chins wobbled.

"That's a crock—"

"What about you, SSA Beddow. Any ideas how the Doomsday Creed found out?"

"How would I know?" Beddow said. "We had nothing to do with this case until two days ago."

"Uh-uh," Kaine said, shaking his head. "That's not exactly true, is it, SSA Beddow?"

"What the hell d'you mean by that?"

"As well as video calling the head of the FBI, Sabrina's grandfather contacted his *other* good friend, your boss, Director Lombardino."

"You don't say?" Griezmann said, the surprise clear in his question.

"I do say."

"And what did Director Lombardino have to say?"

"Not a whole lot, apart from the fact that Sabrina visited the ATF Field Office in Phoenix the day *before* she spoke to you, Special Agent Chang."

"What?" Griezmann snapped, directing the question at SSA Beddow.

"That's the first I've heard of it," Chang said, frowning. "She didn't tell me. And what did the ATF say to her?"

Kaine shrugged. "No idea. Director Lombardino told us he only had the online visitor's log for the Field Office. He promised Mr LeMaître he'd investigate and get back to him as a matter of urgency. And guess what?"

"What?" SA Chang asked.

"Like FBI Director McGregor, ATF Director Lombardino suddenly stopped taking Maurice's calls, too. Strange that, eh?"

"It ain't strange at all," Griezmann barked. "They're Bureau Directors, for cryin' out loud. Busy as all hell."

"Smells of a conspiracy to me," Kaine said. "What do you reckon, Beddow? Still claim to have no idea who leaked Sabrina's identity?"

Beddow curled his sausage-sized fingers into fists. Big, knuckle-popping fists.

"Are you accusing me of something, you little—?"

"Nope. Not at all. Just asking the question. What's the answer?"

Beddow pushed his fists into the desk and used his powerful arms to lever himself to his feet.

"Step outside, son, and I'll answer that question right now."

Chang gasped.

SA Steiner took everything in through piercing, deep blue eyes and a pair of sticky out ears. The aircon hummed.

Kaine stared at Beddow and, for a moment, seriously considered accepting his offer. He'd like nothing more than to turn the big man into a blood-soaked puddle on the floor, but how would that help Sabrina?

"Fair enough, *son*," Kaine said, meeting the ATF man's angry glare. "We can go outside for a dance if you like. Tell you what, to make it a fair fight, I won't even bring my backpack."

Steiner's eyes widened and his full lips parted. Chang stretched out another thin smile and, this time, made no attempt to hide it.

Beside him, Sheriff Hawksworth snorted, then let out a raucous guffaw and slapped the table almost as loud as Beddow had done moments earlier.

"Hell, Griffin," Hawksworth chuckled. "That's a hoot. Gotta love it."

"Okay you two. Quit the dick-measuring contest," Griezmann

said, struggling to regain control. "Beggin' your pardon, Special Agent Chang." He dipped his head in apology.

She shrugged her acceptance, clearly not upset by his words.

"You boys can sort out your differences in your own time," Griezmann continued. "Right now, we've got work to do."

After a moment's hesitation, Kaine nodded.

"I'm happy to park the discussion, but only when SSA Beddow answers my questions in a civilised manner."

Beddow dropped back into his chair, grinding his teeth so hard Kaine wondered how they stood up to the pressure without disintegrating.

"Del," Griezmann said, "what d'you say?"

"You want me to undergo an interrogation?" the SSA demanded, his face darkening even further.

"I think we'd all be keen to learn what the ATF said to Ms LeMaître that day," Griezmann said, rolling his hand forwards in encouragement.

Beddow turned his head away and growled his answer.

"We asked her to put it in writing, and said we'd get back to her." He glanced at Griezmann, eyes hooded. "We also suggested she … might want to talk to the FBI."

Griezmann pulled back his shoulders and looked as though he wanted to scream, but Kaine dived in first.

"So," he said, trying to remain calm, "someone comes to you with information about missing weapons—missing in their thousands—and you just send her away?"

The sinews on Beddow's thick neck stiffened, pressing into his overtight collar. He turned to Griezmann.

"You know what it's like, Al. People call in all the time claiming all sorts of bullcrap. We can't investigate everything. We're stretched even thinner than you guys."

"You passed it off to the FBI?" Kaine asked.

"Yeah, that's right."

"Is that *all* you did?"

Beddow slammed the side of his fist on the table. It made a fearsome crack.

"Now wait just a—"

Kaine raised his hands again.

"Okay, okay, I'll take that back," he said to the SAC. "We'll draw a line under it for the moment."

"The hell we will," Beddow snarled, on his feet once more. "This asshole's virtually accusing someone in the ATF of giving the French girl up to the Creed. I ain't gonna let that pass."

"From what I heard," SA Chang said, "Major Griffin didn't actually accuse you—or us—of anything. He was simply asking a question. And it's a valid one, as far as I'm concerned."

Sheriff Hawksworth knocked on the desk with his fist.

"Look," he said, "this is getting us nowhere. We're running round and round in circles here. I've opened up my department to you people and the longer we sit here spinning our wheels, the more chance there is of the Creed learning about the raid. Am I right?"

Kaine closed his eyes and breathed out slowly. He'd lost focus of his end goal and it had taken a small town sheriff to show it. In the process he'd shown up all the so-called professionals as fools.

You bloody idiot, Kaine.

Allowing his feelings to take over had almost blown up in his face. He'd gone too far and backed his "hosts" into a corner, put them on the defensive.

He put it down to the adrenaline rush of being in a room loaded with Feds and having no idea how to hurry the hell up and find Sabrina.

Shape up, Kaine. Get a grip.

"Okay," Hawksworth continued. "We gonna move this along or what?"

Kaine took a deep breath and nodded.

"Okay, Sheriff. I'm game. What about you, SSA Beddow?"

The ATF representative frowned.

"Accuse the ATF of spilling intelligence to the Creed again and, so help me, I'll tear you a new one."

"Del," Griezmann said, cutting his hand through the air, "that's enough. This is getting us nowhere and time's marching on. Okay?"

Beddow nodded, but his brooding stare remained fixed on Kaine and promised untold future pain on someone.

You'll keep, Del-boy.

"So," Kaine said, turning to the SAC, "are you going to tell me about the upcoming raid on Camp Pueblo?"

After a pause for thought, Griezmann answered.

"Our intelligence picked up some rumblings."

"You have intelligence?" Kaine asked, shooting a sideways and sarcastic glance at Beddow.

"Like I said earlier, we've been monitoring certain people in Pine Creek."

"Marshall Guthrie and Jim-Bob Masters, you mean?"

Griezmann nodded.

"Among others."

"What did this monitoring tell you?"

Beddow snorted and shook his head.

"Not a chance," he said, speaking to Griezmann.

"That, Major Griffin, is 'need to know'," the SAC announced. "And you don't need to know."

"When's the raid planned for?"

"That's none of your damned business," Beddow growled.

"I'd like to help," Kaine said, addressing Griezmann and ignoring Beddow's bombast.

"You have got to be kidding," Beddow said. "Al, for Christ's sake, you can't let this piece of—"

Griezmann raised his hand again and cut Beddow off, mid-rant.

"Out of the question, Griffin," he said more gently. "We're mounting a tactical operation and you'll only get in the way."

Kaine breathed deep. How far could he take this?

"Like I said, I have significant experience with hostage retrieval."

Beddow snorted. "That's a crock."

"No. It isn't," Kaine said.

Chang held up her hand and addressed the SAC.

"If I may, sir?"

Griezmann hesitated before nodding with obvious reluctance.

She turned to face Kaine.

"We can't be certain that Ms LeMaître *is* being held at the camp so we're going in low key, treating the raid as a search for stolen weapons. That's why the ATF is so heavily involved."

"The ATF organised the search warrant," Griezmann said, "and SSA Beddow will be leading the raid."

Kaine nodded. "Okay, makes sense. What time's the raid set for?" he asked SA Chang.

"Sunrise, tomorrow morning," she answered. "On the southwest face of Mount Garrett, that'll be around oh-six-hundred."

Kaine glanced at his watch. He had a little under sixteen hours to find Sabrina before the ATF charged in, armed to the teeth. What he'd seen of the hot-headed SSA Beddow so far didn't exactly fill him with confidence in his ability to remain calm under fire.

"Right, that's enough information," Beddow said. "My warrant, means my rules. And you, *Major* Griffin"—he jabbed an index finger in the air at Kaine—"ain't invited."

This had gone far enough.

Kaine could see the way things were heading. He removed his glasses again and placed them carefully on the table, lenses pointed at the whiteboard. He pinched the bridge of his nose as though fighting a headache.

Time to play nice.

"Mr Griezmann," Kaine said, leaning past SA Chang to win an uninterrupted view of the SAC, "might I have a word with you in private, please?"

"Uh-uh." Griezmann shook his head. "Whatever you have to say to me, you can say in public."

He wants witnesses.

"Fair enough. You've read my CV—my résumé?"

"Yeah, so what?"

"That part where it says I'd completed two tours in Afghanistan, and another two in Iraq, is true. I was a Special Forces operative."

"You were in the SAS?" Chang asked, her expression doubtful.

"No. Not exactly. I was a serving member of the Royal Marines. A Commando. I regularly operated behind enemy lines."

"You expect us to believe that?" Beddow said. "A runt like you was a Green Beret?"

Kaine drilled a dark stare into Beddow's eyes.

"Yes," he said, calm and considered.

Beddow stopped sneering and his expression changed to one of uncertainty. Clearly, the ATF leader couldn't be sure whether he was talking to a real live Commando or a raving nutcase.

"Okay," Griezmann said, "assuming I believe that you really were a Commando—"

"Given time, I can prove it."

"Yeah, well. Let's take that as read for the moment. What's your proposal?"

Might as well give it a try, Kaine.

"Let me go in tonight under cover of darkness. I can recce the camp from the inside. Find out if Sabrina's really there. If I can't get her out, I can at least keep her safe until you and the ATF arrive at sunup."

Beddow's jaw dropped. Shortly afterwards he started laughing—a deep rumbling and humourless guffaw. Griezmann and Steiner did their best not to join in, but failed miserably. SA Chang kept still, her expression serious.

Kaine let them have their moment of amusement.

"Did you hear that?" Beddow said, eyes tearing, still roaring. "The guy's a total loony. Lock him up, Al."

A chuckling Griezmann waved his hand in front of his face as though to cool his heated skin.

"Let me get this right," he said, trying stop himself laughing. "You expect me to let you wander into a camp full of armed radicals, a few hours ahead of a dawn raid, in the hopes of finding a kidnapped woman?"

"Yes, sir. That's exactly what I'm asking."

"And you want to go in solo?"

Kaine nodded. "I work better alone."

"I told you, Al," Beddow said, still laughing. The guy's a crackpot You need to lock him away—for his own good."

"You know what, Del?" Griezmann said, straight faced. "You're right. This *has* gone too far. Sheriff Hawksworth, have you got somewhere safe you can hold *Major* Griffin while we get on with the real business?"

"Somewhere like a padded cell," Beddow added.

Hawksworth scratched his chin and half-turned to shoot a glance towards the entrance. Sometime during the discussions, Deputy Davis had eased his way through the doors. He stood, leaning against the rear wall staring down at them in silence. Kaine had no idea how long he'd been there, but it showed how much his loss of control had cost him in peripheral awareness.

In war, such errors ended up costing lives.

Bloody fool.

He turned to Hawksworth. "You happy with the way this is going down, Sheriff?"

Hawksworth opened his hands in a shrug.

"The Feds carry a load more firepower than this city sheriff and his three deputies," he said. "Not a whole lot I can do to stop them."

Kaine scratched the top of his head, then dopped his hand onto the table, edging his glasses slightly to the right.

"In that case," he said, "there's really no point in continuing this discussion, is there?"

Kaine pressed his hands onto the tabletop and prepared to stand.

"Where you going, bud?" Beddow demanded.

"Heading back to my car. I've had enough of this nonsense."

Griezmann stood. "Afraid I can't let you do that, Griffin." He pointed to the sheriff, who also stood.

"Are you serious?"

"Major Griffin," the SAC announced, "it is clear by your recent outburst that you are not only a danger to yourself, but also to an ongoing Federal operation. In light of that, we're going to take you into protective custody where a medical professional will assess your mental condition. Until I'm satisfied that you are no longer a danger to the community at large and to this operation, you will remain in a safe house." He paused long enough to add an apologetic but clearly fake smile. "Sorry about this, Major. Please think of it as Uncle Sam's way of taking care of his guests."

"You're really doing this? You're arresting me?"

"I'm afraid so. Sheriff, take him away."

Hawksworth dropped a heavy hand on Kaine's shoulder.

"The hell you are!"

Kaine shrugged the sheriff's hand away and jumped to his feet, but only for appearance's sake. There were too many weapons on show for him to make a break for it—not that he really wanted to.

Steiner stood and, after glancing at Griezmann, rested a hand on his, making sure Kaine saw the action. To her credit, SA Chang stayed in her chair and had the grace to look embarrassed.

"Sheriff Hawksworth," Griezmann said, "do you mind showing the Major to your most comfortable holding cell until we can arrange to take him to the safe house?"

Hawksworth faced Kaine.

"Sorry 'bout this, Griffin, but my hands are tied." He dropped his left hand on a pair of shiny handcuffs sticking out of a leather pouch at the side of his belt and offered Kaine a sad smile. "Am I gonna need the bracelets?"

Kaine glanced at the black, textured handle of the semi-automatic sticking out of the sheriff's reinforced nylon holster, a Sig P226. Polymer-framed and short recoil-operated, it happened to be the weapon of choice for many police departments in the US, and for good reason. Even the most cack-handed law officer could learn to shoot the weapon effectively. The steel glint in the lawman's eye didn't offer much wriggle room, and Kaine wasn't about to test the sheriff's firearms skills.

Kaine shook his head.

"No, Sheriff. I'll come peaceable," he said in the worst cowboy accent he'd ever heard. He held his hands up in surrender to add to the image.

"Son, you're such a smartass," Hawksworth said. "That sort of attitude was always liable to land you in a whole heap of trouble."

"Sorry, Sheriff. Can't help myself. As I said earlier. My mouth runs away with me sometimes. Can I lower my hands?"

He dropped them slowly.

Hawksworth snorted, grabbed Kaine's upper arm, and led him away.

"Let's get you out of here, pronto. These Feds mean business."

As they descended the steps at the side of the stage, Griezmann called out, "Keep him under wraps until I can arrange that escort to the safe house, Sheriff. You got that?"

Hawksworth tipped his hat to the SAC and led Kaine away. Kaine dragged his heels a little and Hawksworth slowed to match Kaine for pace rather than exert more force on his arm.

Behind him, Griezmann spoke again.

"Okay, Mark," he said, addressing Special Agent Steiner, "now that the sideshow's over, go tell the guys we're ready for them."

Steiner released his hold on his sidearm and lumbered to the far side of the stage. He trundled down the second set of steps and ducked through a door partly hidden by a fire curtain.

By the time Kaine and Hawksworth reached Deputy Davis at the main doors, Steiner returned, followed by a phalanx of men and women dressed in black and dark blue. All wore holstered sidearms and peaked caps. The majority showed FBI logos stencilled in yellow, but a few wore white ATF decals. Boisterous chattering filled the auditorium as they trooped into the room, but it quietened when they settled into their seats. They took up most of the first three rows.

Kaine counted twenty-three people in all.

A group of armed men and women, platoon strength, keen to show their worth. Kaine shuddered at the idea of Sabrina being caught up in the fallout of an armed raid.

Deputy Davis pulled the door and held it open, a grim expression on his youthful face.

"Okay, Griffin. Let's go," Hawksworth said and ushered Kaine through into a deathly silent hallway.

CHAPTER TWENTY-THREE

The sheriff pointed Kaine down the corridor and they set off, side by side, with Deputy Davis acting as tail-gunner, but staying well back and out of reach. The lawmen had clearly run the perp-walk often enough to know the correct drill.

"That was pretty dumb," the Hawk said as they sauntered down the hallway apparently with all the time in the world.

"What was?" Kaine answered in apparent innocence.

"Winding up the Feds. Pretty dumb if you ask me."

Kaine up-nodded.

"Couldn't help myself. Told you I spout off when I'm nervous."

"Didn't sound nervous to me. Sounded like you were spoiling for a fight."

"It did?"

"Yep. The Feds don't react too kindly to aggression. Honey's gonna catch you more flies than ... you know."

"Vinegar? Yeah, I know. You reckon I should have dragged out the soft soap?"

The corridor ended at a cross junction with another, wider hallway. The Hawk turned left and Kaine stayed with him, keeping a careful note of the directions. Davis still hadn't joined in the conversation.

Hawksworth snorted.

"Soft soap might have been worth a try. Doubt it, though. They weren't never gonna let you join their raid."

"Yep, I know that, Sheriff. But I had to ask."

"You did, huh?"

"Yep."

"Why?"

"Between the three of us?" Kaine asked, glancing over his shoulder at the angular poker-playing deputy.

The Hawk cast Kaine an old-fashioned sideways look.

"Shoot."

Kaine sent the sheriff a conspiratorial smile.

"I'll deny this if you ever ask me in public, but I wanted to make it look good."

The Hawk held out an arm. They stopped and turned to face each other. Davis kept his distance.

"What you mean by that?"

Kaine leaned closer and lowered his voice. Davis edged a shade closer.

"Sheriff," Kaine said, "I'm nothing but a working stiff. ESAPP doesn't pay me anywhere near enough to make me risk my life." He ended with a wink.

The aging lawman jerked a thumb in the direction of the lecture theatre.

"You trying to tell me you engineered that? You *wanted* them to turn you down and kick you out?"

"I certainly did." Kaine smiled. "Worked a treat, too. Didn't it?"

"You that much of a coward?" Davis said, finally barging his way into the conversation. He moved even closer, but not close enough.

"Deputy Davis, I don't want anything to do with that bloody raid. Far as I'm concerned, FBI or the ATF can go ahead without me. To be perfectly honest, I'm much safer here. And you know what's even better?"

"What's that?" the deputy asked, staying where he was—a full three paces away.

Come on, Cal. Step a little nearer.

"Well, think about it, Deputy Davis. When Griezmann tells his boss, Director McGregor, why he had me arrested, he'll tell my boss, Maurice LeMaître. Maurice will hear how I offered to risk my life to save his granddaughter but the Feds wouldn't let me. I'll come out of this smelling of roses. Might even earn myself a nice little pay hike." Kaine rubbed his hands together. "Lovely jubbly."

The Hawk sneered. "And the girl, Ms LeMaître?"

"What about her?"

"You don't give a damn about her?" Davis asked.

Kaine snorted.

"Why the hell should I? She was the one who volunteered to play amateur detective. She was the one who wandered into danger without running the idea past me first. Her recklessness put her in this mess, and I'm supposed to bail her out? Not bloody likely, mate. To be perfectly frank, she's nothing but a spoiled brat."

Sorry, Sabrina.

"Jesus, man," Davis said, shaking his head. "That's so damn cold."

"Yeah, well, I'm more pragmatic and don't see it that way. Hopefully, the ATF will do the business and poor little billionairess Sabrina will be okay. If not ...." Kaine let the sentence trail off and threw them a deep, two-shouldered shrug. "Shame, but either way, I won't be getting the blame."

"Jesus H Christ," the Hawk said, grabbing Kaine by the upper arm. "I've heard enough. Get a move on."

He pushed Kaine on ahead, but Kaine dug in his heels.

"You really taking me to a holding cell, Sheriff?" he asked, scanning the empty corridor for an escape route. None made themselves obvious. Unable to hear Griezmann's briefing, he needed access to his backpack to pick up the live feed, but it was lying in the sheriff's office.

"No, son," the Hawk grunted and pushed Kaine in the back. "Not the lockup."

They started walking again.

"Where *are* we going?"

"We *were* heading for the interview suite. One of them's tricked out like a front room, for when we have assault victims to interview, or little ones in need of gentle handling. But after what you just said, it might be too damn comfortable for you." Hawksworth shot him another sideways glance, this one contemptuous. "I'm inclined to throw you into the holding cells with the rest of the town's drunks."

"Aw, Sheriff. You can't blame a man for protecting himself. And you have no idea how many times I've had to pull Sabrina's nuts out of the fire."

The Hawk sniffed. "Guess not. At least the FIU—that's the Family Interview Unit—has a good lock on the door in case you get yourself a bad case of itchy feet."

The law and their acronyms. Almost as bad as the military.

"Does it have a loo?"

"What in the hell's a 'loo'?"

"Sorry, I meant does your FIU have a rest room? I'd like to freshen up and change my shirt."

The Hawk sniffed the air close to Kaine. "It does, Griffin. And you sure need it. I saw the way that cute little Special Agent tried to change seats when you sat next to her. Man, you smell ripe."

"Smells like a steaming pile of horseshit to me, Sheriff," Davis offered from four paces away, his hand resting on the butt of the Colt in his holster.

Smart boy.

Kaine ignored the deputy's jibe.

"After rolling around in the dirt and fending off the local lowlifes, you'd hardly be smelling too good yourself, Sheriff. Mind if we go by your office so I can pick up my backpack?"

Hawksworth tilted his head a fraction, thinking.

"I need a change of clothes," Kaine added.

"Well … I don't see why not, considerin' I've already searched it an' you travel so light. An' it's on the way, more or less."

They took the right turn at the next intersection and followed it to the end of another deserted passageway. The bullpen was still empty and they made their progress through the silence.

Hawksworth paused at his office door, dug a set of keys from his pocket, and worked the lock.

"Go fetch your pack, Griffin."

"You're not going to lock me in again, are you, Sheriff?"

A crooked smile appeared on the lawman's craggy face.

"Not here, I'm not."

After retrieving his pack, they retraced the route along the hallway and past the fork, ending up at a ghostly custody suite.

The booking desk stood empty, like all the others in the tomb of a facility.

"No one here to look after the drunks in the tank?"

"Uh-uh. The tank's on the other side of the building. Out of earshot. No one can work alongside the noise of their yelling and puking."

The sheriff pointed him towards a door marked, *Family Interview Unit*, and waved Kaine in.

Kaine dropped his pack on a nearby chair and took in the comfortably appointed room—a cross between a three-star hotel suite and a upscale living room, complete with well-upholstered furniture and a wall-mounted flatscreen TV. The colour scheme was restful creams and greys. A kitchenette in the far corner offered the promise of some refreshments. A sign on the only other door in the place read, *Restroom*.

All the mod cons.

"Don't know how long the Feds are gonna be," the Hawk said from the doorway, "but I wouldn't hold your breath none. The TV's hooked up to satellite and carries a whole load of cable channels. Remote's in the drawer. Help yourself." He pointed to the wooden cabinet on the floor below the TV, and then to the far corner of the room. "You'll find some coffee and creamer in the kitchen. Only instant, but it's drinkable. And look hard enough, you might even find some cookies in there, too. Unless the Feds found the place already. Greedy sombitches tear through this place like locusts when they ain't being watched closely. Make yourself at home."

Behind the Hawk, Davis shouted, "Don't get too lonely now, y'hear?"

"Thanks, Sheriff," Kaine said, and meaning it—the elderly lawman could easily have stuffed him into a holding cell, which would have severely cramped his style. "This is the cosiest cell I've ever seen."

"Seen the inside of many cells, Griffin?"

Kaine grinned. "Only on TV. You read my résumé, Sheriff. Did it say anything about my ever having been on the wrong side of the law?"

The Hawk scrunched up his face and shook his head. "They flashed it up so quick and the damned print was so small, I couldn't read the danged thing."

From Kaine's perspective, the bio on the whiteboard had been perfectly legible. His estimation of the Hawk's ability to use his firearm dropped a few notches, although a short-sighted man with a loaded firearm carried a damn sight more threat than one carrying a knife. And for his part, Davis appeared more than competent. In fact, the younger lawman seemed eager to deal with "Griffin the coward" in what he considered to be a suitable manner.

Kaine let the matter slide. He had no intention of mentioning eyesight to the Hawk in case the old lawman noticed his missing glasses.

"Don't bother trying the phone on the table. It's hooked up to the switchboard and Mercy won't give you an outside line. And this here's for emergency use only." The sheriff nodded to the red button on the wall beside the light switch. "Press it, and you'd better be having a heart attack or something even more serious. Otherwise, leave it alone. Get it?"

"Got it, Sheriff," Kaine said, straight-faced. "I recognise when someone's doing me a good turn. And I appreciate it."

He stopped talking, hoping the Hawk would stop hovering and fly away along with his sidekick.

"Okay, Griffin. See you when I see you."

"Bye, Sheriff. Bye, Deputy."

Hawksworth backed out and closed the door. The lock clicked under the action of a key and Kaine pressed his ear to the steel door. He couldn't hear a thing.

Good soundproofing.

For show, Kaine yawned loud and long, headed to the cabinet and grabbed the TV remote. He hit the power button and the TV fired up in seconds. Kaine flicked through the stations until he found the first music channel and increased the volume enough to mask his movements but not arouse suspicion. Then, he collected the backpack and headed for the restroom. Given its function, he made the calculated assumption that the FIU restroom would be the least likely place in the building to contain a surveillance camera or a hidden microphone. But he wasn't about to take it for granted.

Once inside, he surreptitiously quartered the plain but well-maintained room—four white-tiled walls, toilet, wash basin with a mirror above—all sparkling clean. A heated chrome rail held a fluffy white towel and the place smelled of lemons. He'd rented less well-appointed hotel rooms.

No obvious signs of a camera.

Kaine lowered the backpack to the toilet seat and turned his back to the mirror. Hiding his actions, he unclipped the top flap, released the rope tie, and dug through his belongings until he found the rectangular plastic case he was looking for.

Still facing away from the mirror, Kaine opened the case and took out what looked like a battery powered electric razor. When the Hawk searched his bag, Kaine half expected him to ask why a man with a full beard carried such a device.

More fool the Hawk.

He uncoiled the cable and plugged one end into the bottom of the unit and the other into his ear, hiding the bud beneath his long hair. Kaine threw the switch and the razor buzzed into life, sounding exactly like the real thing. The earbud output gave nothing but a slow metronomic bleep, confirming the restroom contained nothing that emitted radio, infrared, or microwave signals. No electronic bugs. The room was as clean as his initial assessment suggested.

Holding the razor up to his cheek, Kaine turned to face the mirror, and inspected the reflection close up. A normal sheet of glass with a silvered back. Not a one-way, reciprocal mirror.

Safe.

He removed the bud from his ear, returned the fake razor to its case, and searched through the pack again, this time looking for his spare glasses case.

As well as giving him a promotion, Corky's update of the Griffin legend included the growing list of medical conditions responsible for his early retirement on health grounds. Not only was Griffin hypertensive and borderline diabetic, he was becoming increasingly longsighted, and he had a serious astigmatism which required him to wear reading glasses.

Not for the first time, Kaine had reason to admire Corky's superb attention to detail.

He removed his spare glasses from the case, slid them on, and tapped the arm once.

"*About bloody time, Mr K. Wondered what was happening.*"

"Sorry, Base. Took me a while to shake my jailors. Have you been following Griezmann's briefing? Over."

"*Yeah, sure have. You need to get a wriggle on.*"

"Why, what's happened? Over."

"*Best you see for yourself. Just done a quick scan of your location. There's a TV close by. Can you get to it so Corky can show you something?*"

Kaine gave Corky his location and confirmed the channel he'd set the TV to, and added, "Give me five minutes to sweep the room before you piggyback onto the signal. Over."

"Don't worry about mics and cameras in the interview room, Mr K. Corky's sorted them already."

While they talked, Kaine stripped off his top, splashed soapy water over his upper body, and rinsed. He towelled off and dragged on a fresh, dark blue polo shirt. No value in arousing the sheriff's suspicions by staying in his dirty clothes, especially since he'd promised to freshen up.

After dressing and reloading his pack, Kaine headed back out to the main room.

"Base, I'm ready now. What do you have for me. Over."

Instantly, the channel on the screen flipped from a scantily clad woman twerking along to a hip-hop beat to the slightly offset picture of the electronic whiteboard and the satellite shot of Camp Pueblo.

"Corky piggybacked into the Fed's satellite feed from earlier, Mr K. You need to take a shufty at this before you hear what Griezmann's saying. Gotta warn you though, it don't make pleasant viewing."

"Okay, Base. I'm ready. Over."

The image on the TV zoomed in and the camp enlarged enough for Kaine to identify a number of individual buildings, one of which was clearly the administration block.

Black and white. Crystal clear and pinprick sharp. The pollution-free air and high altitude made the satellite images the best he'd ever seen. Much better than the ones in Helmand Province where atmospheric dust played havoc with the satellite's acuity.

A compass superimposed onto the top right hand corner of the screen showed north as the top of the picture. It also showed magnetic north as eight degrees to the east. Beside the compass, a digital clock ticked away the time, showing it as 09:57:32 and counting. The previous morning.

The overhead shot, taken at a slight angle of incidence to the nadir and fifteen degrees to the east, allowed a decent field of view with a good resolution and the minimum of distortion.

Uniformed men in straight rows of platoon strength stood facing the camp's administration block.

"What's this, Base? We're missing the briefing. Over."

"Hold your horses, Mr K."

Kaine only had to wait a few seconds for the action to begin.

The doors to one of the smallest buildings in the southwest quadrant flew open. Three people appeared from the shadow of the opening, two men in military fatigues and a struggling woman. The lead man—a hulking figure with massive shoulders and shaggy blond hair—held the woman by her arm. The second, smaller man carried what looked like a shotgun and took up the rear, his gait shuffling and crouched. Hulk walked the woman out onto the parade ground, between the rows of soldiers, and punched her in the chest. She staggered and landed on her back in the dust.

Corky froze the picture with the woman on her back, her face fully exposed to the satellite camera. The picture zoomed in close, pixilating as it did so. Slowly, the pixels reduced in size, and the image cleared to reveal her face, creased in pain.

Sabrina!

No doubt about it.

Kaine clenched his teeth. It was definitely her. In pain and in grave danger. Hulk's cowardly blows might easily have broken her ribs. Although as much a techie genius as Corky, Kaine had no idea whether she'd learned any form of self-defence, or whether she knew how to absorb the full force of a blow. He doubted it. Most of the techies he'd met spent their waking hours sitting at a desk, their only exercise being rippling their fingers over the keyboard, and the heaviest weights they lifted were coffee mugs and glazed doughnuts.

"That blond geezer's a right fucker, Mr K."

Corky sounded as angry and squeaky as Kane had ever heard him. And the hacker rarely swore.

"You gonna give him a good kicking, right?"

Too bloody right, I am.

After what had happened to Danny, he would *not* let another of his friends die. No bloody way.

Damn it.

Watching Sabrina on the receiving end of such punishment had been hard to take.

Kaine took a deep, settling breath. Anger wouldn't help. He needed cool, steady logic.

"First things first, Corky. Let's get her out of harm's way. Okay? Exactly how far away is Camp Pueblo from here? Over."

"'Bout thirty miles, give or take. Cross country and uphill the whole way. Mostly dirt-track roads winding through the forest, too. Good job the Canadian hired you that SUV."

Kaine grimaced. "My Ford's back at the saloon. A couple of miles from here. Means I'll need to borrow one. Over."

"Not a problem. There's plenty of police SUVs parked outside."

Corky's high-pitched and slightly manic chuckle vibrated through the arm of Kaine's glasses.

"Can you identify the sheriff's SUV from the others? I know where it's parked. Maybe hack into it for me? Over." Kaine asked, still staring at the screen and memorising Camp Pueblo's layout.

"What's that? Hack into it? How very dare you! Corky's never hacked into nothing in his life. Corky gains access to technical systems by stealth and cunning, and by—"

"Sorry, Corky. My mistake. But the sheriff's SUV? Over."

"Yep. Already on it. Corky's accessed the SUV's infotainment system. That car ain't going nowhere for anyone but you. Is Corky a talent or what?"

"No doubt about that. Over."

Kaine had lost count of the number of times Corky had not only made his life easier, but actively saved it. The man's genius had saved countless other lives, too. But not even Corky could help save Danny. No one could save ....

Pity's sake, Kaine. Don't go there. Not now!

"Can you show me the auditorium now, and take it back to when I left? Over."

"Coming right up."

Kaine watched the images scroll on the TV and listened to the audio all the way through before he'd seen enough. One part in particular made his blood boil and confirmed his decision as the correct one.

He switched off the TV and shrugged on the backpack. Although it had a sixty-litre carrying capacity and a maximum load of twenty-five kilos, his was only half full. It wouldn't slow him down much. He balanced the load on his shoulders and tightened all the webbing straps, including the one around his waist. Until he reached the sheriff's SUV he'd need to move fast and quiet.

"So, Mr K. Whatcha gonna do now? How's you getting out of that place? Corky's assuming the door's locked."

"Yes," Kaine said, allowing the options to swim through his head. "It'll be alarmed, too. There's no point in my trying to pick it. Give me a moment to think, will you? Over."

"Don't be silly, Mr K. Corky's gonna nobble the alarm for you. Just a tick, eh?"

"Excellent. Thanks, Corky. Over."

While he waited, Kaine pulled the hairbrush from the zipped side pocket of his shaver case and removed the brush's head to expose the specially crafted set of lockpicks.

"Ready?" Kaine asked.

"Nearly there, Mr K. Takes a while to isolate the correct circuit on a system this ancient. Corky don't want to shut down the whole shootin' match. Wait ... wait. There! Alarm's off. You can crack that there door any time you fancy."

"Brilliant. Thanks, Base. Over."

Kaine dropped to one knee and set to work on the five-lever mortice lock. He added the crossbar to the brass tensioner bar, slid it into the keyhole, and fed in the thin tungsten picking wire. He found the first two gates easily enough but fell into a false gate on the sticky third before picking up the fourth and fifth gates. He reset and repeated the process, setting gates four and five before gate three, and presto. Adding a little more torsional force to the tensioner bar did the trick and the lock slid back, making a healthy clunk against the lock's back plate. The operation had taken him a little over two minutes. He should have been quicker, but no one had oiled the lock in years and two of the levers were caked in grease and dust, and stiff as a result.

"Okay, Base. I'm through. I'll be on silent running for a while. Alpha One, out."

Kaine tapped the left arm of the glasses and stood. Before twisting the handle, he pressed his ear to the door panel and heard nothing but silence. He pulled the door towards him ... and walked straight into Sheriff Hawksworth and Special Agent Chang.

CHAPTER TWENTY-FOUR

Pine Creek, Arizona, US

Al Griezmann ran a hand through his close-cropped hair, making sure the flattop was neat and tidy. He paid enough to keep his trademark hair shipshape and saw it as an essential part of his public face. A tidy body made for a tidy mind. And Al owned both.

Yeah, he owned it.

He tightened his abdominals and stood to address the crowd, but their murmuring didn't quit. Mostly the ATF assholes, of course. Their inferior training and lack of discipline made them the joke of the entire federal law enforcement community. But they did have their uses. The word "scapegoats" came to mind.

So far, Al had done pretty good for a guy in his early forties. Nothing stellar, but he'd earned his promotion to SAC of the Phoenix office in close to record time. During his short tenure, he'd reorganised the field office and posted some record case clear-up figures, which made Deputy Director Hallam look good for recommending his promotion in the first place. Joanna Hallam was headed for the Director's office and Al Griezmann was hellbent on riding her coattails all the way to the top.

Yep, making Deputy Director Hallam look good reflected well on Al, which helped his career. In that one respect, Hallam was worth following, but in every other way the woman was a useless pain in his butt.

She should stay at home and push out more babies, leave the real work to the men. Not that he'd ever voice those words in public. Not these days. If he did that in these times of political correctness, he'd end up in the Anchorage Field Office—the Home Team's version of being sent to Siberia. If that ever happened, he'd spend the rest of his career chasing down drunk locals accused of driving their skidoos the wrong way up a goddamn glacier.

Shit no. Not for this good ol' Kansan boy. Go Jayhawkers!

Nope, he needed to protect his back should anything go wrong and the Frenchwoman ended up dead.

Now hang on a minute. There's a thought.

Would Sabrina LeMaître ending up dead be such a bad thing? Might make it easier for Al to bury the way he'd mishandled the situation.

Think on it.

In hindsight, he should have taken her more seriously. Should have listened to her from day one. Hindsight's a bitch. Made every decision look like a bad one, especially if the shit hit the fan afterwards.

Yeah. Think on it, Al.

With the Frenchwoman dead, Colonel Caren—the mad SOB— wouldn't have any leverage over Old Man LeMaître. No way would the colonel be getting his hands on the material he needed to make a dirty bomb. No way Al could let that happen. What a shitstorm that would unleash. His career would never recover. Alaska would be paradise compared to where he'd end up.

Lord help me.

At one stage, Al had considered flooding Brown and Company's storage facility with agents to shore up their security, but that would have drawn even more attention to the place. Way too much. No one in the area was supposed to know what they were actually storing in there. A stockpile of nuclear material within a half-day hike of a civilian population? Hell no. He couldn't let that sort of information out. Heads would roll.

That's why he needed a Plan B. And he had that in the dumb-assed shape of Senior Special Agent Del Beddow and the rest of the ATF.

Yep, having a scapegoat was one of the benefits of leading the Joint Task Force. In the event of a "disaster", he'd shift the blame onto the other guy, easy enough. And if the shit really did start raining down, the ATF would be less able to defend themselves in any federal inquiry.

Granted, *Operation Slingshot* was aimed at locating missing weapons, which made it the ATF's responsibility, at least theoretically. And maybe enough guns, carbines, and ammunition *had* gone missing to arm a full-blooded right-wing insurgency.

On the face of it, the ATF should be in charge, but the trail of missing weapons led from Colfax-Lacy's factories in Maine, to Pine Creek, and from Pine Creek to Camp Pueblo. Added to that, people had been killed and others—mainly women—had disappeared in at least three states between Maine and Arizona. The case crossed half a dozen state lines, which put it squarely in the domain of the FBI, the big boys. And the threat to nuclear material? Well, that added one heck of a new dimension.

Yep. Al had done well to make sure that the ATF dickwads were running the "official" raid so he could shift the blame for any mistakes onto them. Meanwhile, he took on the secondary mission—rescuing the Frenchwoman—if possible. And if he could manage that, he'd soak up all the glory.

In law enforcement and politics alike, size mattered. The team with the loudest voice and the greatest firepower won. And, in this operation, that was the FBI, and the FBI could ride roughshod over the ATF whenever the hell they wanted.

Al raised both hands in the air.

————

"Okay people, settle down, now. We've got a whole heap of organising to get done."

He made his way to the side of the electronic whiteboard and turned to face the troops again. They finally shut the hell up and even the ATF bozos started listening. Made a change.

Al fired a quick look at Mei Chang and nodded. Man, the woman had the cutest little behind he'd ever seen in all his born days. Not that he'd ever make a move on her. No chance of that. Pissing on your own doorstep was a sure-fire way of sending your career down the toilet. He's never make such a dumbass move.

She hit a key on her laptop and five circles got superimposed on the satellite image of the camp. Running in a clockwise direction, they were named, OP1 to OP5.

"Thank you, Special Agent Chang," Al said, glancing at Beddow to show how polite he could be to people who obeyed his instructions quickly and efficiently.

"Okay, let's get down to business."

Al paused a moment before launching into a summary of the operation they all should have read in their briefing packs. That being said, he'd been in the law enforcement business long enough to know that some agents would rather boil their heads in oil than read through a whole report. Given the chance, most would limit their reading to the sports pages. As for the ATF morons, he wasn't even certain they could all read.

He coughed over the laugh he almost barked out.

"Right, in case some of you haven't had the chance to read the briefing pack, I'm gonna review it, bullet points only." He paused to let the loud guffaws from his more experienced men die down—

they'd all heard him say the same thing before. And they all knew his reason for saying it.

"We're here to serve a Federal warrant to search Camp Pueblo. Officially, we're on a normal raid, looking for unregistered weapons, which is why the ATF and SSA Beddow will be leading the raid."

Al nodded at the ATF goon and added a tight smile. Beddow stared back, his face blank. The clown's default expression.

"However," Al continued, "our primary mission is to release any hostages the Creed might be holding. Our intel suggests there may be as many as a dozen women being held against their will in one of the barracks. A building that doubles as a whorehouse." He paused to let the chuckling and murmuring die.

"In particular, our prime target is this woman, Ms Sabrina LeMaître." He nodded and Special Agent Chang posted a still taken from the hostage tape onto the centre of the whiteboard. Underneath the bruises and the cut lip, Al saw a real, dark-eyed cutie. "The Creed's holding her and the ransom they're asking for her release isn't acceptable. I'm not at liberty to say what they're after, but it's big. Very big."

One of the ATF fools in the back row shouted, "The key to the cathouse?"

Al glowered at him and the guys in the audience who laughed at the joke.

"Goddamn it! Take this serious!"

Al paused again and scanned the multi-coloured faces. They were mostly young, mostly fresh, and mostly showing keen interest.

And damn right, too.

Anyone could say what they liked about Al Griezmann, but give him an audience and he could hold its attention. A born showman.

"The Doomsday Creed are dangerous people. They're armed to the teeth and make ISIS look like a Sunday School play group!"

Some members of the audience, FBI agents he recognised, nodded along, stern-faced. Some of the ATF throwbacks, looked at each other as though they'd never heard of ISIS and didn't know what the hell went on in a Sunday School.

The Lord God help us.

"Now, Special Agent Chang, bring up the mugshot of Colonel Caren, please," Al said, smiling at her. It didn't hurt to play nice with the babes since you never knew where it might lead. Maybe he could transfer her to a different field office so it would leave the way clear for him to make his move.

Man, that pert little ass!

The Frenchwoman's picture disappeared from the whiteboard and was replaced by a mugshot of the man in question. Short grey hair, military cut, moustache. Eyes so intensely blue he might have been wearing coloured contact lenses. His tight smile showed no teeth.

"This here's Colonel Richard Caren, leader of the Doomsday Creed. The other two are his Chiefs of Staff." Again, he nodded to Mei and she pulled up two more mugshots alongside the first.

"The fat one's Captain Bernard Boniface"—more chuckling from the audience—"the other's Captain Sven Andersen. Don't let the ranks fool you. Neither of these bozos have ever served in the military. Colonel Caren handed out the commissions when he set up the Creed as his own personal army.

"The three of them look real respectable, right? But don't let that fool you, neither. These men are dangerous SOBs. Any questions so far?"

As expected, a wave of silence blew back at him. No one asked any questions. Al was giving them the opportunity to kick some right-wing butt and that was all they cared about.

"Sergeant Schreiber, show yourself."

Schreiber jumped up from his chair in the front row by the aisle, and the bullnosed, red-faced former soldier stood to attention, chest out, wide shoulders pulled back hard.

"Sir, yes sir!"

"At ease, Sergeant."

Schreiber stamped his feet shoulder-width apart and clasped his hands behind his broad back, assuming the position. A damned fine soldier, he obeyed orders and didn't ask any dumb questions.

"Anyone who's not met Sergeant Dean Schreiber, take a good look. He's leader of Team Sierra, the five-man sniper unit. They'll be taking the high ground overlooking the camp which is indicated here, at OP1."

Al pressed the button on his laser pointer, shone the green light at the appropriate circle on the map, and ran it along the ridge. The position stood on a tree-covered knoll some five hundred yards out from the southern edge of the camp. A perfect place for a snipers' nest, and each one of Team Sierra was more than capable of taking out a fast-moving target from that distance. Dang, most of them could plug the eye of a crow from that sort of distance.

"Your briefing pack contains a list and photos of the seven men we've identified as the colonel's top team. Normal rules of engagement apply. Shoot to save life only. And, you'll take your lead from me and no one else. Understood?"

Delorme Beddow threw up a hand.

"Now wait just one minute there, Al."

Beddow dragged his big black butt out of his chair and marched towards the whiteboard. He stopped in front of Al and they stood nose to nose. Al didn't give an inch. Never did. Never would.

"This is an ATF operation," Beddow said, in a stage whisper.

The veins on the ex-footballer's thick neck bulged, and his ebony skin darkened. No doubt about it, Beddow was struggling to stop himself launching into another hissy fit like he'd done with the dumb-assed Brit.

"That's where you're wrong, Del," Al replied, smiling all sweetness and light. "This here's a joint FBI-ATF task force, remember?"

"Fuck that, Griezmann," Beddow hissed, straining even harder to keep his voice in check. "The ATF swore out the warrants. My name's on them, and we're the ones serving them. The FBI are here as our backup in case things go awry."

Awry? Been reading a dictionary, Del?

Al used Beddow's square head to block his sneer from the audience before turning it into a friendly smile. "Perhaps we should discuss this *after* the briefing, Del. And in private."

Beddow ground his teeth, his expression thunderous.

"Time's too short to pussyfoot around, Al. Me and my team's going to be driving up to the compound's main gates and serving them warrants in less than"—he read the time off his wristwatch—"fifteen hours. We'll be in the firing line. I need to control—"

"Del!" Al barked out, cutting the asshole off mid-rant. "That's enough. We're gonna take this to one side. With me, right now."

He turned and beckoned the blowhard with his index finger like he was summoning an unruly child or a puppy. When they reached the side of the stage, he turned to face the table.

"Special Agent Chang," he called, fixing her with another cheery smile, "please put the photos of the Creed's 'officers' up on the screen while SSA Beddow and I discuss some procedural issues."

The cutie nodded and tapped away on her keyboard.

Moments later, the satellite shot on the whiteboard disappeared behind a whole bunch of mugshots with names and short bios beneath each.

Al then turned to face the AFT leader.

"Look around you, Del," he hissed, pointing to the men and women in their combat gear. "This is a joint task force, and the FBI is the greater force. More to the point, I outrank you here. So, shut your goddamn pie-hole, right now."

Beddow stretched taller and leaned closer, trying to intimidate with his pure animal power. Well, that sure as hell wasn't going to work. In his time, Al had faced down far tougher hombres than the musclebound Delorme Beddow.

"I need *my* men on that ridge, as well as yours," Beddow hissed, spittle flying.

"How many nationally registered sharpshooters have you bought to the party, Del?" Al shot back.

"Party? For fuck's sake, Griezmann. This ain't a goddamn party, it's a strategic and dangerous law enforcement operation, set in a volatile situation. These Creed nutjobs aren't going to give up easy and my men and I are gonna be in the direct firing line."

"Which means you need the best people taking up the best defensive positions. Are you hearing me, SSA Beddow?"

"Yeah," Beddow said, hardly moving his lips, "I'm hearing you. And to answer your question, I have three qualified snipers sitting out there, and I want them on the ridge with Team Sierra. Okay?"

Al stared Beddow down for a count of five before nodding his consent.

"Okay, that seems reasonable." For the benefit of the crowd, Al served up another one of his amiable smiles. "It ain't possible to have too many marksmen in a *volatile* operation like this one. Am I right?"

"And since I'm going to be the man on the ground," Beddow said, "*I'm* going to be calling the shots."

Still smiling, Al shook head. "No way, bud. That ain't happening."

Beddow's hands formed knuckle-popping fists. He was forever doing that shit. If it didn't work on the scrawny Brit, it sure as hell wasn't going to work on Al Griezmann.

"You arrogant piece of—"

"What's likely to happen tomorrow morning if I withdraw my support for this operation and stand my people down?"

"What!"

Beddow stood stock still, eyes wide, jaw set hard.

"You heard me, Del."

"You wouldn't dare!"

"Try me."

"Why the hell would you pull out?"

"Well now, SSA Beddow," Al said, dropping the smile and looking thoughtful. "I might decide this whole situation is heading in the direction of another Waco Siege. There's a whole bunch of innocent souls sitting down there in Camp Pueblo, including—no, especially —the Frenchwoman, and I might decide that serving the warrants under these conditions is way too dangerous. Yep, seems to me that going in might be too great a risk of them getting hurt. I might— reluctantly—stand my teams down and let you guys go in alone."

Beddow shut his mouth and looked fit to explode all over the stage.

Yep. That's got ya, buddy.

"What will you do then, Del? I'm head of this joint operation and the buck stops with me. I ain't gonna have a bunch of AFT jokers callin' the shots. My reputation's on the line here, along with the lives of a whole load of my people. Not to mention those poor civilians."

"Your reputation? Jesus, Griezmann. You're worried about your rep? You sorry son-of-a-bitch. I can't move on the camp without the FBI's support, and you know it. We'd be heavily outnumbered, and you know that, too. I'd have to call off the raid."

"You could always call up more of your ATF agents. Remind me, Del, where's your nearest Special Response Team based? I mean, one with enough spare men?"

Beddow lowered his eyes a fraction and released a loud breath.

"As you damn well know," he growled, "SRT4's based in Los Angeles. They won't be able to get here 'til the day *after* tomorrow. By that time, the date on the warrants will have lapsed and we'll have to resubmit them all over again. All our work will be in the shitter. And to top it all, the longer we wait, the less chance we'll have of keeping the raid secret. Jesus. I'd hate to see what would happen if those nuts in Camp Pueblo get time to prepare. Fuck's sake, Griezmann. You're a real piece of work. You know that?"

"All your work, Del? All *your* work? Fuck's sake, man. If you think I'm gonna let you screw up one of my operations, you can think again."

Al stopped talking and let Beddow chew on the information for a while. He studied the crowd, which was growing more and more restless. Most of their eyes were trained on him and Beddow rather than examining the faces on the whiteboard. Things had gone far enough.

"So, Del," he said, judging that he'd given the big grunt enough time to acclimate to his weakened position. "Are we in agreement?"

"Yeah," Beddow growled, nodding his big, square head. "You've got me over a barrel. But listen up, Griezmann." He edged close enough for Al to smell his aftershave and his coffee breath. "If one of my people get hurt on account of your self-preserving bullshit, I'm coming for you. And nothing on this planet's gonna be able to save you. Nothing. You hear me?"

Al smiled again. He could show magnanimity when he needed to.

"Sure thing, Del," he said, all sweetness and light once again. "And don't worry. Not a thing's gonna happen on my watch." He slapped the big man's powerful shoulder, making sure the whole audience could see his friendly smile. "I've got your back, Del. You can rely on me."

"Asshole!"

Al ignored the insult and returned to his position at the whiteboard, leaving Beddow in the dark shadows where he belonged.

"Okay people," he called, addressing the whole audience, "SSA Beddow tells me there are three qualified snipers in his contingent. Show yourselves, please." He nodded to the two tall men and the equally tall woman who raised their hands. "I'm temporarily assigning you to Team Sierra. Report to Sergeant Schreiber after the briefing. You'll be with him at OP1."

Al tilted his head towards Beddow to show his fairness.

"Now that's settled, we'll move on to OP2." He pointed the laser at the post furthermost from the action. "Team Bravo, where are you, guys?"

Without being asked, Mei had removed the mugshots from the screen, proving she had brains as well as looks.

In the second row, three men and a tall woman with slim hips slowly climbed to their feet. They knew what to expect. One of the men, a barrel-chested sergeant, said, "That'll be us, sir."

Al almost stared in surprise. The guy had said, "sir", and he was an ATF grunt! Wonders would never cease.

"Soon as SSA Beddow and his advance team passes your position, you'll erect the barriers and block the road. Your job will be to make sure no members of the Creed make it past SSA Beddow and his team. You're there to guard the points of access as well as egress." He wondered whether he needed to explain what "egress" meant to the fools, but decided against it. "We also don't want any innocents wandering onto the field unannounced. That clear?"

The sergeant shot a lightning glance at Beddow before answering with a disappointed and grumbled, "Yes, sir."

Judging by his response and the facial expressions of the rest of Team Bravo, none of them seemed too excited by the prospect of being kept so far away from the action.

Tough.

"That meet with your approval, SSA Beddow?" Al asked the cowed leader of the ATF contingent.

Beddow's nod must have hurt his thick neck, judging by the length of time it took him to respond.

"Yeah. We're good."

"Excellent, excellent."

He'd dealt with the majority of the ATF clowns, and only had one detail left.

"Team Charlie," he said, pointing to OP3, which stood on the far side of the camp, way, way up to the northwest. "You're the rear guard. Where are you?"

No one moved.

"Come on," Al shouted. "Show yourselves, we don't have all afternoon!"

Three surly men stood, looking at each other as though none wanted to admit who they were.

"It's likely to take you most of the night to reach your position. You'll have to leave right away. One of the local deputies has agreed to show you the best route up there. Check your weapons and communications systems before you set off. Report into QB when you arrive and take care. No telling what you'll come across up there and we don't want any trouble ahead of time. Keep your heads down, your eyes and ears open, and wait for my instructions. Me and Special Agents Steiner and Chang are going to be quarterbacking the operation from the Command Unit at OP1, with the snipers. Any questions before you head off?"

Team Charlie stood with their thumbs stuck up their butts. Nodding, but saying nothing.

Sheriff Hawksworth had returned from dealing with the Brit, and brought his man along for the ride. Dressed in their smart grey police uniforms with their silver badges glinting under the lights, they looked a picture and stood at the side of the stage in full view of the troops.

"Okay then. Deputy, lead the way, please."

The deputy waved at Team Charlie, signalling them to follow him. The three men filed out, looking like they'd been sentenced to sanitise the company latrines with their favourite toothbrushes.

Life's a bitch, guys. Suck it up, y'all.

With all the ATF clowns dealt with, Al could get down to the real business. He rattled through the assignments and delivered his final, crowd-rallying speech about staying alert and keeping safe. Then he dismissed them, and they filed out of the room to deal with last-minute prep, which would include weapons and comms checks, evening meal, and letters home to be delivered in the event of ....

Yeah, whatever.

Al waited for the auditorium to empty, including Del Beddow—tail curled up tight between his huge, muscly legs—before signalling the sheriff onto the stage.

"Any trouble with the Brit?"

Hawksworth sank into the same seat he had earlier, two up from Mei Chang.

"None. I holed him up in the mother and children's interview room. It's got satellite TV and everything."

"Satellite TV?" Mei asked, speaking for the first time since they'd turfed the Brit out the room.

Man, she had a sexy voice. Deep and hot. Smoking.

"Yeah, that's right, Miss," Hawksworth said. "Ought to keep the guy quiet until you're ready to take him off my hands."

She flinched. "It's Special Agent Chang, Sheriff Hawksworth, not 'Miss'."

Hawksworth dipped his head and tipped a finger to the brim of his hat. "Sorry, Ma'am. Please forgive this old timer's mistake. Can't keep up with what's good and what's not these days."

The touchy woman pointed to the fancy, steel-rimmed eyeglasses on the table in front of her. "How's Major Griffin going to watch TV without these?"

"Dang it, Sheriff," Al said, to support his favourite Special Agent. "You frogmarched the poor man out of the place so quick, you might've left him blind."

"I was following your instructions, Mr Griezmann. Who the heck cares if he can't watch TV?"

Mei grabbed the glasses and held them up to the light. "Looks like he's short-sighted."

"Oh, now ain't that a real shame," Hawksworth said, all sarcastic.

"Are you going to take them to him?" she asked.

"It'll wait. I ain't his servant."

She thinned her lips and turned her head to look directly at Al.

"Is there time for me to take them to him?" she asked. "I know what it's like to be without my glasses."

Al shrugged.

"We're about done here. Knock yourself out," he said, showing that he could be considerate if he wanted—especially if it worked out well for him in the long run. And the way she smiled at him when he agreed to her simple request to go on her mission of mercy, confirmed how good a move it really was.

"You won't be able to get in without me," the decrepit lawman said. "The lockup is unmanned right now and I'm the only one with a key since Cal's in the wind."

Mei scraped her chair back and stood. She hovered over the sheriff, intimidating as all hell for such a little woman. Hawksworth gazed up at her, probably in admiration.

What a magnificent specimen she was, despite her lack of stature. Man, what Al wouldn't do for the chance to climb into them panties.

Wonder if she wears a thong?

After a short standoff, Hawksworth buckled. He struggled to his feet, grunting and moaning the whole way up.

"Have it your way, *Special Agent* Chang. I'll take the man his damn glasses."

He held out his hand but she refused to pass them across.

"If you don't mind," she said, a thin smile on her perfect oval face, "I'll go along with you. Since he's officially been detained under a federal remit, I'd like to see where you put him and how he's doing."

Hawksworth shot a look in Al's direction.

Al nodded. "Strikes me as a good idea, Sheriff. We ought to make sure he's doin' okay. Don't be all afternoon about it, Special Agent Chang. We'll need to be getting out of here before dark. Just take a quick look-see."

"Yes, sir."

She turned, showed him that tight backside, and waited at the side of the stage for the sheriff to catch up and show her the way. Al watched her all the way out. When the doors closed behind her and the bandy-legged sheriff, Al smiled at Mark Steiner, a solid agent he'd brought with him from Washington.

"Sure would like to get me some of that. What an ass."

Steiner curled his lip.

"Don't waste your time, Al. Woman's a cold fish. I tried asking her out once. Turned me down cold. Said she'd never date a work colleague since it wasn't only against the rules, but it could get too complicated. Wouldn't be surprised if she played for the other side. If you know what I mean." He tapped the side of his nose.

"You're kidding me. Woman with a body like that's a *dyke*? Crying shame."

"Sure is."

"You ain't just saying that to keep her for yourself, are you, Mark?"

A pained expression formed on Steiner's chubby face and his baby blues disappeared beneath puffy lids.

"Who, sir? Me, sir?"

The eyes reappeared, big and shining.

"Yeah, you. I don't believe a word of it."

"Just kidding, Al. She's straight, but choosy. You know?" Steiner patted the rolls of fat layering his gut. "I'm guessing she doesn't like men built for comfort. Maybe you've got a chance, though. With your sixpack, an' all."

Al tensed his abs and looked down. Not as trim as he used to be in his college days, but not bad. He still cut a good enough figure for his age.

Maybe he should make the approach to Mei Chang. After all, rules were meant to be broken.

CHAPTER TWENTY-FIVE

Sunday 21st May – Late Afternoon
Pine Creek, Arizona, US

Kaine gave the sheriff his most disarming smile.

Hawksworth's eyes bulged.

"What in God's—"

"You left the door open, Sheriff," Kaine offered, smiling. "I wanted to find out what was happening."

"The hell I did!"

Hawksworth's searching eyes alighted on the pack strapped to Kaine's back—a dead giveaway. His right hand dropped towards his holster, the fingers scrambling to release the popper on the retaining strap.

Kaine threw out an open-fisted, close-order left jab, striking the lawman between the fourth and fifth ribs with his leading knuckle. He followed up with a straight right to the gut, pulling the punch slightly.

Hawksworth grunted, folded over, and collapsed against Kaine, who caught him and stumbled backwards into the room, apparently unable to take the sheriff's weight.

SA Chang, her view blocked by the sheriff's bulky frame, leaned sideways, straining to see what had happened.

"What's wrong?" she asked and stepped into the room.

"God, I don't know. I think he's having some sort of a seizure," Kaine said, lowering the gasping, spluttering sheriff to the carpeted floor.

Hawksworth's streaming eyes searched for Chang's, his arms flailed, struggling weakly to fight Kaine off and pull his gun. Kaine grabbed Hawksworth's right wrist and drove his thumb into the PC6 pressure point between the radius and ulnar bones. Hawksworth gasped and tensed, trembling under what would be piercing pain.

Kaine glanced up at Chang. "Do you know CPR?"

The Special Agent shook herself before answering. "Of course. Move away."

Kaine released his grip on Hawksworth's wrist and leaned in closer. Using his body as a shield, he unclipped Hawksworth's holster, drew the Sig, and coughed as he cycled the slide. He rolled back on his haunches, sprang to his feet, and faced Chang with the gun aimed at her chest.

She froze.

"Sorry about this, Special Agent Chang, but I'm in a bit of a rush. Please don't make a move for your handgun."

Chang spread her arms further away from her hips.

"What the hell do you think you're doing, Griffin? I'm a federal agent, for God's sake!"

"I've already apologised. Kick the door closed."

Kaine beckoned her further inside with his free hand. She obeyed his instructions, staring thunder at him the whole time. He turned his index finger downwards and rotated it anti-clockwise.

She hesitated, looking down at the still-gasping sheriff.

"What did you do to him?"

"Nothing permanent, I can assure you. He'll be fine in a few minutes. Now, turn around."

"You'll never get away with this, Griffin."

Looking doubtful, she spun slowly.

"Probably not, but I have to try. Please stop talking."

Kaine leaned close and reached for the holster clipped to her belt.

"What the hell are you—"

"Don't worry, Special Agent Chang, it's nothing personal. I'm spoken for. And I said, stop talking."

Kaine removed the Glock and made sure it was safe before jamming it into his waistband.

He dug the muzzle of the sheriff's Sig into the small of her back, causing her to stiffen again, and bent at the knees to frisk her for a concealed carry. He found an ankle holster and removed the sub-compact Smith & Wesson Shield it held. Once again, he checked the gun for safety and dropped it into his pocket. He never liked to go visiting bad guys poorly armed and, in the right hands, the light-weight Shield had a decent enough stopping power for most situations. He stepped away. During his pat-down, he found and confiscated her mobile and a spare magazine for the Sig.

"You can turn around now."

Chang dropped her shoulders, but she kept her hands raised and turned.

"What now?" she asked.

"You and I are going for a short drive."

"What!"

"You heard me."

"Griffin, listen to me. You're about to add kidnapping a federal agent to charges of assaulting an officer of the law. That's serious jail time."

Kaine grimaced. "I know, but it can't be helped. Believe me, if I could leave you, I would. But you're my ticket out of here. Lower your hands."

She followed his instructions. Again, she did it slowly. From his prone position on the floor, the sheriff's breathing had quietened.

"Help him into the chair. Must be uncomfortable for him down there. Don't make any rash moves. I'd hate to have to use this Sig, but I will if you force me to."

He wouldn't shoot an innocent woman, of course he wouldn't, but Chang didn't know that.

She struggled with the sheriff's near dead weight, and Kaine added his help with a hand under Hawksworth's sweaty armpit.

"That's good, Special Agent Chang. Now handcuff him to the arm of the chair, if you please."

Chang glowered at him, but did as she was told. Kaine waved her away with the Sig and checked the cuffs were secure. He also removed the sheriff's keys from his utility belt—and his mobile.

"Sorry about this, Sheriff," he said, resting a hand on the lawman's shoulder, but keeping one eye on the Special Agent. "If I could think of a better way to do this, I promise you, I would."

Some colour had returned to Hawksworth's cheeks, and the pain in his teary eyes had eased, to be replaced with the fire of anger.

"When I get out of these cuffs, Griffin," he gasped, "I'll be comin' for you."

Kaine nodded. "I know, Sheriff. I know. And I truly am sorry. I'll be borrowing that nice SUV of yours, too. But I promise to treat it with respect. I'll pay for the gas and any damage done. You can count on that."

Kaine squeezed Hawksworth's bony shoulder once more and stood. He faced Chang and tapped the arm of his glasses.

"*Whatcha, Mr K. Corky thought you was going dark? Ah, right. You've got company.*"

"Is there a back way out of here?" Kaine asked. "A loading bay or something? Over."

"No idea," Chang answered, her tone sour. "I only arrived this morning and we weren't given a guided tour."

"*She don't know your talking to Corky, hey, Mr K?*"

"That's right. Well, is there?" He stopped using the comms protocol to keep Chang guessing. Maybe she'd think the British lunatic was talking to himself.

"*Yeah, there is, but it'll take you through a load of locked doors and*" *right past the changing rooms, and they're full of cops right now. Best if you head for the front doors."*

"At least I'll know the way."

"Huh? What are you talking about?" Chang asked. Her worried frown made it clear she thought she was watching a man in the middle of some form of a breakdown.

"Sorry, Special Agent Chang, but like I said, you're my key out of here. We're leaving now. But remember, I'm armed and extremely dangerous. No false moves."

Oh dear. So many clichés.

Kaine smiled and added, "I've always wanted to say that."

"Fool!"

Kaine tutted. "Is that the way you were taught to speak to a suspect, Special Agent Chang?"

"Bite me!"

"Tempting, but this isn't the time. And, as I said, I'm already spoken for. Now, snap to it."

He stuffed the Sig into his pocket, keeping his hand on the grip but his finger off the trigger. Briefly, he wondered how many badly trained gunmen had shot themselves in the groin when mishandling their firearms? He took hold of Chang's upper arm and turned her towards the door.

"Open it and turn right. If we meet anyone on the way, you're escorting me to my car, okay?"

"There ain't no one in the corridor, Mr K. Right now, you're clear all the way to the front desk. But hurry. No telling when Griezmann's gonna start wondering where his Special Agent's gotten to."

"Relax, Mei. Hope you don't mind my using your first name. Can't keep calling you 'Special Agent' all the time. Far too long-winded a handle. You can call me Bill, if you like."

"I'll see you rot in hell before we're friendly enough to be on first name terms."

Kaine smiled. Chang showed plenty of courage under pressure. In that respect, she reminded him of Lara.

They reached the end of the corridor and she stopped briefly before turning left. Kaine seized her upper arm and tugged her in the opposite direction.

"We turn right here. Don't try my patience."

They took the right and headed down the long corridor leading to the brightly lit main entrance.

"If you're wondering why the sheriff isn't raising all sorts of hell right now," Kaine said to pass the time, "he's probably screaming his lungs out, assuming he's forgotten the family room's sound-proofed. That's the reason I walked right into you when I was leaving."

"When you were escaping, you mean?"

"Corky likes her, Mr K. Special Agent Chang's a real pistol."

"Yep, so do I."

"What?" she asked.

"I said, yes, that's right. When I was escaping. I also disabled the room's emergency alarm. I'm afraid Sheriff Hawksworth's in for a bit of a wait. Still, it'll give him plenty of time to recover from my ... little love taps."

"You beat up an old man."

"He'll recover soon enough. Nothing I did will cause him more than a few hours' discomfort. I know what I'm doing."

Hopefully.

"Look, you don't strike me as a man on the edge, Griffin. What's this all about?"

While she talked, Chang's gait changed marginally. She turned her head slightly and lowered her right shoulder. She'd clearly seen the fire alarm attached to the wall up ahead and wanted to distract Kaine's attention.

"Don't bother, Mei," he warned.

"What do you mean?"

"I imagine you've noticed the fire alarm and want to cause me some distress. Don't bother. My invisible friend has disabled the alarms temporarily. Isn't that right, Base?"

"Sure is, Mr K. Corky's been isolating each alarm as you pass it. Wouldn't want to put the building at risk by cutting them all off at once. By

the way, you're still alone and the entrance foyer is empty, too. But get a wriggle on, eh?"

"You have an invisible friend?"

Still walking slowly, SA Chang half-turned at the waist and squinted sideways at him.

He gave her a cheeky smile and added a shrug.

"Yep, that's right. Can't tell you his name, though. It's a secret. Go on, try the alarm. Break the glass if you fancy it."

She shook her head. "And get a bullet in the back? No thanks. I can wait."

"Suit yourself, but step lively. I don't have all afternoon."

He hurried her along the happily deserted corridor until they reached the half-glass double doors guarding the foyer. She stopped.

"What's wrong now?" he asked.

Chang turned to face him fully, an expression of triumph brightening her young face. She pointed at the keypad attached to the wall.

"The doors are locked, and I don't have the code."

Kaine smiled back. "Give the right-hand door a tug."

"It's locked, I'm telling you!"

He eased her to one side and stole a quick peep through the glass. Empty. Still smiling, he grasped the handle and pulled. The door opened inwards, free and easy. And silent.

"After you, my dear," he said, giving her a gentle shove.

"How did you do that?"

"I told you. My invisible helper's on the case."

"*He sure is, Mr K.*" Corky chuckled in his ear.

As expected, the lobby stood deserted. Kaine took his reluctant companion by the hand and dragged her towards the entrance. The closer they drew to the main doors the more she struggled to break his grip. Thankfully, she didn't call out.

"Calm down, Mei. I really don't want to hurt you."

At the doors, he stopped and gave the place the once-over.

The sun had lowered since his arrival, but it still looked hot and dusty in the parking lot. The sheriff's SUV stood tantalisingly close.

Not far now.

"Special Agent Chang!" a man yelled. "Where the hell are you going?"

Kaine turned. He spotted them through the half-glass doors. Griezmann and the overweight Mark Steiner raced along the internal corridor, guns drawn. Behind them, a line of dark-clad agents followed.

CHAPTER TWENTY-SIX

Sunday 21st May – Early Evening
Pine Creek, Arizona, US

Kaine crashed through the main doors, dragging Mei along behind him by her wrist. It would have been quicker to leave her behind, but their close proximity might be the only thing stopping Griezmann and his buddies from opening fire.

"Let me go!" Mei screamed, finding her voice again.

She dug in her heels and grabbed onto a door handle, stopping them dead.

"Sorry 'bout this, Mei."

Kaine bent her thumb back to break her grip.

She yelped.

"I did say sorry."

He tugged her arm over his shoulder, ducked, and pulled her into a fireman's lift. She kicked, fought, and screamed the whole way. Fortunately, she didn't weigh a whole lot more than his backpack.

Outside, the temperature hadn't fallen by much. Before taking more than half a dozen steps towards the sheriff's SUV, Kaine found himself gasping for breath, and the sweat was pouring out of him—the result of a combination of the heat and the high altitude.

He released his grip on the Sig, took hold of the sheriff's key fob, and pressed one of the buttons. Nothing happened. He pressed another and the indicators flashed orange twice.

"*The SUV's already open, Mr K. Corky told you that back in the lockup.*"

"Sorry, I forgot."

"Forgot what?" Mei asked, still fighting.

"Nothing."

"What are you saying?"

Kaine yanked open the rear passenger door, tossed her in, and slammed the door closed before she could recover. The prisoner cage would keep her secure until he found a place to set her free.

With the backpack shucked off and thrown onto the front passenger's seat, he dived behind the wheel and had the engine fired up before securing his seatbelt. He selected drive, stamped on the accelerator, and they took off at tyre-squealing speed. The all-wheel-drive powertrain and traction control helped keep the wheels on the road and the bonnet pointing forwards.

The SUV's tyres screeched on concrete as Kaine reversed his route from earlier, and they sped through the quiet back streets of Pine Creek.

In the cage behind him, Mei had untangled her arms and legs and started slamming her open hands against the plexiglass and mesh screen separating the prisoner cage from the driver's cabin.

"Stop!" she screamed. "What the hell are you doing? Let me out!"

The rear-view mirror showed her red and angry face clear and sharp.

"Soon," Kaine said. "I promise. Soon as I'm out of town and safe, I'll release you. And stop banging on that panel. It's shatterproof. You'll only hurt your hands."

She kept hammering.

Kaine tapped on the brakes and the Ford slowed abruptly. Mei's face mashed against the panel, her cheek and nose flattening. She yelped. Kaine picked up speed again, and Mei slammed against the back of the seat.

"Seatbelt on, Mei," Kaine called.

He dabbed the brake pedal once again, and she bounced around a little more.

"I can keep this up a lot longer than you."

He made a sharp right onto 5th Street, and another onto Main Street, heading northwest. Since leaving the precinct house, they hadn't encountered a single other vehicle.

Mei righted herself and fought with her seatbelt, struggling to locate the clasp.

Kaine kept glancing in the rear-view, expecting to see blue flashing lights.

Nothing.

The road straightened. Kaine added more pressure to the accelerator, and the big SUV powered ahead, topping ninety miles an hour on the dust-covered highway.

"*In case you're wondering, Mr K, there ain't no one chasing you right now.*"

"Why not? Over."

"*For some reason, the exit doors to the police station are jammed. Right now, the cops are locked inside their own shop! Shame that, eh?*"

"Base," Kaine said, smiling and reducing speed to a more comfortable level, "you are a naughty fellow. Over."

"*Yep.*"

His chuckle squeaked through the comms unit, making Kaine smile.

Finally, Mei snapped her seatbelt into position and glowered at him through the mirror. She swept her hair from her eyes and used her fingers as a comb to pull it into some sort of order.

"You can't get away," she shouted above the quieting roar of the hardworking engine. "This car has a tracker. My people will be on your tail in minutes. The cops will be setting up road blocks, too."

"Thanks for the warning, Mei," Kaine said, grinning into the rear-view mirror, "but I'm happy to take my chances."

Low buildings flashed past on either side of Main Street. Still, the roads were clear. Within half a mile, the houses disappeared and wilderness and mountains stretched up high above them on both sides.

"Take the next left," Corky ordered. *"And take care, you'll be going off-road."*

Mei mumbled something under her breath, but Kaine missed it while fighting to keep the big truck on the road through a series of sharp turns. The dirt track cut through scrubland populated with thick bushes and widely spread conifers. They bucked and bounced on the uneven surface. Kaine eased his foot off the accelerator a little more and their speed fell back to a slightly more manageable bronco ride at thirty mph.

Another glance in the rear-view showed Mei with one hand clamped onto the grab-strap over the door, the other fisted on the seatbelt's strap running across her shoulder, struggling to hold herself in place. Looking at her in the bouncing mirror image, something was off.

Something had changed but Kaine couldn't think what.

With no signs of pursuit behind or ahead, Kaine slowed the car even further, keeping their speed hovering around a bone-jarring fifteen. Fast enough for the terrain.

"What were you doing with the sheriff?" Kaine asked.

Mei frowned and clamped her mouth shut. It made her look like a little girl who'd been refused her favourite soft toy. Kaine laughed and repeated the question with more force.

Still, she refused to answer.

"Come on, Mei. Loosen up. Relax a little. You should be trying to gain my trust. If you wanted to ask me some questions, now's your chance. Ask away."

Mei's eyes finally turned to the rear-view. She took a preparatory breath, but hesitated.

"Come on, Mei. What does the training manual say about hostage situations? Look, let's make it a quid pro quo. You answer my questions and I'll answer yours. We'll take it in turns, and I'll go first."

"Why do you get to go first?"

"Because I have all the guns."

He winked at her through the mirror. She scowled back.

"Tick tock, Mei. I'll be letting let you out soon and it will too late. You answer one of my questions and I'll answer one of yours. Deal?"

Her scowl eased and she nodded.

"Great, now we're getting somewhere. So, why did you accompany Sheriff Hawksworth to the cells?"

"Your glasses," she said, barely loud enough for him to hear above the bouncing, chattering SUV.

"My glasses?"

"You left them on the table and I wanted to return them."

Really?

"That was very kind of you." Again, he smiled into the mirror and tapped the side of his frames. "But I had another pair in my backpack. I always keep a spare set."

Glasses!

The Special Agent wasn't wearing her specs. No wonder she looked different. Without her glasses, she looked even younger. She could easily have passed for a college student.

"Were you worried about me not being able to see properly?"

She nodded, but didn't speak.

"Where are your specs?"

She sniffed.

"They fell off when you threw me over your shoulder."

"How well can you see without them?"

This time, she shrugged.

"Well enough, thank you."

"And you brought me my glasses because you felt sorry for me?"

"And to check on you. Wish I hadn't bothered now."

She released her hold on the straps and folded her arms, petulance evident in every abrupt movement. If she'd pushed out her lower lip again, it would have completed the picture.

Kaine laughed.

"I appreciate the thought, Mei. I really do, but there's nothing wrong with my eyesight. In fact, I have better than normal visual acuity."

"That's not what it says on your résumé. And I checked the lenses. They're really weird."

"Résumés aren't always one hundred percent accurate, Mei."

"Stop calling me that. I'm Special Agent Chang to you, Griffin."

She uncrossed her arms and turned her head to look out the window.

They drove in silence for ten miles, climbing uphill all the way, until Kaine felt safe enough to search for a stopping place. To the left, the treeline backed away into a small clearing. Kaine rammed on the brakes, tweaked the wheel, and turned the SUV into the patch of open ground.

Kaine slid the gear selector into park, rolled down his window, and the raucous cheeps, barks, and howls of the neighbourhood wildlife instantly crowded out the momentarily silence. A distant waterfall crashed over rocks and dived into a deep plunge pool, the noise unmistakeable. It promised to be a place of great beauty, but he wouldn't be staying long enough to see it in full daylight.

He released his seatbelt and twisted in his seat to face the back.

"Mei," he said, quietly, "I am not your enemy."

She stared at him. If she could shoot daggers from her eyes, he'd be dead in a heartbeat.

"You incapacitated the sheriff, escaped from lockup, and kidnapped a federal officer. What part of that sentence suggests that you are *not* my enemy?"

"Good point," he replied, evenly, "but I didn't hurt Sheriff Hawksworth. At least, not permanently. Apart from a couple of small bruises, he'll be none the worse for wear in an hour or two. As I've tried to tell you before, I do know what I'm doing."

"And what is that, Griffin? What exactly are you up to?"

"You know precisely what I'm up to. My friend is being held in Camp Pueblo, and I'm going to get her out before your people arrive and put her in even greater danger."

Mei opened her mouth to say something, but changed her mind and closed it again.

"Why did you really visit me in the lockup? And don't give me that nonsense about my glasses."

She turned her head and stared through the side window again, her eyes scanning the terrain through the gathering darkness.

"If you're wondering why your people aren't here yet, don't. My invisible friend has disabled the car's tracking system. Your buddies aren't coming anytime soon. And my friend also tells me the nearest police helicopter is more than ninety minutes away. We're all alone out here, you and me."

She snorted and shot him a look that was both derisive and angry.

"And to think I took pity on you. You belong in an asylum."

He laughed. "Is that the way they teach you to talk to fugitives in Quantico? I'd have thought you'd try to keep me calm and lucid. After all, if I really was a nutter, I might be offended. Who knows how I'd react. I might even throw a wobbly."

Mei frowned deep and long, clearly finding it difficult to come to terms with the way her day had panned out.

"What's a 'wobbly'?"

"Loosely translated, it means 'throwing a fit of rage'. Now, do I look like I'm throwing a wobbly, or do I appear calm to you?"

Mei studied him for a moment before shaking her head.

"You appear calm, but looks can be deceiving. I have no idea what's going on beneath the surface. For crying out loud, you think you're talking to an invisible man!"

"He has a name, you know. But like I told you back at the police station, it's a secret."

"*Tell her it's Bob. Corky's always wanted to be called Bob.*"

Kaine tilted his head. "Apparently, he's happy for you to call him Bob."

She raised an eyebrow. Not by much, but enough for Kaine to make it out, despite the increasing gloom of dusk.

"Bob?"

Kaine dipped his head.

"That's right."

"And this Bob's in your head?"

"Nope," he answered, smiling and shaking his head. "He's in my ears. I can hear him through my bones."

"For pity's sake. You're not making any sense."

He grinned and held up his empty hands. "All will become clear, my dear."

"'My dear'?," she scoffed. "That's even worse than calling me by my first name."

"Okay, Mei it is, then. Right now, shall we get down to business?"

"What business?"

"The Q and A. Why did you really come to visit me in my cell? And don't give me that nonsense about returning my glasses."

"You don't got all day."

Kaine checked the time on the dashboard clock and nodded, but didn't answer. Speaking to himself—again—might undo the little progress he'd made so far.

"I don't have long, Mei. So let's make this quick and truthful, okay. No lies. Why the visit?"

She frowned. "Okay, the truth. I *was* bringing you your glasses, but that was only my excuse. You were clearly worried about your friend, and I wanted to reassure you we weren't about to go in all guns blazing. We're not like that. At least, that's what I thought, but …."

"But?"

"The way SAC Griezmann organised the raid … it worried me. The man's an opportunist. Ambitious, you know. Doesn't care who gets hurt so long as it helps him climb further up the ladder. The way he talked to SSA Beddow. Goading him, almost. I didn't like it one little bit."

"Agreed," Kaine said, nodding slowly. "It looked to me like Griezmann was setting up Beddow to take the blame if things turned pearshaped."

She jerked upright. "How the hell do you know that?"

Kaine shrugged. "Do you still have my glasses?"

"Hold on. Quid pro quo, remember?" she said. "You're supposed to answer *my* question next."

"I am. Do you still have my glasses?"

She leaned to one side, giving herself room to reach into her jacket pocket. "I popped them into my glasses case for protection."

"Put them on."

"No, I tried them. They don't work for me."

"Put them on," he repeated. "Trust me."

Hesitantly, she did as he asked.

"Okay," she said, "they're a little heavier than mine and the lenses are clear. So what does that prove?"

"Hullo, Ms Chang. This is Bob, Bill Griffin's invisible friend."

Kaine heard both the words and the ensuing chuckle through his backup glasses.

"What the hell!"

Mei yanked the specs from her face and peered at them. She turned them over, examining the arms closely.

"Damn me! It's a radio."

"They're much more than that, Mei. Put them back on."

She obeyed.

"The arms act as receivers and transmitters," Kaine said.

"Yep," Corky added. *"They use bone conduction technology. Hang on a tick while Bob adjusts them to your prescription ... wait. There, you go! Neat, eh?"*

Mei jerked her head back. Her eyes widened as Corky worked his magic.

"How the hell—"

"Don't get him started on the techie stuff, Mei. He'll blind you with the science. Or should that be deafen you?"

She shook her head and glared at Kaine.

"I know about liquid crystal focal adjustment, Griffin. What I'm worried about is how he got my prescription."

"Now, that's a different story, Special Agent Chang. But Bob ain't saying nothing 'bout that. It's what's called proprietary info. Want Bob to show her the camera, Mr ... ah, Mr G?"

"Later. We need to crack on."

"Oh my God," Mei said, more to herself, and removed the glasses again. "These things are brilliant. I can see perfectly and the sound's clear, too. I could hear him inside my head. What was that about a camera?"

"Later," Kaine answered.

"This is how you knew what Griezmann was saying in the briefing, yes? You left the glasses on purpose?"

"Exactly. Now it's my turn. Given your reservations about SAC Griezmann, what did you hope to gain by talking to me in the family interview room?"

Mei brushed the fringe away from her eyes and replaced the glasses.

"Since your boss, Mr LeMaître, is so tight with Director McGregor, I hoped maybe he could put some pressure on Griezmann. Rein him in a little. I don't know, really. But our informant says there are at least a dozen innocent civilians in that camp."

"You have an informant inside Camp Pueblo?"

She shrugged and shook her head.

"We're not sure. The Bureau's tip line received an anonymous email two days ago, before we knew of Ms LeMaître's abduction. When Special Agent Steiner verified the contents of the email, I told Griezmann we should pull her out of Pine Creek, but by then—"

"Hold on. By 'pull her out of Pine Creek', you mean you *were* running her as an agent?"

"Yes, but by the time we received the email, it was already too late."

"Did the anonymous tip mention Sabrina by name?"

Mei shook her head again.

"So, you still don't know whether she's in the camp?" he asked, keeping his intel to himself.

"Not for certain, but if the Creed are holding other women at the camp, it seems likely that Ms LeMaître's there too."

"Okay, next question. What's the deal with Griezmann?" Kaine asked. "Why's he winding up SSA Beddow?"

"To cover his tracks," Mei said, lowering her eyes. "He should never have sent Ms LeMaître undercover in the first place. Since the moment she disappeared, he's been in a panic. His career's in the balance and he's desperate to save his ass."

"How's he going to do that? If Sabrina dies in the crossfire, the blowback on him will be horrendou—"

"That's just it, Griffin. There's no firm paper trail. The only people who know for certain that Griezmann was running Ms LeMaître as a CI are Mark Steiner ... and me. And Mark's been with Griezmann since FBI boot camp. They're practically blood brothers."

"But you know the truth, right?"

"So long as I'm still alive to tell it."

Kaine paused for a moment.

"Now who's sounding paranoid?"

"Yes, I know what it sounds like, but I'm serious. When Al Griezmann made me part of his QB Team—"

"QB Team?"

"His Quarterback Team. The three of us, Griezmann, Mark, and me are going to be locked together for the whole raid. If the raid falls apart there's going to be mayhem. You ever heard of Waco?"

"Yes," Kaine said. "I have."

"Right. No telling what's likely to happen when the bullets start flying. The way Al's been looking at me lately, it feels like I'm in the crosshairs, like he's keeping his enemies close, you know?"

"So, you came to me in the holding cell to—"

"Break you out."

Kaine snorted. "Really?"

"Don't look so doubtful, Griffin. I could have taken you down any time I wanted."

"You *let* me abduct you?"

"Yes."

She spoke with absolute confidence. She believed it, too.

"Why?" he asked. "Why let me take you?"

"Seemed like the best way to get out from under those same crosshairs. Now, I'm free to act."

"Act how?"

"Ms LeMaître and those poor women are in danger, and I don't want any of them getting hurt."

Me neither.

"So, what's your plan Special Agent Chang?" Kaine asked.

If she had a plan, Kaine wanted to hear it. It wouldn't have taken much to improve on his.

CHAPTER TWENTY-SEVEN

Mount Garrett, Arizona, US

Kaine waited for Mei to speak. It didn't take her long to disappoint him.

"Your boss is ESAPP's Chairman, Maurice LeMaître," Mei answered, using her index finger to push the overlarge glasses to a more comfortable position on her nose. "You have a way to contact him directly, right?"

"Maybe."

She pointed to the glasses that had again slipped down her nose.

"Using these and your invisible friend, Bob?"

"Possibly. What do you want me to tell him?"

"Tell him to get Director McGregor to call off the raid. There's still time."

"Ah, I see. I don't think that'll work. Maurice LeMaître isn't really my boss, and I'm not sure he has as much clout with your Director as he thinks. Bob, how's Mr LeMaître getting on? Over."

"He's hit a brick wall. Director McGregor's currently incommunicado.

259

He's in a meeting with the Joint Chiefs of Staff and the Director of Homeland Security. Apparently, they're expecting POTUS to drop by any minute. Could be an all-nighter. They can't be disturbed."

"What about Deputy Director Hallam? Over," Mei asked "Bob" directly.

"Apparently, she's in the same meeting. At least that's what her PA keeps telling him."

"Damn. Not good. Over."

"Too right, Mr G. Too right."

"Okay, next question," Kaine said to the rear-view mirror. "How many teams do you have watching the camp right now?"

"What makes you think—"

"Come on, Mei. There's no way you don't have eyes on the camp this close to an op going live. My guess is they've been on station for at least the past twenty-four hours. At least, that's the way I'd have set it up. Only an idiot would organise a raid at sunup without having spotters on the ground overnight. Not even Griezmann would rely solely on satellite imagery. Anything could go wrong."

"Okay, okay. You're right. There are teams in situ, but I'm not about to give up their locations without getting something from you first."

Kaine studied her for a moment before replying.

"What do you propose?"

"You need to convince me that you're one of the good guys. For all I know, you're selling me a crock. If I give you the information, what's to stop you killing me and warning Colonel Caren? With all the money he has at his disposal, he'd pay you pretty well."

"Mei," Kaine said, meeting her eye, "my friend's in that camp. All I care about is getting her to safety. If I can help the other women at the same time, I'll do that, too."

"Can you prove that?"

"Nope. All I can do is give you my word."

"Your word? What the hell's your word worth to me? I don't know anything about you!"

Here we go. Economic with the truth.

"Despite what it said on my CV, I wasn't just a Royal Marine Commando."

"Yeah? What were you?"

"I ended up as a member of the Special Boat Service."

"The SBS? I've heard of you guys. Like our Navy SEALs, right?"

Kaine nodded.

She leaned forwards in her seat and took a closer look at him.

"Most of the Navy SEALs I've seen are huge, beefcakes. You're a bit on the ... light side."

"So I'm told."

Kaine stole another glance at the dashboard clock. Corky wasn't wrong about the time passing quickly. He had to wrap up the Q&A, pronto.

"SBS, huh?"

"That's right."

"You had it redacted from your résumé?"

He nodded. "SOP."

"Yeah, I guess so."

She nodded slowly, as though taking in the new information. Her frown suggested doubt.

"People in my line of work like to keep a low profile. Black Ops, you know?"

"Hmm, I guess so ... still."

"You still haven't answered my question," Kaine said, moving swiftly along. "How many spotters do you have at the compound?"

"There are three teams of two," she answered after a momentary delay.

Progress of sorts.

"Locations?"

"It's my turn to ask."

"Go ahead."

"What's your plan?"

"Not sure yet, I'm working on it."

"You're going to try and bust your friend out before the raid."

"*This here's one smart cookie, Mr G.*"

"Yes, I am, Bob," Mei said, "and don't you forget it."

"Okay," Kaine said, "assuming Mr LeMaître can't contact Director McGregor in time to force Griezmann to call off the raid, I'm going to have to pay Camp Pueblo a visit. And really quickly."

"Will you take me with you?"

Not a chance.

"We'll see. Convince me you're worth it. Your obbo teams," he asked, "where are they and how are they equipped?"

"They're at positions OP1, OP2, and OP4."

"Night vision glasses? Sniper scopes?"

She nodded. "NVG and each team has at least one sniper."

"If they're spotted, what are their orders?"

"Griffin, these are some of the best in the business. If the teams don't want to be seen, they won't be."

"Yeah, sure. So what are their orders in the 'highly unlikely' event they're seen. Will they engage or withdraw?"

"Withdraw," she answered, instantly. "They'll hightail it to the agreed RV point and await further instructions."

"Thanks. Bob, exactly how far away from Pine Creek are we? Over."

"Nine and a half kilometres," Corky shot back so fast it was almost as though he was expecting the question.

Kaine flinched. Mei looked fit and strong. Even taking her time and yomping in the dark, it would take her less than two hours to reach help and raise the alarm. Too soon. On top of which, although they'd encountered no traffic so far, she might flag someone down and speed up her return to the police station. He'd have to drop her off much further out. Unless ...

He reached up to the overhead instrument cluster, and flicked on the courtesy light. Mei blinked hard, momentarily dazzled by the brightness.

"Okay," he said, staring into her eyes, "I'm taking you with me. But we need to get the ground rules straight."

She met his eyes.

"What ground rules?"

"I've lost count of the number of night-time incursions I've made."

"So?"

"So, I'm in charge. I give the orders. Okay?"

She dipped her head in a nod.

"Okay? Let me hear you say it."

"Okay, I agree. You're calling the shots."

"I say jump, you ask—"

"How high?"

"Good," he said, shooting her a grim smile. "Now we can go rescue Sabrina."

"And the other women?"

"If we can. Settle in, it's likely to get a little more bumpy back there."

Kaine started the engine and reversed back onto the narrow track. He gunned the motor and headed into the growing darkness, climbing higher with every wheel revolution.

The sidelights picked out eyes in the darkness—a mountain lion crossing the track. Kaine eased the pressure from the accelerator to allow the big cat to cross before gunning the engine and picking up speed to a full-bore twelve mph. The sheriff's SUV bounced and yawed like a RIB crashing through the breakers of a rocky cove.

Kaine almost felt at home.

———

During the drive, Mei sat with her head turned towards the window, apparently watching the sun setting over the western mountains. Every now and again, her eyes closed and she seemed to be dozing off until they hit a bump, she butted the window, and woke with a start.

They hadn't talked for twenty minutes.

He took his chance and tapped the left arm of his glasses three times.

"Alpha One to Bravo One, are you receiving me? Over."

He spoke quietly but received no response.

In the back, Mei didn't stir.

Kaine repeated the call.

"*Bravo One to Alpha One,*" Dubois answered, sounding tired and disheartened, "*receiving you strength five. Over.*"

"Sitrep. Over."

"*I've hit a bit of a snag. One of the guys I need to talk to is dragging his heels, but I should receive the final intel by early tomorrow morning. How's it going your end? Over.*"

"Tickety-boo, thanks. Don't worry about the ransom, we won't be needing it. Bravo One, I've located the target. Over."

"*You've got her? That's fucking—that's great. How is she? Can I talk to her? Over.*"

"No, I don't actually have her yet, but I do know where she is. Over."

"*Where—Goddamn it. Where the hell is she? Over.*"

"Camp Pueblo, Renshaw County. I'm on my way there right now. Night-time infiltration. Over."

"*Camp Pueblo? Yeah, I've heard of it. It's on my list of Caren's properties. How you getting there? Over?*"

"Overland. Where are you right now? Over."

"*In my SUV, waiting for my contact. Why? Over.*"

"Power up your GPS. Over."

"*It's already on. I've got the engine running, too. Freezing my butt off out here. Over.*"

"Okay, plug these numbers in." Kaine read the co-ordinates from the GPS on the sheriff's SUV. "Got them? Over."

"*Christ, Alpha One. Looks like you're in the middle of nowhere. Over.*"

"I'm on a dirt track hugging the southwest face of Mount Garrett. At this speed, I'm still more than an hour out. Over."

"*Yep, I got you. Jesus, you're miles away. You got an RV in mind? Over.*"

"One moment. Over."

Kaine tapped the arm of the glasses to cut the connection with Dubois.

"Alpha One to Base. Have you been listening? Over."

"*Sure have, Mr G. About ten kilometres up ahead, there's a lookout post for fire wardens. It's a couple of hundred metres below Black Buck Ridge.*

Looks plenty big enough for a meet. The coordinates are on the screen now."

"Brilliant. Thanks, Base. Over."

"You is welcome, Mr G."

Kaine re-established the link with Dubois.

"Alpha One to Bravo One. You still there? Over."

"That's an affirmative. Over."

"There's a small open space about five clicks southeast of the camp, just below Black Buck Ridge. Looks like a decent spot for an RV. Plenty of tree cover, too. 32.709 degrees north, 109.896 degrees west. Over."

"Hell. That's at least three hours away. Over."

"I can't wait that long. Over."

"Goddamn it, Griffin! Don't you fucking dare go in without me! You need my help. I'll be there soon as I can. Bravo One, out."

Kaine nodded to himself. No way was he going to wait three hours. It wouldn't leave enough time before sunup. He'd have to run with his original plan and go in alone.

He glanced in the mirror and found Mei sitting up straight, staring back at him.

"Who were you talking to?" she asked. "I couldn't hear anything through the glasses."

"A friend."

She rolled her head to one side and massaged her neck.

"You have friends?"

"Believe it or not."

"Anyone I know?"

"Doubt it. He's a senior ESAPP employee. One with the ear of Maurice LeMaître."

That much was true.

"He also knows Sabrina."

As was that.

"You gave him our location?" she asked, looking at the GPS screen in the middle of the dashboard.

No doubt about it, the woman didn't miss much. Under different circumstances, they might be able to work together, but Corky hadn't had time to run a full background check on her. Kaine had no idea whether she'd be an asset or a liability in the field.

She had to go.

———

"That's twenty kilometres from Pine Creek, Mr G. By the way, Corky's closed the comms with Special Agent Chang. She ain't hearing this."

"Thanks, Base. How far are we from the RV point? Over."

"Er, couple of kilometres."

"Thanks, Base. Alpha One, out."

Kaine hit the brakes and the big SUV slewed to an abrupt stop. The tyres threw up dust and small stones clattered against the skid pan. He released his seatbelt, pushed open the door, and climbed out into the chilly night. Cicadas chirruped and trees creaked and groaned as they lost the heat of the day. Wildlife rustled through the underbrush. An owl hooted to its mate and, in the distance, water cascaded over rocks.

He tapped on the rear window.

"Out you get."

From her angry expression and her vigorous headshake, Mei had worked out the reason for Kaine's instruction.

He open the rear passenger door and held out his hand.

"No," she said, her tone insistent. "No, Griffin. You can't. This is the middle of nowhere. You promised to take me with you!"

She struggled with her seatbelt.

"No, Mei, I said 'we'll see'. I'd rather not drag you out of there, but I will if I have to."

"You can't leave me out here. It's dangerous. There are black bears and mountain lions in these hills for fuck's sake!"

"They're more scared of you than you are of them. Keep quiet and still, and wait for daylight. You'll be fine."

The moment she released her seatbelt, he took hold of her wrist, yanked her out of the car, and released his grip. She dropped into the dirt, kicking and throwing punches. Most missed, but the ones that landed had no real power behind them.

Feisty, but a lightweight.

No match for him.

"Mei, I don't have time for this nonsense. Behave yourself."

Still on her backside in the dirt, she stopped struggling and held up a hand.

"Help me up then, you pig!"

Kaine stepped away.

"I'm sure you can manage. Wouldn't want to have to restrain you."

In the backwash from the SUV's parking lights, Kaine watched her scramble to her feet, glowering at him the whole way up. She dusted herself off and stood facing him, arms crossed.

"I thought you Brits were supposed to be gentlemen."

"I didn't want you to try anything. Hated the idea of having to cuff you. You might have ended up being hurt."

Mei uncrossed her arms and made fists, but she kept them lowered.

"So, what now?"

"You know what."

"You're really planning to leave me out here all night?"

"Afraid so," he said. "Can't think of an alternative. Like I said, if you stay still and keep quiet, you should be safe enough."

"Look, I can help you."

"In what way?"

"How are you getting past the OPs?"

"I'll manage. I've done this before."

"They've got night vision goggles. You'll be seen."

"I have my ways."

"You'll hurt them, won't you?"

"Not if I don't have to."

"But I can get you through. I know the point guards and they know me."

"Sorry, no can do. I can't take the risk. I really am sorry."

He took a stride towards her.

She screamed, spun on one leg, and snapped out a kick in one fluid, lightning fast movement. Kaine forearm-blocked the heel strike aimed at his jaw, and narrowly avoided the follow-up straight-fingered jab to his throat. She threw a roundhouse chop, and another, and another. All missed, but not by much.

Krav maga, the Israeli special forces martial art.

Kaine backed away and Mei burst forwards, raining vicious blows and kicks to his face, knees, and groin. Most missed, but a rising knee to his groin grazed his outer thigh. Any more force would have resulted in a dead leg.

Crap.

Mei circled to the right, stepping in close. Kaine danced to the left, mirroring her actions. She bobbed and weaved, searching for an opening.

Gasping for breath, she threw a left uppercut, aiming to land the heel of her open fist on the point of his chin. She followed it with a right elbow to the cheek. Both blows missed, but he felt the breeze of their passing.

A well-aimed and vicious toe-poke grazed his shin.

Too close. End this.

Kaine weaved right, jagged left, threw an open-handed right, clapping her left ear hard. She yelped, staggered backwards, shook her head.

He held up his hands and backed away, blocking any chance of her diving into the SUV.

"Sorry, Mei. That must have stung. Now, stop it. I can keep this up longer than you, but I don't have the time. The next blow I land will end this fast, and it's going to hurt."

Mei backed off, lowered her hands to her knees, and bent over. She pulled air into her lungs as though it was about to run out.

"Okay, okay. I'm done," she gasped, waving one hand in front of her bowed head. "You win."

Kaine stayed well back.

"It won't work, Mei. I'm not falling for it."

Developing the technique she'd just demonstrated would have

taken hours of gym-based training. Despite the altitude, she had no reason to be blowing so hard so soon.

Kaine pulled the Sig from his waistband and racked the slide.

"On your knees, Mei. Raise both hands and cross one foot over the other."

Mei looked up, straightened, and stopped gasping. She stood still, breathing deep and slow. Her eyes found the Sig. She smiled and shook her head.

"Give me the gun, Griffin. You don't have it in you to shoot an unarmed woman."

"Are you willing to risk your life on that?"

She hesitated for a moment before stepping closer.

"The way you defended yourself without really hurting me proves it. You won't shoot. Now pass it over."

Kaine nodded slowly. He lowered the Sig and de-cocked it.

"You're right, Mei. I'd never hurt an innocent."

Not intentionally.

"So, where does that leave us?" she asked, her arm still outstretched, hand open, palm up.

"Mr K, you got a sec?"

"Give me a moment, Mei," Kaine said, raising his hands and backing further away.

"Go ahead, Base. Over."

"While you've been pigging around in the dirt, Corky's finished running the check on Special Agent Chang."

"What have you found? Over."

"Nothing but good. She's as clean as the driven, Mr K. For what it's worth, Corky likes her."

"You do? Over."

"Yep. It ain't Corky's job to tell you what to do, but look how she's behaved since you took her. Pretty cool, Corky reckons."

"Okay, Base. I'll think on it. Alpha One, out."

Without taking his eyes off Mei, Kaine reviewed her actions since he'd abducted her. She'd been calm under pressure and had given up intel Corky confirmed as the truth. She'd had plenty of opportunity to attack him before this point and hadn't. She'd ignored her own safety to check on the sheriff in the FIU, and hadn't tried to earn his trust by playing him like an interrogation. She also hasn't done anything particularly sly or underhanded.

"What's wrong?" Mei asked. "What's taking you so long?"

"Look," Kaine said, "I don't really want to leave you out here. It is dangerous. But, I don't trust you, not fully, and you clearly don't trust me."

"So, we've got a standoff. What's the answer?"

"Bob."

"What do you mean, 'Bob'?"

"He's recording everything we say. If you double-cross me, or Sabrina dies as a result of anything you do—like giving a safe word to your OP teams—he'll go public with it, and you'll lose everything."

Her jaw clenched.

"You're threatening me, Griffin?"

He shrugged. "Sorry, but it's the only way this is going to work."

Mei balled her hands and pushed them into her thighs. She glared molten lava at him, turned her back, and yelled a string of swear words into the forest surrounding them. After a deep breath and a final frustrated roar, she faced Kaine, her expression one of simmering fury.

"So, now what?"

"Hop in the front. There's still a couple of miles to go to the RV point, and I'm going to have to run without lights."

Kaine open the front passenger door and offered to help her climb in, but she slapped his hand away.

"Don't you dare."

"Wanted to prove I haven't lost all sense of gallantry."

"Asshole!"

"Charming."

Smiling, he raced around the front of the SUV and dived behind the wheel. He fired up the SUV's crinkling-hot engine. He drove without running lights, slow and cautious, and they travelled at little more than marching pace. If nothing else it gave him time to plan the next stage.

It took more than an hour and three course corrections before they reached the lookout point. Mercifully, she kept silent to let him concentrate. The GPS' tracking showed an incomplete route and Kaine had to rely on gut instinct, moonlight, and his innate sense of direction.

Eventually, the SUV crested a steep rise. At the apex, the track turned sharp right and climbed further up the mountain, heading towards Black Buck Ridge. A narrower spur cut straight into the forest, heading sharply downhill. He took the spur and crawled fifty metres off the main track until he found a patch of pale ground that absorbed more moonlight than the surroundings. He pulled in beside a clump of red-stemmed dogwood bushes and well out of sight of the main dirt track.

He killed the engine and absorbed the ringing silence.

CHAPTER TWENTY-EIGHT

SUNDAY 21ST MAY – Evening
Mount Garrett, Arizona, US

The lookout post for fire wardens, a flat outcropping of rock below Black Buck Ridge and two miles from the summit of Mount Garrett, held space enough for the SUV to park but not to turn. When the time came to leave, he and Dubois would have to reverse to the nearest turning spot—where the trail forked. On the plus side, the tree line stepped well back from the ridge, and bushes and thick undergrowth hid the vehicle from the camp.

The parked SUV jerked and swayed in the heavily gusting mountain wind.

"This it?" Mei asked, straining to see through the windscreen and into the blackness.

"According to our travel guide."

"How did you manage to drive at night with no lights?"

"Practice. And, as I already told you, my eyes are pretty decent."

Kaine released his seatbelt and twisted to study her. He shook his head.

"That won't do."

"What won't?"

"Your white shirt. It'll stand out like a beacon."

"What do you suggest?"

"There's a dark t-shirt and sweater in my pack. They'll be way too big for you, but it'll have to do."

"You want me to strip off in front of you?"

"Mei, I'm an English gentleman. I promise not to look."

"Yeah, I believe you."

"Excuse me, please."

Kaine waved her to lean back into her seat and reached into the passenger footwell for his backpack. He searched inside by touch alone and fished out his final set of spare clothes.

"Here you go."

He offered her the bundle.

She snatched them from his outstretched hand and scrambled for the door release.

"Wait!" he snapped. "The courtesy light."

"Nobody's going to see it in this hollow."

"I said wait, damn it."

He found the roof-mounted light cluster and threw the switch.

"Okay, you can go now."

"It's pitch black out there. You're being an asshole."

"No, I'm trying to develop my full night vision, Special Agent Chang. And you'll need yours, too."

"Oh, I see," she said, offering nothing in the way of an apology.

She climbed out and the gusting wind immediately whipped her shoulder length hair into her eyes and mouth. The wind brought with it a faint but familiar sickly-sweet smell of battlefields and smouldering bodies.

Hell!

Kaine's stomach roiled.

She leaned back inside the cab.

"Do you smell that?" he asked.

She stood and sniffed the air before ducking into the cab again.

"Smell what?" Mei said, shaking her head, "can't smell anything but dirt and damp."

Really?

She grimaced before adding, "I ... er, need the rest room. Don't suppose you have any tissues in your backpack?"

Kaine resisted the temptation to roll his eyes, but he had discovered how much she knew about fieldcraft.

"Nope. Can't carry everything. Hang on a tick."

He searched the SUV's dashboard and found a packet of wet wipes in the dropdown glove compartment.

"These do?"

"In a pinch."

She snatched the packet from him and backed out of sight. Twigs crunched under her feet and undergrowth rustled as she fought her way deeper into the gloom.

"Crap!"

Kaine leaned over the passenger seat and pushed the door open, gripping the handle tight to prevent the wind sucking it out and tearing it from his grasp.

"You okay?"

"Yeah, yeah. Stay back. I dropped the wet wipes. But it's okay, I found them again."

"If you tried really hard, do you think you could make any more noise?"

"Shut it, Griffin."

"Steer clear of anything that looks like poison ivy."

"It's pitch black out here. Can't see a damn thing."

"There's plenty of starlight. Let your eyes get used to it."

"And what does poison ivy look like, anyway?"

"You're kidding, right?"

"Yes, I'm kidding! Now, close the door and leave me alone."

Kaine pulled the door and let it rest on the half-catch.

Once certain she was fully occupied, Kaine pulled the Swarovski Optik case from his backpack and removed the powerful EL Field Pro 10x42 binoculars. He unscrewed the right rear lens and tipped out the ceramic throwing dagger hidden inside. He rebuilt the binoculars, returned them to the case, and clipped it to the side of his belt, settling it comfortably on his hip. Smuggling the dagger through Tucson International had been a risk, but the ensemble failed to trip any of the scanners or raise any border guard attention. His and Alain Dubois' entry into the US had been a breeze.

He slid the blade into the sheath sewn into the leg of his chinos and tugged his heavy-duty socks outside the cuffs to hold it securely in place. The handle settled nicely against the outside of his calf. Well-hidden but with easy access.

Finally, he removed the tin of camouflage makeup and set to work, transforming himself for a night-time incursion by daubing it on his face, forearms, and the back of his hands. He checked the result in the rear-view mirror.

Satisfied with the effect, he tapped the arm of his glasses once.

"Alpha One to Base, are you receiving me? Over."

"*What's up?*"

Kaine sighed. Still no formalities.

"Are you still monitoring the police and FBI radio traffic? Over."

"*Yeah. The radio signal in and around Pine Creek is holding up steady enough. Griezmann's having kittens. Can't work out how you disappeared so quick. The guy don't know nothing 'bout old Corky's skills.*"

Kaine smiled. Corky had inadvertently given him an idea.

"What was that about the radio signal? Over."

"*It's like Corky told you this morning. The radio signal can be a little spotty in the mountains, 'specially when the weather turns nasty. Some of the outlying comms traffic's been breaking up.*"

"Is that so? Over."

"*Yep. Sure is. And mobile phone signals don't stretch out as far as where you is. There ain't no masts for twenty miles.*"

"What about the comms at the OPs? Over."

"*Holding up pretty good right now.*"

Kaine waited for the penny to drop.

"*Wind's blowing in the right direction—oh, hang on. Right. Corky gets you. Just a tick. Let's see what a little Corky magic can do ....*" The line fell silent for a full forty-five seconds. *"Yep, there you go. Houston, we have a teensy little problem. Ha!"*

"You haven't killed their radio signal completely? Over."

"Nah. That would be real sus. Corky's bleeding a local radio station into their signal. Intermittent, like. Don't want to make it too obvious or they'll be on their guard. But it is gonna drive 'em nuts. The station plays nothing but country."

Corky's infectious chuckle lifted Kaine's spirits. For the first time since leaving Pine Creek, his mood lightened.

"Corky, I don't know what to say. Over."

"Ain't nothing, to say. Anything to help Ms F. Get her out safe, will ya?"

"I'll do my best, Base."

My very best.

"Next bit of business Corky, are you able to show me the satellite view of the camp and add the FBI's observation points, please? Over."

"Yep."

Seconds later, Corky replaced the GPS map on the SUV's dashboard screen with the satellite image from the whiteboard in the auditorium. One by one, the five circles marked OP1 to OP5 appeared in the same positions as earlier. OP4, to the southeast of the camp seemed the obvious choice, since it was closest to the building from which Sabrina and Hulk had emerged.

"Thanks, Corky. Can you zoom in on that area in and around OP4, please? Over."

"Not without losing resolution. Best Corky can do is use the most recent satellite imagery and superimpose a topographical overlay on the image."

"Okay, give me the best you have. Over."

The screen changed to a close-up map view of the terrain around OP4. Kaine studied the map for a full five minutes, committing every icon and contour to memory. He latched onto a narrow hunting trail that ran alongside a stream through the densely packed woodland. It ran close by the observation post. More importantly, the stream would cover any noise he made, allowing him to move relatively quickly.

276

He closed his eyes, pictured the map on the image behind his lids, and opened them again to confirm and reinforce the memory.

"That's it, Base. I'm as ready as I'll ever be. Over."

"Will you be taking the specs with you?"

"No. I won't. Over."

"Why not?" He sounded disappointed.

"They're too heavy. I'll use the earwig."

"Corky won't be able to act as your eyes. Not until the next satellite pass, and that ain't 'til twenty-three minutes after sunrise. You'll be travelling blind."

"I've done it before. Over."

Kaine ran the calculation in his head. By the time the satellite had reached its optimal position over the camp—06:17—he'd either have found Sabrina and taken her clear of danger, or he wouldn't be in a position to use Corky's eyes anyway.

"Corky don't like it."

"Can't be helped, my friend. Hold on one moment. I'm swapping units. Over."

Kaine removed the heavy specs, stowed them in their case in a side pocket of his backpack, and removed the earpiece case from the same pocket. He fitted the bug into his left ear, tapped it once, and rubbed the soreness from the bridge of his nose.

"Comms check, Base. Over."

"Hearing you perfect."

"Excellent. In that case, I'm good to go. Alpha One, out."

He tapped the earpiece into inactivity.

"Are you done yet?" Kaine called.

"Yeah, I'm coming."

"No, stay right where you are. I'll be with you in a sec."

He eased open the driver's door, bent at the waist slightly, and ghost-walked around the rear of the SUV, moving as silently and smoothly as necessary for the demonstration. The twelve-metre journey would take the best part of five minutes.

One minute in, Mei called out, "Griffin, what's taking you so long?"

He ignored her and kept moving. Slowly. Soundlessly.

Three minutes in.

"Griffin, this isn't funny."

Anger made her shout. Fear made her voice quake.

Kaine approached from the side and crouched within touching distance, making sure to not to block the wind—which would be a dead giveaway.

He waited.

"Goddamn you, Griffin. If you've left me here …."

Arms outstretched, scrabbling the air, Mei stumbled towards the SUV. His dark sweater, three sizes too big for her, flapped and billowed in the blustery gale.

Kaine stood and followed, keeping close, and staying silent.

"Griffin, I swear to God …. Where are you?"

"I'm right here, Mei," he whispered, tapped her shoulder, and backed away.

She roared, spun, and threw a backhand punch aimed at where his head had been.

"Easy, Mei," Kaine said, holding up both hands. "Let's not go down that route again."

She regained her balance and stood still, panting.

"Damn you, Griffin. What the hell was that for?"

"A demo."

"A what?"

"A demonstration. You were expecting me, and you knew the direction I was coming from, but you heard and saw nothing."

Her shoulders relaxed.

"Okay, Griffin. You've got skills and I didn't see you coming. What's your point?"

She needs to ask?

He shrugged.

"No point. Just a demo."

"You were showing off?"

"Something like that."

She scowled, deep and hard. He could see her expression clearly, despite the gloom.

"Idiot!"

"Guilty as charged. Here, I found this in the car."

He held out his hand and gently touched her arm.

"What is it?"

"A rubber band, for your hair."

She snatched it from his hand and used it to tie a ponytail.

"Thanks," she mumbled. "Appreciate it."

Her first show of gratitude made a pleasant change.

She stared hard at his face, squinting into the darkness.

"Nice makeup job," Mei said. "Got any spare?"

"Just a sec."

Walking normally, but still taking care, Kaine returned to the car, retrieved the tin from his backpack, and offered it across. This time, Mei took it without resorting to snatching. Progress indeed.

"Need any help?"

"No thanks."

She dug two fingers into the thick paste and swiped it on, making a good fist of breaking up the shape of her face and killing the starlight reflecting off her smooth, pale skin.

"Okay, so, what have we got?" she asked.

"Come with me."

He took her forearm and led her towards the edge of the lookout point where a faint orange dome glowed the distance.

Kaine dug the binoculars out of their pouch and dropped down to lie prone at the edge of the ridge. The damp, musty earth failed to overpower the familiar odour that had been assaulting his nostrils from the moment he'd stepped out of the SUV.

Mei took her place beside him, but left a gap.

Below them to the northwest, some fifteen hundred metres distant, a wide, sharply descending valley cut between two steep-sided, tree-covered ridges.

Kaine found the source of the light easily enough—Camp Pueblo.

He raised the field glasses to his eyes, rotated the thumbnut, and the out-of-focus image sharpened.

A brazier-shaped bonfire burned bright and hot on the far side of the parade ground, bathing the front of each building in a demon radiance. No lights showed in any of the windows. Two men wearing dark boiler suits, facemasks and heavy gloves tended the flames. They tossed a huge log onto the fire and sparks erupted into the air around their heads.

Two more men patrolled the parade ground's perimeter. Each carried an M4 carbine at port arms, the muzzles pointing skywards as though they'd actually been properly drilled.

Kaine orientated himself to the terrain between OP4 and the camp, using both the light thrown from the bonfire, the four weak floodlights surrounding the parade ground, and the descending moon. He matched it to his memorised topographical map.

"That bonfire's weird," Mei whispered, sniffing the air.

"You can smell it now?"

"A bit late at night for a hog roast, isn't it?"

"It's not a hog roast," he said, darkly. "And that's no bonfire."

"What is it then?"

Kaine hesitated a moment before responding, but she needed to know the truth. If the demo hadn't done its job, the stench might be the final convincer.

"It's a funeral pyre."

Mei frowned, raised her head a little higher, and sniffed the air again. The skin showing beneath her hastily applied camouflage makeup blanched.

"Oh my God!"

She scrambled way from the edge and melted into the gloom. Seconds later, she started heaving into the bushes.

While Kaine studied the valley below, the retching eventually stopped, and Mei crawled back to his side. She'd tied a handkerchief over her nose and mouth.

"Sorry," she said.

"Not a problem," he said, reaching out a hand to squeeze her shoulder.

She jerked away from his touch.

"You don't think it's your friend on that fire, do you?"

Kaine was thinking exactly that and it turned his guts into knotted rope.

"Nope. Not a chance. We still have a couple of days before the ransom deadline. Why kill her now?"

"God, I hope you're right."

Me too, Mei.

"What's your plan?"

The pallor beneath her makeup remained, but her voice sounded stronger.

"The info you gave me earlier, was it true?"

"About the observation points?"

Kaine nodded.

"Yes, it's the truth."

"Do you know who's manning OP4?"

"No. Sergeant Schreiber allocated the OP teams. Why?"

"Just wondering. They're in my way. I'm going to have to pay them a visit."

"You know exactly where they are?" she asked, staring into the distance and frowning.

Kaine handed her the binoculars.

"Can't exactly see them from here, but take a look for yourself. See that stream shining in the moonlight?"

"I'm not blind, Griffin. I see it."

Wonders will never cease.

"Follow it down to where it cuts right and dives into the waterfall. Got it?"

"Yes."

"Take a left at that point and run the arc fifty metres or so. There's a tree with a broken branch showing white against the background. See it?"

"Yep, I see it. That where OP4 is?"

"Pretty much. I'll know for certain when I get down there."

Mei turned to face him.

"When *you* get down there?"

"Yep, just me. You're staying here to begin with."

"And then what will you do?" she said, anger flashing in her eyes.

"I'm going to introduce myself to OP4, nice and friendly. Then, and only then, I'll call you down."

"Why don't we go down together?" she asked, teeth gritted.

Kaine arched an eyebrow and waited for her to join the dots.

"The demo?" she said.

"Yep."

"But it'll take you ages to reach them. We can't afford to waste that much time. We should head down together."

"You'd make too much noise. They'd hear you coming a mile off."

"But whoever it is down there, they know me. They'd never—"

"With a supposed kidnapper on the loose and an agent missing, there's no telling how jumpy they'll be. Might even start shooting before we can identify ourselves. I can make it down there faster and more quietly alone than with you in tow. And that's an end to it."

"But they're fully trained federal agents. They won't shoot on sight."

No, of course they wouldn't.

"You're being ridiculous," she added.

"I'm not arguing, Special Agent Chang. You either stay here voluntarily and wait for my call, or—"

"Or what? You'll tie me up and leave me here to the mountain lions?"

"I'd rather not, but if you insist."

"Okay, okay. Point made."

Finally.

"Can we keep in touch through these?" She pointed to her glasses.

"Nope." He shook his head. "I'll need radio silence to concentrate during my approach. Keep the binoculars and try following my progress. It'll help pass the time."

"If I'm following you through these"—she held up the binoculars —"how are you going to call me when you get down there?"

He sighed. This was like training a rookie. Didn't the FBI teach their agents anything?

"Wear the glasses on the top of your head to keep the arms in contact with the bone. That way, you'll hear me when I call. Got it?"

"Yeah, yeah." She nodded. "Got it."

"It'll take me an hour or so to reach OP4," Kaine said, staring at her and making sure he had her full attention. "Don't get antsy. Wait for my call. Okay?"

"Yes, okay."

Before she could change her mind, Kaine slipped over the edge of the ridge and scrambled towards the bubbling stream.

CHAPTER TWENTY-NINE

Underfoot conditions stayed firm and relatively clear, and Kaine covered half the distance to OP4 in good time—less than fifteen minutes. The rest would take longer. Much longer.

Mountains stretched up dark around him, craggy and imposing, a heavy and barely visible weight in the near distance. Trees creaked and swayed on either side of the narrow trail—Ponderosa pine, Douglas fir, spruce, and aspen. The sharp tang of pine helped mask the stench from the diminishing pyre. The cicadas had quietened during the night, and mosquitoes weren't a problem at this altitude.

Small mercies, since he didn't have any insect repellent.

Not that he could use repellent during a covert approach. The smell would be a real liability. In Afghanistan, his sharp sense of smell had provided an efficient early warning system. The stench emitted by unwashed insurgents had saved his life more than once.

The stream he'd followed slowly veered away from the trail and shifted to the northeast, the burble of fast-flowing water growing more and more distant as he continued.

Clouds rolled in front of the moon. He dropped to one knee beside a feathery bush and took a short breather. The stiff north-easterly breeze dried the sweat from his face and drove away any noise he'd made during his overly rapid approach.

Somewhere below him, close by, OP4 and its two spotters lay in wait.

The clouds floated clear of the moon and, below him, the tops of the trees shone silver in the darkness.

Ahead, the thin trail he'd been following split in two. The right fork wound forwards, heading northeast, towards the stream and the mountains. The left fork cut a darker line into the trees, curving northwest, pointing straight towards the camp.

Kaine chose the right fork, taking the long way around and keeping the bonfire, the floodlights, and the breeze on his left.

One hundred metres, and twenty minutes later, a narrow gully split from the track, doubling back towards the camp and OP4. On the topographic map, it had shown up as the thin sinuous line of a dry gully. He sat on the edge of the lip and slowly wriggled his way into the void.

Sharp rocks grazed his palms, scraped his sweater, and caught on his chinos. His clothes wouldn't survive the night, but so what? His careful descent dislodged small rocks and stones, which rattled down the slope.

After ten minutes slow going, the gully levelled off, the ground opened out, and the rock walls spread away into the night. Trees stretched up around him. Fragrant, thorny bushes scratched his cheeks, clutched at his eyes, combed his hair. Slowly, barely breathing, he climbed into a sprinters' crouch.

Hidden somewhere close by, to his left, the two observers studied the camp.

Movement to his right in the pitch black.

He sensed rather than saw it.

A twig snapped.

He froze.

Five metres away. Something rustled the bushes. Something big.

A throaty growl. The foul stench of rancid breath—the breath of a mountain lion. The big cat snarled and leapt. Behind Kaine and to his right, another, smaller animal screeched. A snap of powerful jaws followed by more rustling and scraping as the big cat dragged its prey off to a quiet place. The animal would sate itself on the carcass and, if any meat remained, bury the leftovers and return to feast later.

Kaine breathed easier. Although mountain lions were reportedly afraid of humans, having a fourteen stone hunter-killer within striking distance of his throat didn't rate as the most comfortable situation he'd ever experienced.

"Fucking hell, Butch!" a man whispered, up ahead. "Did you hear that?"

Once again, Kaine froze.

"'Course I heard it, man. I'm not deaf."

Kaine heard Butch's hushed response clearly. Too clearly.

OP4 were close.

He'd almost stumbled right on top of them. Thankfully, their position lay northeast of him, upwind. With any luck, they wouldn't be able to hear, smell, or sense him.

Kaine tucked himself into the bole of a pine tree and peeked around its sharp-smelling trunk.

The bright gibbous moon and the camp's dim floodlights revealed Butch and his oppo as pale orange outlines. On the left, a heavyset man wearing his FBI ball cap reversed, lay propped up on his elbows, his back to Kaine, staring through a pair of long-range field glasses. He raked the binoculars through a narrow arc, taking in the whole of the camp.

The other man, much slimmer than his buddy, sat up, cross-legged. His glittering eyes searched the area where the mountain lion had downed its prey.

"Mountain lion, d'you think?" he asked, his voice hushed in awe.

"Wasn't a bear, that's for sure," Butch answered without turning from the binoculars. "Might have been Sergeant Schreiber, though. You ever heard the old man chow down?"

"Ha! Sure have," the other one said, trying to suppress a chortle. "Don't let him hear you saying that or we'll both be on a charge."

"Keep your voice down, Doofus," Butch hissed.

"How many times I gotta tell you, man. Quit callin' me that," Doofus said, almost talking aloud. "It ain't cool. And anyway, with this wind in our faces I could stand up and sing the *Star Spangled Banner* at the top of my voice, and those morons in the camp wouldn't hear a damn thing."

Kaine smiled. Doofus had a valid point, but his voice carried clear enough to Kaine, as did the crackling of the dying funeral pyre and the cloying smoke from some five hundred metres away.

On the plus side, the stiff breeze would make Kaine's final approach slightly less challenging.

"Goddamn it, Shane," Butch said, hurling it out as a forceful hiss. "This is all kinds of wrong. Why are we still here? I don't like it. Don't like it one little bit."

"Yeah, I know. You keep telling me."

"Mei's one of our own."

Kaine craned his neck and held his breath to make sure he didn't miss anything.

"I know that, too, man. And you still got the hots for her, huh?" Shane-Doofus said, his tone gently mocking.

"Shut the fuck up."

"I can understand why, too. She's real cute. If I weren't a happily married man, I'd have taken a shot at her myself. Yes, sir."

"Christ sakes, Shane. Will you let it go?"

"Sorry, buddy. My bad."

"Shit, man! We should all be out there searchin', not sitting here, freezin' our butts off. Fucking *Griezmann* should have called off the raid. This is so many shades of wrong."

The way Butch spat out the SAC's name showed disrespect bordering on insolence. Kaine half expected Shane-Doofus to dress his buddy down.

"The raid's still going ahead and we've got a job to do here," Shane said.

"You still watching our six?"

"Yeah, but like I said before, there's no chance of the Brit heading this way. The guy's in the wind."

"Mei could be lying dead in a ditch—"

"Don't go there, man. No value in it."

"This is so wrong, man."

"You already said. Repeating it won't change anything."

"Yeah, but—"

"No 'buts', Butch."

"What I wouldn't give to have the British asshole in my sights."

"Ain't gonna happen any time soon. How's he gonna sneak up on us through all that scrub without making enough noise to wake the dead?"

"Griffin's ex-Army. He'll have skills, so keep your eyes and ears open. What time you got?"

Shane peeled back the cuff of his jacket sleeve and pressed the nightlight on his wristwatch. The green glow showed a bearded face wearing a deep frown.

"It's oh-one-twenty-eight. I'd better get ready to call in."

"Better had, Doofus. Your turn."

"Butch, I swear to God—"

"You don't wanna be late again or Sergeant Schreiber will tear you a new one. And don't forget to ask what's happening with the search."

"Like I'm gonna forget about Mei!"

Pine needles rustled as Shane stretched out a hand and picked up an object from the ground by his side. He clicked on a handheld radio, and its green power LED brightened the gloom.

He pressed the PTT button.

"OP4 to QB. Come back. Over."

Shane paused for a second, repeated the call, and awaited the response. The response came as nothing more than an intermittent tinny hiss. A musical hiss.

"Hello? Repeat that, QB. Over. Fuck's sake."

"Radio still playin' up?" Butch asked.

"Can't hear anything but AZBC. Damned station's busting in on our channel again."

Butch pulled his eyes away from the field glasses and turned to his oppo.

"This is for shit, man. When are the bean counters gonna stump up for satellite phones? Fucking SOBs. This could cost lives."

"Hold on, they're back." Shane hit the PTT button again. "No. It's all quiet here, QB. Nothing's happened since the convoy left."

Kaine frowned.

Convoy?

"Quiet as the grave, here," Shane continued. "Any news of Mei—I mean, Special Agent Chang? Over."

He paused to listen to another response Kaine couldn't catch.

"No sightings at all? What about Griffin? Over."

More intermittent hissing followed before Shane ended the call with, "Thanks, QB. OP4, out."

The radio clicked, the green light disappeared, and once again, their little corner of the forest dimmed to an orange darkness augmented by the white light reflected by the rapidly descending moon.

"Nothing?" Butch asked.

"Not a damned thing," Shane answered. "Griffin's still in the wind."

"Mei?"

"No sign." Shane shook his head. "Far as anyone knows, she's still alive, though."

"God, I hope so. She's good people."

"I'll check in with the guys."

Another click foreshadowed the reappearance of the green LED, and Shane ran a monosyllabic tour of the other two OPs.

"They've seen the same as us. Bupkis," Shane reported. "None of them's happy 'bout leaving the search for Mei to the LEOs, neither."

"Yeah," Butch responded, "but I guess the locals will know the lay of the land. They'll be manning roadblocks, too. Which is no more'n we'd be doing."

"Okay, that's my work done for another hour," Shane said. "My turn for some shuteye, right?"

"How you gonna sleep with what's happing to Mei?"

"You know me, Butch. I can sleep on a porcupine. In any case, I won't be no help to her if I'm out on my feet."

"What about Griffin? You're supposed to be guarding my six."

"I told you, he'll be clear out of the state by now."

Kaine smiled.

No he won't.

"Wake me in fifty." Shane yawned long, hard, and loud. "You can call in the next report."

"Thought it was my turn for a break," Butch muttered, his eyes still attached to the binoculars.

"Like you're gonna be able to rest."

"Always envied you your ability to catch the zees."

"Sleep only comes to the innocent and the pure of heart, Butch, my man." Shane chuckled.

With twenty-five minutes to meteorological moonset—less until it disappeared behind the western mountain range—Kaine leaned against the tree trunk and forced himself to settle back and wait. The sun would be up in less than five hours, and predawn would arrive sooner. As he waited, his window of opportunity shrank.

Sitting on his backside, leaning against the rough and sticky bark, waiting for the moon to set couldn't have been any more excruciating, but he had no alternative. To close in on OP4 before moonset would be impossible.

Patience, Ryan. Patience.

––––––

Fifteen minutes earlier than scheduled, the moon dipped behind the western ridge, leaving a slowly diminishing haze of silver in its wake. In the middle distance, the sickening bonfire had burned itself into a glow of embers, and the sparse floodlights illuminating the valley dimmed the sparkling dots of a billion stars.

While Kaine endured the wait, Shane's breathing had settled into the long slow pattern of sleep, interspersed with the very occasional quiet snort. Each light snore caused Butch to mutter a curse under his breath.

Time to go.

Keeping the tree between him and his target, Kaine stood slowly, making sure his clothing didn't rustle or scrape against the bark. He stepped out from behind the tree and ghost-walked towards OP4.

CHAPTER THIRTY

MONDAY 22ND MAY – MICHAEL "BUTCH" Elkins
Camp Pueblo, Arizona, US

Michael "Butch" Elkins pulled away from the binoculars and tried to rub the grit from his tired and dry eyes.

Goddamned asshole of an SAC.

Griezmann, the glory-seeking SOB, should have called the raid off as soon as the Brit broke out of the cell. A jailbreak, for fuck's sake! How could the shit-for-brains have let that happen? No doubt he'd be blaming the local sheriff's department—or maybe even the damned janitor. Anyone but himself.

Whenever the moron screwed up, he always managed to shift the blame onto some other poor schmo, and he was forever backed up by the kiss-ass, Steiner. Fat fucking weasel.

Griezmann was a total fuck-up. Must have the juice on someone higher up or no way would he be in charge of anything more important than a school crossing.

Why let the raid continue when they should be searching for Mei? Like as not, the Brit would be on his way to warn the camp.

Drop a dime on the raid and earn himself some running away money.

Shit!

Damn, but Shane was dead right. Butch liked Mei. Liked her a whole lot. Hoped one day to pluck up the courage to ask her out. Never had the nerve, though. Not so far. Maybe not ever. Woman was out of his league. Too damn hot. And Griezmann obviously had his eye on her. Way he stared at her butt whenever he thought no one was looking.

Slimy prick.

The thought of Mei being at the mercy of a British nutjob made Butch's blood run cold. Why were they lying in the dirt while Mei was in danger, fighting off a madman?

Not right, damn it.

Jesus, Mei. Please be safe.

When they eventually found the guy, Butch would push his way to the front of the line to dish out the punishment. Griffin would suffer. Maybe Butch could engineer another escape attempt. Or an accident. Griffin wouldn't be the first prisoner to break his neck falling down the stairs.

No, sir.

And wouldn't that be a fitting end for anyone who'd abduct a federal agent.

A fitting end, sure enough.

Frontier justice.

Butch shook off his thoughts and resumed the position.

Eyes open, Butch. Concentrate.

The two fire-tenders had disappeared ages ago. They'd left in a truck after letting the bonfire die down. What the hell was that smell? Not quite pork, but something similar. Lamb, maybe? Definitely not beef though. His mouth watered at the thought of hot barbeque sauce being dribbled over some ribeye steaks.

Damn.

How could he be thinking of his stomach while Mei was out there somewhere, fighting for her life?

Peering through the Bushnell Lynx Gen 2 Night Vision goggles, Butch peeled back his upper lip and formed a snarl.

He swivelled the Bushnells to the left and found the lit end of Che's latest coffin nail. He called the first guard Che, on account of his wispy beard and the scraggy hair flying out from beneath a stupid red beret. The fool had chain smoked the whole night. Must have lungs of pure leather.

Che's patrol had reached the farthest point from the embers. He stood in his camouflage jacket and trousers, together with a scuffed pair of sand-coloured desert boots. He waited for his buddy, a guy Butch called Slabhead, on account of the huge, bald skull sitting on top of a pair of the narrowest shoulders he'd ever seen on a man.

Jeez, what a freakshow.

When Che and Slabhead met, they exchanged a couple of quiet words, turned, and retraced their steps back towards the embers. A pointless exercise. They wouldn't be able to see anything outside the pool of light thrown by the floodlights.

Butch scanned the darkened buildings surrounding the compound. No lights showed, and nothing moved.

Why did he always get the bum end of the deal? Shane-the-Doofus was lying there on his sleeping bag, snoring like a son-of-a-bitch, while Butch was doing all the work, as per usual. It was his turn to rest, not Shane's. Just 'cause he had seniority—by two fucking months—he led the partnership.

Another thing that wasn't right about life.

Where are you, Mei? God, I hope you're okay.

He raised his arm and read the time. 02:27. Time to radio in.

"Shane," Butch whispered.

The fool didn't budge.

"Shane!" Butch repeated, this time adding a kick to his skinny rump.

Shane grunted.

"What the—"

"Time to report in, Doofus. Take over the binoculars for me."

Shane groaned.

"Already?"

In the near total darkness, Shane rolled over and sat up, his dark silhouette barely visible since the moon had set. He yawned, long and hard.

"Right in the middle of a damn fine dream, too."

"Don't tell me. I don't wanna know."

"Me an' Ella-May were going at it like—"

"Land sakes, Shane," Butch hissed, throwing a wild punch that connected with the man's upper arm and received a snorted guffaw for his troubles. "Shut your mouth. Talk dirty 'bout my sister again and I'll slice off your dick next time you start snoring. Now swap places!"

"Jesus, man. I was only kidding. You can be a real shit when you don't get your way. Here, take the damn radio."

Butch handed the radio across the narrow space between them.

"Jeez, it's cold. Anything happened down below?"

"Nope. Not much since the convoy left," Butch answered, sliding back and away from the binoculars, allowing Shane to take his place. "Che and Slabhead are still circling, but the other two have driven off. Bonfire's died right back."

"That's why it's darker then, huh?"

"Yes, Shane. You know, you can be really sharp ... for a doofus!"

While Shane took over the binoculars—and spent an age doing it —Butch flicked the power on the radio.

"OP4 to QB, are you reading me? Over."

"*QB to OP4, reading you loud and clear. Over.*"

"Nothing to report. The target is dark and quiet. Any news of the search? Over."

"*That's a negative, OP4. Road blocks are up and the whole state's on alert. We'll find them soon enough. Over.*"

You'd better, or Griezmann's toast.

Butch wasn't above reinstating the old Vietnam tradition of fragging a senior officer, strictly for the good of the unit, and to extract some payback. Shane would volunteer to help in the process, too. Not that Butch would ever accept it.

"OP4 to QB, any change to our orders? Over."

C'mon, Griezmann, call this disaster off and pull us out.

The radio crackled. Three bars of Dolly Parton's *Jolene* cut into the transmission before QB's, "*...your position. Over.*"

Shit!

"OP4 to QB. Signal's breaking up. Repeat your last message. Over."

"*Signal's perfect this end. What did you miss? Over.*"

Butch ground his teeth.

What a crock.

"OP4 to QB. Any change to our orders? Over."

"*That's a negative, OP4. The SAC says to stay put. QB, out.*"

Butch clicked off the radio and whispered, "Fuck you, asshole!" into the dead microphone.

"No sign of them?" Shane asked.

Butch answered with his special look. The look that could boil water.

"Griezmann still going ahead with the raid?"

"Sure is—"

Butch would have finished the sentence and said a whole lot more, but the cold circle of steel pressing hard into his temple cut off all thought and stunned him into silence.

Hot breath and whispered words warmed his ear.

"Don't move, Butch."

The British accent froze the blood in his veins.

Griffin!

CHAPTER THIRTY-ONE

On his knees, keeping Butch between himself and Shane, Kaine eased forwards and pressed the muzzle of the Sig against Butch's temple. The breath caught in the FBI man's throat. Kaine leaned closer and whispered into his ear.

"Don't move, Butch."

Butch stopped moving. Stopped breathing.

"The cold circle of metal you feel against your temple is the muzzle of a Sig Sauer P226," Kaine continued, in a hushed whisper. "Tell Shane to back away from the binoculars and throw up his hands."

Butch didn't respond.

Kaine rammed the muzzle harder into Butch's temple.

"SAIC Griezmann probably told you how desperate I am," he whispered. "Well, he's dead right. I don't want to hurt you, but my friend's down there in that camp and I don't know you from Adam. Do it!"

Butch breathed in gently, careful not to twitch in case it set the "desperate Brit" off. He wasn't to know that Kaine hadn't primed the Sig and the weapon was as safe as any loaded semi-automatic would ever be.

"Shane," Butch said, a little too loud, "come here, will you?"

Kaine jammed the Glock even harder.

Butch groaned.

"What?" Shane asked.

"You heard me. Slide away from the glasses and come here. Raise your hands, too."

"Butch, stop goofin' around, will ya?"

"Shane, I have a gun to your mate's head," Kaine growled deep and slow. "Do as he says and everything will be fine."

Shane flipped onto his back and sat up.

"Griffin?" he gasped. "How the fuck—"

"Shut up. Do as I say."

Kaine pulled the gun away from Butch's temple and racked the slide. It clicked loud and metallic in the windblown quiet.

"What the hell was that?" Shane shouted.

Butch moved, lightning fast.

Kaine weaved away.

Butch's wildly swinging arm whistled past Kaine's nose. In the darkness and the undergrowth, Butch lost his footing and staggered. Kaine leapt forwards, slammed the butt of the Glock into the back of Butch's head, hard enough to stun but not to cause serious damage unless the Special Agent had a particularly thin skull.

Butch grunted. Fell to the ground and lay still.

"Don't bother, Butch," Kaine said, speaking quietly. "I'm not falling for it, mate. I didn't hit you that hard. Roll onto your back and slide towards Shane. Please don't make another move on me, or I will shoot."

Butch rolled over, sat up, and shuffled closer to Shane.

"No you won't," Butch said, rubbing the back of his head. "A gunshot's gonna wake the whole goddamned camp."

"In this gale?" Kaine asked, having to speak up against the wind whistling through the pine needles. "I doubt that."

Behind and to Butch's right, Shane kept quiet. Too quiet.

"Shane. Don't try anything stupid, son. Whatever you're thinking, it won't work. From this distance, I won't miss. Keep those hands up and away from your gun. You too, Butch."

Kaine risked a quick glance downhill. The glow from the remains of the fire had almost faded into nothing, but the floodlights shone steady enough to form a small dome of orange in the gloom.

"What do you want with us?" Shane mumbled, his words barely audible over the wind.

"We'll get to that."

"Where's Mei—I mean, Special Agent Chang?" Butch asked, rubbing the back of his head.

"She's close."

"What'd you do to her?"

"Nothing. She's unhurt. I promise you."

"Prove it."

"Yeah," Shane said. "Prove it."

"Happy to. Give me a second."

Kaine tapped the earpiece once.

"Alpha One to Charlie One. Are you receiving me? Over."

Butch and Shane glanced at each other, but stayed put. Kaine pointed the Sig at the middle of Butch's chest. Although both men would be wearing ballistic vests, the effect of a 9mm bullet striking at such close quarters would be debilitating and both men knew it. Neither fancied risking broken ribs and internal damage. They'd bide their time. Hopefully, giving Kaine an opportunity to explain all and maybe even bring them aboard.

"*Charlie One here. Is everything okay? You took so long. What happened? Over.*"

"OP4 is neutralised. You can come on down. Take the direct route, but be careful, there are plenty of trip hazards. Alpha One, out."

Shane found his voice again.

"Who the fuck was that?"

"Special Agent Chang. Shouldn't take her too long to reach us."

"You expect us to believe that?"

Kaine shrugged.

"What choice do you have?"

"If you've hurt her—"

"Butch, she's okay. I promise. You can ask her yourself in a few minutes. Oh, and you can lower your arms, but please keep them away from your sidearms and we'll be cool. We're all friends here."

"You and I ain't friends, Griffin."

Shane lowered his arms first and rested his hands on his thighs, in plain sight. Butch dropped his left, but kept rubbing his head with his right.

"Sorry about the crack on the nut, Butch. Hope it doesn't hurt too much."

"It doesn't," Butch growled.

"Bleeding?"

"Nope."

"Good. Now let's settle down and wait for Mei. Don't start twitching though. I'm a nervous kind of guy."

"Don't seem nervous to me," Butch mumbled under his breath.

"How come you know our names?" Shane asked. "You beat them out of Mei?"

"Nope. I told you, she's fine. Actually, you told me yourselves."

"Huh?"

"I've been listening to your chatter for the past hour or so."

"Bullshit," Butch blurted out.

"I mean," Kaine continued, "while you were awake, that is. Tut, tut, Shane. You really shouldn't sleep on the job. You snore too much."

Shane jerked upright.

"Snore? The hell I do!"

"Tell him, Butch."

Butch lowered his head and allowed his shoulders to slump. "Yeah, you snore, Shane. Been telling you the same thing for years."

"If you like," Kaine said, "one of you can still keep watch on the camp. After all, that's what you're supposed to be doing. Shane, it's still your turn, I think."

"Bite me, Griffin," Shane snarled.

"No thanks. I'm a vegetarian."

"Funny guy."

"Sorry, that was my first and only lie of the night."

So far.

"I really do eat meat."

"Can I ask a question?" Shane asked. Always alert, his eyes scanned the darkness behind Kaine.

"You just did, but be my guest."

"Why are you here, busting our asses?"

"I need access to the camp and you're in my way. I'd never have made it past your NVGs. What are you using, Zeiss? Bushnells?"

He stretched his neck to win a better look at their setup.

"Ah, Bushnell Lynx Gen 2s, if I'm not mistaken."

Butch and Shane shared a glance.

"Okay, so you know your binoculars," Butch said. "Big deal."

"What were you gonna do? Crawl up behind us and slit our throats?" Shane asked.

Kaine shook his head, hoping they could see him clearly in the dark.

"If I was going to do that, you'd be dead already. No, I'm looking for your help."

"You're looking for what now?" Butch said, his jaw dropping.

"Way I heard it earlier, neither of you think too highly of your boss, and Butch, here, has a soft spot for Mei. I hoped she'd act as my calling card, and I'd be able to persuade you two to guard my six."

"Are you serious!"

"It's either that, or I'll revert to Plan A."

"Which is?"

"Truss you up and leave all three of you here while I go rescue my friend."

Saying it aloud made it sound ridiculous. No wonder everyone had started calling him a nutcase.

"You really expect us to sit here and let you cuff us together?"

"No, not really. I'd expect to have to force you into it. And I have zip ties in my backpack. Cuffs are too heavy to lug around all night. They rattle, too."

A second lie. Choosing to travel light, he'd left his backpack in the sheriff's SUV.

Naughty boy, Ryan.

Shane turned to his friend. "Do you believe this guy?"

Butch shrugged his wide shoulders.

"No, Shane. I don't. And I don't think he's gonna fire that gun, neither."

"I agree," Shane said. "Too much of a risk. If he wakes up the camp he'll never get his girlfriend out. He's bluffing. There's two of us. We can take him. What d'you reckon?"

"I don't know, Shane. He's holding a loaded gun on us, and Mei's on her way. Assuming he ain't lying."

"I'm not lying, Butch," Kaine said. "And Sabrina's not my girlfriend, Shane. She's just a friend."

A very dear friend.

"You're risking life imprisonment for a buddy?"

Again, Kaine nodded.

"I owe her my life and my freedom." He paused long enough to gauge the windspeed, which had fallen a little. "While we wait, it's my turn to ask a question."

"We won't tell you nothing, Griffin," Butch spat. "Not until we see Mei and make sure she's okay."

Kaine ignored the outburst. In Butch's position, Kaine would be pretty pissed off, too.

"I'm not asking you to spill state secrets, Butch." He pointed between the two men, towards the obbo setup. "Is that a Remington 700 I see lined up alongside the Bushnells?"

Butch frowned in surprise and turned to Shane as though looking for permission. Shane answered for him.

"Yeah," he said. "It's the 700P. Police version. You know your weapons as well as you know your binoculars."

"So I'm told. Laser night 'scope?"

Shane nodded.

"Who's the sniper? You or Butch?"

"Shane is," Butch said, "I'm good, but he's better. Or so he keeps tellin' me. Where are you going with this?"

"Just passing the time. I hate awkward silences, don't you? What other weapons do you have?"

"I carry a Glock 17. Shane prefers a Sig. Why? You want us to hand them over?"

"No thanks. We're cool as we are. By the way, I prefer a Sig, too." He raised his weapon. "It's a good handgun at close range."

"So's the Glock," Butch noted.

Kaine turned his attention to the sniper.

"Shane, what's your estimation of the wind speed down there at the bonfire?"

"Why?"

"Like I said, I hate awkward silences."

"You checking my skills?"

Kaine shrugged.

"Might be."

"Fifteen miles per hour, gusting to twenty."

"Close. It's eased a little in the past ten minutes. Do you use a range finder?"

"Nope. They're for amateurs."

"What constant do you use to calculate your minute of angle?"

"None of your damn—"

Before Shane could continue the rant, Mei stepped around the tree Kaine had hidden behind. She'd made better time than he expected, and slightly less noise, although Kaine had followed her stumbling approach for the final twenty metres or so.

"Mei!"

Butch jumped to his feet. A fraction of a second later, Shane did the same.

"It's her," he said to Shane, relief flooding his voice. "Mei, it's me, Butch—I mean Special Agent Michael Elkins."

She stepped closer, moving almost soundlessly, for her.

"I know who you are, Butch."

"Told you she knew you," Shane said, elbowing Butch in the ribs and relaxing his shoulders.

"Are you okay, Mei? Did he hurt you?"

"Only my pride. I'm good, thanks."

Butch beamed at her. Ignoring Kaine completely, he marched right past him and stopped only centimetres away from his diminutive colleague.

"Where've you come from?"

"Up there." She pointed behind her. "A lookout point below Black Buck Ridge."

"That close? I—we've been worried sick. Haven't we, Shane."

"Yeah. *We* have." Shane smirked and turned to Kaine. "So, you're for real, huh."

Kaine assumed the statement didn't need a response.

Butch's arms twitched, as though he wanted to throw them around Mei, but he fought off the temptation.

"You sure you're okay?" he asked quietly.

"Yes, Butch. I really am fine."

"Okay," Kaine said, "now the meet and greet's over, can we get down to business?"

"What business?" Shane asked.

"My friend's down there in that camp, and I'm going to pull her out before the raid. That's all. I don't care what happens after that. Are you going help or stand in my way?"

"Fuck's sake," Shane snapped. "Sorry, Mei. You expect us to help? You expect us to break the law?"

"Not exactly, I just hoped you'd turn a blind—"

"Jesus, Griffin," Butch said. "You go down into that camp and you'll screw everything up. We know what we're doing. You're friend's safer where she is."

"Bullshit," Kaine said. "When the ATF turns up, who knows what'll happen. There are dozens of militiamen down there, armed to the teeth."

"No there ain't," Shane said.

"What?"

"He said, 'no there ain't'," Butch said, smiling wide.

"What d'you mean?" Kaine asked.

"Couple of hours ago a convoy of trucks tricked out as battle buses rolled out of camp. Made plenty of noise doin' it, too. Me and Shane counted thirty-seven board up and ship out."

"Was Colonel Caren with them?"

Shane answered. "Couldn't tell for sure. They were all in full camo gear and makeup. Captain Andersen was with them, though. He's distinctive enough and was giving the men a whole load of hurry-up. They were all loaded for bear, too. Can't be more than a handful of militiamen left in the camp. A skeleton crew. Plus the captives, of course."

Kaine took a moment to consider the implications. Not least, why hadn't Corky updated his intel.

"You reported this to SAC Griezmann?" Kaine asked.

"OP1 did," Shane said.

"What did he make of it?"

"He reckoned they set off on night manoeuvres and would be back before dawn. Apparently, Colonel Caren's well known for springing them on his troops without warning. Did it all the time when he was in the service."

Alarm bells rang in Kaine's head. Suddenly, the funeral pyre held a whole new relevance. The Creed were shutting up shop. Cleaning house. He might already be too late. A deep, dark hole opened up in his belly.

"Butch, I need to get down there, right now. Before the Creed return. If they return." He turned to Mei. "Can you explain it to them?

"Yes, sure. Go ahead, we'll watch your six."

"Thank you," he said, reaching out and touching her upper arm. This time, she didn't flinch.

Kaine turned towards the lights.

"Griffin!" Shane called out. "Hold it right there!"

Butch and Shane unclipped their sidearms, but Mei stood

between them and Kaine, holding out her arms to block their aim. Butch's eyes widened. He probably wondered how long it might take a captive to develop full-blown Stockholm syndrome.

"What's gotten into you, Mei?" he demanded, his tone plaintive.

"Griffin's one of the good guys," she said. "Which is more than any of us can say about the SAC."

"What do you mean by that?" Shane asked.

Mei glanced at Kaine. He nodded.

"Tell them what you told me."

"Tell us what?" Butch asked.

"Why we're going to help Griffin," she said.

While she spoke, Kaine watched the camp, searching for the best way to approach and watching the two guards walk their slow circles.

A century later, Butch tapped him on his shoulder. Kaine turned and stared into the agent's eyes, trying to read his intentions.

Butch pursed his lips and spun to face the camp.

"Which way you planning on heading in?" he asked.

Kaine released his pent-up breath.

"Thought I'd follow the course of that dry gully that took me here. Why?"

"I've been studying the terrain all day. That gully leads to a whole bunch of wolfberry bushes and crucifixion thorns."

"Crucifixion thorns?"

"Yeah. And they're as bad as they sound. Fetch up in there and you'll be torn to shreds."

"Thanks for the warning."

"You want my advice?"

"Wait for the raid and hope my friend doesn't get hurt?"

"Apart from that."

"Okay, I'm game."

"Take the eastern side of the gully and follow the course all the way down to the treeline. It'll take you to within twenty-five yards of the fence."

"I don't suppose you have a pair of wire cutters?"

"As it happens ... we do," Shane answered. "We always come fully prepped, but you won't need them. Look hard enough and you'll find plenty of breaks in the fence. It ain't been repaired in years. There's a huge gap in front of the PX. That's the double height building you can see at three o'clock to the admin block. There's another break near the barracks."

"Thanks, Butch. I appreciate the intel."

The angular Special Agent sniffed and shook his head.

"You didn't hear a single thing from me, Griffin. In fact, you and I have never even met. Never will neither."

"I suppose not. Are you going to keep eyes on me?" he asked Butch.

"We'll be watching. We'll have to, since it's our job."

"Will you be reporting in?"

"We'll try, but the dang radio's been playing up. We keep getting interference."

"Shame that, eh?"

Butch smiled and his teeth showed white in the darkness. "The moment it clears, I'll report to QB and tell them Mei's safe and they can call off the search. I'll say we don't know how you got past us."

"Thanks, Butch."

"The SAC's an asshole. And the way Mei tells it, she could be in danger, too. Griezmann's gonna pay. Go get your friend out. We've got your back."

"Thanks, Butch. I appreciate it."

"No idea what you mean. I've never even seen you. We've got a spare radio. You need it?"

"No thanks."

"How we gonna keep in touch?"

"Mei knows how to contact me."

"She does?"

"Yes, I do," Mei said, repositioning the glasses which kept slipping down her nose.

Butch raised his eyebrows. "Wondered what you were wearing them for. They're way too big for you, if you don't mind me saying."

"No, I don't. They are too big. Heavy, too. But they do have certain advantages."

Kaine held up his hand.

"Special Agent Chang, please look after those glasses. I'll be needing them back at some stage. Cheers."

He turned towards the orange lights and headed out.

CHAPTER THIRTY-TWO

Monday 22nd May – Predawn
Camp Pueblo, Arizona, US

Kaine dropped onto his front, squirmed over the edge of the ridge, and scrambled towards the right rim of the little gully. The same owl that had been hooting derisively at him all the way into the valley started up again, swiftly answered by its mate. The wind chose that moment to ease and a deathly quiet descended on the valley.

Kaine took a knee behind a large tree and tapped his earpiece once.

"Alpha One to Base," he whispered, barely taking a breath. "Are you receiving me? Over."

"Corky's here. What's up?"

"Why didn't you tell me about the convoy leaving? Over."

A pause.

"Corky's been ... busy on other things. You ain't his only 'client', you know."

"Sorry, Corky. I forget you have another life. Over."

"*And anyway, you said you was going dark. Corky didn't want to butt in. Might have been dangerous. Anyhoo, you okay?*"

"I will be when I have Sabrina away and safe. Any news of the convoy? Over."

"*Not a dickybird. They've gone radio silent.*"

"What's the law up to? Over."

"*Local plod's set up road blocks, but they don't got a clue where you are. Griezmann's having kittens and fielding calls from Deputy Director Hallam. And his troops are running through their final weapons and comms checks. They'll be rolling out of Pine Creek within the hour. Better get a chivvy on, Mr K.*"

"Am doing, Corky. Can you hold on while I contact Bravo One? Over."

Kaine tapped the earpiece three times.

"Alpha One to Bravo One. Are you receiving me? Over."

He waited a full ten seconds before repeating the call. The response came in as an intermittent and garbled mess.

"Alpha One to Bravo One. Repeat message. Over."

"*Bravo One to Alpha … strength two. The road's … rock slide. I'm … alternative route. Over.*"

"Message received, Bravo One. What's your ETA? I repeat. What's your ETA?"

"*Maybe an hour. Over.*"

"I can't wait for you. I'm going in. Over."

"*Fuck's sake, K …*"

The comms unit hissed and fell silent. Kaine tapped the earpiece again.

"Corky, can you do anything to boost the signal? Over."

"*No can do, Mr K. The weather in the mountains is causing havoc. Corky can't even tell where the call originated. The bloke could be fifty miles away or up your tailpipe. Told you that ESAPP gear were a load of crap. Not a patch on Corky's equipment, eh?*"

"You said it, mate. Okay, I'm going dark again. Alpha One, out."

Kaine twisted and looked over his shoulder. He tried to pick out OP4's location, but it had already blended into the blackness. Apart from the dim glow from the camp's floodlights, which didn't illuminate much beyond the parade ground, the only other lights came from the pinprick dots of the stars.

The prickling sensation at the base of his neck he'd felt since leaving OP4 continued. He couldn't decide whether knowing that either Shane or Butch was following his every move was a good thing or not.

Slowly, he stood and faced front.

Stretched out ahead, the darker shapes of trees and bushes showed against the paler spaces between and the orange glow of the camp's floodlights. He continued his painfully slow progress, picking up the pace only slightly.

In the dead of night, the remaining members of the Creed would be in their deepest sleep. Only the two patrolling guards would be awake, and even they would be at their least vigilant. Oh-three-thirty, the witching hour. The time when most nocturnal incursions would be set for. The time when the enemy would be at their most vulnerable.

Underfoot, the dead pine needles lay thick and soft as carpet, deadening his footfalls and making his progress easier. He picked up his feet and increased his speed. He needed time to enter the compound, break into the cell, and rescue Sabrina.

He ploughed on as fast as he dared, arms up to protect against branches, feet testing the ground before adding any weight.

Fifty more metres to the treeline.

His earpiece clicked.

Corky knew better than to interrupt his concentration. Kaine placed his lead foot on the ground. A twig snapped underfoot, too damn loud. He stopped moving and tapped the earpiece awake.

"*Griffin, this is Shane. I'm watching you through the Bushnells. You're real close to the treeline now. Don't say nothing, just make a fist with your left hand so I know you can hear me. Over.*"

Kaine clenched his hand and relaxed it again.

"*Okay, good. I really gotta get me a pair of these radio glasses, man.*"

They're something else. I can talk you in from here. You okay with that? Over."

Kaine clenched his hand again. He had no choice but to trust the slim Fed.

"Okay, cool. Five yards ahead of you is a fallen tree trunk. No way you're climbing over it. You need to head right, but there's a big-ass Thornberry bush in your path. Retrace your steps a couple of yards and then make the turn. Over."

Kaine turned about-face and followed the instructions. Thorns plucked at his left sleeve and trouser leg. After five root-strewn and scrubby paces, Shane told him to make the turn, and he headed deeper into the gloom. Trees blocked out the starlight, and bushes and undergrowth hid the radiance from the floodlights. He had to take things even more slowly.

"That's it, Griffin. You're past the trunk now. Turn forty-five degrees to your left and go straight ahead for fifteen yards. Then you'll be at the treeline. There's a couple of big pine trees in your way, but the undergrowth looks fairly clear and you're good to go. Over."

Kaine opened and closed his left hand again and nudged into the darkness. Fifteen minutes later, he reached the wide open space of the clearing. The oppressive and humid confines of the woods crowded in on his back, and the fresh, open land ahead promised hope tinged with danger.

He stopped and listened, the silence overpowering.

"There's two guards patrolling the compound. Me and Butch call them Che and Slabhead. Che's a chain smoker. You'll likely be able to smell him when he's close. They meet in front of the final building and then retrace their steps.

"Che's heading toward you right now. You won't be able to see him on account of the barracks being in the way. Stay where you are. I'll tell you when they move off. Over."

Again, Kaine clenched his fist. He took a slow knee and waited.

Five minutes ticked by with the speed of a comatose sloth. The orange glow of a lit cigarette marked Che's arrival, but even if he'd not been actively smoking, the rancid stench of stale sweat would have announced the guard's presence. The wind picked up again, driving the foul body odour inexorably ahead of him and deep into Kaine's nostrils.

Wonderful.

Che strolled in front of the last low building in a row of ten and pulled into view. He coughed loud and wet, spat a glob of brown mucus into the concrete, and lit a fresh smoke from the glowing butt of the other. He dropped the butt to the earth, stamped it out, and turned to face the parade ground, his back to Kaine.

Seconds later, Che's buddy, Slabhead, arrived and Kaine immediately understood the reason for his nickname. He had a huge head balanced atop a pair of narrow shoulders that looked too weak to take its weight.

Che and Slabhead exchanged a few quiet words before turning and retracing their steps.

Kaine waited until they were well out of sight before making his move.

He dropped prone and crawled through the knee-high grass until stopped short by the rusty chain-link fence. He twisted to the right and squirmed towards the PX building and the nearest gap in the fence.

Thanks Shane.

Before he reached the PX, another, smaller break in the fence, one part-hidden by the rippling grass, allowed him an earlier entry. Once through, he doubled back on himself and retraced his route to the flat-roofed, single-storey and windowless bunker from which Hulk and the man with the shotgun had dragged Sabrina.

Keeping to the deepest shadows, he kitty-crawled to the bunker, stood, and leaned his back against the rear wall.

Sabrina was close, so close he could almost smell her.

"*Shane to Griffin. You hear me?*" Kaine gave the signal. "*Che and Slabhead have their backs to you. You're clear to go. Over.*"

Kaine trailed his fingers along the bunker's rear gable wall and stopped when he reached the far edge. He pressed himself against the concrete and poked his head around the first corner.

The floodlights' glow destroyed his night vision, but it couldn't be helped. He held his breath, listening to the wind whistling through the buildings and hearing nothing to cause alarm.

The bunker's solid form stood between him and the patrolling guards.

Perfect.

He crawled along the side wall and poked his head around the next corner. The bunker's windowless front face, lit by the orange floodlights, contained a single opening. A doorway.

The door stood ajar.

Kaine's heart thumped.

Why keep a cell door open if the prisoner was still alive?

Bastards! Fucking cowardly bastards!

Breathing hard, Kaine pulled back into the shadows.

No! Not again.

The painful memory of Danny dying in his arms mingled with the more recent memory of the smell from the funeral pyre. The hopelessness and the anger threatened to overwhelm him.

Colonel Caren, the cowardly bastard, had killed Sabrina and run away.

No! Oh, God. No!

CHAPTER THIRTY-THREE

MONDAY 22ND MAY – *Predawn*
Camp Pueblo, Arizona, US

Kaine shook his head. No. He couldn't make the assumption. Sabrina might still be alive.

He flattened his back against the rough wall, allowing its cold surface to soak in and pull the heat from his blood—cool his rage. He pulled the Sig from his waistband, slowly racked a bullet into the chamber, and rolled around the corner to the front of the bunker-jailhouse.

The open door stood flat against the wall, held in place by a rusted metal clasp. The rectangular doorway, a black and open maw, stood waiting.

Leading with the gun, he crouched and ducked through the opening, immediately stepping to the side and out of the rectangle of light.

The smell hit him first—a pungent, sickening brew of sweat, urine, faeces, and vomit. Then came the silence. No shout of alarm, no breathing, just silence.

Kaine stood with his back pressed against the inner wall, waiting for his night vision to recover.

Slowly, the contents of the room appeared. An empty metal cot stood against the far wall, its mattress thin and stained. Filthy bedding piled in a heap lay crumpled on the floor beneath. An interior door stood open and lay flat against the side wall. Keeping away from the light, he crossed the cell, and peeked inside. The inner room housed a stained and cracked toilet and washbasin. Nothing else.

He exited the foul-smelling but empty cell, and ducked back around the side, hiding in the shadows once again.

What next?

If she was still alive—a hope he needed to hold onto for fear of losing it completely—where would they have taken her? With the whole of Camp Pueblo to search he had no chance of finding her without help.

The guards, Che and Slabhead, might know. If not, they'd be able to point him in the direction of someone who did.

Kaine breathed deep and slow, and waited.

In the distance, Che and Slabhead had already met near the dead bonfire and were on the outbound route. As usual, Slabhead tested a few doors on his side religiously. Che, the atheist, ignored his obvious orders and sauntered along, puffing merrily on his cancer stick.

Kaine had a choice to make. Ordinarily, he'd give people, even bad people, the benefit of the doubt, but he didn't have time to play nice. He'd read the FBI files on the Creed and had seen photos of their tortured and murdered victims. None of its members deserved leniency.

Che approached the jailhouse, halfway through his latest cheroot. He puffed, the lit end glowed, and he carried on walking until he reached the end of his well-worn track. The painstaking Slabhead was still thirty metres from the rendezvous.

Kaine de-cocked the Sig and returned it to his waistband. He picked up a nearby stick and dragged it slowly along the cell wall. Wood scraped and scratched against concrete.

Che spun towards the noise and bit on the cheroot to empty his hands. He pulled back the charging handle on his M4 and raised the carbine to his shoulder, pointing it at the jailhouse.

"Who's there?" he called, his voice clogged and sticky with phlegm.

Che coughed and spat from the side of his mouth, still biting the cheroot. Brown sludge dribbled from his mouth. It ran down his chin, dripped onto his shirtfront, and glistened under the lights. He swiped it away with his sleeve.

Kaine dropped the stick and backed deeper into the shadows.

"Who's there?" Che repeated.

"What's wrong, man?" Slabhead asked, his accent local, but the speech slow and deliberate.

"I heard something," Che answered, edging closer to the side of the building.

Slabhead hurried towards his mate, breathing heavily, the breath condensing into a thin cloud the moment it left his mouth. As he pulled alongside, Che threw out a hand to stop him.

"I don't hear nothing," Slabhead said.

"Where's your flashlight?"

"In my pocket."

Che punched Slabhead's shoulder. "Take it out and—"

Kaine leapt up and slammed the heel of his hand into the point of Che's jaw. It snapped closed with a crunch of broken teeth. He grunted and dropped like a stone.

Slabhead staggered backwards, dragging his heels in the dirt. Kaine followed him into the open.

Slabhead tried to work the bolt of his M4 but the knob caught on the flap of his jacket. Eyes wild, he sucked in a deep breath, making ready to yell.

Kaine slammed a fist into his midriff and followed it with a clubbing side-fisted blow to the temple. Slabhead's eyes rolled up into the back of his oversized head, and he joined Che in a heap on the ground.

Both men lay in the dust, unmoving, barely breathing. Che's breath rattled in his chest.

"OP4 to Griffin," Shane said. *"Nice work, man. Real slick. But soon as anyone wakes up, those guys are gonna be missed. How's that gonna work with our raid? Over."*

"I don't give a flying fart for your bloody raid," Kaine snapped. "All I care about is my friend. Over."

"Griezmann's gonna skin you alive, Griffin. Over."

He'll have to catch me first.

"Cover me, OP4. Griffin, out."

Loath to move any closer to Che than absolutely necessary, he dragged the reeking man around to the back of the jailhouse by his feet and did the same for Slabhead.

Once he had them out of sight of the compound but in full sight of OP4, Kaine removed the laces from their boots and threw both pairs into the deep grass. He used the laces to tie each man's thumbs together behind their backs, binding Che's thumbs so tight they turned red immediately. The rank-smelling man rolled his head and groaned, showing an impressive recovery rate. Che spat out shards of broken teeth, and dribbled bloody saliva into his scraggy beard. Muttering, his words garbled, he struggled to lift his head.

Kaine pulled the men into a seated position, back-to-back, and propped them against the wall. He removed their belts, linked them together, and strapped the extended belt around their waists, pulling them as tight as they'd go. A decent stopgap, but it wouldn't stop them shouting or struggling to their feet if they worked in tandem.

Using pieces of their clothing as gags would restrict their breathing dangerously and he had no reason to want either man dead. Besides, he'd thought of a better way to guarantee their silence.

Happy he'd secured them as best he could, Kaine fought his gag reflex and leaned close enough to slap Che's cheek. At the same time, he drew out his dagger and held it up to the man's nose.

Che coughed a wave of vile stench into Kaine's face. Once again, he overcame his gag reflex, but this time, it took a lot more effort.

He slapped the sunken cheek again. Che's eyes crossed as they found focus—on the blade of Kaine's ceramic dagger. Kaine held a finger to his lips.

"Raise your voice and you die. Understand?"

Che jerked out a nod.

"Yeah, yeah. I-I understand," he whispered, his eyes never leaving the blade.

"Good, good," Kaine whispered. "Looks like I ain't gonna have to gut you after all."

He used the best American accent he could manage, which Rollo once described as sounding like a Brummie fighting bellyache.

Can't be good at everything.

Kaine pressed the dagger's razor-sharp edge against Che's greasy neck and added enough pressure to nick the skin. Che whimpered as a thin line of blood trickled into the gap between neck and collar. He tried to pull away but ended up cracking heads with the still comatose Slabhead.

"N-No," Che stammered, sparkling eyes wide and staring at Kaine's hand. "P-Please, don't. I'll keep quiet. Are you a Fed?"

"Quit that. I'm asking the questions, bud," Kaine whispered.

He pulled away to a gag-safe distance but left the dagger resting against the parted flesh.

"I'm gonna keep this real simple, partner. Answer my questions and you live. Got it?"

Che swallowed. It caused the blade to bite a little deeper and the blood to ooze a little faster. The foul-smelling man whimpered.

"Y-Yeah, I-I get it. Wh-What d'you wanna know?"

"Where's the woman?"

Che looked into Kaine's eyes for the first time.

"Which one? There's plenty of women here, man. They ain't all dropping like flies."

Kaine flinched.

"What d'you mean by that?"

"Some of 'em took ill, man. Couple even died, an' we had to burn 'em."

Jesus.

"That's what the bonfire was for?"

Kaine pressed the knife a little harder before easing it off again. It

319

wouldn't have taken much more pressure to sever a carotid or a jugular, but he needed Che alive. For the moment.

"Y-Yes," Che said. "P-Please don't hurt me!"

Tears filled the reeking man's grey eyes. Kaine knew terror when he saw it. He'd seen it often enough on the battlefield. Good. Terror suited him well enough.

"What about the French woman?"

"Frenchie?" Che asked. "You here for her?"

The fear in Che's eyes turned to hope. The same sensation surged through Kaine, only the reason differed.

"Is she still alive?" He almost didn't want to ask.

"Yeah, yeah. She's okay."

"Are you sure? Lie to me and I'll gut you right now."

Kaine lowered the knife to the quivering man's belly.

"No, no," Che squealed, much louder than he'd intended. "I-I ain't lying. Honest."

He squeezed his eyes tight shut in the expectation of a gutting, but opened them again seconds later and sighed when he saw the knife had yet to do its work. Tears rolled down his sunken cheeks.

"Keep your noise down, *asshole*," Kaine hissed.

"Sorry, man. Sorry. But Frenchie's alive, man. I swear to God she is. I saw her a few hours ago."

"Where is she?"

"Let me go and I'll take you to her."

Kaine shook his head slowly.

"You think I'm stupid, shit-for-brains? That ain't happening. Where is she?" To add emphasis to the question, Kaine raise the knife and rested the flat of the blade against Che's sodden left cheek, the point millimetres away from his eyeball.

"Oh, God. No! Don't."

"Where is she?"

"The infirmary," he whispered, spittle flying.

Kaine twisted the knife enough for the blade to slice into Che's cheek. He whimpered.

"The infirmary?" Kaine said. "I thought you said she was okay? What's she doing in there?"

"Sh-She's looking after George. The colonel's nephew. She's okay, the French girl. I-I swear it, man."

"Which one's the infirmary?"

Che tore his eyes from the point of the knife and locked them onto Kaine's. "It's on the right ... the big hut three buildings down from the PX. You can't miss it. There's a sign on the door, man."

Kaine leaned away, taking the dagger with him. He wiped the bloody blade on the sleeve of Che's jacket, which probably made it even dirtier, and slid it into its sheath. He stood over the trussed men, looking down.

Che had to crane his neck to see him, which opened the neck and cheek wounds and made the bleeding worse.

"If you're yanking my chain," Kaine said at a little above a whisper, "so help me, I'll come back and slice off your pecker. Then I'll make you eat it."

"I ain't lying, man. I swear to God."

"While I'm gone, stay quiet and you live. Make a ruckus and you die. You hear me?"

"Y-Yes, I hear you, man. I'll keep quiet."

Kaine tapped the earpiece. "Griffin to OP4. Mind lighting him up? Over."

Moments later, the red dot of a laser sight blinked on. It lit a point on the grass between Che's legs.

The terrified captive held stock still. His eyes widened as they followed the little dot of death as it crawled upwards. When it reached his groin and lingered for a second, Che whimpered and snapped his legs together as though they would offer him some protection. By the time the red point reached the centre of his chest and held steady, more tears poured out of Che's eyes, and he started mumbling something that could have been prayers.

"Shane to Griffin, the guy doesn't look so tough now. By the way, man. That's one God-awful accent. Over."

Kaine sighed.

Everyone's a critic.

"Sorry, pal. It's the best I can do. Griffin, out."

Kaine kicked Che's bare foot. He stopped praying and stared up at Kaine through panicked eyes.

"You got keys for the infirmary?"

Che swallowed hard.

Kaine kicked him a second time, this one even harder.

"Don't make me ask again. My friend up the hill's got an itchy trigger finger!"

Inwardly, Kaine grinned. He'd always wanted to say that, and the accent made it even better.

"J-Jacket pocket."

Che pushed out his chest and indicated with his eyes.

Kaine confronted the stench again, tugged the jacket open against the restriction of the belts, and reached inside. He grabbed the heavy bunch of keys he found in the inner pocket and fixed Che with a death stare. He held the keys up in front of the goggle-eyed captive.

"Which one opens the door?" He didn't want to waste time searching for the right one while standing in the open.

"Big one. Brass."

Kaine identified the key in question—one of only two brass keys on the loaded ring—and nodded.

"Any guards inside the infirmary?"

Again, Che hesitated.

"If I'm interrupted, my men have orders to kill you first. Now, are there any guards inside the infirmary?"

"No, no. Only George and Frenchie. And the sick women."

Behind Che, Slabhead groaned. His head jerked up and cracked against Che's. He snorted, and his underslung chin dropped back onto his chest.

"When your buddy wakes up, explain the situation to him. Do it carefully. He kicks up a ruckus and you both die tonight. *Capisce*?"

Kaine chalked off something else he'd always wanted to say.

"Don't move. Don't even breathe heavy. You got that, bud?"

With his lower lip trembling and his watery eyes pleading, Che nodded.

Kaine climbed to his feet again and stared down at the sorry-looking captives. Reluctantly, he reached down and tugged the beret from Che's filthy mop. He held it at arm's length. It might come in handy, but he prayed he wouldn't have to stick the greasy thing on his head.

"I'll be back!" he said in his best "Arnie".

Dear, oh dear.

They were all coming out one after the other. Next, he'd be using, "Reach for the sky".

News that Sabrina was alive and well almost made him giddy.

He turned away from the quietly muttering Che and made his way to the far side of the jailhouse—the darker side.

Keeping to the deep shadow at the foot of the wall, Kaine crawled back to the fence and scurried the long way around, passing hut after dark and silent hut.

Fifteen minutes later, he reached the large clapboard building Che had called the infirmary. It didn't look like any medical facility he'd ever seen. Some of the worst field hospitals he'd been treated in were palaces in comparison.

Kaine crawled along the deep grass at the foot of the side wall and stood, pressing himself flat, his nose touching the rough clapboard. He slid his head around the corner.

A gusting breeze pushed dead leaves in eddies around the wide open space of the parade ground. The compound stood glaringly empty. Any Creed insomniac would notice the lack of patrolling guards in an instant.

He couldn't hang around any longer.

Braving the contamination, Kaine dropped Che's beret on the top of his head, promising to shave off his hair if the filthy item gave him head lice. He stepped out into the open and tried to mimic Che's shamble-footed gait. They were of a similar stature and he might just pass for the scrawny guard.

Heart pumping fast, he shuffled out and around to the front of the infirmary and headed straight for the large double doors. Kaine inserted the heavy brass key into the lock and turned. The ancient mechanism creaked and the lock clunked as the reluctant deadbolt scraped back against its mortised strike plate.

Only one barrier remained.

Unlike the shuttered and barred windows running along the side walls of the barn-like building, a rusted hasp and staple held the right-hand door firmly against its partner. This was secured in place by a matt black Abus padlock. Kaine held Che's keychain up to the light and counted seven padlock keys. Fortunately, only one would fit the Abus. He separated it from the others and slid it into the lock. The stainless steel shackle opened with the smooth click only apparent with a well-made and well-maintained mechanism.

Kaine removed the padlock, snapped it closed, and dropped it to the gravel at his feet. He levered the hasp away from its staple and pushed at the door. Its hinges let out a sad but loud creak and it opened inwards. He stepped over the low sill and into a dark and cavernous area that smelled only slightly better than the cell in the jailhouse. The place would have given Che a good run for his money in the Pungency Stakes.

"Hey, Banner!" a guttural voice boomed out, close behind. "What the fuck you doin'?"

CHAPTER THIRTY-FOUR

Kaine jerked and dropped the keys into the darkness.

"Fuck, man!" he said, rasping the same way Che did. "You scared the shit out of me."

He bent low, making himself small and more difficult to identify, and scratched about on the dark concrete floor inside the doorway as though searching for the keys.

A heavy hand landed on Kaine's shoulder and spun him around.

"I asked you a question, shit-for—"

Kaine spun and sprang upright, putting his whole weight behind a right uppercut into the belly of a huge man. His blow landed in a relaxed gut and drove upwards towards the chest cavity. The breath whooshed out of the man, sounding like the air exploding from a punctured tyre. He crumpled to his hands and knees, winded, gasping for breath. Wavy blond hair hung in a curtain around his drooped head. Kaine recognised him as the animal from the satellite stream—Hulk.

Bastard!

The huge man recovered fast and pushed up with his hands, trying to stand. Kaine ended his efforts with a boot to the temple.

Hulk fell forwards onto his face, toppled onto his side, and lay in a messy, arm splayed heap. Kaine's steel toecap had opened up a nasty gash on the side of Hulk's head. It bled into his eyes and over his forehead and puddled on the floor.

Tough.

The bugger deserved much worse.

Hulk's gasping eased into a wheezing burble, but Kaine wouldn't care if the pig stopped breathing altogether.

Kaine tugged Hulk's legs fully inside the infirmary and swung the door shut, enclosing the room in near total darkness. He stood with his back against the doors and, once again, waited for his night vision to recover.

In the gloom, the silence was broken only by Hulk's ragged gurgling and something else he couldn't identify.

He stood still, held his breath. The narrow gaps around the double doors allowed slivers of light to filter into the interior but they did little to dispel the darkness.

Off to his left, metal clanked on metal, a chain rattled. Quiet crying. Weak, wet coughing. A woman sobbed gently, quietly, seemingly oblivious to his and Hulk's presence.

"Sabrina?" Kaine called out softly. "Are you in here?"

"Ryan? *Mon Dieu.* Ryan?"

The chain clanked again.

She's alive. She is *alive. Thank God!*

Kaine could barely believe it.

"Ryan, I am chained to the wall. Where are you?"

"By the doors. Stay put. Don't move. I'll come to you."

Hulk grunted, shifted position. Boots scraped on the concrete floor. Cloth swiped against cloth. The big man groaned.

"*Merde*, who is that?"

"Don't worry, lass, I'm on it."

Kaine stepped closer. Reached out and down. Found a broad

shoulder and followed it across to a head of thick, long hair. He grabbed a handful and yanked it back hard, simultaneously dropping a knee between the man's shoulder blades, slamming him into the floor.

Hulk gargled, pushed up with his powerful arms, trying to ease the strain on his neck. He struggled, fighting for breath.

Kaine wrenched the tuft of hair back even harder and twisted his head to the side. Merciless. No time to mess around.

"Stop fighting me, or I'll break your goddam neck, *asshole*." He switched back to his cod US accent.

The huge man stopped struggling, but still gargled, unable to swallow.

Kaine eased off the force enough for Hulk to suck in gasps of the foetid air. Two, three, four. Deep and fast. It must have tasted so sweet to the vicious prick.

"Who the fuck—"

Kaine snapped Hulk's head back again. "Shut up, *dumbass*. If I wanna hear you speak, I'll ask you a question. You get me?" He tugged harder, neither wanting nor expecting an answer.

"Sleep tight, buddy. Just be thankful I ain't ending you."

Kaine shifted position, applied a choke hold, and squeezed until Hulk stopped bucking and kicking and his arms flopped to his sides. He maintained the pressure for a further count of six. Any longer might prove fatal.

He released the hold and allowed Hulk to drop, face first to the floor and stood. His head hit the concrete and made a satisfyingly wet thud.

Not enough light made it through the gaps around the doors or the cracks in the clapboard walls for him to see anything and he couldn't risk lurching around in the dark. Who knew what he might step on or stumble into. He patted Hulk down, found the outline of a mobile phone in the back pocket of his jeans, and tugged it free. He needed some light and had to take the chance.

"Ryan, where are you?"

"Be there in a minute, lass."

On the top edge of the phone, he found a power button. He covered the screen with the palm of his free hand, pressed and held the button down until the device buzzed into life. The display's light shone red through the skin of his fingers, a darker outline showed the bones.

He slid his hand part way down the screen to expose a little more light and pointed it in the direction of the rattling chains.

"Jesus!" he muttered.

The newly lit scene could have made a shock point in a horror movie.

A dozen steel-framed beds stood out from the wooden walls. Three contained a human outline covered in a stained cotton sheet. Two of the figures didn't move and Kaine feared the worst, the third coughed weakly. Chains fixed to the head of each bed ran to the left wrist of its occupant.

In the furthest corner, a dark mass moved. Not a bed, but a mattress on the floor. He couldn't make it out in the gloom and removed his hand fully from the screen. The brighter light made the more aware patient jerk her hand up to cover her eyes. Her chain rattled louder—the rattle of a ghost roaming castle walls.

The mass in the corner was sitting up. Long, dark hair hung in front of her face, lank and unwashed. She raised her free arm to protect her eyes from the glare.

"Ryan, is that really you?" she called, her voice weak but familiar, its accent undeniably French.

"Sabrina."

She jerked upright. The long hair parted to reveal a dirty, haggard face with dark bruises under swollen and bloodshot eyes and a cut lip. Gone was the beautiful young woman who'd saved his hide back in London so many months ago, replaced by a dreadful apparition who'd taken a real beating.

Unluckily for him, Hulk chose that precise moment to revive. He groaned and tried to roll onto his back. Kaine, incensed, took one stride and landed a vicious boot to the point of Hulk's jaw. The huge man's teeth snapped together the same way Che's had done earlier.

Kaine followed the kick up with one to the gut and another to the groin.

Hulk lay still, his breath whistling through a headful of shattered teeth.

Serves you right.

He left Hulk in a limp puddle on the floor and raced across the open space to the corner.

As he approached, Sabrina backed away into her hovel and held up her hands to stop his approach.

"Stay away!" she said, crying the words.

He stopped a coupled of metres short and dropped to his knees in front of her.

"Sabrina," he said softly. "It's me, Ryan."

She scrunched further away until stopped by the wooden walls at her back.

He tore off Che's filthy beret, raised the phone and turned it to light his face from above—a less horrific angle.

She nodded.

"I know," she said, "I know it's you, but you shouldn't be in here. They are sick. Contagious."

She pointed to the women in the beds.

"It doesn't matter. I'm here to get you out."

Kaine reached out and gradually lowered her hands to her lap. Slowly, lightly he brushed the hair away from her damaged face.

She gasped and fell into his open arms.

He hugged her as tightly as he dared and gently rubbed her sweat-dampened back. Her ribs stuck out through empty skin. The vital, healthy Sabrina he'd known so briefly in London had turned into a bag of bones.

What the hell had they done to her?

Gently, Kaine eased her away from his embrace. He shone the screen on her wrist. Like the other patients, it was handcuffed to a chain, but this one was bolted to a support beam against the back wall. A suppurating wet gash encircled her wrist where rough metal had rubbed the skin red raw. She gasped when he reached for her hand and pulled it away.

"Forgive me," he whispered. "Do you know where they keep the keys?"

He had a thousand questions, but the others could wait.

"W-Who's th-that?"

A voice, that of a young man, called out from behind a screen to Kaine's left. He spun. The screen hid another bed.

"It is okay, George," Sabrina said, "this is a friend of mine. His name is ..." She glance at Kaine in mute question.

"Bill," Kaine said. "Bill Griffin."

He pulled the screen aside. The mobile's dim light showed brown eyes glistening out of another battered face, the bruises livid and fresh. Someone had given the poor kid a real going over within the past two days.

Kaine held a hand out to the lad, who squirmed further back into his bed, shaking his head and trembling all over.

"It's okay, George," Sabrina said. "It really is. Bill is going to help us."

George stopped shaking and looked up.

"N-No, he c-can't be here," George whined, his voice rising in volume and pitch. "The c-colonel's g-gonna be m-mad. Real m-mad."

"Quiet, George. Hush," Sabrina said, "you will wake Mary and the others."

The lad snapped his mouth shut and nodded. He brought a finger to his lips and held it there.

Sensing no danger from the youngster, Kaine left the lad and returned to Sabrina. He held up Che's key chain. None of the keys would open a set of handcuffs.

"Sabrina, the keys to the cuffs, where are they?"

"*Les clés ... dans sa poche*," she answered. "Tex keeps them in his pocket." With her free hand, she pointed to the fallen Hulk.

Kaine backed away.

Sabrina gasped.

"Please, don't go," she cried, reaching for him with both hands, stretching the chain. "Don't leave us!"

"I won't be long, lass. We need those keys."

Using the minimal glow from the mobile's screen, Kaine retraced his steps to Hulk—Tex.

The big man lay where Kaine had dropped him. As far as Kaine could tell, he hadn't moved. Out of one nostril, a bubble of pink snot grew and popped, showed the evil bugger still lived.

Shame.

Kaine found a set of keys in the pocket of Tex's jacket and stood with his back to the front doors.

He flipped the mobile over, found the torch icon, and closed his dominant right eye before taking the risk of switching it on. The powerful white LED shot a narrow beam which illuminated the horror-filled scene. Kaine closed his mind to the human suffering and ran the beam around the room, looking for a rear exit. The only other door in the so-called infirmary stood ajar. He headed towards it, and found a small store room with one glazed window, but no way out.

He hurried back to Sabrina's corner. George, with his finger still raised to his closed lips, followed his every move through shining eyes. Kaine gave the kid an encouraging smile and dropped to his knees in front of Sabrina. Gently, he inserted each key and twisted. On the fourth try, the cuff opened and the chain clattered to the floor.

She was free.

"Can you walk?"

Sabrina frowned, nodded.

"But of course."

She leaned forwards and tried to push herself to her feet but failed. Kaine grabbed her good arm, gently pulled her into a fireman's lift, and stood. She didn't weigh a whole lot more than Mei.

Without warning, Sabrina started squirming on his shoulders.

"Ryan," she grunted, "what are you doing?"

"Taking you out of here. You need a hospital."

"No. No. We cannot go! Put me down!"

With an unexpected burst of energy, she kicked, punched, and writhed, desperate to get down. Fear was setting in. Delirium overtaking logic.

"Sabrina, stay still. Keep quiet!"

Much more noise and she'd wake whoever was left in the camp.

He lowered her to the floor and she stood on unsteady feet, sucking in great gasps of air. Her cheeks had regained some colour. Whether flushed from the exercise or from fever, Kaine couldn't tell.

He shone the light at her, but kept it out of her glistening eyes.

"Sabrina, what's wrong?"

"We cannot leave these people. They will die."

He shone the light around the infirmary. The more aware woman was sitting up, arms raised to protect her eyes from the sudden glare. A pitiful sight. Bare shoulders, thin and shaking. Lank hair covered her flushed face, hanging like dirty drapes.

"The FBI and the ATF are on their way. They'll look after your friends. They have medics."

Sabrina stood taller, straighter. She stopped swaying and seemed to pull in strength from the dank air around them. Shaking her head, she grabbed his forearm and squeezed tight. Her grip held more strength than he expected.

"Ryan," she said. "What did you say?"

"The FBI and the ATF will be here at sunrise. An hour or so, no more, but I want you out of here long before then. In case there's any trouble."

"Oh my God," she said, eyes wild, voice rising in volume. "Everyone will die. The colonel, he is totally insane. He will kill everyone. Everyone."

Behind her, George lowered his finger from his lips. "I d-didn't say n-nothin'." His lower lip trembled and tears started flowing.

The woman in the first bed slumped back onto her pillow.

Kaine raised his hand, trying to quieten them both.

"Sabrina, hush. You'll wake the whole camp."

She let go of his arm and waved at the other beds.

"Ryan, you don't understand. Listen to me. Please. Colonel Caren, he will not let the police or the authorities in here. If they try to break in he will destroy the camp."

"What?"

"It is true, Ryan. He has enough explosives to obliterate the whole of the camp and blow up half of this mountain."

"Sabrina, slow down. You're not making any sense."

"The colonel, he is insane. The Creed has kidnapped women from all over the country. They are being used as sex slaves."

"I know. So do the Feds. How many are there and where are they being held?"

"I don't know. But listen to me, Ryan. He has booby trapped the armoury and the barrack huts. He calls it his Shield of Death. If the authorities set one foot inside the Camp he promises to kill everyone in here. He is convinced that every member of the Creed is prepared to die for their cause. You have to go. Get the authorities to call off the raid!"

"I'm not leaving without you."

"But I will only slow you down. You must go. Tell the FBI—tell SAC Griezmann about the Shield. He must call off the raid."

"Who told you about this Shield? The colonel?"

She shook her head and turned to the lad crying in his cot.

"George told me."

"N-No, I d-didn't. I-I d-didn't say n-nothin'. Keeps my secrets, I d-do."

George's lower lip still trembled, but at least he'd stopped bawling.

Kaine paused. Short of beating Sabrina insensible and dragging her from the place—something he seriously considered—he needed time to think. Precious time he didn't have.

He glanced at Tex. How long would it take for someone to notice his absence and raise the alarm? Che and Slabhead's disappearance would soon be noticed, too. Even a skeleton crew of Creed nutcases could kick up a real fuss.

What the hell was he going to do?

CHAPTER THIRTY-FIVE

"Sabrina," Kaine whispered. "We don't have time. Please come with me."

She shook her head. Stubborn to the last. She reminded him of Lara—and every other woman he'd been close to.

"Only if George and the others can come too." She indicated the women in the beds.

"I can't take them all. We'll be lucky if the two of us get out without waking the place. I've already pushed our luck too far."

Sabrina crossed her arms. "You are resourceful, Ryan. You must go and warn Griezmann."

"Okay. Give me a moment to think." He held up the keys. "Can you unlock the others? If I think of something, they'll need to be free."

She snatched the keyring from his hand and rushed towards George.

Kaine grabbed Tex by the ankles. By the time he'd dragged him to the corner, George's chain lay puddled on the floor by his bed. He hadn't moved, but stared at Tex in wide-eyed wonder. A weird smile twisted his bruised and battered lips.

"You k-killed T-Tex?"

"No, George. He's sleeping."

"D-Don't look like he's s-sleeping to me. He's unc-conscious, huh?"

While Sabrina moved to unchain the woman in the first bed, Kaine closed George's cuffs around Tex's right wrist, snapped the lock in place, and ratcheted it as hard as it would go. Its tight fit restricted the blood flow to Tex's hand which quickly started to redden.

"George, can you come here, please?"

"W-Why?"

"I think you might be able to help me."

"Y-You do?"

"Assuming you want to save the women. Do you?"

George tilted his head. A frown furrowed his brow. He shrugged.

"You'd be a hero, George. Would you like that?"

The lad looked up through a pair of the bushiest eyebrows Kaine had ever seen in a man younger than seventy.

"I-I ain't never b-been a hero afore."

"Better than being laughed at and beaten up, eh?"

George touched his swollen cheek with a dirty hand.

"That's a f-fact, sir."

"No need to call me sir, George. You can call me Bill if you like."

The youngster canted his head to one side and his frown lines deepened.

"Is there a problem, George?"

"Why do I g-get to c-call you Bill when Miss L-LeMaître c-calls you R-Ryan?"

Kaine grinned, seeing more to the boy than he expected.

"You don't miss much. Do you, George?"

The lad's frown relaxed and he returned Kaine's grin.

"Uh-uh!" he said, shaking his head.

"No," Kaine added. "I'm betting you're a lot smarter than others think you are. And I'm also betting that's exactly what you want them to think. Am I right?"

The lad's right shoulder hiked up in a mini shrug.

"M-might be. J-Just 'cause I st-stutter, d-don't mean I'm st-stupid."

Kaine dropped his hand onto the same high shoulder and squeezed. The lad's smile remained in place and he seemed delighted to let Kaine in on his life's secret.

"So," Kaine said, leaning closer, "you want to be a hero, George?"

The frown returned.

"Wh-What I g-got to do?"

"Only answer a few questions."

The kid relaxed a little more.

"I c-can do that."

"Even if it means letting me in on a secret?"

"D-Depends on the s-secret."

"It's a big one, George."

Kaine tapped the earpiece once, hoping both OP4 and Corky were listening.

"You want to know a-all about the Shield, huh?" George asked, arching one of his bushy eyebrows.

"That's right, son. Will you tell me what you know?"

"Well, i-it ain't really my secret if I'm not s-supposed to know about it anyway, right?"

"What do you mean, George?" Sabrina asked, having returned after completing her task as turnkey. Behind her, the three released women seemed unaware of their new-found freedom and simply lay in their beds as before, unmoving.

George studied Sabrina long and hard before answering.

"Well, if I overheard the c-colonel talkin' to the c-captains and Tex, an' I didn't do no pinkie swear ... it ain't really my secret to keep, is it?" He smiled, proud of his logic.

"Is that why you told me about the Shield in the first instance?"

"Y-You sure d-do talk funny, Miss LeMaître."

"That's because I'm French."

"I know that. Some of them w-words you use are real f-fancy, but I g-get what you mean."

"So," Kaine said, keen to move things along. "What can you tell me about the Shield?"

"Wh-What d'you w-wanna know?"

"Thank you, George," Sabrina said.

She planted a peck on the lad's cheek. He blushed and his bruises darkened into purple. Kaine imagined he'd just witnessed the kid's first kiss.

"Okay, George," Kaine said, "first things first. Do you know where the trigger is?"

George straightened.

"'Course I d-do. Th-That's an easy one. The Colonel c-carries it around with him all the t-time."

"Have you ever seen it?" Sabrina asked.

George looked at her and the blush deepened. With that simple peck, she'd made a deep and permanent conquest.

"Couple o' times. Wh-When he didn't know I-I were around."

"What did it look like?" Kaine asked.

"Weren't n-nothin' s-special. Looked just like a c-cell phone. A real s-small cell phone."

The implications of a cell-phone detonator were enormous. The colonel could destroy the camp on a whim from anywhere in the world, but only if the detonators could receive the call.

"A radio-controlled detonator?" Sabrina asked Kaine.

"Sounds like it. George," he asked, turning to the lad who clearly revelled in his role as hero, "earlier, a couple of hours ago, did you hear the trucks leave?"

"Uh-huh." George nodded. "Happens all the time. Night m-m-manoeuvres. Uncle Rich—I mean, Colonel Caren orders 'em all the time. Never lets me go on 'em, though. Says I'd only g-get in the way."

"Does he always go with them?"

"Mostly, but not always. S-Sometimes, he lets the Swede, take ch-charge. That's C-Captain Andersen." George scowled. "D-Don't like the Swede. He's worse than all the others, 'cept Tex."

"Thanks, George. Where's the colonel's billet? His bedroom, I mean."

"The t-top floor of the b-big house."

The lad pointed in the general direction of the admin block and the officers' mess.

Kaine nodded. Already, he had the kernel of an idea.

"The communications block on the far side of the camp, is that the only place with a radio receiver?"

"Y-Yeah, th-that's right."

For the next few minutes Kaine asked question after question, which George answered as best he could.

"Thanks, George," Kaine said after running out of questions. "You've done really well."

"S-So," he asked, sitting up straighter on his bed, shoulders thrown back proudly, "am I really a h-hero?"

Kaine clapped his shoulder one more time.

"Yes, George. You are."

The lad's chest expanded, and he seemed ready to burst with pride. He smiled at Sabrina.

"You hear that, M-Miss LeMaître? I's a h-hero."

"I heard, George. And I agree."

"Sabrina," Kaine said, "I'll be off now."

"Where are you going?"

The big house via the communications block.

"Not sure yet, but while I'm gone you need to do something for me."

"What can I do?"

He pointed to the storeroom-cum-office. "That's about the safest place in the infirmary. Move everyone into the office and barricade yourselves in. Use the mattresses for protection. Are you strong enough to do that?"

She nodded.

"With the help of George, I can."

Kaine slid a glance at the lad.

"Well, George?"

"S-Sure I'll help. I'm real st-strong, I am. I can c-carry them mattresses for you, M-Miss LeMaître."

Kaine turned to leave, but Sabrina grabbed his arm.

"Be careful, Ryan."

He winked. "You know me, lass. I'm always careful."

Without waiting for her response, Kaine pried her fingers from his arm and left.

———

Kaine ducked around the side of the miserable excuse for an infirmary and settled into the shadows. Since he'd entered the building, the wind had picked up even further. It whistled through the surrounding trees and howled over the mountains. He couldn't have wished for anything better to cover his movements.

He tapped the earpiece.

"Griffin to OP4. Come in. Over."

"*Shane to Griffin. Reading you okay. Over.*"

"Did you hear any of that? Over."

"*Every last word. Over.*"

"Did you relay the message to Griezmann? Over."

"*About the Shield? Over.*"

Griffin ground his teeth.

What the bloody hell was wrong with these people?

"Of course, about the bloody Shield. Over."

"*Yeah, I told him we overheard the guards talking. Couldn't exactly tell him we learned about it through you now, could I. The SAC already went ape when I told him how you got past us. Said we should have shot you in the back. Me and Butch are already in deep shit over this SNAFU. Over.*"

Hardly a surprise.

"And? What did he say about the Shield? Over."

"*He says it's a crock and the colonel's bluffin'. Over.*"

"What do you guys think? Over."

"*We reckon the kid definitely thinks it's true. But whether it is or not's anyone's guess. What do you reckon, Griffin? Over.*"

"According to George, there are a dozen female captives being held in one of the barracks. I can't take the risk that the Shield's a bluff. Over."

"What's your plan? Over."

"Going to check things out. See what I can find. Will you back me up? Over."

"Dunno how we're gonna do that. Our orders are to sit here and watch. Nothing else. Over."

"Shane, if it comes to taking a shot, will you do it? Over."

"Er ... We got rules of engagement. You know that, right? Over."

Federal agents in America weren't allowed to shoot people?

Yeah, right.

"You're authorised to shoot in defence of innocent life, aren't you? Over."

"Under certain circumstances, yeah. We are. Over."

"Good. You noticed the increase in wind speed? Over."

"'Course I did. Reckon it's gusting at about twenty miles an hour. Over."

"Make that a force four gusting to five. Adjust your aim to compensate for a twenty-five-mile-an-hour peak. You can ignore the air mirage over the parade ground. Over."

"You tryin' to teach me how to shoot again, Griffin? Over."

"Trust me, Shane. The mil dot on your scope's going to tell you the distance, so you can work out the drop angle range yourself easily enough. But you need to use a constant of twelve for your minute of angle calcs, not the standard thirteen. Your target will be really small and there's no room for error. Do you understand what I'm saying? Over."

"Yeah, I got you. And you've made your point. You know what you're talkin' about, but that ain't got nothing to do with whether I'll take the shot or not. Over."

Kaine ignored the comment and kept on talking. "If the wind down here changes significantly, I'll let you know. Don't forget to allow for the value of the wind at the different targets. Over."

"Now you're starting to piss me off, Griffin. I'm no rookie. Over."

"Keep your ears open for my shout. Over."

"*Might do,*" he said, entirely non-committal. "*By the way, as senior agent in attendance, Special Agent Chang has taken command on the ground. She's told the other OPs to stand down and take a watching brief. Over.*"

"She has? Over."

"*Thought you'd want to know in case you're wondering why they weren't jumping all over your ass. Over.*"

"Thank her for me, Shane. Griffin, out."

"*No! Wait. Griffin are you still there? Over.*"

"I'm still here. Over."

"*There's a vehicle hammering along the main route into Camp. Its lights are out. Over.*"

Hell. Now what?

"What type of vehicle? Over."

"*Looks like an SUV. Black. Could be a Ford Explorer. It's pulled off the road a quarter mile out. Now it's reversing into the trees. The driver's door just opened and a guy's climbed out. Big guy. Tall. He's standing by the hood with his hand to his ear. What you make of that? Over.*"

Kaine's earpiece clicked three times. He smiled.

About bloody time.

"Not to worry. The Mounties have arrived. Over."

"*The Mounties? Griffin, have you flipped? Over.*"

"He's a friend of mine. Watch my six and listen for my call. Griffin out."

He answered Dubois' second triple click.

"*Bravo One to Alpha One, are you receiving me? Over.*" He sounded stressed, urgent.

"Alpha One to Bravo One, receiving you loud and clear. What's taken you so long? Over."

"*Up yours, Alpha One. I damn near busted an axle getting here so quick. Those mountain roads, man ... never mind. Where are you? Over.*"

"Behind the PX store. You can't miss it. I found her, Bravo One. Repeat, I found the target. Over."

"*You did? Oh my—how is she? Over.*"

"A little the worse for wear, but she's alive. Over."

"Thank God. Where is she? Over."

Kaine gave him Sabrina's location and a brief outline of the situation.

"You sure she's okay? Over."

"She will be when we neutralise the Shield. Over."

"Shield? What shield? Over."

Kaine gave him a brief outline. Ever the professional, Dubois listened without interruption.

"What's your plan? Over."

"I'm on my way to the admin block. Hopefully Colonel Caren will play nice and hand over the detonator without too much of a fuss. Assuming he's home. Over."

"What's my job? Over."

Kaine nodded to himself. One of the things he liked most about the *Quebecois* was his ability to assimilate information without the need to ask a stream of inane questions.

"Fancy laying waste to the radio room? It's the opposite side of the camp to the admin block, and I can't be in two places at once. Over."

Dubois laughed.

"Consider it wasted, Alpha One. Bravo One, out."

The earpiece clicked into silence.

Kaine relaxed a little. With the *Quebecois* on board, life had just become a whole lot easier.

CHAPTER THIRTY-SIX

Monday 22nd May – Parker "Tex" Scarborough
Camp Pueblo, Arizona, US

Tex twitched.

Groaned.

Consciousness swam up from the black void and, with it, came pain—booming, thumping pain. His face felt like it had been stomped on by a rodeo bull, and his guts and his balls were on fire. Something had torn up through his belly and scrambled his innards. The side of his head throbbed like it had been stove in, and he couldn't breathe through his nose. Hurt like a bitch, too. Probably broke again. His mouth tasted of copper and his tongue rasped against cracked and busted teeth.

Jesus. What ... the ... fuck ... happened?

Slowly, the fog lifted. The little bastard fucked him over. Stomped him big time. An ambush. The asshole who wore Banner—wore that stupid red beret—and had a punch like a mule, had gotten the drop on him. Worked him over real good.

Sneaky little shit.

He moved.

Face scraped on something hard. Concrete. Stank of sweat and vomit. Had he puked? Maybe. Maybe not. Didn't taste like it, but with the taint of old pennies in his mouth, he couldn't tell one way or the other.

Where was he?

The reek of puke and sweat.

Shit.

The infirmary! The little fucker left him to catch the bitching plague.

Jesus! I'm gonna die!

Get up. Move. Run.

No. Wait. He might be watching.

Distant sounds filtered through to his consciousness. Scraping. People whispering.

Lie still.

Play dead.

Play dead 'fore you are dead.

Tex wasn't in any condition to defend himself. Not yet. The small fucker with the punch like a club hammer striking an anvil might come back to finish him off.

Lie still.

Without moving his head, he tried opening his eyes, but only one worked properly. The left was swollen shut.

Dark. All around, pitch black.

No. Not quite.

Across the way, dim lights moved above his head. Cautiously, he raised his chin. No. Not lights. One light. Behind the door to the medic's office, the store room. The people carried on whispering. Tex concentrated hard, tried to listen, but couldn't make out the words.

Couple of minutes later, the door opened and closed. Darkness descended again. Footsteps padded above Tex's head, coming from the store room heading towards him.

Shit.

Tex closed his eyes. Held his breath. Tensed for the finishing blow. Tensed long and hard until the quiet footsteps faded into silence. Darkness descended again. More throbbing pain in his head.

Oblivion.

———

A door squealed open and light hit the front of his closed lids. The headache returned with added power. Movement all around. More mumbled words.

Scraping. Cloth being swept back. A woman's groan.

What the fuck's happening?

Tex held his breath. One of the voices sounded familiar. Halting. Stilted speech. Stuttering.

George!

The other, a woman. Frenchie. What the hell were Frenchie and shit-for-brains George doing?

Another soft moan was followed by a grunt.

"Be careful," Frenchie whispered, close by Tex's feet. "Protect her head."

"S-Sorry. D-Didn't expect her to b-be so heavy."

He spoke louder than Frenchie, an idiot's version of a whisper.

Didn't make sense. If it was a break out, why the hell weren't they gone?

Tex held his breath again. Listened hard. Apart from the whispered mumbling, he couldn't make out a thing. He lifted his throbbing head from the floor. Taking a risk, but he had to know what was going on. He scanned what he could see of the place in the darkness.

Black shadows. Beds sticking out from the walls. From his position on the gritty floor, he couldn't tell whether or not the beds were empty, but nothing moved and no one made a sound. No sign of the short guy who wore Banner's beret, neither. Maybe he'd gone.

Tex had nothing to lose. He needed to move.

His arms were still splayed out from his sides in a parody of Jesus on the cross. He hadn't moved them in case the tough guy, Shorty, noticed. Tried flexing his fingers. Electric fire shot out from his right hand.

Shit in a bucket.

His hand was on fire, lying in a pool of acid. The pain. Why hadn't he noticed before? Involuntarily, he jerked his arm into his side. Metal rattled. A chain. They'd cuffed him to a chain, and the cuff was too tight.

Jesus, it hurt! Started throbbing, pulsing, the moment he moved his arm.

Christ.

How long had he been lying there?

Not long. There weren't no daylight showing around the gaps in the doors, only the floodlights. Still dark outside. Night time.

Pain coursed through him. His heart thumped against his ribs. Tex fought the blind panic rolling up from deep in his gut. Fought the need to scream. Shorty might still be around.

Working his left hand, he rolled onto his back and pushed himself into a seated position. The chain rattled as he pulled his right hand tight into his chest, biting back a squeal of agony. Pins and needles attacked his fingers and thumb as he tried to move them.

"Wh-What was that?"

Shit!

The kid heard him.

The storeroom door opened. A flashlight cut into the room, and George popped his head through the opening. Stooped and twitching, his head swivelled left and right just like the shit-scared coward he always was. The flashlight's beam crawled over the floor. Creeping. Snaking. Searching.

The light moved closer to where Tex huddled in the darkest corner of the infirmary, leaning against the wooden walls. Holding his right hand tight to his chest, Tex scrunched deeper into the shadow.

Would George notice he'd moved?

One chance. Tex only had one chance. He couldn't call out. No telling what might happen. Didn't want to startle the inbred moron.

George had to come to Tex. He couldn't force it to happen the other way around.

The door opened wider and George straightened. The flashlight's beam crawled ever closer. Soon, it would reach Tex's corner. Except, it wasn't a flashlight. It was the harsh white light from a cell phone. Slowly, so he wouldn't rattle the chain again, Tex moved his left hand, searched for his cell.

Shit.

The pocket he kept it in was empty.

The imbecile was searching for Tex with his own damn phone. The irony slapped Tex in his damaged face.

Fuck.

If he ever caught up with Shorty again he'd be more prepared. He'd kill the little squirt. No warning. No quarter. A swift but painful death.

George the moron shuffled out of the office and further into the infirmary. Frenchie whispered something Tex couldn't hear properly.

"T-Thought I h-heard s-something," George said, stepping further into the room. "G-Gonna ch-check it out. K-Keep them patients quiet."

What was that? George giving orders like he knew what he was doing? Didn't make no sense. The world had turned upside-down.

Perhaps the kid was play-acting. Pretending. Tex had seen him doing it a few times when he thought no one was watching. Talking to himself and giggling.

Moron.

George moved and the light snaked to the left, away from Tex's corner, leaving his place relatively darker.

Closer, George. Come closer, now.

George tiptoed forwards.

Five more steps. That's all.

The cell's light tracked to the right, lifted up from the floor, hit Tex square in the face. Dazzling.

"T-Tex!" George gasped.

347

Tex squinted against the brightness and beckoned George closer with his free hand.

George shuffled forwards, but stopped out of reach. Tex shielded his eye with his good hand.

"George," he whispered, "what the hell you doing, dummy?"

The kid stiffened. Stood taller. Stuck out his chest.

"Don't c-call me a d-dummy!"

Ignoring the pain shooting through his mangled face and cut lips, Tex smiled. "Sorry, George. My mistake. I just wanted to know what you was doin', is all. Didn't mean no offence by it."

"Y-You's always t-talkin' to me like I was d-dumb."

"Sorry, George. Didn't mean nothing by it. Trying to toughen you up, is all. Wanted to make a better soldier out of you. It's what the colonel wanted. Weren't nothing personal."

The kid's lower lip trembled and his chin dimpled. Close to crying.

Goddamn halfwit.

"You k-kicked me in the f-face."

He raised his right hand and for the first time, Tex noticed the shotgun. Until that point, the kid had kept it hidden behind his back.

Take it easy, Tex. Be cool now.

He could outsmart the dopy, stuttering kid fifty ways from sunset.

"You made me mad, George. Disobeyed a direct order. Got in my way. I had to punish you, son. Don't you see that?"

George squinted, using his thoughtful face. Tex had him.

"Whatcha say, George? Are we friends?"

"B-But you k-kicked me in the face ..."

"And I apologised, son. I'm sorry. I'm hurt, too. You can see my face and look here." He held up his damaged hand. "My hand. Can't feel nothing. Can you help me, George? Please?"

The kid shuffled a shade closer.

Not far now. Tex pulled his feet closer to his butt and braced his back harder against the wall. Making ready.

"Wh-What you w-want me to do?"

Got him!

"Loosen the cuff, George. Please. My hand's dying. Can you see? I can't move my fingers."

He turned his hand. It looked ugly and grey under the harsh light. Felt better than it had, though. Since he'd started moving it.

George closed another two feet.

"But Mr G-Griffin said—"

Tex pushed away from the wall and sprang up. He grabbed George's gun arm, twisted and yanked it up behind his back. The kid screamed as Tex damn near tore the arm out of its socket.

George dropped the shotgun. It rattled on the floor, out of reach. The cell phone fell next, landing face down, throwing the beam at the ceiling. Tex hooked his chained arm around the kid's neck and pulled him up and off his feet.

"Sass me, dummy?" Tex hissed into George's ear. "Sass me, would ya? You fucking moron."

George kicked and struggled, but Tex dodged, and the kid's flailing heels missed their target. He squeezed harder. Choking the idiot.

"Quit kicking, dummy. Else I'll break your scrawny neck."

George stopped moving. His hands held onto Tex's forearm, trying to take the pressure off of his throat.

"That's better, boy. Where's the key to my chain?"

The kid garbled a response. Tex relaxed his hold a little and lowered George enough for him to stand. The kid took a huge gulp of air.

"The keys, George. Where the fuck are they? I ain't asking again."

George released one hand and pointed to the office.

"M-Miss LeMaître's g-got 'em."

Shit. Of course she had. Nobody'd trust George with a set of keys.

"Frenchie!" Tex called out, all sing-song. "Oh, Frenchie! You hear me in there?"

He shouted plenty loud enough for her to hear, but not loud enough to arouse the camp. If the others found him trussed up like a Thanksgiving turkey, it'd be as embarrassing as all hell. It'd certainly cost him his lieutenant's bars. Might even cost him his life since the colonel didn't take kindly to screw-ups. Tex had seen it once before when the colonel lost his rag. Up and killed a Creed man outside of Omaha City just 'cause the guy jumped a red light in a truck carrying liberated munitions. Doing it, he drew the attention of a state trooper. Stupid-assed move.

After killing the trooper where he stood in the middle of the road, the colonel summarily executed the driver for "gross dereliction of duty". A simple driving error had cost two men their lives.

And all that happened over twelve hundred miles away.

As for Tex, he'd let a man get the jump on him inside the camp when he was in charge of night security. If he couldn't put things right, it didn't bode well for his long term survival.

"Frenchie! Oh Frenchie! Come out here, Goddamn it! Right now."

Scraping from inside the store room turned into movement at the door. A hand grabbed the jamb, and half her face showed at the side of the door. One bloodshot eye glinted in the backwash of the cell phone's beam.

"That's better," Tex said, taunting. "Come closer, darlin'. Tex needs you."

She shook her head. Stayed where she was, half-hidden behind the open door, using it for protection. Fat lot of good it would do her. Tex held all the cards.

Tex tightened his hold around George's throat, squeezed harder, and hauled him off his feet again. The kid gagged, started kicking again, weaker than before. Still missed Tex's shins.

"I said, come here, bitch, and bring the keys with you. Damn it, move your scrawny ass!"

She pushed the door. Hinges creaked as it swung away and banged against the wooden wall. She stood in the opening, shaking. Either with fear or from the plague, Tex couldn't tell. If she had it, so did George, and likely, so did he, now.

Fuck, what a shitstorm.

"Let George go. I am here."

She held up a bunch of keys. Tex's keys. Shorty must've taken them from his pocket. Fucking bastard was going to pay. Big time was he gonna pay.

"Uh-uh, honey."

He tightened his choke hold even more. Tex felt something pop in George's neck. The kid stopped moving and hung limp, like a rag doll.

"Better hurry. George's stopped breathing. He ain't gonna last much longer."

"Let him go, *putain!*"

She rushed forwards, holding the keys out in front of her.

Still keeping his choke hold tight, Tex twisted at the waist, turning George away from her. His skinny arms and legs dangled, lifeless. Still, Tex squeezed. George was already gone. Had to be. His dead weight hung heavy on Tex's chained arm.

Tough shit.

Frenchie drew up beside him. He dropped George in a heap and snatched the keys from her hand. She fell to her knees beside the body, calling George's name and wailing.

While Tex found the right key and opened the padlock, she rolled George onto his back, checked for a pulse at his throat, and gave him the kiss of life, crying between each breath.

The cuff clicked open, and the chain fell to the floor in a clattering, tangled heap. Blood started pumping into the near-dead hand. Pins and needles came first, but soon exploded into agony. Excruciating, unrelenting pain coursed through his hand and crept up his wrist, his forearm, spreading through his arm and into his body. At least his fingers moved the way he wanted them to.

His eyes watered, and his vision blurred. Heat built up from his core and sweat flowed, bathing him in its sticky moisture. Headache. A thumping headache.

The plague?

Christ knew.

Frenchie breathed for George and his chest expanded as air filled his dead lungs, but the kid didn't move on his own. Wouldn't never move on his own again.

Ignoring his throbbing hand and arm as best he could, Tex bent low and snatched up the shotgun, gripping it by the fore-stock. He flipped the gun around and jabbed the butt into the back of Frenchie's head. She slumped forwards and flopped on top of the kid. Looked like they were making out. Tex stared down at them and snorted. The closest George would ever get to being with a real woman and he was already dead.

Cryin' shame.

He righted the shotgun and braced the butt against his thigh. He tried pumping a cartridge into the chamber, but nothing happened. A jam? No. Damn thing was George's gun. Tex almost forgot. The colonel stopped his ammo allowance after the last time he fired it. The old man shouldn't never have let the little squirt have a loaded weapon. Too damn dangerous for everyone. Moron kept tripping over hisself.

He threw the shotgun aside, grabbed Frenchie by the hair, and yanked hard. She groaned, started struggling. He shook her head 'til she woke, tugged her to her feet, and marched her to the wall. He pressed her face into it, and held her firmly against it with his throbbing arm. Using his good hand, he patted her down all over. She was firm and soft in all the right places. A little bony maybe, but nice, just the same.

If he had more time and his balls didn't hurt so much, he'd make her pay the old fashioned way.

Tex leaned closer and kissed her exposed cheek. Kissed it wet and rough, suffering the pain throbbing through his mouth and nose. If she had the plague, so what? They were both dead anyway and he might as well have some pleasure afore he got too sick.

"You and me are gonna have some fun, honey."

"George is dead," she said, her face scrunched into the woodwork. "You killed him!"

"Uh-uh, honey. Shorty killed him, not me. I got here too late to save poor George."

"I will tell the colonel the truth!"

"How you gonna do that if'n you're dead?"

Tex yanked on her hair and she squealed and struggled against him. Her movement turned him on, made him hard in spite of the throbbing pain, but he didn't have time to take advantage of her. Not yet.

"Where's Shorty?"

"Who?"

"The guy who broke in here wearing Banner's stupid beret. Where's he at?"

She bucked against him, trying to throw him off. Such a turn on.

"I do not know."

"Why'd he break in to save you and then leave you here?"

"I will tell you nothing."

Tex stepped back. Punched her in the kidney. She squealed, doubled up, and crumpled to the floor. He dropped to one knee beside her.

"Where is he?"

He grabbed the back of her head and mashed her face into the concrete floor.

"Where the fuck is he!"

She whimpered, tried to struggle, but her efforts were pitiful. Eventually, she'd break, but it would take too long. He balled her hair into his fist and yanked her to her feet again. By the cell phone's light, he searched the room. All the beds were empty. Where the fuck had the sick bitches gone?

The office, of course.

He dragged her, kicking and squirming, into the storeroom.

Yep, he was right.

All the movement and scaping earlier had been Frenchie and George setting two mattresses on the floor beside each other. Three women lay on top of them, covered in the threadbare army blankets. Two more mattresses were propped up around them like they were preparing a gunfight.

"What you do that for, Frenchie?"

She shook her head.

"Answer me, damn it."

Again, she shook her head.

"Fuck's sake, woman. Don't try my patience."

He released his grip on her hair and thumped her in the back. She stumbled forwards, bounced off the desk, and fell, gasping, into the chair. Keeping a close eye on her, Tex crossed to the mattresses.

"Why'd you move the women in here?"

Again, she refused to answer.

Tex sighed.

"I'm gettin' awful sick of askin' the same question, woman."

He leaned against the storage shelves, raised his foot and rested the arch of his boot on the throat of the nearest patient. She barely even twitched.

Frenchie sat up straighter.

"No! What are you doing?"

"If I have to ask again, I'm gonna crush her damn throat. Then I'll do the same to the next one."

"Wait. I'll tell you. It … It's for their protection. Mr Griffin suggested it. Please, leave her alone."

He shook his head.

"Uh-uh, honey. Not until I'm finished asking."

Tears rolled down Frenchie's face. He'd broken the bitch.

Smiling, Tex leaned a little harder. The sick woman opened her eyes and tried to remove his boot but didn't have the strength in her arms. He had the power over life and death.

Christ, what a turn on.

"Please! Leave her alone. I will tell you everything I know."

Tex removed his foot and kicked the woman in the ribs to emphasise the control he had over their lives.

"*Connard!*"

Frenchie jumped up but flopped back down when he raised his foot again.

"No idea what you said, Frenchie, but I'm guessin' it weren't no compliment. Now start talkin'."

"Mr Griffin—"

"Who's he?"

"The one you called Shorty. The one who did that to your face!" she snapped, sneering the whole time.

"Stunted little worm got the jump on me, is all. Won't happen a second time. Where's he at?"

"He knows about the Shield."

"Shield? What fucking shield?"

More bullshit.

Confusion spread over her damaged face.

"You don't know?"

"What shield?"

"The explosives. The colonel has threatened to blow up the whole camp if the authorities move on him."

"Bullshit! Where d'you hear that?"

She lowered her eyes and made fists. If he ever lowered his guard, she'd pounce. Tex smiled. Let her. The bitch wouldn't stand a chance.

"George told us," she said, talking to her fists.

Tex tensed his right hand. He flexed the fingers. More pins and needles shot through his hand and forearm, but at least the pain had subsided. Apart from the headache and the sweats, he'd started feeling more like his old self. Stronger, mightier.

"George told you? George the idiot told you?"

She looked up at him, her eyes red and teary.

"George was not an idiot! He overheard the colonel talking to Captain Boniface and Captain Andersen. You did not know?"

Tex didn't answer.

"Ha! The colonel didn't trust you enough to let you in on his big plan. His secret. It is obvious."

"Shit, woman. I'm his most trusted lieutenant. Colonel Caren tells me everything. If I ain't heard nothin' about a shield, it means there ain't no such thing. You hear me?"

She swiped her eyes clear of tears.

"Are you trying to convince me, or yourself, *Lieutenant* Scarborough."

Again, she sneered. The bitch was laughing at him. Taunting him. Well, he'd show her ....

He braced his standing leg, pulled back his foot, and aimed a finishing kick at the same sick woman's head.

Frenchie screamed, sprang from her chair, and hurled herself at him, arms outstretched, grasping. Something in her hand flashed. Something metallic. She landed on his braced leg. Pain bit the inside of his thigh. He kneed her in the face, and she fell to the floor in a gasping heap. A small knife with a plastic handle—a scalpel—fell from her hand and rattled on the floor.

Warm wetness flooded the inside of his pants leg. He looked down. A three-inch slice parted the cloth just below his crotch. Blood stained the jeans. It flowed down past his knee and spread to his calf.

So much blood.

A river.

His vision blurred. A flush warmed his face and neck. Bile rose to his throat.

"Bitch! You fucking bitch! I'm gonna kill—"

Movement caught his eye. Behind him and to the side.

Tex twisted around. A tall man with wavy, light brown hair stood in the doorway. He carried a gun.

Tex staggered. His vision dimmed.

"Alain!" Frenchie screamed from the floor.

The man smiled. He raised the gun and fired in one smooth action.

Pain exploded through Tex's throat. Light faded to dark, then to black. Muscles turned to water. Legs collapsed beneath him and the floor rushed up.

The world ended.

CHAPTER THIRTY-SEVEN

MONDAY 22ND MAY – Predawn
Camp Pueblo, Arizona, US

Kaine scampered around the back of the infirmary. Hugging the fence, he kept low until he reached the last of the barracks. He crept to the front of the hut and took a knee. A large open space spread out between him and the next piece of cover, and beyond that lay the parade ground. If he hugged the fence all the way around the perimeter to the admin block, it would take forever.

Time to take a risk.

Kaine stood and pulled Che's stinking beret from his pocket. Braving the stench and the grease, he planted it on his head, hopefully for the last time, and stepped out into the floodlit parade ground. Assuming Che's stooped, shuffling gait, Kaine picked up the man's semi-circular route, heading in an anticlockwise direction from the barracks area towards the glowing embers of the bonfire and the admin block beyond. Although he felt the prickling of a sniper's crosshairs tickling the back of his neck, he kept his pace slow and shambling. Anyone looking from a distance should mistake him for Che, as Tex had done to his cost.

As he drew ever closer to the two-storey admin block and the squat officers' mess off to the side, the cooling breeze dried the sweat from his face. He breathed deep, his lungs needing to draw more oxygen from the thin air.

His earpiece clicked three times.

Dubois.

Kaine tapped his system awake.

"Bravo One to Alpha One, are you reading me? Over."

"Alpha One here. I hear you. Over." He spoke quietly, just above a whisper.

"What the hell are you doing out there in the open? Over."

Kaine kept on walking.

"I know what I'm doing, Bravo One. This is the shortest route. Where are you? Over."

"Closing in on the PX. Not far from the infirmary ... Shit, what was that?"

For an extended moment, silence filled Kaine's ear. He hitched midstride before carrying on towards his target and heading further away from the infirmary. Kaine held his breath and shuffled even more slowly.

"Bravo One, what's happening? Over."

"Something's wrong! Screaming ... the infirmary. Bravo One, out."

Kaine shot a look over his shoulder. The infirmary stood two hundred metres away on the far side of the drill square, downwind. No wonder he hadn't heard any screaming.

Sabrina!

Kaine tore Che's beret from his head and took off, racing across the parade ground. Boots pounded the dust, all pretence at stealth gone.

Bloody idiot.

Why had he left her?

Why hadn't he dragged her away to safety.

Stupid, stupid, stupid.

Heart thumping, the chill air scorching his lungs, Kaine pumped his arms and drove on, pushed by the wind. The thin air and its reduced oxygen were taking their toll. Thighs burned, calves cramped up. The stifling effects of high altitude coupled with the lack of acclimatisation slowed him.

His vision greyed, but still, he careened forwards.

If Dubois heard the scream, the skeleton crew might have, too. In his peripheral vision, the barracks windows remained dark.

Why?

He barely had time to register the question.

Halfway across the open ground, the percussive blast of a gunshot cracked the air and echoed around the nearby buildings.

Sabrina!

Kaine drove himself even harder. Sucked in more and more of the empty air.

Thirty metres …

The infirmary drew nearer. The storeroom window shone yellow against the black rectangle of the building. Someone had turned on the light.

Alain?

Twenty metres …

Kaine whooped cold air into scorched lungs. Swung his arms, drove his feet into the ground, ignored the burning in his thighs and calves.

Move, man. Move!

The wind drove him forwards, but the dusty, leaf-strewn ground held him back, the slight incline working against him. He aimed at the lit window, using it as his guiding beacon.

Fifteen metres …

To the right of the window, the entrance doors stood shut.

Which way did the doors open? Out or in?

Ten metres …

Inwards. They opened inwards.

Five …

Without hesitation, he shoulder charged the right hand door and crashed through into near darkness. He dived forwards, rolled, and made his feet in a single flowing movement.

"Alain?" he gasped, panting hard.

The light from the storeroom cut a yellow, door-shaped rectangle into the darkness of the infirmary. Kaine raced across the room, towards the light, and dived inside.

The hot metallic tang of fresh blood and spent gunshot hit his nose. Tex lay spreadeagled on the floor, floating in a lake of red. The bullet that punched a hole through his throat had exploded out the back of his head. Blood, bone, and brain matter spackled the shelves above and behind his corpse. Three women lay on mattresses, eyes closed, unmoving.

The rest of the room stood empty.

Sabrina. George.

Where the hell were they?

Behind him. Shuffling.

Boots scraping on concrete. Cloth rustling.

Kaine spun and reached for the Sig tucked into his waistband.

Too late. A million years too late.

He froze.

Sabrina floated in the darkened infirmary, her feet dangling a few centimetres off the floor. A black-sleeved arm encircled her throat, holding her aloft, its elbow pointed towards Kaine. Sabrina's hands grasped the sleeved arm, taking the weight of her body and off her neck. Shock and fear carved into her ravaged face.

Kaine breathed deep, slowed his heartrate. Preparing for whatever was to come.

The tall man carrying her shuffled forwards. Alain Dubois' grinning face appeared in the rectangle of light.

"Hi there, Captain. How the devil are you doing?"

CHAPTER THIRTY-EIGHT

MONDAY 22ND MAY – Predawn
  Camp Pueblo, Arizona, US

In his right hand, Dubois held a Colt Defender, aimed at Kaine, its hammer cocked, and his index finger hooked around the trigger. Kaine couldn't see the Colt's thumb safety, but he knew it was disengaged. The confident glint in Dubois' eyes confirmed it.

For all the good it would do, the Sig still tucked into Kaine's waistband might as well have been back in Sheriff Hawksworth's SUV. He'd never be able to draw, cock, aim, and fire before Dubois turned him into a colander.

His heart rate slowed further, along with his breathing.

"Don't move, Captain," Dubois said, and the annoying grin widened. "This time, my weapon *is* loaded."

Kaine held his arms out from his sides, hands open, towards Dubois. He stood in the doorway, framed in bright yellow. Nothing stood between him and the Canadian apart from Sabrina.

From Dubois' perspective, Kaine would be haloed in the bright light. A perfect outline. A perfect shot.

Kaine leaned to one side. Closer to the open door.

"Uh-uh, Captain. Stay right where you are. I'd hate to have to shoot you in front of the only woman I ever loved," Dubois said, his tone mocking.

Kaine held still.

"Alain, what's this? Have you gone mad?"

Still smirking, Dubois shook his head slowly.

"You know full well what this is, Captain. This here's a Colt Defender. Not the most reliable or well-balanced handgun ever made. Not as good as that Sig in your waistband, but serviceable enough—and pretty accurate at this distance. You know I won't miss."

Slowly, Dubois raised the Colt and pressed the muzzle hard against Sabrina's temple. She stopped struggling, and her terrified eyes locked with Kaine's.

"What the hell are you doing?"

"Well," Dubois said, "for one thing, I'm cleaning up Colonel Caren's mess. The moron should have tied up all his loose ends before skedaddling out of here, but he was too keen to save his own worthless hide. Still, he did leave me a little present."

He lowered Sabrina enough for her feet to touch the floor. Even as slightly built as she was, he couldn't carry her dead weight forever.

As Dubois moved, Kaine lowered his right hand a fraction.

"Neither of you move, now," Dubois said. "I need to show you something."

Dubois scrunched lower, hiding more of himself behind Sabrina. With the Colt's muzzle still pressed against her temple, he released his hold completely. Sabrina sagged but stayed upright, gasping for air.

Dubois' left hand disappeared behind her and re-emerged a moment later, holding a black object half the size of a mobile phone, but twice as thick. He held it up for Kaine to see.

"In case you're wondering, this here doohickey ain't a cell phone, it's a triggering device. It turns me into a magician. I press one button and release it, and a part of the camp disappears in a puff of smoke. Press and release another button and a different part of the camp vanishes. I have no idea which button blows up which bit. The colonel didn't hang around long enough to tell me." The grin widened even more, showing his perfect white teeth. "He did say that one of these buttons is attached to a whole bunch of Semtex in the weapons store. If I work that one, the whole camp is vaporised, along with part of this mountain. I reckon it's this big red one in the middle. What d'you think?"

His thumb hovered over a button in the middle of the pad.

Kaine couldn't see its colour.

"Press that button and you'll die, too."

Dubois lowered the hand and tilted his head as he glanced down at the trigger.

"Duh! You don't say! Better not press it then, hey? Not until I'm miles away."

"Why?"

"That's for me to know and you to die wondering about," he said finally dropping the smile. "I suppose this is where you say something like, 'you'll never get away with it'. Right?"

"Well, you won't."

Dubois shrugged and raised the cell phone a little higher.

"With this, I might. They'll discover Sabrina's body in the debris. They'll have to use her DNA for identification since the body's gonna be unrecognisable. The Feds will assume the colonel did it to clean house. As for me, I'll be mortified, of course, but I'll soldier on. And I'll be a rock for a poor, grieving Maurice. He loves me, you know. Like a son. Believed every word I told him about me and Sabbie here." He kissed the back of her head. "You did, too. Didn't you, darling?"

Sabrina stiffened and braced her shoulders.

"*Putain*! I saw through your every advance. We never even kissed."

"But that ain't what *grand-père* Mo-Mo thinks, my sweetheart. In the end, he'll believe what I tell him. Because he wants to. And because he'll need someone to hand over control of the company to when he retires, grief-stricken."

"Is that what this is all about?" Kaine asked, still trying to calculate his options, inching his right hand further away from his side. "You want control of ESAPP?"

Dubois shrugged.

"At first, I just wanted to make my eventual retirement a little more comfortable. You know, you move a little inventory from one place to another, some gets lost in transit. Then you sell it to some freaks for a few bucks. Well, a few *million* bucks." He laughed again. "No harm, no foul. Especially since the weapons were due for destruction anyway. Then Sabrina started her damned investigation. You see, I know what she's like. Tenacious ain't the word. She'd have traced the losses back to me eventually. It was only a matter of time."

"So, you sold her out to Colonel Caren?" Kane asked.

"Sure did," Dubois said, his face downcast, feigning sadness. "Didn't feel too good about it, but couldn't be helped, eh?" He sighed. "The asshole was supposed to make it look like she died in an accident. These mountains are dangerous, you know? But he got too greedy and kidnapped her instead. Then Maurice brought you aboard and it messed with my plans. Which is why I had to tag along for the ride."

Kaine leaned a fraction to his right and reached for the door handle. The thin pine wouldn't offer much protection, but he had nothing else to hand.

"Uh-uh, Captain. You can stop moving. That door ain't gonna save you. Time to lose that Sig you've got stuck in your waistband. Use your left hand, index finger and thumb only. Be careful doing it, too."

Slowly, Kaine lowered his left hand. He rotated his wrist and, as instructed, pinched the handle between finger and thumb. He held it in place.

"Why didn't you shoot me when I burst in?" he asked, desperate to keep the arrogant prick talking.

Fire burned in Sabrina's eyes. The fire of hatred superimposed over the swelling and the bruises. She kept blinking and glancing to her right, towards the Colt. She was trying to tell him something, but Kaine couldn't work out what.

"Playing for time, Captain?" Dubois asked, dropping the sickening smile.

"Just interested."

Kaine tugged out the Sig and held it out to his side, in the pincer grip.

"I thought about it," Dubois answered, keeping his focus on Kaine's weapon. "And if you'd been carrying that Sig at the time, I would have done. But it didn't seem right to shoot an unarmed man in the back. Especially a man like you. Whatever you may think, I'm no coward."

"No?" Kaine sneered. "I can see how brave you are."

"Hiding behind Sabrina, you mean?" Dubois shook his head. "That isn't cowardice. That's taking advantage of all the cover available. Basic fieldcraft. Now toss the Sig over there." He nodded towards the darkest corner of the infirmary.

"I'll need to make it safe first, Alain. Wouldn't want it to go off when it landed. Someone might get hurt."

Dubois smirked and shook his head again.

"That's unlikely, Captain. But I'm willing to take the risk. Toss it!"

"Okay."

Kaine flicked his wrist and threw the Sig.

Dubois followed the gun's trajectory and watched it clatter into one of the bed frames. Couldn't help himself.

Kaine dived backwards, pulling the door with him.

Dubois fired four times.

Sabrina screamed.

CHAPTER THIRTY-NINE

Pitiful. Goddamned pitiful.

As though Alain would ever fall for such an old trick.

Alain pretended to watch the Sig arc through the air, but when the captain made his inevitable move, he was ready and waiting.

The moment Kaine twitched, Alain fired. Again and again.

One thing surprised him, though. Kaine didn't dive forwards as Alain anticipated, the asshole dived *backwards* and away. He ran. The so-called action hero ran. And Kaine had the gall to accuse Alain of cowardice.

How fucking dare he.

Didn't do him any good though. Alain plugged him. Must have done. The first shot aimed high, might have winged him, but Alain adjusted. The next three slugs had drilled through the door's middle panel.

They'd smashed a three-inch diameter hole through the thin screen. Perfect grouping. They'd all have hit their target. All of them.

Sabrina fell to her knees, screaming.

"Shut up, woman!" Alain slipped the electronic trigger into his pocket, knotted a bunch of her hair in his fist, and rammed the Colt's burning hot muzzle into the side of her head. "Can't hear myself think, Goddamn it."

She stopped howling, but started whimpering. Still annoying, but a definite improvement.

"That's better. Now, up you get. C'mon, darlin'. Stand up."

He yanked on her hair. She squealed and grabbed at his hand, scratching with talons as fingernails. He shook her head hard.

"Quit that, woman, or I'll blow your fucking brains out."

Her hands dropped away. Alain eased his grip.

"Good girl. Now shut it while I check on our friend in there." He took a breath. "Captain, you still alive in there?"

He listened but didn't really expect a reply. With the desk, the shelving, and Tex, not to mention the sick women on the mattresses, the storeroom was overcrowded. Not much bigger than a closet. Even if he was still alive and mortally wounded, Kaine had no place to hide.

"Oh Captain, my Captain, if you can hear me, better answer. I've got Sabrina and you've got nothing but dead people in there. I checked the place for weapons before you blundered in here. And George's shotgun's empty. Come on now, better call out if you don't want me to shoot this little darling here."

Again, he listened, and again, he heard nothing.

"I'm gonna count to three. If you don't call out, I'll shoot her anyway. Ready?"

Alain paused for emphasis before starting the count.

"One ..."

He released Sabrina's hair and encircled her waist with his left arm. He picked her up and shuffled closer to the punctured door.

"Two ..."

Silence. Not a single sound made it out of the supply room.

With Sabrina the best shield in the world, he edged closer to the door. He added more pressure to the trigger.

"Three!"

Nothing. Not a murmur. Not a squeak.

Alain twisted Sabrina to one side. He bent at the knees to peer through the hole he'd blasted in the door panel.

Kaine lay on his back, in the middle of the room, alongside Tex, feet tucked under his butt. The gutless piece of shit must have fallen to his knees and then toppled backwards. Happened so fast, the poor sap didn't have time to register any emotion before he died. Mouth open, face and neck covered in blood, mouth agape, Kaine's sightless eyes stared up at nothing.

Alain stayed where he was for thirty seconds, watching for movement, looking for signs of life.

Nothing. Just a body cooling in death.

Alain burst out laughing.

Quel dommage. Such a shame.

He released his hold and Sabrina collapsed to the floor.

Alain kept his eyes on Kaine, trying to ignore Sabrina's howling. Such a horrible noise.

"Sabrina, my darling," he said, smiling at her distress. "Why all the fuss?"

"*Tu l'as tué.* You killed him!"

"Easy, honey. That was the evil terrorist, Ryan Kaine. I just saved your life. Maybe even earned myself a big reward in the process."

"No! He was my friend. And you know it. *Meurtrier!*"

"Sabrina, this is America. Speak English, for Christ's sake."

"*Meurtrier!*"

He kicked out. The toe of his boot connected with her tight butt. She yelped.

"Stand up, bitch."

She scrambled to her feet.

"Get in there!"

She entered the office, sidestepped around the fresher of the two corpses, and backed away until stopped by the desk.

"Why?" she demanded. "Why did you shoot him? He came to save me."

Alain stopped in the doorway and nodded, unable and unwilling to take his eyes off Kaine's unmoving form.

"Yeah, I know. And I couldn't allow that to happen. You were supposed to be dead already, damn it. Serves me right for getting into bed with a lunatic like Dickie Caren. I mean, the 'Doomsday Creed'. Jesus! I should have known better."

He stared down at Ryan Kaine's crumpled corpse, almost feeling sorry for the former national hero and current patsy. For a man such as him to die so easily didn't sit right, but those were the breaks. In the end, it was either Ryan Kaine or Alain Dubois. One of them had to die, and it wasn't going to be Alain. No way. He'd waited too long and worked too hard to let things fall apart when he was so close to the end game.

"The whole of the UK establishment has been hunting Kaine for the best part of a year, but who finally caught up with him? Who killed him? Me, Alain Dubois, that's who."

Alain Dubois.

"Still, better make sure, eh?"

Alain raised the Colt and took careful aim at Kaine's head. He needed to make absolutely certain. This was too dangerous of an asshole to take any chances.

Sabrina screamed and leapt at him, arms outstretched, fingers clawing. He swung his left arm and swatted her aside. She yelped, slipped on the Texan's blood, and carried on going.

Kaine jerked up.

What the fu—

His right arm shot out. Something white flew through the air. Alain jerked his gun arm up to protect his throat. A sharp pain lanced through his wrist. The Colt slipped from dead fingers.

Fuck!

The pain.

He couldn't breathe. Couldn't swallow. A dagger stuck through his forearm, an inch above his wrist. Blood spurted out. A nicked artery.

Fuck, fuck, fuck!

How long did he have?

Kaine was up on his feet, lunging forwards, his bloodied face a mask of horror. He slid through the blood. It slowed him down. He couldn't brace his feet.

Alain blocked a roundhouse blow with his good arm. A heel strike glanced his thigh.

Run!

Get moving!

Vision blurring, blood pumping from the wound, his right hand useless, Alain stumbled backwards out of the storeroom into the welcome darkness of the infirmary. He scrambled, staggered towards the exit doors. Towards the outside. Towards safety.

Hurry, Kaine's coming.

CHAPTER FORTY

Monday 22nd May – Predawn
Camp Pueblo, Arizona, US

Kaine spat a glob of blood from his mouth, and wiped the sticky excess from his face with his sleeve. He stank of Tex's blood. Stank of death.

Not for the first time.

Sabrina stared at him, wide-eyed and open-mouthed. Battered and filthy, she looked as bad to him as he must have done to her.

"But ..." she gasped. "You were dead. I saw you. Your eyes were open and you didn't move. Didn't breathe. For so long. How?"

"I'm a freediver."

"Excuse me?"

"Explain later. Dubois still has that trigger."

Kaine grabbed the Colt from the puddle of Tex's blood and brains, and studied the arterial trail as it wound through the store-room door and out into the infirmary. So much spilled blood and probably more to come.

Before easing fully out of the storeroom, he checked the Colt.

Although the handle and stock were tacky with part-congealed gore, the muzzle was clean and clear. It would still function properly. To make certain, he racked and released the slide to eject the bullet up the spout and load a fresh one.

The blood trail led straight through the open door and around to the right, glistening under the yellow floodlights. Kaine tapped the earpiece twice.

"Griffin to OP4. Over."

"*OP4 to Griffin. I hear you. Over.*"

"Did you see him? Over."

"*What the hell was all that shooting? Over.*"

"Dubois, where did he go? Over," Kaine asked, bypassing the question.

"*He's in the shadows at the side of the infirmary. I don't have a shot. Over.*"

"Hold your fire, Shane. He's got the trigger. Over."

"*Okay, understood. You got some time, though. There ain't no lights come on anywhere. Looks like the camp's pretty much deserted. Over.*"

"Okay. Understood. I'm going to try drawing him out. Listen for my shout and aim carefully. Griffin, out."

Kaine left the comms line active, edged forwards, and paused at the side of the open doorway, exhibiting the caution he should have used earlier.

Schoolboy error.

Never again.

He crouched low and poked his head through the gap, ready for anything. The parade ground stood empty. Dubois' blood drops led around the side of the infirmary and trailed out of sight.

"Alain, are you still alive?"

After a short delay, a cough spluttered out from the darkness.

"Sure am, buddy. You can't get rid of me that easy."

Kaine shook his head.

"You should have kept quiet, Alain. I might have stumbled around the corner, but now I know where you are."

The Canadian could never have stayed silent. Loved the sound of his own voice too much. He had to crow. That point alone explained why Dubois hadn't shot him through the hole in the door. Kaine's calculated gamble had paid off. He breathed deeply, pulling in the fresh, sweet air, paying back the oxygen debt from his desperate 'freedive'.

Dubois coughed again. Sickly, wet.

"Like, you can't see all that ... claret I already spilled?"

He sounded tired, weak. A ploy? How much blood had he really lost? The trail looked heavy, but looks could be deceptive in the poor light.

"I can see it. You've lost quite a bit of it, too. How you feeling?"

Another cough. This one drawn out longer, wetter.

"I've ... had ... better days."

Kaine wouldn't fall for it.

"You deserve worse."

"I'm not such a bad guy," Dubois said, sounding sorry for himself.

If he was pleading for sympathy, Kaine wasn't about to offer any.

"You armed a group of murderers. Homegrown militants hellbent on killing innocents and overthrowing their government. And you did it for pure greed. How good does that make you?"

"Guess you've got a point there, Kaine. How we gonna play this?"

Kaine ground his teeth at the use of his real name and considered closing the comms, but he needed it open. Another gamble.

"Step out into the light with your hands in the air and I'll make sure you get to a medic."

"That's gonna be a bit difficult. That fucking knife of yours damn near cut my hand off."

"Do it, Alain. I won't shoot, you have my word."

"The word of Ryan Kaine, a hunted terrorist? What's that worth?"

Kaine flinched. How would Shane and Butch react to hearing his real name? Mei would be okay with it—probably. No time to worry about that, though.

"A damned sight more than yours, Alain Dubois, traitor to Canada, the United States, and the United Kingdom."

A pause.

"Yeah, yeah. Guess so." His extended sigh degenerated into another bubbling cough. "Hold on a ... second. I'm on my ... knees. Standing's an effort."

"Take it slow and easy."

"No other way I can ... do it."

Dubois grunted and the rasp of cloth scraping against clapboard indicated movement.

Kaine took aim, lining up the spot where he expected Dubois' chest to appear, but an arm broke the line of the wall first—a left arm. Its hand held the trigger device, the thumb hovering over the buttons.

With his left hand outstretched and clearly visible, the Canadian stepped smartly out from around the side of the building and headed into the light. He stood tall and straight, and held his blood-soaked right forearm upwards, tucked tight against his chest. Kaine's ceramic knife remained in place, buried hilt-deep through the wrist, the thin blade's point showing clear through the other side. Dubois had wrapped his belt tight around his forearm, immediately above the knife.

"That's far enough," Kaine barked.

Dubois smiled and waved the trigger in front of his face, making sure Kaine could see his thumb hovering over the keypad.

"Cut the crap, Captain. This little doodad means *I'm* calling the shots. Come out where I can see you. Ryan Kaine ain't the kind of guy to hide in the shadows."

Kaine pushed out of the doorway and adjusted his aim. The Colt felt strange in his hand, unbalanced. He'd never liked Colts' trigger action, either. Always found them way too stiff. He tried to line up a shot, but Dubois kept his left hand moving. Even at so short a range, ten metres, the shot was impossible.

"Nice tourniquet," Kaine said, nodding to the damaged arm. "Probably stopped you bleeding out."

Dubois shrugged and stretched his lips into another annoying, taunting smile.

"Nah. Didn't bleed all that much. I've had worse cuts shaving."

"Hurt much?"

"Like a bitch. Think you might have severed a tendon. Can't move my trigger finger."

"That's a pity."

"Yeah, a real shame. I'm gonna have to pay you back for that."

"At some stage," Kaine said. "Now I'd like my knife back."

He held out his free hand.

Dubois dropped the smile.

"Uh-uh," he said, shaking his head, "the knife's staying put until I can get to a surgeon. It's plugging the wound."

The whole time Dubois spoke, he kept moving his left hand. It never stayed still long enough for Kaine—or Shane—to risk a snap shot.

"Don't forget Captain, I read your file. Even with your skills, think you can hit a moving target with an unfamiliar weapon at this range?"

"I don't want to shoot you, Alain," Kaine lied and smiled while doing it.

"Yes you do. I know you better than that. You're a killer. It's been drilled into you." He paused for a second to swallow, before ploughing on. "Ever stopped to count the number of people you've killed? And I don't mean those eighty-three poor schmucks on the airplane. That wasn't really your fault. ... No, I mean all the others. The insurgents. The towelheads. Do you lie awake at night, counting your kills? I bet you do." He paused for breath, but the trigger kept moving. "Better not miss, though. I'd hate for this thing to blow. Any idea what'll happen if you *do* hit the trigger?"

"Not really. You?"

"Not a clue."

"So, where does that leave us?"

Dubois sucked a breath between his teeth. He wasn't as strong as he tried to make out. A sheen of sweat glistened on a face a few shades paler than its usual suntanned mahogany.

"Well, it leaves me in need of a car and a driver."

"Sorry, Alain. All I can promise is a hospital bed—in prison."

"Goddamn it! Get me a car and a driver!"

"Look around, Alain. There's no one else here."

His eyes glistened.

"Sabrina can drive."

"She's in no fit state."

Dubois growled.

"Sabrina! Get out here right now, or I'll blow up the whole fucking camp. Including your precious girlfriends."

"She's not going anywhere with you, Alain."

Dubois screamed and rushed towards Kaine, brandishing the trigger ahead of him. Madness and desperation shone in his eyes. A mere eight metres separated them. It might as well have been a kilometre.

"Do it, or everyone dies!"

Kaine raise his hands, pointing the Colt skywards.

"Take it easy, Alain. You don't want to die any more than I do."

"Don't tell me what I want!"

He pointed the trigger device at Kaine's face and pressed a button.

Kaine screamed, "Now!"

The side of Dubois' head exploded an instant before the crack of the rifle shot reached Kaine's ears.

Dubois's body stiffened, swayed ...

For a brief moment, the world stood still.

...then crumpled, backwards. His left arm lost tension, dropped. The hand opened and the trigger slipped out.

The blood-soaked trigger tumbled through the air.

CHAPTER FORTY-ONE

Kaine lunged, arms outstretched.

A desperate, fingertip grab.

Kaine caught the slippery device centimetres before it struck the deck, and he hit the ground at full stretch. His elbow struck the hard-packed earth.

The heavy trigger spilled from his grasp and clattered into the gravel.

Shit!

Kaine covered his head with his arms, squeezed his eyes shut and held his breath, expecting the concussive roar of the camp's obliteration. He heard nothing but silence.

He counted to ten.

Still nothing happened.

He released the breath in a whoosh.

What the hell?

Kaine pushed himself to his feet and dusted himself down. The trigger had landed face up, the middle of nine buttons—the red one — still depressed. It hadn't released when Dubois' thumb lost its tension, nor when it had struck the ground.

A dodgy switch?

Dare he risk touching it?

No choice.

Kaine knelt beside the device, pressed his thumb to the button, and dug his fingers underneath. He picked it up, gripped it tight, and stood. It was heavier than he'd imagined. Twice the weight of a standard mobile phone. No wonder he'd dropped the bloody thing.

His earpiece buzzed.

"*Butch to Griffin. I've taken the glasses back. Are you there? Over.*"

"Griffin here. Shane missed. He was supposed to aim at the hand, not the bloody head. Over."

"*Fuck's sake, Griffin. You dropped the trigger. What the hell happened? I repeat, what happened? Over.*"

"Get down here and see for yourself." Kaine breathed again. "Oh, I don't suppose you have some insulating tape, do you? Over."

"*Yeah, I always carry a roll. What d'you need it for? Over.*"

"To hold down a detonator button. Better hurry, though. My thumb's already getting tired. Ask Shane to stay where he is. We might still need cover. Griffin, out."

He tapped the earpiece inactive and turned towards the infirmary. "Sabrina, you can come out now."

He moved closer to Dubois' cooling corpse. Like the trigger, he'd landed face up. Unlike the trigger, he wasn't in one piece and looked a lot like Tex.

Sabrina appeared at Kaine's side, trembling under a threadbare blanket, and he tucked her under his arm on instinct.

"You okay?" he asked.

She nodded.

"*Oui, merci.* Much better now. When you dropped the device, I thought we were going to die."

Me too.

"Always been useless at cricket. Never could catch worth a damn.

Can't hold a bat and as for bowling ...." He smiled and hugged her tighter. "Still, can't be good at everything, eh?"

"Ryan, must you make a joke of everything? We might all be dead!"

"Not on my watch. Let's get you into the warmth."

He tried to turn her, but she held firm, refusing to move.

"No, please. They have kept me locked up for days. Fresh air is ... wonderful."

She took in a deep breath, tilted her head back, and breathed out long and hard. Her head rolled forwards and her eyes landed on the trigger in his hand.

"I saw everything through the window. When Alain dropped the trigger, why didn't it work?"

"No idea."

"A hoax after all?"

He shrugged. "Perhaps. Either way. I'm not letting go until Butch gets here."

"Butch?"

"A friend. You'll meet him in a minute."

She seemed steadier, stronger. Kaine removed his arm from around her shoulders and they stood together in the fresh air, watching the silvery brightness behind the eastern horizon announce the onset of sunrise. The strong wind died to a hush.

Kaine de-cocked the Colt and lowered it to the ground at Dubois' feet. No point trying to wipe away any fingerprints or DNA. Corky had deleted his biometrics from every system in Europe and would continue to do so. No Federal database would ever be able to link Bill Griffin with the fugitive Ryan Kaine.

He turned to face Sabrina.

"Griezmann and his people will be here soon. He'll be hopping mad to have missed his chance to scoop up Colonel Caren and his lunatic Creed. Probably blame me for the whole thing. I'll need to make myself scarce soon."

"Go now, I can hold down the button."

She reached out for the trigger, but he jerked his hand away.

"Oh no, you don't. I'm holding onto this baby until Butch arrives with that tape. Too bloody dangerous."

While they waited, he placed his arm around Sabrina's shoulders again, giving her what support he could as she started to come to terms with what she'd seen and heard. With what had happened. Minutes passed before Mei's twig-snapping approach broke into his thoughts.

He smiled to himself. If they were still on talking terms, he'd advise the Special Agent to attend a fieldcraft course at the earliest opportunity.

"Griffin?" Mei called out behind them.

As they turned, Kaine leaned closer and whispered into Sabrina's ear.

"Remember, my name's Griffin. I've just started working for your grandfather, and you've never seen me before tonight."

"Okay, *je comprends.*"

Mei and Butch stood behind the fence, staring at them. Butch towered a full twenty centimetres over the diminutive Mei and a huge smile split his angular face. He was, no doubt, delighted to be standing so close to the woman he'd admired from a distance for so long.

"You guys okay?" Butch shouted.

"Yes thanks," Kaine answered and held up the trigger. "Where's that insulating tape?"

Butch waived a roll of black tape in the air.

"I'd throw it over the fence to you, but I've seen the way you catch. Wait there a minute."

He and Mei scrambled through a nearby break in the fence and jogged towards them.

"Are you hurt?" Mei asked, studying his face and looking concerned.

"This isn't my blood. I borrowed it from a dead man." He turned to Butch. "What the hell took you so long? My thumb's starting to cramp up."

"That's rough ground, Griffin," he answered, "didn't fancy falling and breaking my neck." He shook the pack from his back, knelt and placed it on the ground in front of him. He removed a penlight from the pack and switched it on. The thin beam lit a bright circle on the pack. "Let's see what you got there, buddy."

Kaine dropped to his knees in front of Butch and held the trigger device under the circle.

Mei ushered Sabrina to one side. "It's really good to see you again, Ms LeMaître. How are you?"

"Don't worry about me. My friends, though. They're really sick," Sabrina said pointing towards the infirmary. "Can you call for medical assistance? And there are more captives in the Camp. Perhaps in one of the dormitories."

"There's a paramedic in the lead assault team and a chopper *en route* from Tucson. We've got doctors and nurses on their way from Pine Creek, too. They'll be here soon."

"I need to make sure my friends are okay. Please help me."

Sabrina nodded a surreptitious *au revoir* to Kaine and tugged Mei towards the infirmary.

"Now, will you look at this," Butch said, sitting back on his haunches and smiling up at Kaine. "This thing's safe as houses. You can relax your thumb, Griffin."

"I can?"

"Surely can. I've seen these things before. You can buy them in hardware stores. See these here LEDs?" he said, pointing to three tiny glass domes running along the top edge of the trigger. "They should be lit up green, but they're all dead. This fool"—he dipped his head towards Dubois—"didn't know enough to switch the damn thing on."

"Are you sure?"

"Yep. You'll find a toggle button under that flap right there." He pointed to a square panel alongside the LEDs. "It's covered like that so you can't activate it by accident."

Kaine puffed out his cheeks.

"Wish I'd known that earlier. Would have saved me soiling my trousers. You can buy these things over the counter?"

Butch smiled and hitched a shoulder. "Well, not exactly. It's specialist stuff. In most states, you'd need an explosives licence."

"You certain it's safe?"

"Sure I am. Attended a training course at Quantico last fall. One of the modules taught us how to deconstruct one of these things. Good job your buddy didn't know what he was doing, huh?"

Kaine shrugged.

"Unless he did."

"What d'you mean?"

"Alain Dubois didn't strike me as the suicidal type. Maybe he knew it was safe. We'll never know."

Butch held out his hand.

"Wanna pass it over?"

"You absolutely certain?"

"Come on. We don't have all day."

He beckoned with his fingers.

Kaine sucked in a breath, squeezed his eyes tight shut, and lifted his thumb.

"Boom!" Butch yelled. He burst out laughing and plucked the dead trigger from Kaine's open hand. "Man, the look on your face. A real picture."

Kaine glowered at Butch for a moment and ground his teeth.

"You know what happened to the last man who did something like that to me?" he asked.

"No," Butch said, still chortling. "What?"

Kaine thought better of pointing at Dubois. He stood and watched a slightly more sober Butch remove the back panel from the trigger and rip out the square battery.

"There you go," he said "No way that's going to detonate any explosives today."

He climbed to his feet and waited for Kaine to join him before holding out his hand.

"Sorry 'bout that little joke, Griffin. We cool?"

Kaine took the hand and they shook.

"We're cool. Any idea when Griezmann's likely to arrive?"

Butch frowned and tilted his head.

"Damn, didn't I tell you?"

"Tell me what?"

"Griezmann ain't coming. Not for a while."

"Why not?"

"Turns out that on their way here to set up for the raid, the ATF ran straight into Creed's column. Took the bozos completely by surprise. They didn't have time to draw their weapons or get off a single shot. Right now, Colonel Caren and thirty-six of his men are under Federal arrest. ATF found a whole load of illegal weapons in the trucks, too. SSA Beddow's real pleased about it, I can tell you."

"What about SAC Griezmann?"

"Yeah," Butch said. "What about him?"

"I bet he's happy, too."

"Doubt it. He missed the whole shebang."

"Shame."

"Sure is."

Kaine put a hand to his stomach.

"Oh dear."

"What's up, Griffin? You look a little green, buddy."

"Feeling a tad queasy."

"Right. Delayed shock, I guess."

"Mind if I take a stroll?"

"Sure, be my guest. But don't go too far. Griezmann is still on his way in with the medics and the search teams. He'll want a full debrief. I'm guessing he'll be stoked to meet the fugitive, Ryan Kaine, in person."

Kaine sighed and allowed his shoulders to droop.

"I was wondering if you and Shane picked up on that."

Butch nodded. "While lining up his shot, Shane relayed every word of your conversation with Dubois to me and Mei."

Dubois. Bloody man couldn't stop talking.

Kaine glance up in the direction of OP4, where Shane lay in wait with his rifle.

Butch shook his head.

"Don't worry. Shane and Mei have never heard of the legendary Captain Ryan Liam Kaine of the British SBS. Here, take these."

He reached into his pocket and held up the spare glasses Kaine had given Mei what seemed like ages ago. Gratefully, he took them from Butch's outstretched hand.

"You follow the British news?"

Butch nodded.

"Now and again. Fascinating story. A decorated SBS officer—a war hero—accused of blowing up a passenger plane? Couldn't get enough of it. Always wondered what kind of a man you were." He glanced down at the dead Canadian. "Guess I found out, huh?"

"What happens now?"

"I tidy up here and wait for the troops, and you ... well, you still look a mite queasy to me. Better skedaddle before you puke your ring."

Kaine smiled.

"You're a good man, Butch."

"I sure am." He winked, beaming.

"Mind if I take my knife? It's my favourite."

"Be my guest. But hurry, I think I can hear sirens."

Kaine stooped low, yanked the knife from the dead man's wrist, and wiped the blade clean on Dubois' sleeve before returning it to its scabbard.

"Cheers, Butch. See you later," he said, hurrying towards the nearest set of latrines.

Once he'd passed behind the low buildings, out of sight of both Butch near the infirmary and Shane in his eyrie, he ducked low and kept on walking.

CHAPTER FORTY-TWO

Kaine leaned back into the plush leather seat and stretched out. Although travelling west to east always worsened his jetlag, the ESAPP Gulfstream G550 Maurice had placed at his disposal turned out to be even more luxurious than the one he'd shared with the turncoat, Dubois, on the outbound journey.

How many hours' sleep had he missed since that flight? He didn't have the energy to work it out—the time zones being a complicating factor.

He yawned long and hard without bothering to cover his mouth. No one to upset since he was the only one in the plush cabin. No doubt about it, this was the way to travel between continents. Ridiculously expensive and so environmentally destructive he'd be paying tens of thousands into a green bank to offset his carbon footprint as soon as he had a moment, but nice, just the same.

The plane's intercom dinged and the pilot, Captain Giraud, announced they'd reached their cruising altitude and invited Kaine to avail himself of the galley and the bar. She also told him the satellite link was now available.

About time.

His watch read thirteen hundred hours, Phoenix time—Mountain Standard. A nine-hour time difference made it four in the morning in Paris. Although predawn, Lara should be expecting his call. He'd left her a voice message during his drive to Tucson, telling her he was safe and on his way to the airport.

She hadn't replied in person, just sent a perfunctory text message:

Glad to hear it. L.

She'd clearly not forgiven him for dumping her in Paris. Even though he'd done it with the best intentions, he'd screwed up badly and they both knew it.

A rush of nerves clenched his gut and worry flooded through his system. He stared at the button on his armrest, hesitant. He stretched out a hand and withdrew it.

Suck it up, Kaine.

In his time, he'd tackled some of the most evil people in the world—jihadists, insurgents, terrorists, power-crazed lunatics—without batting an eye. Now all he faced was a veterinary surgeon whom he loved more than anything in the world.

What's the worst that can happen?

Nervously, he pressed and held down the button. A flatscreen TV popped out of a compartment in the bulkhead near his lap. He flipped it down and swivelled it around to face him. The screen lit up with a video window above a virtual keyboard. Fingers shaking unexpectedly, he typed in the secure URL and hit enter.

It took a few seconds to make the connection.

"Hello, Bill? Is that you?" Lara asked, unsmiling, her delivery flat, deathly serious.

He smiled and his chest swelled. God, he'd missed her.

Judging by her background, *Le Mandarin Oriental*'s bedrooms were significantly less impressive than he expected. Striped wallpaper in dull shades of yellow and green looked tired and, it had to be said, a little tatty.

Shabby chic?

No. Not at all what he'd expected.

"Who else would be calling you so early in the morning?" he asked, aiming for lightness but feeling as though he'd swallowed a pebble.

"Yes, well, it's about time, Bill."

She spoke quickly.

"It's okay," he said, "we can speak freely. This video call is on the modern equivalent of a scrambler and I'm alone."

"Great," she said.

Her pent-up anger bubbled through the screen. He could tell by the jutting jaw and the deepening frown. A few fences to mend there, but they had time. Lara must know why he'd done it.

"How's Sabrina?"

"Alive, thank god. Been through the wringer, but she's tough. Maurice told me the Feds rushed her to hospital for a thorough workup, and they'll be monitoring her for infection."

"Did Maurice survive the flight over okay?" Still, she didn't smile.

"Looked pretty chipper to me, but I only saw him for a few minutes. As you can imagine, he was more keen to see Sabrina than me. I ducked out of sight when the FBI's Deputy Director Hallam arrived to escort him to the hospital. It's amazing the doors you can open when you're a multi-billionaire."

"He was horrified when he learned about Alain Dubois' part in Sabrina's abduction."

Kaine nodded. "I can imagine."

"Same way I felt when Maurice told me you'd buggered off to Arizona without me."

Kaine shuddered. Lara rarely used bad language.

"About that, love ..."

He hesitated, waiting for the inevitable explosion.

"We'll talk about that later," she said, glancing to her left. "Assuming there is a later."

Ouch!

She wasn't about to make his job any easier.

"You know why I did it, right?"

She clamped her mouth shut and waited.

He never could stand being on the receiving end of her silent treatment.

"After what happened to Danny—"

"Don't you dare blame Danny for this. *You* dumped me here! *You* decided I was a liability. *You* thought I couldn't be trusted to help."

"I didn't know what to expect. Arizona's the Wild West, love. They all carry guns over there."

"You left me alone ... with a bunch of strangers—"

"In Paris, love. Shopping!"

Lame, Kaine. Bloody lame.

He spread his hands in appeasement.

"Strangers," she continued, pointing at the screen for added emphasis, "who were working for Alain bloody Dubois!"

"Ah," he said, thinning his lips. "I see your point."

He scratched his beard.

"I did send you Rollo, though."

She glanced off to the side and focused on the screen again.

"Yes, I know. And he drove through the night to be here for me. But it's unacceptable, Ryan. We need to talk about this—"

"Oh dear. That sounds ominous," he said, smiling and aiming for casual, but feeling as though she'd stabbed him through the heart.

She looked directly into the camera.

"It was meant to."

"I ... I'm sorry," he mumbled. "I love you, and I—"

"I'm sure you do. And we will talk about this, but not now." Again she glanced off to her left. "Rollo's listening and looks like he's about to throw up. You can continue to make this up to me later. Perhaps forever."

She jutted out her jaw, discussion over and plenty of fences still left to mend.

Kaine dipped his head.

"Sorry."

She leaned closer to the screen, but her expression remained cold. "How are you feeling? Any symptoms after your time in the infirmary? Thirst? Elevated temperature?"

"None so far. And I've kept a safe distance from everyone since leaving the camp."

"Good. Make sure you stay hydrated. Take plenty of fluids. I'll have some *ciprofloxacin* waiting for you when you arrive. And you *will* complete the whole course. You hear me?"

She does still care.

Kaine placed a hand over his heart. "I promise. Thanks for looking after me, darling."

Lara frowned at him and shot another glance to her left.

Kaine sighed. "Tell Rollo not to be such a wimp."

"Tell him yourself."

She shuffled to one side and Rollo slid into shot, an awkward smile on his chiselled face. Since marrying Marie-Odile, he'd shaved his greying beard and allowed his hair to grow out. He looked totally different and ten years younger.

"Morning, Colour Sergeant. Everything okay?"

"Er, well … I—"

"Actually, you look exhausted," Lara said to Kaine, frowning at Rollo again.

What's going on here?

"That's a shame," Kaine said. "You look wonderful."

"I'm serious, Ryan. You need to get some sleep."

"I plan to do just that. This aircraft has a fully equipped bathroom and luxurious sleeping quarters. Double bed and everything. A real home away from home."

"Better make the most of it, sir," Rollo said, brow creased and looking as nervous as Kaine had ever seen him.

"Why?"

"Um, well …" He glanced to his right, his green eyes showing discomfort.

"Rollo. What's up?"

"We received another emergency message from the website," Lara answered for him.

"One of *The 83*?"

"Definitely. I've double confirmed their credentials."

"Who and where?"

"We'll tell you all about him when you arrive."

"He's in Paris?"

Lara shook her head.

"No, you'll have to ask Captain Giraud to register a new flight plan."

"Where am I going?"

"Cardiff Airport. I'll see you here in six and a half hours."

Here? See you here?

"Hang on a minute," he snapped. "You're in Wales?"

"Ryan, you aren't the only one who can rush off to help members of *The 83* at the drop of a hat."

"Lara, what have you done?"

She ended the call and the screen froze on her beautiful, unsmiling face.

"Lara!" he shouted to the silent screen.

Kaine tried reconnecting, but his call bounced back, unanswered.

Idiot!

He slammed a fist into the arm of the chair and left the screen powered up. After a few minutes staring at her unmoving but glorious image, he climbed out of his seat.

Where the hell do they hide the bar in this plane?

ADDENDA

Former Army Colonel arrested for treason along with 48 other members of the outlawed Doomsday Creed.

PHOENIX, Arizona – Today, Colonel Richard Caren, 55, of Copper Strike, Renshaw County, Arizona, was arrested under the Counter Terrorism Act, 2001.

Yesterday, Monday, May 22, in a Joint Task Force, the Federal Bureau of Investigation, the Bureau of Alcohol, Tobacco, Firearms, and Explosives, together with the Renshaw County Sheriff's Department, conducted a dawn raid on Camp Pueblo, a former military base. Numerous arrests were made and thirteen hostages were released. Details to follow.

Case Number: CR-18-2416-TUC-JGZ.

Release Number: 1212-005_Chang.

Staff Changes in the FBI's Arizona Field Office.

PHOENIX, Arizona – Today, the Federal Bureau of Investigation has the sad duty to announce that Special Agent in Charge, Allman Griezmann, has been forced to take early retirement on medical grounds. SAC Griezmann joined the Bureau in ....
Release Number: 1217-006_Hallam.

FOR IMMEDIATE RELEASE Friday, May 26.

Staff Changes in the FBI's Arizona Field Office.

PHOENIX, Arizona – Today, the Federal Bureau of Investigations is delighted to announce that Special Agent, Mark Steiner, has accepted a post in the FBI's Field Office in Alaska. Special Agent Steiner will take up his new role with immediate effect.
Release Number: 1218-005_Hallam.

FOR IMMEDIATE RELEASE Friday, May 26.

Staff Changes in the FBI's Arizona Field Office.

PHOENIX, Arizona – Today, the Federal Bureau of Investigation is delighted to announce the appointment of Mei Lu Chang as the new Special Agent in Charge of the Phoenix Field Office. SAC Chang has vowed to improve on the excellent work of her predecessor, former SAC Allman Griezmann, who retired on medical grounds ....
Release Number: 1219-005_Hallam.

The End.

THE RYAN KAINE SERIES

On The Run: Book 1 in the Ryan Kaine Series

On The Rocks: Book 2 in the Ryan Kaine Series

On The Defensive: Book 3 in the Ryan Kaine Series

On The Attack: Book 4 in the Ryan Kaine series

On The Money: Book 5 in the Ryan Kaine series

On The Edge: Book 6 in the Ryan Kaine series

On The Wing: Book 7 in the Ryan Kaine series

On The Hunt: Book 8 in the Ryan Kaine series

On The Outside: Book 9 in the Ryan Kaine series

For a free Ryan Kaine origins novella, go to
fusebooks.com/ryankaine

PLEASE LEAVE A REVIEW

If you enjoyed On the Outside, it would mean a lot to Kerry if you were able to leave a review. Reviews are an important way for books to find new readers. Thank you.

https://geni.us/ontheoutside

ABOUT KERRY J DONOVAN

#1 International Best-seller with *Ryan Kaine: On the Run*, Kerry was born in Dublin. He currently lives in a cottage in the heart of rural Brittany. He has three children and four grandchildren, all of whom live in England. As an absentee granddad, Kerry is hugely thankful for the invention and widespread availability of video calling.

Kerry earned a first-class honours degree in Human Biology, and has a PhD in Sport and Exercise Sciences. A former scientific advisor to The Office of the Deputy Prime Minister, he helped UK emergency first-responders prepare for chemical attacks in the wake of 9/11. He is also a former furniture designer/maker.

kerryjdonovan.com

facebook.com/KerryJDonovan
twitter.com/KerryJDonovan

Printed in Great Britain
by Amazon

40655156R00229